SISTERS
of the
RAVEN

SISTERS
of the
RAVEN

BARBARA
HAMBLY

WARNER BOOKS

An AOL Time Warner Company

Aspect® name and logo are registered trademarks of Warner Books, Inc.

Warner Books, Inc., 1271 Avenue of the Americas, New York, NY 10020

 An AOL Time Warner Company

Printed in the United States of America

ISBN 0-7394-3017-3

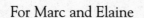

For Marc and Elaine

THE YELLOW CITY

BLUFFS

FARMS

BLUFFS

Flowermarket
Gate

Circus

Citadel Of The
Sun-Mages

OLD VILLAS

Flowermarket
District

AQUEDUCT

THE RING

House of
Marvelous
Tower

AVENUE OF THE SUN

Slaughter House
District

Grand Bazaar

Tannery
District

BoSaa's
Square

Dyers
Yards

TRACKWAY TO AQUEDUCT CAMP

Fishmarket

Redbone
Hills

FARMS

LAKE

REALM
of the
SEVEN LAKES

Sulpher
Lake

Lake of
Slaves

MARSH

Mud
Lake

The Lake of Reeds

MARSH

Ith

Lake
of
Gazelles

MARSH

City
of
Reeds

The Great Lake

The White Lake

The City
of
White
Walls

Mountains of the Eanit

Sun Canal

Lake of
Roses

Lake of the Sun

The Yellow
City

Dead
Hills

Oasis of Koshlar

D E S E R T

D E S E R T

Lake
of
The Moon

The Singing
World

SISTERS
of the
RAVEN

ONE

I f the other novice wizards on the row hadn't broken into Raeshaldis's rooms the previous day, pissed on her bed and written WHORE and THIEF on the walls, she probably would have been killed on the night of the full moon.

It was the seventh night of the Summoning of Rain, and magic filled her like a cup brimming with holy light. Her soul rang with it, nearly effacing the memory of her eighteen months in the College of the Mages of the Sun: the petty tricks, the dirty scrawls, the male novices' unrelenting hate. If that was the price she had to pay for the joy of feeling magic flow in her, she thought as she made her way across the moon-drenched North Terrace, she was more than willing to pay it. Nothing was too much for this ecstasy, this knowledge that the dreams of all her life had been true.

But yesterday's memory made her wary. The filthy bed and violated walls, the derisive look the Master of Novices had given her when she'd complained to him . . . *Shouldn't a student of your* great *abilities be able to guard herself against the jests of boys?*

And behind his resentful anger, the unspoken wish that she'd leave the college, as if her departure could make all things as they had once been.

So she approached the stair that led down into the darkness

of the novices' row with caution, half expecting further mis-
chief.

Between walls of stucco and dressed stone at the bottom of
the stair, darkness clotted thick, like blindness cut into slabs.
Shaldis's ability to see in darkness was new—it had opened
like a flower only a few years ago, almost unremarked in the
greater birth of her other powers. After a day in the open ring
that crowned the Citadel, pouring her concentration and her
power into the Summoning of the vital rains, Shaldis wasn't
surprised that her eyes couldn't pierce those shadows.

Still she slowed her steps, braced herself, listened into that
silent blackness for the sound of breathing. Moonlight flooded
the indigo infinities of sky. From the stony heights to the east
and south of the high Citadel bluff, the endless wasteland to
the north, the wind carried only the scents of sand and dust.
After seven days of Summoning the sky was still clear, but
Shaldis understood that the rains took time. They would come.
How can they not? she thought, reliving in her flesh the music
of the Summoning Song. *Magic is here. Magic is alive.*

How can people say it is gone?

She smelled her attacker the moment before he struck. As
she came down the dark unrailed stair from the terrace into
the black seam between the northern wall and the novices'
quarters, she felt—she didn't know why—as if someone called
to her in a language she didn't understand. Then, in the second before hands grabbed her out of the dark, she thought, *The
boys are here after all. . . .*

Her stomach curdled with dread.

But it was no boy who seized her. Hands crushed her arm,
twisted the lacquered knot of her hair. Only the merciless hazing she'd endured for a year and a half had her curling her
back, tucking her chin, so that she took the impact with the
wall on her shoulders and not her skull. In that same instant

spells of defeat and confusion smashed at her mind like a blow. Magic that took her breath away: malice, poison, sick despair.

She called a thunderclap of fire in the air between them and of course none came. Tried to remember how to make white light explode to blind this man and couldn't. Her only awareness was breathless terror: She lashed with her feet, ripped with her nails, kicked into swirling masses of heavy wool and screamed.

Will anyone come?

Or are they all in on it?

She got a foot behind her and thrust off the wall, drove her head hard into her attacker's middle. When an iron grip tried to haul her back, she skinned out of her over-robe, plunged up the stairs again in the pitchy dark. Magic reached after her, smoke in her eyes, panic that screamed at her to circle back into that waiting dark. Its strength was terrifying—*Not a novice.* She stumbled, scraped her palms, rose and fled.

And whoever it was, she knew instinctively she *must not* let herself be caught.

It wasn't late—a few hours before midnight—and freezing cold. Adepts and masters, numb with exhaustion after the Summoning's daylong fast, had all fallen into their beds; she alone out of all who'd sung today had had enough energy to sneak out to the pantry in quest of honey and bread. Now she fled across the terrace, not daring to look back. Praying someone, anyone, would be abroad, would save her . . .

Who, in this place, would care if they heard her scream?

Three years ago, when at fourteen she was too old to be sneaking out to the marketplace in her brother's clothes but was still doing so anyway, she'd been recognized as a girl by a bunch of half-drunk camel drivers. They'd chased her through the tangled alleyways around the Grand Bazaar, herding her with the brutal efficiency of wolves. The terror she'd felt then was as nothing to what she felt now, for even then, she suspected, she'd felt the first stir of power in her, and had known she could get away. . . .

This man was a mage. And he was stronger than she.

She fled up the stairs beyond the terrace. Night cold gashed through the pale wool of her robe. Her pursuer's steps weren't the thudding tread of the camel drivers but the light wind-touch of one trained to cross sand without leaving a track. Shadow wouldn't hide her. Magic wouldn't hide her. The Summoning had drained her, taken everything she had. She couldn't make a cloak spell work. The air like broken glass in her lungs, she threw herself up the narrow stairway to the rock tip of the Citadel, the summit, the Ring, her mind reaching to the magic that still clung around the place.

Break his vision, even for an instant, she thought, dodging behind the waist-high wall that set it off from the drop on all sides. Mage-born eyes could see right through the cloaks—the spells of unseeing—and her panic-sickened thoughts couldn't summon the words. She wadded her long legs and skinny body into a ball in the few hand spans of rock between the wall and space: a drop of sixty feet to the pavement of the library court. She hid her face, the lingering magics left from five hundred Spring Summonings flowing away like water from her groping mind. Only the old nonsense spells remained, words she'd made up for herself when she'd hide from her brothers in the kitchen yard of her grandfather's house.

But that childish spell—if it really was a spell—had sent the camel drivers roaring and cursing down another alley and had convinced her—almost convinced her—that the powers she'd begun to dream about might actually be real.

A child's chant, silly and simple: *Zin, zin, I am the wind. Zin, zin, blow. Ping, ping, I am the starlight. Ping, ping, shine.* Words to focus her mind, to make her body melt into the icy drift of the desert wind that sidewindered across the Ring's bare flag-stones. Different words every time. Words to make her shadow melt into the blue moon shadows without appearing to do so. To dislimn her form into the black lines between the blocks of the wall. *Whiss, whiss, I am the dust. Whiss, whiss, sneeze.*

Don't let him see me, she prayed desperately to Rohar, the braided-haired god of women. *Please don't let him see me. . . .*

The drop, an inch beyond her feet, turned her sick. The Citadel clung like a succession of swallows' nests to the golden sandstone of the bluff. Below it the Yellow City spread. An intricate jumble of walls and domes, roof tiles and vines, pigeon coops and cisterns and marketplaces no bigger than the Citadel's dining hall, baths and Blossom Houses and dyers' yards and stables. Like a moth pressed to the wall, Raeshaldis saw the topaz speckle of the few lamps still burning far below, the knot of torchlight that would be the Circus district against the flank of the bluffs and the hot clump of jewels that marked the Night Market. Plowed fields lapped the city like dark velvet, north and south along the lake's still darker shores. The lake itself—the Lake of the Sun—burned with the fierce platinum moonlight, stretching out of sight into the west.

I'm going to die.

And yet the lake and the city and the sky are so beautiful. . . .

She smelled, and felt, her pursuer. The smoke in his robes, the revolting halitus of decayed blood filled her nostrils, and beneath those stinks the tingly whiff of ozone. She dared not look up, dared not even think, lest he hear her thought. Then like a shadow the smell winked away, and she found herself thinking, *Silly me, I slipped and fell and thought it was someone attacking me. I'd better go back to my room. . . .*

Her belly went soft with dread. Not even an adept could call spells of concealment like that. *A master wizard.*

He hears me, she thought. *Hears me breathe. No matter how still I sit, I can't stop breathing.*

Zin, zin, I am the wind. . . .

Please go away. Go away and let me alone.

The other novices were boys. Angry like boys, but like boys, even cruel boys, limited in what they could and would do. That one of the masters who should know better should have this much anger terrified her.

Zin, zin, blow.

She pressed her hands over her mouth and waited. She didn't even dare to reach out with a counterspell to put aside the illusions of safety that came like vagrant wind into her mind.

Shadow gathered at the head of the stair to her left. She tucked her face into her arms so as not to catch the moonlight. Her long brown hair, torn free from its pins, trailed out over the abyss. She felt him seek her, a thin alien jangling in the air, as if her flesh were scourged with a thousand icy chains. Utterly different from the magic of the Summoning, different from any magic she had felt before. She felt him scan the moon-frosted flagstones of the Ring, from which even the tiniest particles of the gypsum, iron dust, and ocher that had made the great power curves of the Song had been meticulously cleaned away. The core of his anger was a column of freezing shadow, the heart of an unimaginable storm.

She felt him cross the Ring, listen for her breath, for the beating of her heart. He stopped near where the Archmage had stood all day in his ceremonial robes of blue silk and gold. His listening touched her, like cold fingers groping. Then he moved on. Soundless as darkness down the marble stair to the outer courts of the college. Shadow passing over the painted dining hall, the tiled scrying chamber, the library where the wisdom of a thousand years dreamed in its cases of pickled oak.

The reek of his rage settled like filthy smoke into the dust.

They heard me scream. Trembling so badly she feared she would lose her balance, pitch over the edge, Raeshaldis crept along the wall to the stair that would lead back down to the terrace, then to the walkway to her room. *When he seized me, every boy in the novices' three dormitories heard me scream.*

And none came.

She had to support herself on the balustrade. Eastward, level with the Ring and the Citadel's uppermost roofs, desert stretched back from the flat-topped bluffs that bounded the Realm of the Seven Lakes. Below her, around her, the range-land that lay beyond the tilled arable of the lakeshore showed dark patches, herds of cattle and sheep. Their thirsty lowing carried up to her through the stillness. Rangeland thinned to scrub—bounded by the cliffs or merging gradually up the slope between them, range gave way to desert. Stringers of rock marked the low hills surrounding the valley north of the cliffs, where jackals cried among the tombs.

At the bottom of the steps she found her over-robe, novice white and thick against the freezing desert nights. Though the blindness that had covered her eyes had vanished and she could again see clearly in the darkness, she almost feared to stoop and pick it up, expecting someone to jump out of one of the deep-set doorways along the seam between wall and wall.

Secure in the knowledge that she wasn't going to tell.

You could run crying to the masters only so many times: *The boys hit me. The boys aren't being nice.*

Shouldn't a student of your great abilities . . . ?

Fingers fumbling, she touched the secret spots on the door of her own tiny cell. It had once housed the prefect of this corridor, and sometimes she could detect, deep in the wood, the spells some long-ago adept had put on it to warn him if the boys under his charge had broken in. Her own spells to ward away intruders were usually stronger, but on this occasion they hadn't worked. They often didn't. She didn't know why, and the masters weren't able to tell her.

It didn't require a spell to tell her the room had been entered when she'd sneaked out to slake her craving for sweets. The stink that hit her as she opened the door informed her of that. Tears collected in her eyes as she pulled the blankets from the bed, dumped a dead pigeon to the floor and carried it by one wing to the window. Maggots crept confusedly around in the sheets and pillows. Shaldis stripped the bed and found another blanket in the cupboard. It wasn't thick enough to stave off the spring night's bitter cold, but she didn't care.

She bolted the door and the window shutters, laid every spell of ward she could think of on them, rolled up in the blanket on the bare cotton tick and cried herself to sleep.

Corn-Tassel Woman had long ago become adept at gauging the depth of her husband's slumber by his snores. Even before she'd felt the first strange stirrings of power in herself—those terrifying awarenesses that she was unlike any of her friends, unlike any woman she'd ever heard of—she'd taught herself to listen, to walk through her father-in-law's house with mind and ears, identifying the breath of each servant girl in the harem, each child in the nursery, each teyn in the sheds—latterly each mouse in the loft. The house was silent.

Corn-Tassel Woman slipped from the quilts, wrapped her thickest shawl around herself. It had taken her a long time to realize she could see in the dark, for she knew every inch of the house so well she could walk it end to end blindfolded. The night outside was rich with moonlight, but her husband Enak was a deep sleeper. When she cracked the modest bedroom's outside door she didn't even need that little mental hush-a-bye that she'd learned recently was enough to deepen his dreams. The air was piercing as she descended the pine-pole ladder to the kitchen below. It would have been warmer to go downstairs through the house, but she thought Number Four Flower—the youngest maid in the harem—carried tales to her father-in-law. Her life was difficult enough without that.

All the scents of the Glassblowers Quarter rose up to meet her, scents that blended in daylight into one great smoky reek. Each was sharp and distinct now as the note of a flute: the rabbit hutches along the back of the courtyard, the heaped charcoal beside the furnaces, the privies, the wet, sour aroma of the laundry next door. A ghostly whiff of frankincense blessed the air from the high Citadel where the Sun Mages had spent the day calling the rain.

Sheep Woman had said she'd wait for her in the alley, outside the kitchen-yard gate. Sheep Woman was the wife of one of her father-in-law's workmen. A small woman of the brown-skinned desert breed, her round face disfigured now by a black eye, a blot between the indigo swaths of her veils. Corn-Tassel Woman guided her silently across the yard and into the warm kitchen, where Cook had banked the fire but left a pot of water steaming on the back of the hearth for tea.

"He's not a bad man," Sheep Woman said, putting back her veils and accepting the teacup. "Please don't think that of him. But when he drinks it's like he turns into someone else. And he spends more and more of each day in the cafés, and it seems he's always drinking now. I went to a wizard"—her voice hushed with respect—"but he said it wasn't something he could do, to put a spell on a man's heart so he wouldn't drink so much. Then I heard about you."

"Isn't that just like wizards." Corn-Tassel Woman shook her head, exasperated, and grated a little more sugar from the heel of the loaf. She was a tall, stout woman, the blond hair for which Enak had named her at their marriage returning, slowly, to its original brightness under the influence of little cantrips and spells. Of course Enak would never hear of her bleaching it, though he had plenty to say about graying old mares who couldn't give a man a decent ride anymore. Her movements were brisk, but her big hands were gentle as they patted the other woman's bowed shoulder. "They can't do this and they can't do that, and nowadays they can't even make a mouse ward that works, or keep the mosquitoes out of the house." Old ward signs, the ocher faded with years and overlaid with generations of kitchen soot, ringed the windows and stretched across the thresholds of the kitchen's three doorways: one into the yard, another into the tiny storeroom, and a third into the *seryak*—the public area of the house. Only the outside one had a wooden door. The others were curtained with weaving of Corn-Tassel Woman's own bright, lively work.

"Don't you worry, doll baby," she added kindly, giving the smaller woman a hug. "I've been thinking about Vorm's drinking, and what I think is this: I'll put a spell on him"—she held up a little tube of copper into which a rolled-up paper could be tucked in the manner of Earth Wizards' spells that she'd observed—"so that when he drinks he'll get sick: headache, throwing up, joints hurting, itching—everything I can think of. Ordinarily I wouldn't put those kinds of bad spells on anyone, of course, but in this case I think it's justified. That would be enough to stop anyone from drinking, don't you think?"

Sheep Woman nodded eagerly, eyes swimming with relief. The majority of the folk of these poorer quarters were of the neat-boned desert breed, like the farmers whose villages thickly dotted the shores of the Seven Lakes. Corn-Tassel Woman, like her husband's family, was of the taller and fairer stock of the High Houses and the old merchant clans. "The wizards all say—I've been to them before—that it's a man's own decision whether he wants to drink or not," Sheep Woman said. "But that isn't right. There has to be some way to stop him."

"Well, if this doesn't," Corn-Tassel Woman said with a grin, taking her special bag of powders—ocher and silver and lamp-black and ash—from its hiding place beneath the hearth, "he can't *be* stopped. And if he knew, he'd thank us."

Sheep Woman's smile of gratitude was all the reward Corn-Tassel Woman needed. She felt a bright glee in herself as she spread out a slip of papyrus paper on the hearth. She was always happy to help, as she wished she could have helped her mother in the face of her father's drunken violence—both had died long before Corn-Tassel Woman had realized she could make crying children sleep with a word and could take the sickness off the kitchen cats.

Briefly she consulted the almanac for her own moon aspects and those of her friend, then whispered spell words as she ground a little ink onto the stone and mixed in water and spit. Sheep Woman huddled beside her in her thick, bright-colored shawl as Corn-Tassel Woman took up her quill, watching in fascination by the glow of the tiny fire.

Corn-Tassel Woman thought for a time, pulling the magic out of the secret part of herself—the magic women weren't supposed to have, had *never* had. . . .

Never until now.

At last, she thought, marking the paper with those few High Script glyphs she'd been taught, *at last I can help people. Can make people what they ought to be, for their own good.*

Maybe that's why the gods are taking magic away from the wizards and giving it to us.

Raeshaldis remembered very clearly when first she heard the rumor that magic was dying. She'd been nine then, old enough and big enough to climb over the stable-yard gate and walk about the market in her brother's clothes. She'd been tall and thin even as a girl, and in the baggy trousers and embroidered shirt, tunic and short coat, with her delicate, rectangular jaw and her hair braided up under a rough hat, she'd looked enough like a boy to be taken for one. That was when she'd taken a boy's name, calling herself Raeshaldis if anyone asked.

The news that magic was dying had made her want to weep.

Isna Faran, the gruff, elderly Earth Wizard who healed the sick in the Grand Bazaar and laid wards to keep mice from the granaries, had bristled his black whiskers and sworn it wasn't true. Others agreed. How could it be true? That was like saying dogs would cease to be dogs—what else would they be, if not dogs? Like saying all the musicians in the world would simultaneously forget what tunes were. That birds would lose the ability to fly.

A hundred contrary anecdotes were produced. Only last week Khitan Redbeard, the old Blood Mage over in the Tannery District, had written wards for the new king on the city granary, and everything over there was well. And Urnate Urla, another Earth Wizard who was court mage for Lord Sarn, had cured two of Lord Sarn's teyn children of scorpion sting just by laying his hands on them. Of course magic lived.

Well, there were charlatans—more every day, it seemed. Their spells wouldn't work, that went without saying. But that didn't mean magic itself was dying.

Then Isna Faran hanged himself in his house. And Urnate Urla was called to lay words of healing on the Quail Concubine, Lord Sarn's favorite, just to take a little summer fever off her. After tossing in delirium for three days the girl died, as had the next person the healer had tried to cure, and the next.

People began to look more closely at their neighbors.

If spells were less efficacious—nobody dared to say more than that at first—how would the landchiefs keep control of the teyn who tilled the grainfields and worked in the silver mines, who picked and milled the cotton? Teyn had no magic—there was even debate about how much of anything the slumped, white-furred humanoids understood—but they did have cunning. In addition to the thousands domesticated around the Seven Lakes, there were wild bands that roved the desert. How would they be kept at bay?

How would the sick be healed if the hands of the wise men lost their power to cure?

How would mice be kept from the great clay storehouses of the city's grain? What would happen the next time black clouds of locusts billowed down from the desert wastes?

And, most critically, how would rain be brought each spring, to fill the Seven Lakes and quicken the growing crops along their shores?

The new king, fat and lazy and bejeweled, roused himself from among his concubines and called a meeting of his landchiefs, of the other great clan lords and of the lesser rangeland sheikhs, and of the mages from all the cities around the Seven Lakes that comprised the realm. But nothing much was done.

It simply wasn't true. And it couldn't be true.

Walking about near the Southern Gate, where the camel trains came in from far-off Ith and the Towns of the Coast with their loads of fine porcelains, of amber and pig iron, or from the deep-desert nomad sheikhs with longer-lived and hardier wild teyn, Raeshaldis one day heard shouting and cursing and ran to see. She was eleven by that time, and knew all the wizards around the Bazaar District where her grandfather's house was—Urnate Urla, and Aktis, and old Ghroon the Pyromancer—and those from other districts of the Yellow City as well. She was careful around them, well aware that if she called attention to herself they could probably see through her boy's disguise. They had always fascinated her, and when she heard the rumors about magic failing she'd felt horrible, as if something were being taken away from her. Of course that was absurd, since women had no magic and never had.

She ran down the little crooked street near the southern wall where the crowd was gathered, and so was in front and saw everything clearly. It was the street of the dyers, and everything stank of dye and soap and the piss that the dyers used to set the color: a tangle of little houses, white or brown or pink-washed stucco piled up on top of each other, all marked with mouse runes in ocher and indigo, with ladders and little windows and sometimes vegetable gardens growing on the roofs. The gutters flowed bright with streams of blue and red and green from the round dye-yard vats.

A woman was sitting on the threshold of a dye yard making fire without touching the wood.

The sight went through Raeshaldis like the blade of a knife. Like the noon blare of sun unshuttered suddenly into a darkened room.

The woman looked to be about thirty, chubby and ordinary. Like most women of the working people, she didn't veil her face, and the veil that covered her hair didn't hide its coarse, black straggles. Her sleeves were rolled back, her brown arms and legs bare, her breasts saggy under a couple of layers of rough linen and goat hair. The bunch of friends gathered around her were of much the same type. She'd made a little pile of sticks and cotton fluff before her on the yard's wide stone threshold, and she pressed her hands together and looked at the wood, and the wood caught fire.

Then she scooped up a handful of dust and smothered the flame and scattered the wood. And rebuilt the pile and looked at it again. First smoke curled forth, then pale bright tongues of light, almost invisible in the day.

A boy named Seb Dolek, Urnate Urla's apprentice, who was fifteen then and had been the god of his father's house since his powers first became evident when he was five, jeered, "Yeah, you right—" marketplace slang to express his mocking disbelief. "Show me another, Mama." Someone else went into the nearby house to find the wizard there who was really starting the fires, but he came out shaking his head and said, "Place is empty." Other men—fair-skinned merchants from the cotton market, some of the dyers and a silversmith from the next street—looked in every house on the street.

But even then Raeshaldis knew.

And the whole core of her quivered with wonderment, and she thought, *It's true*.

Young Seb Dolek kicked the burning twigs into the street, scuffed them out with booted feet. The woman looked up at him with her dark wondering eyes, then looked at the charred twigs lying around in the widened circle of the spectators. . . . And all the twigs burst into flame again.

"You see?" The woman's smile was gap-toothed with childbearing, brilliant with relief. "Magic isn't dead! It isn't dying!"

Shaldis felt that she would throw up, or weep, or laugh.

It was the first time she had seen a woman work magic.

The first time anyone present had.

There was a word for men who weren't wizards—*kyne*, they were called, though she'd learned later at the college that wizards called them Empties among themselves. There wasn't a word for women who weren't wizards, because magic was a thing that had never appeared in women before. It was like asking for a word for a woman who wasn't a man. And there definitely wasn't a word for a woman who did magic. Looking around her in the crowd, Shaldis—aged eleven, in her brother's clothes—saw in the faces of the men all the expressions she'd later see when men looked at her. Disbelief, mostly, and annoyance that she'd say it was so.

And anger.

The anger of the other novices in the college, cheated of the birthright they'd come to take for granted.

The anger of the Master of Novices, who hadn't been able to work a spell in seven years. *Shouldn't a student of your great abilities . . . ?*

A man came out of the crowd, parted the front of his pantaloons and pissed on the fire, putting it out. The woman looked up in shock, and Shaldis saw her face change from joy to terror, and knew this was the husband. He grabbed the woman by the arm and slapped her, said, "I told you not to go running around the town playing these tricks! Making me a laughingstock!" And men began to call out jovially, offering to buy her—"Bet she had to learn magic just to get your sword in battle order!"

There was laughter all around them as he shoved her away down the street.

Shaldis didn't know what ever became of her.

But she had thought of her today, whoever she had been. Had thought of her the day before, and for the four days prior to that, in the chill brittle glory of the Citadel Ring, from sunrise to the final fading of the light.

Thought of her as she'd focused all her energy, all her magic, on calling the rain, in a ceremony that according to college records had not taken more than two hours, sixty years ago. Not more than half a day as recently as thirty.

Shaldis had come back from the market that day six years ago not knowing whether to laugh or to weep, and had told her father that magic wasn't dying. It was only turning into something that women could work, instead of men. Her father had slapped her for lying and sent her back to the women's side of the house with instructions for her mother to beat her.

But what you know, you cannot unknow.

TWO

Pomegranate Woman dreamed about the Citadel of the Sun Mages, and a girl with amber eyes.

She'd never been to the Citadel, of course. Up until a few years ago no women were even admitted past its outer gates. But she'd dreamed about it for as far back as she could recall.

Back in the days when she'd been married—when she'd been the mother of girls, and had lived in a regular house, albeit a tiny one, near the great Eastern Gate, and had gone about the streets selling pomegranates from her husband's orchard—she'd had a game with her daughters at bedtime. They'd bring her an object, an old earring found near the local baths, or some neighbor's slipper, or a piece of broken pottery, and she'd make up a story about it. About the woman who wore the earring, and how she'd wanted to marry a handsome young neighbor but her father had given her instead to a fat middle-aged merchant who came to love her dearly; about the cobbler who made the slipper, and how he'd worked long and hard to buy a beautiful dog in the market from the caravans that came across the desert, two months' journey, from the towns of the barren coast. After the girls went to sleep, Pomegranate Woman would sometimes dream about these people, seeing their lives go beyond the borders of her tale. Occasionally, she'd see people in the market who could be them.

On the days of the Rain Song, when the antiphony of the Sun Mages' chants flickered on the wind, when the slow, atonal crying of the horns whispered in every corner of the city and the air smelled of ozone and frankincense, she would dream of the Citadel Ring. See the novices in their white robes and the adepts in gold-figured blue, the masters burning like flame in panoplies of sapphire and crystal. See every gesture and sign, every sigil written on the peach-colored sandstone flooring, each cloud as they gathered in the infinite sky.

So she felt she knew the Ring, and wasn't surprised to find herself walking there again.

It was empty at this hour. The full moon balanced a handbreadth above the quicksilver waters of the Lake of the Sun, the stars just beginning to lose their intensity above the cliffs in the east. She was a little surprised in fact that the mages weren't there already, laying out anew the sigils and runes, the glyphs and lines and triangles on the stone to focus the power of the air and the light. Though in all her other dreams the Ring was an open circle of space, tonight she saw a shoulder-high stone block there, like the altar of some unknown god.

"That isn't right," said Pomegranate Woman to Pontifer Pig, who trotted at her side as he had trotted for years. He cocked his big, white, silky ears at her, regarded her with bright black eyes. "That shouldn't be there."

She walked over to investigate, even though she knew this was only a dream.

A girl lay on the stone block, her thin silk shift torn half off her and her flesh gleaming like the petals of a lily. Soft, straight hair, dark gold like sage honey, rippled down off the edge of the block, hanging nearly to the ground.

Bright scarves or rags bound her hands above her head and roped her ankles to the corners of the block. She must have heard the rustle of Pomegranate Woman's shabby garments, the click of Pontifer's little cloven hooves on the stone, for she turned her head and her eyes were honey colored like her hair, and wide with terror and pain.

"Don't be afraid, dearest," said Pomegranate Woman, though she herself was profoundly uneasy. "This is only a dream."

But she looked around her at the cold stillness of the dawn and thought, *This isn't right. It isn't the right dream.* The Ring looked all right, but now there was no Citadel around it. The cliffs of wind-carved golden sandstone had vanished, replaced by strange rock-strewn hills half seen in darkness. Pomegranate Woman often argued with her dreams: It had driven poor Deem to distraction, the Good God bless his faithful heart.

Wondering if, when she woke, Deem would be there alive again, Pomegranate Woman searched through her mismatched assortment of dresses and shirts for the scissors she usually carried, to cut this poor girl free. But she couldn't find them, and she couldn't wake up, and someone was coming.

If it was the Archmage she'd be in trouble. They wouldn't want to see any woman here, much less a raggedy old beggar-crone whose unruly cloak of ash-gray hair hung about her shoulders unveiled. But if it was the Archmage she'd have to go over and tell him that the poor young girl had no business in this dream that was frightening her so, and then they'd cast a spell on her, Pomegranate Woman, that would prevent her from dreaming about this place ever again. And that would be worse than anything.

This was the reason she hurried to one of the three stairways that led down from this high place and crouched behind a baluster at the edge of the down-plunging cliff. She snapped her fingers for Pontifer, who'd stood on his hind legs with his forehooves against the stone block, sniffing worriedly at the girl with his pink snout; the white pig dropped down and ran to join her, crouching at Pomegranate Woman's side.

It wasn't the Archmage who came.

Pomegranate Woman tried to see his face and couldn't. Maybe he didn't have one. It was like trying to see into the heart of a moving storm. Cold wind flowed out of that blackness, and she saw blue light flicker, flashing as if far off and creeping over the stones.

Pale hands held a thing that glittered as it moved.

What the girl on the table saw Pomegranate Woman didn't know. But she began to fight, trying to thrust herself away; dark blood bloomed on her bare heels where they scraped and shoved at the granite. Hips and back arched, head thrashing from side to side, and that dark shape within the darkness watched her, silhouetted against the searing stars, lambent with invisible fire and holding the moving thing of gold and crystal close at its breast.

Pomegranate Woman thought, *No. No, leave her alone. . . .*

And then *Wake up. I have to wake up.*

Because she knew that what she was going to see was hideous, was something she wouldn't want to remember, ever, dream or no dream.

The white hands set the glittering thing on the stone between the girl's knees, reached back within the darkness of itself to emerge with a knife. The girl's body bucked and twisted as she screamed, but her voice rebounded from those scraggy bare hills, the dead obsidian sky.

And the glittering thing moved, tiny, like a jeweled scorpion, flashing its barbed pincers, its four-jawed glittering tail.

Its jointed iron legs moved like a spider's, as it climbed up on the girl's bare thigh. Its claws left beads of blood.

Wake up! Wake up, girl—you don't want to see this.

Was there a way to wake the poor girl on the table?

But Pomegranate Woman knew—more clearly than many things she knew in waking life—that to cry out, to call attention to herself, would bring that horror upon herself as well.

It's only a dream, she thought desperately—and understood that this was not true.

Somewhere this is actually happening. Why don't the Sun Mages hear? Why don't they come and stop this?

A second white hand took the girl by the hair, twisted her head to one side. The knife pierced the flesh just beneath her shuddering breasts, the blood spilling out blackly as the blade drew down. Pomegranate Woman saw the thing crawling up the girl's slim white leg, over her bucking hip and belly. Saw it only distantly and in the confusion of starlight, heaving shadow, wrenching terror. It crept to the bleeding wound and crawled in. Blood fountained out, as if the thing had found the heart, and the girl's scream ripped the night, her last breath shrieking to the stars that heard, but did not care.

Pomegranate Woman jerked awake with a sensation like falling, to find Pontifer Pig shoving at her feet with his flat round snout. Gasping, she sat up, and the pig planted his hooves on the bed and regarded her worriedly with those bright, too-intelligent black eyes. Hand trembling, Pomegranate Woman pulled the blankets tight to her sagging breasts and tried to rid her brain of images that would not disappear.

When she opened her eyes again the room seemed dark. For a moment she wondered if she was forty again, and Deem still alive. Would she have to grind his breakfast corn for him in an hour or so, and then go out herself into the lively early-morning streets to sell pomegranates? When she opened the door would she see the Salt-Pan Quarter as she remembered it, the streets brisk with vendors' cries and the jingle of donkey bells?

Would she have to face Deem again, knowing he was going to miss his footing while repairing Lord Nahul-Sarn's rain tank and drown?

Knowing that she'd have to go through all those weeks and months of madness again, of sorrow that no healer could lift from her, of lying quietly in the dark talking to Pontifer?

No. She touched her long gray hair, the badge and reminder of her years.

He saw me hiding behind the wall. He's looking for me.

Pomegranate Woman scrambled out of bed, pulled from the top of her blankets all the rest of her clothes—dresses of wool and camel hair and quilted cotton and a heavy old robe of silk given to her by a merchant's wife—put them all on, one on top of another, and thrust her feet into her old boots. Without bothering to latch them she shot open the door bolt, hurried out into the etiolated dimness of the street, Pontifer trotting soundless at her heels. Drifts of sand and tumbleweed heaped the north-facing walls, and the dead, bare, gray tangles of vines hanging from roof garden and terrace scratched and fumbled in the predawn wind. Pomegranate Woman stopped long enough to latch up her boots, then hurried again not toward the city, whose wall rose blank and lightless at the end of the avenue, but outward to the open desert.

She glanced toward where the Citadel was hidden by the towering bluff, black on the ashen sky. *The moon's nearly down—first light will be in an hour.* Against the somber bulk of the city wall, specks and sprinkles of gold gemmed the Slaugh-terhouse District, which lay outside the Eastern Gate and between these ruined villas and the city. Wives lit breakfast fires, ground corn in the flickering light. Sheep bleated plaintively as they were driven to the markets. Pigs squealed in the shambles, a sound she hoped Pontifer didn't understand. A cock crowed.

At one time the whole Salt-Pan Quarter had been a comfortable and stylish suburb where villas stood among groves of date palm and tamarisk and even willows, fed by their own rain tanks, or by wells along the foot of the cliffs. The Slaughterhouse District had lain farther off, south of the road. But now even the beggars had abandoned these streets. The wind blew cold across the open desert, and it was a nuisance to walk all the way back to the Bronze Leopard Fountain for water— not to mention paying Xolnax and his thugs their fee.

There was a law, of course, against enclosing public fountains, but the kings had never bothered much with the Slaughterhouse. She wondered, as she passed among the square brick pillars of this new construction they were building—this aqueduct—whether the water bosses would find a way to take it over as well.

Beyond the suburbs, when first she'd lived here with Deem, there had been a strip of market gardens salvaged from the desert. When the rains were summoned the whole vast Valley of the Seven Lakes drank the blessing, out onto the ranges and scrubland of the desert's edge. Wildflowers grew almost to the feet of the cliffs, and those who served the House Sarn and its subsidiary clans—which owned all this land to the northeast of the city around the bluffs—would farm a little, though personally Pomegranate Woman had always thought the wild pomegranates that grew in the canyons to be sweeter. Now, like the suburb, those market gardens were gone. Only little ridges marked where the fences between them had stood.

Still, she found where Deem's orchard had been. She could still feel under her fingers the prickly echo of the melon leaves that had grown there; still taste the sweetness of the new-picked corn at summer's end. Still hear the women singing thanks to Darutha, god of rain, as they decked themselves with flowers. Sand filled the ridges of the ground as she walked over them, slid beneath her boots. Sand skated in over the lift of the desert and hissed across the ground.

There wasn't even a god who ruled the desert; the desert was a place where the gods didn't go.

Far out on the sand beneath the dimming stars, Pomegranate Woman gazed into the darkness. The darkness was clear, like something viewed through a polished sapphire, and she could see what looked like little fingerlets and flickers of greenish fire flashing among the sagebrush and ocotillo. She'd heard all her life about djinni, the Beautiful Ones, creatures of starlight and wind. The ones who did rule the desert. Mages could speak to them, and sometimes they went for a time to live in their crystal palaces, in their realms built all of magic, invisible to all but mage-born eyes.

But this she had never heard of, these green whispers of light.

She sat down and put her arm around Pontifer's neck, trying not to think about the knife, and the girl, and the blood bursting out after that foul insect of crystal and gold had wriggled into the curled-back lips of the wound. Tried not to think about the way the girl had screamed.

There was nothing, she thought, in all she had ever heard, in all the stories she had absorbed from walls and stones and people, about this.

Pomegranate Woman hugged her little friend in the bitter cold, taking comfort from his round, solid warmth, and wondered if she were the only one who knew.

She stayed sitting on the desert's edge with her pig until full

dawn came and the clamor of the market carts could be heard
entering the city's gates.

THREE

S o, just how long, exactly, *are* we to wait?"
Oryn Jothek II, lord of the Seven Lakes and high king
of the Yellow City, folded plump, bejeweled hands and considered the lords around his council table, mentally laying out a
gaming board and putting wagers on each man's response.

*Lord Sarn: His brother Benno's the rector at the College of the
Sun Mages and in line to become Archmage when dear old Hathmar steps down. A first-quality ruby and a thousand bushels of
wheat that he'll find some really good reason to give the Sun Mages
more time. And he'll take all the lesser Sarn landchiefs with him.*

*Lord Jamornid: Five hundred bushels and a hundred yards of
second-quality silk says he'll go along. Can't give dancing girls as
take-home presents to your guests after a feast if he's paying the
extra taxes my plan will require. The rangeland sheikhs will back
him because he controls their rights-of-way to the lakeshores.*

*I'd wager a thousand acres of prime agricultural land and the
teyn that work it that Lord Akarian will throw up his hands and
refer the entire matter to the Prophet Lohar, the Mouth of the Great
God Nebekht—provided I could find a taker. And perhaps the guild
sergeants will go with him—Nebekht has many followers in the
city—though it's a safe bet the priests will find some reason to say
nothing at this time.*

Lord Mohrvine . . .

Oryn turned to consider his uncle's profile, generally spoken of as hawklike but actually much more reminiscent of a trained cheetah who's just killed your dog and hidden the body where you won't find it until later.

There is never any telling what Mohrvine will say.

"Has it ever occurred to you . . ." Lord Akarian leaned forward, balding brow furrowed with earnestness. "Has it ever occurred to you, my lord, that these events—the delay of the rains, the death of wizards' powers—are all part of a vast single intent, a great test, to which mankind is being put?" He had a narrow face like a mummified camel and the curiously clear skin and attenuated appearance of a strict vegetarian. In the course of twelve years' reign and the some twenty-two years of life that had preceded it, Oryn had heard from Lord Akarian all about divination from lizard dung, the wisdom gained through lying in vats of tepid water (with and without rare herbs added), clarification of the thought processes by the burning of still other rare herbs in one's navel, and petitioning the djinni for advice about field re-allotment—a notion that still made Oryn shudder almost as profoundly as did the half-cropped hairstyles affected by his lordship's current cult. Each time he thought he had plumbed the depths of the great clan lord's credulity, more was revealed.

He said, "I *beg* your pardon?" Quite politely, he thought.

"For centuries," intoned Lord Akarian, clasping his fussy, brown-spotted hands before his chest, "mankind has been given the opportunity to learn, to grow and develop spiritually, under the sheltering care of a great commander who rules all the universe." He used the same words—and precisely the same delivery—that Lohar, the Mouth of Nebekht, boomed out when proselytizing in the temple courtyards of every other god in the Yellow City. Oryn wondered if he'd taken notes or had been given a script by his mage.

"But instead of using this time of shelter to seek out and do the bidding of that mighty power, we have ignored it, and turned to sorcery to heal our sick and protect our families. Now that the Iron-Girdled Nebekht has taken away these toys as a wise and loving parent will take a dagger from the hand of a foolish child . . ."

Hathmar Enios, the white-haired old Archmage of the Sun, straightened up sharply on his leather cushion. "Don't be ridiculous!"

"And I suppose *you* didn't have those ten court mages living in *your* house all those years mixing elixirs to make you wise?" retorted Lord Sarn. "Or rich, or able to see djinni, or whatever it was you were after in those days?"

"I too was deceived." Lord Akarian leaned back on the divan and turned sunken eyes ceilingward, as if to address Nebekht in his heavens. "Now that I have seen the ineffable truth that Nebekht has revealed through his holy Mouth . . ."

"You were born deceived." Lord Sarn's sharp blue glance flicked to Hathmar, then on to Oryn, who sat on peacock-embroidered cushions at the head of the low table of purple bloodwood. "Your father was my best friend, my lord," Lord Sarn said—which wasn't true, but Oryn had better manners than to call him on the lie before the clan lords, landchiefs, and rangeland sheikhs assembled in the pavilion—"and I set you on your first horse as a child." That was something else Sarn never failed to bring up, though the event had taken place thirty years ago and the poor pony had been heavily drugged. Even at four years old, Oryn had known the difference—had known, too, that he was being patronized. But his soldierly father had been delighted, considering his son far too taken up already with music, kittens and flowers.

"So I think I may speak freely," the big lord went on, "when

I tell you that you may be over-hasty in this scheme of yours to build a whatever-it-is you want. . . ."

"An *aqueduct*," said Oryn with the scrupulous politeness that had been his only defense against his father's murderous rages.

Sarn gestured impatiently, as if the word—and the concept—were too ephemeral for him to waste valued brain space on. Not that he need have worried, reflected Oryn—he quite clearly had empty acres to spare. He reminded Oryn a great deal of his father, being built, like the dead king, along the lines of a granite cube on which a thin crop of yellowing grass had grown. "That's understandable—you're young."

"Well, I keep trying to think so." Oryn picked up his peacock-feather fan, an affectation he'd begun in his youth to annoy his father but had kept up—why should women enjoy portable breezes while men sweated in stoic dignity? "As it happens, I'm not too young to know how to count, and by my count the Sun Mages have been singing for the rains for seven days now. Isn't that so, my lord wizard?"

He hated to hurt old Hathmar's feelings, but the Archmage nodded matter-of-factly. "That is so, lord." His long hair glistened like marble in the soft light that came down through the pavilion's windowed dome and suffused the room from the screens of oiled paper and lattice that covered the terrace door.

"Nor am I unable to read," Oryn went on, rising in a great whisper of pleated teal-green silk and going to the door. "And never—not back to the beginnings of the Sun Mages' records—have the rains been this late in coming, or taken so long to be called."

He slid the screen aside with a light hiss. Beyond the thin lacework of leafless vines, past the inlaid pink-and-gold marble of the terrace pillars, stretched the Lake of the Sun. As far as the eye could see, its banks were fringed with the spinach-green barrier of trees, the brown patchwork of waiting grain-fields. Between the fields, darker smudges marked the beds of canals. But no glint of water threaded the snuff-colored earth. Bucket hoists, just within the line of the fruit trees, ranked naked and awkward looking fifty feet inland from the water's edge, dipping up and down with the pale stirrings of the teyn who worked them. Like lines of beggars waiting for a handout, smaller makeshift hoists stretched across the intervening distance, the water poured from trough to trough. The pale, shelving shore was already beginning to blow as dust.

"Never have the waters of the lakes fallen this low." Oryn turned back to his gathered lords, a tall, stout, curiously grace-ful man whose foppish clothing and carefully arranged chest-nut lovelocks should have made him ridiculous. Stepping into the shoes of the fearsome Taras Greatsword—not that Oryn would have ever contemplated donning anything so clumsy as the old ruffian's war boots in his life—he was aware that he could not be regarded as other than a poor second to that ter-rible old man. Greatsword's attempts to make him other than he was, to kill his fondness for exquisite food, beautiful silks, perfect blossoms and interesting books, had only exaggerated his determination to make his reign a work of art in itself, an elegant balance of scholarship and dissipation.

And so he would have, Oryn reflected. Had not, ten years ago, magic begun to fail.

"For ten years now we've faced the possibility"—he would have said "fact," but with Hathmar sitting at the table the word would have been both an insult to the college and hurt-ful to the old man—"that magic is changing. That what once we had we have no more."

He looked around the Cedar Pavilion's council chamber. The great clan lords occupied the nearer ends of the cushioned divan that circled the chamber on three sides; the lesser landchiefs of each clan, sergeants from the guilds and families that owed them allegiance, and the priests of the Great Gods—Ean of the Mountains, Darutha of the Rains, Oan Echis, the lord of law—farther away—audience, not participants. The range-land and near-desert sheikhs, and the representative of the merchants, occupied cushions of dyed leather at the end of the room. They'd have stood in his father's time.

No one contradicted. Mohrvine folded slim brown hands on his knees, his narrow face inscrutable. Though, like Oryn and Taras Greatsword, Taras's younger brother Mohrvine had been raised in the palace called the House of the Marvelous Tower, these days Mohrvine affected the style and manners of the nomad sheikhs of the deep desert, among whom the House Jothek had many allies. He wore their simple white robes and wound back his silver-streaked dark hair on ebony sticks as they did. His jade-green eyes slid sidelong to Oryn, consider-ing him with watchful contempt. Greatsword too had affected the same simplicity—and spoke loudly of the deep-desert no-mads' reputation for manliness, which Oryn took to mean abstention from bathing—without ever trusting them.

In these days, with the drought spreading and the nomads pressing in on the rangelands all around the Seven Lakes, Oryn suspected they could be trusted still less.

At Oryn's side, his younger brother Barún looked thought-ful and scratched something on the wax note tablet he took from his trim military tunic. Probably, reflected Oryn sadly, a memorandum to himself about ordering golden arrowheads rather than silver for the palace guards to carry at the next cer-emonial parade. Lord Nahul-Sarn, Lord Sarn's cousin and most important landchief, whispered something to the mer-chant.

"This isn't just a matter of having no more cascades of fire at parties, no more clouds of butterflies dancing to the music in our gardens," Oryn went on. He gestured with his fan to the corner of the pavilion, where Mohrvine's court mage, an Earth Wizard named Aktis, sat next to the somberly brooding Blood Mage Ahure, who for many years had been Lord Jamornid's adviser and pensioner. Beside him on the divan, Gray King, the biggest of the palace cats, sat up gravely and began to wash his paws. "It's not even a matter of having to sleep in gauze tents nowadays because mosquito wards no longer operate, nor of finding herbal medicaments for what could once have been cured by the laying-on of a healer's hands. Each year the rains have come later. Each year they have been thinner when they came. A man may walk across the Lake of Roses, and the Lake of Gazelles is barely a quarter the size it was in my father's reign—a bare twelve years ago! Most of the Lake of Reeds is a marsh now and parts of it not even that."

"They are always thus, in dry years, my lord," retorted Sarn.

"How many dry years can we endure?" Oryn replied. "It takes longer for the Sun Mages to summon the rains, and it takes more mages each year—isn't that so, Hathmar?"

"It is, King." The Archmage met his eyes squarely from behind spectacle lenses of ground and polished rock crystal whose use had become necessary to him, suddenly and terrifyingly, one morning eight years ago. Wizards' eyes did not age like the eyes of ordinary men. Most mages routinely laid spells on them when letters began to blur with time or when the light began to seem less bright than it had.

Hathmar looked exhausted, Oryn thought with a stab of pity. Eyesight was not the only thing mages preserved by means of their spells. With the silk-backed lattice drawn aside, the drift of voices from the Citadel floated faintly on the golden air—the melancholy whisper of frankincense, the echo of sonorous horns. The Song had recommenced with the first lift of the sun above the horizon, and would continue until light was gone from the sky.

Oryn guessed why Hathmar had decided that his presence among the singers could be dispensed with in favor of the council, and his heart ached for the old man. It would be, thought Oryn, as if his own hands had been cut off, so that he couldn't play music anymore. He couldn't imagine what it would be like to pick up his harp one day and have only silence in his heart.

"Last year the rains appeared on the fifth day of the singing," the Archmage went on. His light, sweet voice could hold a note for a minute together, then leap into the illuminative scales of power without drawn breath. Even in normal conversation it was a joy to hear. "In the later years of your father's rule they would come on the following morn, or afternoon at latest. In those days only the core of the singers went up to the Ring. The rest of us went about our business."

Ocher, gold dust, gypsum and doves' blood stained his fingers as he gestured toward the sterile sky. "We have tried everything that we know to do," he said. "Last year a longer ceremony seemed to work. The year before, greater numbers of mages. We have even admitted a woman-who-does-magic to our ranks. . . ." His tongue stumbled awkwardly over the construction of contradicting terms. "But nothing has changed."

"Exactly!" Lord Akarian lifted a portentous finger. "Nothing has changed because magic is *against the will of Nebekht*."

"Don't be an ass," snapped Lord Sarn—possibly because the House Sarn had been at odds with House Akarian over the vineyards along the shore of the White Lake, but more probably because his brother was heir to rulership of the college. "If it was against the will of Nebekht why didn't Nebekht say something about it before? Nebekht isn't even the god of wizards! Or the god of rain. Or the true god of war, for that matter, just the one they worship in the City of White Walls."

"Iron-Girdled Nebekht is the god of all things and commander of the universe," pronounced the old lord piously. "He has always been. But for many centuries he hid himself among the ranks of the gods, *pretending* to be merely a war god."

"Why would he do a stupid thing like that?" demanded old Lord Nahul-Sarn, whose quarrels with the lord of the House Akarian stretched back to their mutual boyhood and an uncle's preemptive marriage of an heiress. "You're full of—"

"Gentlemen!" Oryn cut in, having heard this argument many, many times before. "Whatever the reasons, the fact remains that the rains are harder to bring. The fact also remains that we must find another way to bring water to the fields and the cities else we perish."

"We must trust wholly in Nebekht. Only by doing nothing, by casting ourselves utterly on his mercy—"

"Remind me never to travel with you through bandit country."

"We can trust," said Oryn. "And we will. But while we trust we must work on the aqueduct." He crossed back to the table, where note tablets lay scattered like roof tiles after a storm. "And after it, others like it. We *must*."

"My lord!" Nahul-Sarn threw up his hands impatiently. "How do we know it will even work?"

"It's only a canal, after all," reasoned Oryn. "They seem to work quite well between the lakes, and from the lakes to the fields. The Towns of the Coast have transported water this way from the mountain springs quite successfully in centuries past."

"For a dozen miles," protested Sarn. "And only according to some notes your wizard found the gods alone know where. The men of the coast no longer use such things."

"The Springs of Koshlar are two hundred miles to the east!"

put in Marsent-Jothek, the wealthiest of the rangeland sheikhs. "That thing you're building extends only a dozen miles so far! The country beyond the Dead Hills crawls with nomads and robber barons and bands of wild teyn where it can support any life at all. We've already expended tens of thousands of bushels of corn, uncounted gallons of oil, fish and horses and supplies and herds, just in surveying the route, in preparing the ground. Now you're asking us for *more?*"

"I'm asking for more because I think we have less time than I at first believed." The king looked around the pavilion again, saw Lord Sarn stubbornly disbelieving, Lord Akarian only waiting for his moment to resume his sermon. The lesser landchiefs, players in the endless negotiations over water rights, grazing rights, rulership of the clans and families who made up the Realm of the Seven Lakes, watched their lords, their lords' rivals, and one another: the lords of the Nahul and Gathement branches of the Sarn; the lords of the Marsent, Terrnyi and Troven Jothek; Akarian's two warrior sons with their heads cropped, like their father, in the striped pattern required by conversion to the True Way. All—and most especially the rangeland sheikhs—watched the nomad sheikhs whom Mohrvine had brought, wondering if Greatsword's alliance with the deep-desert riders would hold through a rainless year.

"And I'm saying there will be other aqueducts because we will need more than a single source. What if the rains never come?" Oryn had a deep voice, like dark brown velvet, strong and insistent at need. Up until a few years ago it had never occurred to him to use it as a tool, as a means of making men listen to anything other than the punch line of an elaborately told after-dinner tale.

He missed those days. Missed being a scandal and a disgrace. Standing before his vassals—before the rivals of his house—he had a terrible sense of being an actor in a farce who has walked onstage into the most deadly of dramas scriptless and not at all properly costumed for the part. He would have laughed had not lives been at stake.

And all of this, he thought, they did not see.

"What if the lakes sink away to nothing? It is happening—it *has* happened, in the north."

"Hundreds of years ago." Jamornid's jeweled fingers flicked impatiently.

"And what if the sand-wights that inhabit the desert waste decide they don't want your"—Lord Sarn deliberately mispronounced the word—"aqueduct coming through their haunts? What if the djinni take it into their heads to destroy the work crews, or the caravans that provide for them? They've destroyed caravans before. They can call sandstorms, bring the illusion of water to lead men astray. They can call men out of the night camps with the voices of their family and friends and lead them to their deaths in the waste. They can bring on plagues among man and beast. All these things djinni have done in the past. You take mages away from the Summoning to put wards of protection on the camps and heal the workers, and it's no wonder they haven't the strength to bring the rains. Just let them do what they're best able to do."

"My lord." The Blood Mage Ahure rose from his place on the divan and salaamed. His rich, portentous voice easily filled the Cedar Pavilion, at odds with the scabbed and crusted cuts that crisscrossed his shaved head and the stink of his uncleaned black robes. "If my lord will permit me, *I* shall lend *my* voice, *my* power, to this Summoning."

"The very thing!" Lord Jamornid bounced to his feet in a coruscation of topaz and gold. "Traditionally, of course, only the Sun Mages are involved in the Summoning—"

"As they should be!" cut in Hathmar, rising to look up with indignation at the tall Blood Mage. "The sourcing of blood spells is completely incompatible! It would waste your time at best. At worst, it would interfere with the sourcing in the sun's power."

"As if having a female-who-does-magic doesn't?" retorted Sarn.

"Oh, folly!" Lord Akarian flung up his hands in theatrical despair. "When will we learn to trust utterly in the bounty of Nebekht?"

"When he sends some, I suppose." Oryn never could pass up a good opening but, fortunately, Akarian wasn't listening.

"This isn't only a question of the mages, you know." Mohrvine's cool voice sliced through the rising din, soft as always, and with the judicious tone of one who has cogitated deeply on aspects of the problem overlooked by all except his wise and long-suffering self. "Nor simply of getting the aqueduct to the Springs of Koshlar. Levies of guards will be needed to keep the robber sheikhs from piercing the pipes to water their camels. We'll have to fight one war at least, and possibly more, with the tribesmen of the Koshlar Oasis who will object, once they notice how the springs diminish when we're drawing off a river's worth of water for our cities. And those armies too will need to be supplied, and the supply caravans to *them* guarded. For all I know the Koshlar tribesmen have mages, who may *not* have suffered a diminution of their powers, and in any case I cannot imagine the djinni letting armies and caravans pass unmolested. Yet no one has ever managed to get an arrangement of any sort with the djinni, or even to know whose side they would favor. Is that not so, Lord Soth?"

He lifted one inquiring eyebrow—a trick Oryn had tried for years to imitate—and turned for confirmation not to his own court mage Aktis, but to Lord Soth, the man who for twenty years had been court mage to Taras Greatsword, until his powers left him, and then to his son. It had been one of the griefs of Oryn's life to see that alert and scholarly old gentleman grow sloven and silent, sinking into his own private darkness.

Now Soth Silverlord looked up and said, "The djinni look human sometimes—if it amuses them." He looked as bad as Hathmar did, and nearly as old, though he was fifteen years younger; though his gingery hair had retreated from the top of his head and grayed down to his shoulders, the end of the long braid was still bright. Behind thick lenses of crystal his blue eyes were tired, and their color too seemed pale, as if rinsed away with weariness and pain. "It is true they do not think like humans. I'm not sure they would even appear if asked."

"I have had some degree of success," intoned Ahure, "in summoning the spirits of the sands." He threw a note of modesty into his voice, rather as Horbecht, the god of the sun's rising, might have said *I have had a little experience with Light.* "I place my powers at my lord king's disposal."

"Someone catch the king before he faints with joy," muttered Aktis, who like most Earth Wizards had little use for Blood Mages. Ahure turned to glare, and Oryn said smoothly, "Thank you, my lord wizard. We're extremely grateful."

"I'm sure we are," put in Mohrvine, in his cheetah purr. "But surely it would be better to ask ourselves if we are overstraining our resources to meet a threat that is no threat at all? Isn't it true, Lord Hathmar—Lord Soth—that during the reign of the last of the Akarian kings there was a period of—what was it, twenty years?—when the rains were slow in coming? When in fact it took longer, and more mages, to bring them?" And he raised one eyebrow again.

"That was a matter of two days, of three at most." The Archmage spoke grudgingly, for he had never liked Taras Greatsword's youngest brother. "Not seven. And it was seventy years ago."

"But there *was* a time of diminution. And the rains *did* return.

Was there any record at that time of the might of wizards be-coming less powerful? Perhaps having greater difficulty in bring-ing the rains? Of their spells requiring more repetitions to work?"

The pale eyes blinked warily behind their heavy rounds of crystal. "That I do not know, my lord."

Mohrvine made a small gesture as if his point were proved, and smiled.

"And the fact that something of the kind may have taken place seventy years ago," put in Soth irritably, "doesn't explain why now certain women are beginning to manifest power."

"I'm sure that many of these ladies are convinced that their abilities are genuine." The royal uncle inclined his head conde-scendingly, carefully keeping from looking anywhere in the vicinity of the pavilion's latticed and silk-curtained inner wall. "But I'm sure that if you investigated each case carefully, you'd find a real wizard somewhere in the background."

"For what purpose?" Oryn's plucked eyebrows shot up not at the implication, but at the number of lords in the room who murmured agreement and nodded wisely to one another. "Why on earth hide behind a woman's skirts if you have power yourself? Particularly these days?"

His uncle widened jewel-green eyes at him. "My lord, I'm only a simple soldier. What men think will bring them power is frequently beyond my ken. But I've seen enough dogs and horses and teyn doing mathematical proofs in marketplaces to know how those tricks are worked"—he glanced at the men around him, the dry quirk of his lips inviting them to share the jest—"and I don't think anyone really believes Banzoo the Wonder Camel actually knows the square root of four. If you ask me, nephew, the teyn you're putting to work on your aque-duct—which is a good idea, by the way, if you can find a closer source—would be more efficiently utilized in digging new wells and deepening the existing ones to last us through this dry period until the rains return in strength." He gathered his gloves, his ivory-handled riding whip, and brought his feet under him. "Was there anything further?"

This was insolence, but Oryn knew better than to invent a final item in council simply to assert his power to keep them there. He'd spent his childhood watching Mohrvine use his charm, his hospitality and his air of injured reasonableness to make Taras Greatsword appear to be a brainless braggart and to imply that Greatsword's sons were, respectively, an obese poltroon and a gorgeous blockhead.

The fact that there was truth in those portrayals only played into his hands, of course, reflected Oryn ruefully. His uncle was a caricaturist, like most political men. It is always easier to snicker at a caricature than to study a portrait in detail.

"Far be it from me to keep you from your dinner, my lord." Oryn gestured graciously toward the door with his fan. "And you, Lord Hathmar," he added immediately, cutting off whatever riposte his uncle might unsheathe. "Will you take anything before returning to the singing?" He offered the old man his arm. "I know you're eager to return."

The Archmage shook his head. Oryn guessed Hathmar would consume nothing until full dark; the mages who participated fasted through the Summoning. The cup of coffee and the small plate of heavenly morsels—dumplings, kebabs, moonjellies and the divinely delicious confection known as gazelle horns—that servants had set before him had gone untouched. Even as he spoke Oryn kept a corner of his eye on the various lords and landchiefs as they rose from the divan, and after helping Hathmar to his feet went to the door, to open it himself for their departure.

As he was bowing the first man out—Lord Akarian, owing to that house's ancient royal blood—Mohrvine paused and salaamed deeply to the latticed inner wall. "Madam, my best regards to you." Head high, he took his proper place in the line and strolled from the pavilion and into the garden beyond.

FOUR

Y ou know the man can't be permitted to live." Lord Sarn placed a broad, red hand on Oryn's arm as the king moved to escort old Hathmar out of the pavilion and through the long Green Court, the outermost and greatest of the palace gardens, to the Golden Court and so to the outermost gates. "I've said so before and I don't care who knows it."

"My dear Lord Sarn"—Oryn widened his hazel eyes at the man—"I can't possibly do away with every man who's insolent to the woman I love; I'd have to start by executing my cook."

But the stocky clan lord clearly wanted a further conference, and Oryn, who ten years ago would unhesitatingly have extricated himself from the conversation with a choice epigram, had come to learn that power had its price not in the dire and bloody deeds of ballads, but in terms of the sheer tedium of dealing with people one would prefer to avoid. And power was what he would need, not—alas—to scale the rarefied heights of ultimate dissipation, but simply to pilot the realm through a desperate and frightening time.

So he caught Soth's eye and transferred the Archmage's hand from his own arm to that of the court mage: "Would you be so kind as to see that Lord Hathmar has a couple of guards to walk with him back to the Citadel? Thank you." He smiled and turned back to Sarn. "He only bade her good day, you know, and quite politely. If I had him murdered in his bed what on earth would I tell the rest of the house?"

"Nothing," snapped Sarn, the red in his face concentrating in unsightly blotches on the bones of his cheeks. "Don't pretend you don't know what I'm talking about." Sarn had been Greatsword's rival and drinking companion, a hardheaded warrior who, like Greatsword, detested the court with its preoccupations with orderly procedure. "Your uncle may have had a hand in your father's death and he'd have a hand in yours if he thought he could get support from the other houses in killing Taras Greatsword's son."

The blue eyes narrowed in a fierce glare, and the breeze from the lake ruffled his short-cropped pale hair. The House of the Marvelous Tower was the only dwelling in the Yellow City that actually overlooked the Lake of the Sun, for the greater part of the city was set back, where it would not impinge on expensive agricultural land. But like the lake waters, the wells within the palace precinct were low. The gardens that were one of the wonders of the realm had a parched look under the wintry sun, yellowed and a little dusty, like a floured biscuit.

"He's courting not only the rangeland sheikhs; he's been inviting your own landchiefs to little conferences in Blossom Houses around the city. And not just in this city—in all the cities of your realm. His sons have been courting Garon up near the Lake of Reeds, and Brodag and Gremm. . . . Every word he says is to turn them against you. It'll work, too, if you increase the taxes to pay for this aqueduct of yours."

He pronounced it correctly, that time. Oryn folded his hands over the elaborate knots of his sash, seeing in the man's eyes the contempt that underlay the wariness but seeing, mostly, calculation. When Oryn had been only an overdressed dilettante prince they'd each had the luxury of despising the other. But Oryn understood now that Sarn had brains, even if he didn't bathe particularly often and kept an inferior valet and a worse cook. And Sarn understood . . . what?

"Thank you for your warning, my lord."

"Will you take it?"

"I'll certainly consider it."

The clan lord's thin mouth turned down at one corner. "You'll need allies," he said, "if Mohrvine consolidates the nomad sheikhs. My sister's come of age to be married—my full-blood sister, youngest of my father's daughters. She's a beautiful girl. Better bred than many you'll find these days."

He didn't glance toward the pavilion. Nor did Oryn, though he knew that no shadow stirred within. The woman behind the screen had been strictly trained in proper decorum and would no more have shown herself at a council than she'd have danced naked in the market.

"Her children will be kinsfolk of House Sarn. Your brother can tell you how the ladies of our house are raised."

"He can indeed." Oryn smiled again, warmly. "Barún speaks nothing but praise for your niece Blue Butterfly Woman." Of course, his brother spoke nothing but praise for anything he encountered in life except unshaven chins on the palace guards. But that, Oryn reflected, was scarcely the worst fault a man could have.

"Come to dinner once the rains begin." Lord Sarn manufactured an enormous smile and draped an avuncular arm around Oryn's shoulders. "It goes without saying, of course, that my sister has been raised to know her place and would never dream of trespassing on the privileges of the Summer Concubine. But as a musician"—his voice sank into a conspiratorial man-to-man whisper—"you know there are different songs for different moods."

"I do indeed." Oryn clasped Lord Sarn's hand politely in parting. "And I shall certainly look forward to dinner. I shall also," he added aloud, once Lord Sarn had made his way the entire length of the Green Court to the bodyguard and the other clan lords waiting for him in the shadow of the Marvelous Tower's gaudy arches, "certainly think twice before I let *you* step into the role of wise old brother-in-law."

"That mighty-thewed arm about your shoulder didn't strengthen and comfort you in your distress?" Silk rustled on tiles. The Summer Concubine emerged from the pavilion, wrapping a spider-work woolen shawl about her thin shoulders in the morning's chill. "You didn't leap at once at the opportunity to hear how his good old friend, your father, would have ordered the House Jothek and the realm it ruled?" Her eyes twinkled like aquamarines. "Too many books and baths for you, my lad." In the pavilion behind her, Gray King picked his way along the council table, gravely dipping his paw into the coffee cups and licking the sweet droplets from his toes.

"I felt too faint with joy at the prospect to leap at anything. What are you doing?" For she'd stepped back from him and walked in a little circle, hands behind her back. She halted, and gravely struck the marble pathway twice with one small, pearl-decked foot.

"It's the square root of four." She widened her enormous eyes at him. "Can I have a carrot now?"

"My dear . . ." He caught her up, lifting her effortlessly from her feet—people underestimated how strong he was—and kissed her too-wide mouth. "I shall give you orchards of apricots and boatloads of crimson lilies, warm from the lovemaking of the sun."

The Summer Concubine had a mouth too big, a chin too pointed, and the flat, thin figure of a girl; her enormous blue-topaz eyes had, in moments of repose, a kind of delighted crystalline silliness that women of her age and position were supposed to have long outgrown. When she was eighteen,

Taras Greatsword had paid a hundred thousand gold pieces for her to Peach Woman, the mother of the most prestigious Blossom House in all the Realm of the Seven Lakes—actually to the rabbity nonentity who was Peach Woman's nominal husband, but everyone knew how such matters were worked.

Two years later she had encountered Oryn—whose affectations and aphorisms had amused her from a distance—playing his harp in the gardens, and had realized that the dandified court clown was in fact a watchfully intelligent young man who steadfastly refused to let his father turn him into something he was not.

They had loved at sight.

"Why in the name of all the gods," said Oryn now, "would anyone believe a man would mask his powers behind a woman? Much less that *several* men would set up a cabal of women pretending to work magic? It's ludicrous."

"They believed it." The Summer Concubine took his hand, and handfast like children they walked along the path between the winter-clipped rosebushes, toward the eight-faced glittering pylon of mosaic, statuary, gold and glasswork that gave the palace its name. A gardener picking the tiniest weeds from between the bushes inclined his head to them—the palace gardeners had from the start respected Taras's heir for his formidable knowledge of botany and horticulture. In the trees around them, gold and crimson ornamental finches sang in their lacquered cages, enviously observed by the kitten Black Princess. One of the palace teyn, lugging water in buckets from the central pool, bowed but gave a shy smile at the sight of the king, odd to see on the jutting, doglike face.

"Did you see their eyes?" the Summer Concubine went on. "The landchiefs and the sheikhs? They wanted to believe."

"In the name of all that's holy, why?"

"Why don't kings dare marry the well-bred and gracious sisters of clan lords?"

Oryn's stride checked momentarily: He met the woman's eyes, seeing in them the memory of angry battles with his father over marriage alliances that had never come about, the delicate jugglings of status, power and fear. It had been generations since a high king had taken a formal wife—Blue Butterfly Woman was the first wife of a king's heir in centuries, and if Oryn died sonless Lord Sarn would hold unbelievable power in the land. Taras Greatsword himself had inveighed righteously against the realm being ruled by the sons of concubines from who knew what background, but in the end he, too, had been unable to bring himself to surrender even that much power to any one of his clan lords.

And had he raised a mere concubine to the position of wife, he would have lost them all.

"Every man assumes that a woman will be another man's tool."

"Hmn." Oryn folded his arms, rather like an enormous, exotic blossom himself in his robes of peacock green, his turquoise-striped pantaloons. "I'll bet you gold pieces to your second-best hair ribbons that this girl of House Sarn will be, anyway. Considering Lord Sarn's been lord of his house for twenty years, this sister of his probably 'came of age to be married' quite some time ago."

"You'd turn up your nose at a woman because of her age?"

"My darling, any man who would do so has never encountered Spotted Serpent Woman of the House of Ten Lilies, who has to be sixty-five if she's a day, or was when I had the privilege of being galloped nearly to death by the lady in my dissolute youth. It's an experience I wouldn't care to undergo again—at least I don't think I would—and considering the number of love spells the clan lords throw in gratis when their women marry men of power, I think I'll find some good reason to avoid dinner at House Sarn. It shouldn't be difficult. The man's cook is apparently under the impression that it's polite to boil asparagus to mush in order to spare the teeth of his lordship's guests."

"Just because Lord Sarn means to rule you through his sister doesn't mean Mohrvine isn't a danger." They slowed their steps as they approached the red-lacquered gate beneath the tower. Two young guardsmen waited there with the king's horse, which was tall and caparisoned in turquoise and green. The guardsmen were likewise caparisoned and tall: Oryn greeted them by name. Oryn's valet, Geb, materialized out of the shadows to trade the king's flowing iridescent robe for a shorter riding jacket in the same extravagant hues. "An aqueduct is a farmer's bounty," the Summer Concubine went on softly. "The herds of the sheikhs live by wells."

"How deep does he plan on digging them?" Oryn worked his large, soft hands into embroidered gloves. "The well we dug last year out beyond Mud Lake is close to two hundred feet deep, and it's nearly dry. We've had three of those deep wells collapse, with dozens of workers killed, and not a drop to show for them. Is he right?" He looked down into her eyes; she was like a child beside his tall bulk. Her eyes, within the frame of the pale green veils she'd drawn down as they neared the public area of the Golden Court, were grave and perplexed. "Is this something that comes in cycles, like winter and spring? Long cycles? Too long for generations to remember?"

"It would have been written somewhere," she said. "In the records of tribute if nowhere else. As for the magic"—she shook her head—"there isn't even a word for this . . . this fading. Just as there is no word for a *woman-who-does-magic*. How very awkward it will be," she added, and though her mouth was veiled he saw her eyes smile, "if more and more women *do* come to power, and everyone has to mumble around like that because there is no female form for the word 'mage.' "

"In that event I trust"—Oryn kissed her hands in parting, and the taller guardsman, a big glowering youth named Jethan, looked shocked—"that you and your ladies will come up with one better than any poet could devise."

There were servants who would have escorted her back to the pavilion whose name she bore, but the Summer Concubine wreathed herself instead in the lightest of white cloaks—the spells of not being noticed—and walked back through the palace gardens alone. Her daughter Rainsong Girl would be at her lessons—at eight years old the little girl was making astonishing progress not only in the simple Scribble of women but also in the complex and nuanced High Script of literature, law and men. The Summer Concubine paused on the yellow marble brink of one of the Green Court's long reflecting pools and, kneeling, brushed her hands over the water.

Briefly, like a reflection between sun flashes, she saw Rainsong Girl kneeling before her low table copying out runes under her tutor's watchful eye.

She is well, the Summer Concubine told herself, and let the image fade. *She is well.*

Last night was . . .

Was what?

She rose from the edge of the pool, walked on, barely a shadow passing over the dusty grass.

A *dream?* If she'd dreamed she couldn't recall it—only the waking, the terrible sense of panic, of horror, that had sent her first to her mirror to call her daughter's peacefully sleeping image, then to the nursery itself, padding along the icy tiles of the arcades wrapped in Oryn's fantastic peacock-feather cloak that he'd left lying across the foot of her bed.

And of course Rainsong Girl had been asleep exactly as the Summer Concubine had seen her in her scrying mirror minutes before. Dark braids like silk ropes on the pillow. Hazel eyes like raw amber flecked with gold—Oryn's eyes—closed in dreams. The child's nurse, Rabbit Woman, had been awake and alert, puzzled and worried over the fear that she so clearly saw in the Summer Concubine's eyes.

And the fear had grown as the Summer Concubine had walked slowly back through the candle-pierced predawn darkness to her bed.

It was with her now, as if the daylight were stained. As she entered the shadowy lower floor of the Summer Pavilion, the chilly dimness there seemed, for a moment, alien to her, as if there were someone there besides herself. Though of course that was ridiculous, she thought, standing in the doorway of the little salon and looking around carefully. The indigo silk hangings that all winter mitigated the piercing desert cold had been taken down from the blue-and-white-tiled walls. The screens of pierced sandalwood, and of lacquered lattice as finely worked as lace, stood back from the door into the dining chamber; no one could have been concealed behind them.

And in any case, who could—or would—be hiding in her pavilion?

It was absurd.

Yet so strong was her feeling of dread that she checked in the jewel-tiled dining chamber, and in the enclosed garden beyond it, and even the small and exquisite baths tucked into the garden's foliage, before she climbed the spiral stair.

There was no reason to feel fear. The dream had been only a fright, a noise in the night.

If dream there had been at all.

The Summer Concubine sat at her dressing table, drew her mirror to her again.

Soth Silverlord had taught her that a mage could not scry another mage—could not summon the image of one who had magic born into the flesh—and this seemed to hold true for women-who-did-magic as well as for wizards. Certain spells wouldn't work on mages, either, depending mostly on the strength of the mage who was casting the spell. Addressing a brief prayer to the god of wizards, the Summer Concubine passed her hand across the silvered glass and conjured the broad, fair face of her friend Corn-Tassel Woman, called to mind the Sigil of Sisterhood that they had made between them, to touch one another's magic.

Nothing. Did that mean something terrible had happened to Corn-Tassel Woman, or only that her friend's obnoxious husband or still more obnoxious father-in-law were keeping her from some reflective surface in which she could reply?

Her mind went into the sigil, and she brushed the mirror again. This time she called to mind the round face of Pebble Girl, who had come to her nearly eight months ago—*I hear you been asking about them that can work spells, lady. . . .*

Almost at once she saw her, the angle of her image in the mirror telling the Summer Concubine that Pebble Girl was bending over a basin in her father's kitchen, an expression of astonished delight in her dark eyes. "Oh, madam!" the girl whispered. "Oh, madam, it's really true! You really can speak to me like you said, through water. . . . Oh, madam. . . . Oh, what can I do for you? How can I serve you? Oh, madam!"

The image faded as abruptly as it had come into focus. The Summer Concubine guessed that Pebble Girl's excitement had broken what concentration she had. She'd have to send her a message, reassuring her that everything was all right, or the girl would drop everything to hasten to the House of the Marvelous Tower, possibly getting herself into trouble with her father thereby. Since she'd first begun inquiring, nearly three years ago, for other women in whom the powers of magic had begun to grow, the Summer Concubine had encountered the most problems from the families: fathers, husbands, fathers-in-law. Some of the women she'd sent word to couldn't come to her—their husbands would not let them leave the house. Some had sneaked to her, like thieves in the night—and afterward, she learned, had been beaten.

Cattail Woman, a big-voiced and harsh-featured laundress from the Fishmarket District, had been suspicious, answering her summons sullenly and asking at once whether she meant to interfere in her affairs. Cattail Woman didn't respond to the Summer Concubine's carefully conjured mental summons on this occasion. That might mean she was busy gossiping—or laying out a spell to do some favor for one of her cronies—or it might mean she simply wasn't hearing. The Summer Concubine tried to scry her house, but again got nothing. Soth said that it was far more difficult to call the image of a place where you had never been than it was to see a place you had visited.

Maybe it was only that.

Maybe she was being foolish, placing too much weight on the dread she felt.

She couldn't conjure the image of Turquoise Woman's little room in the Slaughterhouse District, either. Turquoise Woman was supposed to have come to her yesterday, to share in Soth's lesson, but the shy, self-effacing young woman often wasn't able to walk in from that outer district beyond the Eastern Gate. The Summer Concubine worried about her with an uneasy guilt. It had only been after Turquoise Woman had begun to study magic with the Summer Concubine that she had left her husband, had taken up residence in the rough and dangerous slums outside the city walls.

And what about the other women? The Summer Concubine sat back on her heels before her low dressing table, pressing her fingers to her aching head. What about the women whom she hadn't found yet? Who had not yet admitted to themselves that the mice that stayed away from their storerooms, or the cats or birds or teyn who'd recovered their health, weren't accidents? Weren't chance coincidences?

They were out there. She knew there were others.

The thought of them made her feel suddenly afraid. . . .

"Lady?"

The voice spoke in her head and she snapped her attention to the mirror. Passed her hand over it, carefully forming the spells in her mind.

It was Corn-Tassel Woman.

"Great gods, what . . . ?"

"It's all right." The big, fair woman shook her head, gestured reassuringly, as if her bruised cheek and swollen, red-rimmed eyes were of no more importance than an untimely pimple. "It's just my man. Are *you* all right? I felt your calling. . . ."

"I'm well." The Summer Concubine forced down her rage, her frustration; this wasn't the first time Corn-Tassel Woman had borne evidence of her husband's surly angers. "Did anything happen last night? Any ill, any danger that you know about? I felt . . . I don't know. Something."

And she saw, for just an instant, a look of worry or guilt in her friend's eyes.

Then the glassblower's wife shook her head, and said, "Nothing, bar that I was awake, and working just a little bit of a spell for my neighbor; there was no harm in it, and it was all for the good. But Enak got word of it somehow, and has got one of his rages going."

She turned her head sharply, as at a sound—a shout from the door of the kitchen, perhaps, or the crash of a thrown log.

The image faded.

Around her, the Summer Pavilion felt suddenly cold and filled with darkness. The Summer Concubine slewed around on her knees, her heart in her throat.

But there was nothing. Not even shadow or dimness, for the midmorning sun lay bright on the terrace garden, casting lace-work shadows from the vines onto the lapis mosaic of the floor.

Yet for one moment the room had seemed to breathe with a presence other than her own.

There was nothing in the shadow of the bronze bed with its golden vines; nothing where the screens stood near the wide windows; nothing hidden in the rows of gold-rimmed niches where lamps awaited the touch of flame. The wall cupboards with their inlays of shell and gold were closed, and none was big enough to hide so much as a child, let alone . . .

What?

She could not even say what it was she feared. What she thought, for one instant, had been in the room with her.

Dreams, she thought. Dreams and nightmares.

Still she went out onto the terrace, carefully drawing her veils close to protect the porcelain perfection of her complex-ion, and remained outside until the chimes on the Marvelous Tower let her know that Rainsong Girl was finished with her lessons, and she could go and play with her child.

With the sun's sinking, Oryn rode back along the beaten road-way that ran between the dry fields and the wide brown stretches of crocodile-fringed lakeshore. From far off he heard the groan of the Citadel's horns and shivered. On either side of the Yellow City the sown fields lay brown and waiting, the turned tops of the soil crumbly-pale between the rows where last year's seed wheat slumbered. Between the wheat fields, teyn labored at clearing the last debris of the winter cotton crop, watched by mounted overseers. As Oryn and his two bodyguards rode past, one of the shaggy little hominids raised a long arm and waved.

Like the smile of the gardener's teyn, the gesture made Oryn wonder—not for the first time—what they thought about, those long days in the fields. Set any band of the children of humankind to a tedious task, hauling a canal barge or grinding wheat or churning butter, and someone is bound to start a song. Oryn was fascinated by these simple tunes, the heartfelt words, old tales of love and work and heartbreak.

Teyn didn't sing. As a child he'd asked one of the teyn who worked in his father's stables about this and had gotten only a blank look from those pale blue, slit-pupiled eyes. He wasn't even sure his question had been understood.

What did they think of any of this? he wondered, and slowed his horse beside the high mud-brick wall of one of Lord Sarn's teyn villages.

His guards drew rein as well, young men chosen by Barún for looks and height as well as skill. Why surround oneself with ugly guards? The fair one, bronze and blue eyed, looked about with his hand on his sword, assuming that the only reason anyone would stop near a teyn compound was if there was trouble. Iorradus, his name was, Oryn recalled. A relative of House Akarian. Jethan, dark and dour and built like one of those standing stones one saw far out in the deep desert, merely looked disapproving. He'd ridden with his king before.

Most farming or mining villages had a walled teyn compound nearby, particularly where there was a crop requiring heavy labor, like cane or cotton, or where long chains of hoists were needed to bring up water from the lake. Ocher and white and black, the runes of fear and obedience were traced along the wall top and around the village's single gateway. Oryn remembered riding out with his now deceased uncle Polmec to watch Soth and Lord Sarn's then court mage, the Earth Wizard Urnate Urla, renew them, as they were renewed every few years. They were fresh-marked now. He wondered who Sarn had found to do it after he'd turned Urnate Urla out.

And what would happen if those spells were to fade?

For centuries innumerable generations of those short-lived, silent little creatures had been controlled by the magic of humankind. Attacking bands had been driven off from the fields along the lakes. Spells had been laid on the leaders of the tame villages, to make them fear their human overseers, to make them remain in the boundaries of the villages at night. To fill them with content at a good day's work well done, and at a small ration of corn at night. Having no magic themselves, the teyn in their turn relied on their human owners for healing, and seemed grateful as far as anyone could tell.

Those whom spells could not cow, spells could defeat—and destroy.

From his horse in the shade of the drooping date palms along the dried lake brim, Oryn watched the slumped little forms. They worked neatly, loading stalks and dead leaves onto sledges to be hauled to the kindling sheds and pulping mills of Lord Sarn's domain. Did they sense that those spells were growing weaker every day?

Did their wilding brethren, roving the mountains on the western shores of the lakes, the dust-colored rock hills and wastelands to the east?

Teyn minders were just finishing up the stewing of the cornmeal porridge that the village lived on as the king and his guards rode under the gate arch. The men hurried out of the round central pavilion, but Oryn gestured with his fan. "My dear sir, I'm just having a look about," he called out to the senior of the two. "I shall think much the worse of you if you lay your rightful work aside to fawn upon the powerful." The teyn minders laughed, and told him to give them a shout if he did need anything—he was aware of Jethan's deeper frown.

He feared that the boy found him unconscionably frivolous. Apparently it was perfectly legitimate for kings to go about in disguise—for they did in all the best tales—and have humble folk tell them home truths because they weren't aware of their kingliness. But if a monarch were there in his curly-toed shoes and peacock-embroidered riding jacket, a certain amount of fawning was in order just on general principle.

Shaking his head, Oryn reined his horse slowly around the perimeter of the village, as close to the wall as he could, to feel the terror spells imbued in the bricks. Flies swarmed—teyn villages were uniformly filthy—and Oryn swished vainly at them with his fan. As a child, he recalled, he'd been made almost sick by the sense of cliff-brink fright that began a foot or so from the wall. He didn't think he was any farther away now than he had been then. Old Sunchaser didn't seem to be having any problems, but then for all his prancing and tail flashing, Sunchaser was really a very calm horse. Cats had avoided the walls, too, and would always walk in and out of the teyn villages by the gates—always, Oryn had observed, in the exact middle of the arch.

A big tabby basked between the sharpened stakes on the top of the wall now, catching the last brazen glimmers of evening light. Oryn wondered how long it would take the teyn to notice.

Or had they noticed already?

But all seemed quiet. A young female—jennies, they were called—swollen with child, waddled from one of the round huts to the cooking pavilion: bent-legged, long-armed, silvery arm and head hair neatly shaved. Oryn called down, "Good evening, Mother," and she looked up at the tall, stout, gorgeous man on his tall, gold-maned steed, bared her tusks and patted her belly proudly.

"Mother," she agreed in the thick bass mumbling characteristic of the teyn. When she passed another hut—the huts lasted anywhere from twenty to fifty years, and were rebuilt on the same foundations until some villages stood on mounds a dozen feet high—an old boar teyn crawled from the low, round door. He was crippled with arthritis and bleached to the roots with age. Oryn saw him take the jenny's hands, exchange a kiss with her on the lips. Neither spoke. Teyn did not, among themselves.

The first gangs were coming in from the fields, settling around the troughs as the minders scooped meal into the hollowed wood. They were all silent, though they'd sometimes nudge or kiss. The children—pips—ran squeaking around with high, shrill calls like birds or piglets, but didn't seem to want or need to speak any more than did the adults.

Queer. Very odd.

Oryn had studied for years in Soth's library, had sent repeatedly to the other cities, and even to the rocky little towns of the faraway coast, for any volumes concerning the teyn, and had never learned more of them than he knew.

"My lord?" Young Jethan's voice was deferential, but he sat his horse as if someone had put a poker up his back. His right hand never got more than a finger's width from his sword hilt, though it was quite clear they were in no danger of attack. The lovely Iorradus simply looked bored, glancing at the sky as if he had other plans in town the moment he was off duty and surreptitiously fixing the hang of his cloak. "It is growing dark. If you'd like us to find torches or lanterns . . ."

"No." Oryn glanced back over his shoulder at those silent, shifting, pale forms around the troughs. "No, we'd best be going." It was nearly time for supper, and young Iorradus wasn't the only one who had other plans for the evening. If he were going to accomplish tonight what he hoped to accomplish, Oryn knew he'd need a few hours' rest. In many ways dissipation was an entirely preferable way to spend one's life; he couldn't imagine why he'd given it up. In his palmier days he'd barely be awake at this hour of the afternoon—well, awake, maybe, but just finishing in one of his three private bathhouses. And it had been weeks since he'd spent time with his music, or sorting through his collections of rare gems, rare books, rare instruments of music.

Perhaps, instead of sleeping, he could spend an hour examining the rubies that had been brought in from the mines in the Mountains of the Eanit west of the Lake of Reeds—dark jewels the hue of bulls' blood with strange pink stars sunk in their depths.

Or maybe just having tea with the Summer Concubine and their daughter.

As he bent his head to ride under the gate again he saw a rat skitter along the top of the ward-written village wall.

A bad sign, he thought.

A very bad sign.

FIVE

Do you think he's really in love with Honeysuckle Lady?"
"What if he buys her contract? Makes her his own?"
"It's the fifth time he's asked for her, and you know what Chrysanthemum Lady charges for the supper room!"

"Well, Iorradus is rich. . . ."

It isn't true, thought Foxfire Girl coldly, silent among her giggling fellow fledglings as they walked back through the tiny garden of the House of Six Willows to the stair that led up to their attic rooms. Their chatter washed over her like the breezes that rippled their thin pastel dancing frocks.

"He isn't, either—he's only a guardsman."

"He's a cousin of Lord Akarian. He could even marry Honeysuckle Lady!"

"I think it's romantic!"

I think you're an idiot, Foxfire Girl fought not to say. *It's only a blind, Iorradus coming to see Honeysuckle Lady. It's me he's in love with.*

And the thought of the young guardsman's long golden hair, his broad shoulders like brown silk and the dazzling sapphire of his eyes, sent a shiver through her limbs and a lance of amber warmth into her heart.

Once through the little gate at the far end of the garden, which was smaller and narrower than the big dining hall in the home of Foxfire Girl's father, the fledglings broke into a run. They dashed along the cramped passageway to the kitchen yard where old Gecko Woman would have water and sponges and towels laid out on the long worktable under the ramada of pine poles that shaded the back of the kitchen. They had to be out of their dancing dresses and into the plain, exquisitely tasteful everyday costumes for their poetry lesson, every bow tied and not a hair out of place, in a little less than an hour, something Foxfire Girl would bet a month's candy money Honeysuckle Lady couldn't do if her life depended on it.

Not that she'd ever be asked to, of course. It was understood that though Chrysanthemum Lady charged enormous fees to teach young girls perfection—in taste, in service, in accomplishments, in manners—it was the payment charged for ex-

clusive suppers with the two Blossom Ladies who worked there
that supported the House of the Six Willows.

The girls stripped, laughed, speculated about Iorradus and
Honeysuckle Lady as they scrubbed each other's backs and
took turns at the four small tubs of steaming water in the
striped black-and-yellow shade. Blossom Ladies were distin-
guished, among other things, by exquisite cleanliness, which
could get expensive if you were buying wood to heat wash
water three times a day. A quick scrub in the kitchen porch
was all the fledglings got; they would then bear cans of hot
water up two flights of stairs so that Honeysuckle Lady and
Poppy Lady could wash in the secluded comfort of their own
rooms. At least they only washed twice, a scrub in the morning and a regular bath midafternoon, in the small but elegantly
appointed bathhouse that was part of every Blossom House,
before getting ready to entertain at supper. Although it was
understood that a Blossom Lady would arrive at an accommo-
dation with a patron to spend the night—not always the patron who had paid the supper-room fee—pillowing was only
one of her talents. As Gecko Woman put it, "Any old whore
can spread her legs."

To be a Blossom Lady was to amuse, to entertain. To direct
the whole of her attention and soul to making her patron
happy.

That was what the girls were truly at the House of Six Willows to learn.

Iorradus can't really be in love with Honeysuckle Lady, thought
Foxfire Girl, gathering up her discarded dancing silks and
wrapping a towel around her. It was a quick bolt across the
kitchen yard to the attic stairs, and the late-afternoon sun was
already fading. Though spring had well and truly come, the af-
ternoons were still sharply chill, the nights bitter. *Honeysuckle
Lady is thirty-six at least, and such a bitch.* She hid it around her

patrons, of course—though her salty tongue and wicked imitations of landchiefs and actors and well-known gladiators were famous throughout the town. But the Blossom House fledglings and servants knew her hidden side too well.

"I'll help you with your hair, sweetheart," offered Opal Girl, who roomed with her, as they climbed the narrow stair.

"Thank you, baby." Foxfire Girl spoke the words without really listening to them. *Surely Iorradus would be able to see through Honeysuckle Lady to the rotten person she is inside?* The last time he'd had supper at the House of Six Willows—eight nights ago, when the year's third moon, the Moon of Rains, waxed like a segment of tangerine above the desert horizon—he'd listened to the Blossom Lady's gay chatter but his eyes had sought the jade-green eyes of Foxfire Girl. She'd felt his glance follow her as she and her fellow fledglings carried mint tea and heavenly morsels, couscous and honeyed chicken, figs and coffee, to him and his guardsmen friends. She, Foxfire Girl, might be only a fledgling training in the accomplishments of womanhood to make her a graceful and entertaining wife . . .

But she had felt the warmth of his love.

And why not *his* wife?

"We're both on the list to help with supper," whispered Opal Girl as she deftly brushed out and coiled her friend's long black hair. "What do you want to wear? My horoscope says I should wear blue as long as the evening star is in my third chamber, and I look dreadful in blue."

"You can settle your third chamber with hair ribbons," advised Foxfire Girl promptly. "That's what I always do. I'll lend you mine—my brothers sent me new ones from the City of Reeds." She studied herself in the polished glass of the mirror on the wall, another gift from her father, which she let Opal Girl use too. "I'll let you wear some of my cassia perfume tonight, too."

Opal Girl clapped her hands with delight and hugged her. Unlike Foxfire Girl, whose father had placed her in the house for her education to become a perfect consort, Opal Girl was the daughter of a carpet weaver who'd sold her to one of the prestigious brothels in the Flowermarket District when she was five to pay for her brother's education. The mother of that house was having Opal Girl educated at the House of Six Willows because of her beauty, which would eventually bring in high-paying clientele. There were a few Blossom Houses that specialized in training the daughters of the wealthy or the noble—and had a reputation for turning out unsophisticated prudes—but none that trained solely those girls destined for careers as courtesans.

Perfection was perfection, Foxfire Girl reflected as she slipped on her white chemise, her underdress of spotless white linen and over it a pleated gown of breath-fine, dark blue silk. Of course there were women who used their training simply as a tool to earn money for money's sake. But there were whores in any profession, including that of wife. The ladies of the Blossom Houses, whether wives or concubines or courtesans, were trained to be perfect. Perfect in pillow matters, perfect in cooking, perfect in fashion, perfect in deportment.

Most perfect of all were the Pearl Women, the ones they wrote songs about. The ones men killed themselves for, gave up everything for, lived for and died for.

And a Pearl Woman was what Foxfire Girl had determined in her heart to be.

Given her own family, it wasn't impossible for Iorradus to ask for her hand. *I'd be a Pearl Woman for Iorradus.* Foxfire Girl turned the matter over in her mind as she followed the others down the steps again, along the garden pathway toward the cypress-shaded pavilion where the poetry master waited for them. Cloud Girl had said after the last supper they both had waited on that Iorradus had asked who Foxfire Girl was. Every night since she'd heard this, Foxfire Girl had pictured the scene in her mind when she lay in bed at night: the young guardsman lingering in the doorway of the supper room as Honeysuckle Lady bade a (too loud) laughing good-bye to his friends. His handsome face was wistful, longing. Cloud Girl was clearing away the last of the coffee things from the table. He'd go to her, touch her shoulder—she'd been wearing her gray robe with the yellow birds on it that night, Foxfire Girl remembered, and the yellow underdress. And he, she recalled, wore the gold and crimson of the king's guard, the bullion that embroidered his breast not brighter than the mane of his fiery hair. The scene was as clear to her mind as an episode in a play. *Who was the girl in black?* he'd asked. Or maybe, *That tall girl in black, with the green eyes . . . what is her name?*

Foxfire Girl, Cloud Girl would have said.

And as she turned away with her laden tray, Iorradus would have sighed a little, and whispered the name to himself. *Foxfire Girl . . .* Treasuring it like a flower against his heart. (*He should have held a flower—maybe picked up one dropped from my hair,* Foxfire Girl thought. Only of course Pearl Women didn't lose pieces of their coiffures at dinner. She wasn't sure about where he could have gotten the flower.)

"Foxfire Girl." Honeysuckle Lady emerged from the rather dusty bamboo thickets of the garden court. The yellow and white of her gown perfectly suited her delicate complexion and amber-hued hair, and if her makeup was applied rather thickly under her pansy-blue eyes, it would take another woman to detect it. Men, Foxfire Girl had already learned, never noticed a thing.

As always, even when she was in bed, Honeysuckle Lady wore an assortment of protective amulets, silver and jade and glass. Every girl in the Blossom Houses had a protective talisman or two. Foxfire Girl had three. It was entirely too easy for a rival to find someone—usually an Earth Wizard who unlike the Sun Mages didn't live in an organized college and hence wasn't as scrupulous about who he worked for—to put words of illness or ill luck on a girl. Even a badly timed pimple on the night of an important supper could be disaster.

"Would you be a darling and go to the Ointment Market for me?" crooned Honeysuckle Lady, standing in front of her while the other girls disappeared through the garden gate. "I've already settled the poetry master to let you. That old whore Gecko Woman is out of sheep cream in the kitchen. I need the good-quality kind, not that curdly stuff they have for the maids here. I just found out, and I have a supper at dusk." She pressed a silver piece into Foxfire Girl's hand.

Foxfire Girl manufactured a bright smile, thinking, *You ratty old slut—you're doing this to make me late because I'm prettier than you.* "Of course. Just let me go get my veils." *And find one of the juniors to bribe. Thank the gods I didn't spend all my candy money this month.*

"You darling!" Honeysuckle Lady put a hand lightly on either shoulder, pecked two cold little kisses on her cheeks. "I'll wait here for you and walk you to the gate. You're the only one I can trust—you have such excellent taste."

Seething at being thus trapped into the errand, Foxfire Girl shouted for Gecko Woman on her way through the kitchen yard, then flounced up the steps to the attic again. Having remained to set out their clothing for the supper, Opal Girl was still dressing for class. She was short where her friend was tall, warm brunette to Foxfire Girl's dramatic pallor and darkness, at age fourteen curvaceous already. Foxfire Girl snatched up the veils without which no decent woman appeared in public, her fingers tangling in the lacquered whorls of her hair.

"I won't have time for a real bath," she snapped, barely able to breathe with anger. "So make sure they don't empty out the tubs by the kitchen until I get back."

Opal Girl nodded. She was half afraid of her roommate, partly because, as the daughter of a great house, Foxfire Girl had grown up with an arrogance that would not take no for an answer. "I'll have everything laid out ready for you," Opal Girl promised. "I'll try to stay here to help you get ready."

"Thank you, baby." Foxfire Girl bit back the torrent of oaths and recriminations on her lips, stepped over to the other girl and kissed her lightly, then pinned the face veil in place with just the proper coquettish gather of folds at the side. "But don't make yourself late." Her tone implied, Not *too* very late, anyway. "I'll be as quick as I can."

But, as Honeysuckle Lady had undoubtedly been aware, by the time Foxfire Girl and Gecko Woman reached the Ointment Market near the Baths of Killibek where the fancy milk sellers had their pitches, most of them had closed up for the day.

There wasn't a question of buying any old thing, either. Honeysuckle Lady brought in too much money for Chrysanthemum Lady to ignore a complaint from her about a fledgling. By the time Foxfire Girl found something remotely acceptable and got back to the House of Six Willows it was dark, and the horns that had groaned so tediously through the day from the Citadel—*Can't they just get on with it?* she'd wondered impatiently—had ceased.

They'd already emptied the tubs.

Her room, when she reached it, was pitch black, but as she opened the door the fusty reek of cat urine stung her nostrils. *Oh, no,* she thought, aghast, furious. *Oh, no . . .*

She fumbled with striker and steel, lit the candle by the door.

Oh, yes. Opal Girl, true to her promise, had left her best

white dress and black-and-white flowered outer robe spread out on the bed. And one of the half-dozen cats that spent their days hunting mice in the kitchens (in spite of what Chrysanthemum Lady spent each year on mice wards—*What was wrong with wizards these days, anyway?*) and loafing around the garden had desecrated not just one garment, but both.

Damn her. From the window Foxfire Girl looked out across the tiny garden court, past the pavilion that held the dancing floor and the classrooms, across to the warm lights of the supper room. Bright figures moved in the verandas, shadows flickered on the stiff bleached papyrus shades of the windows. If Iorradus and his guardsmen cronies weren't there already they would be soon, far too soon for her to get herself washed and perfumed—and her hair fixed; it was still dressed for poetry class, not for serving at a supper—in time to participate.

I'll kill her, she thought, with the cold, perfect, towering fury of fourteen. *I don't know how yet. . . .*

And unbidden, a thought flickered across her mind. A dream, maybe, or something that was almost a dream.

Her eyes narrowed and she thought, *Well, maybe I do know. Or anyway, I'll certainly try.*

With a single slashing gesture she hurled the ruined garments on the floor and carried her candle to the painted chest where her other robes were, to see what else she might wear.

The Citadel's horns had ceased and luminous darkness had settled on the face of the desert when Oryn scratched at the door of the wisteria-covered pavilion behind the library. Lamps burned among the trees of the Green Court, visible beyond a screen of mostly bare foliage. One of Oryn's cats—Candy or Black Princess, barely a silhouette in the darkness—stalked crickets, its eyes flame-soaked mirrors. The silence that was so sweet a component of the House of the Marvelous Tower—set as it was between the city and the lake, with open fields on two sides and water on the third—lay like a blessing over the pebbled paths.

The tall windows of the library still showed lamps burning, and Oryn wondered if Soth had forgotten the time. Time was not something that wizards commonly forgot. It was almost unheard of, for Soth.

At least for the Soth Oryn had known as a youth.

He scratched the door again. When no reply came from within, he pushed on the carved panel gently and called the wizard's name. "Are you there?"

"No." The soft, husky voice came out of the darkness. Oryn knew the pavilion well enough to cross its outer vestibule to the inner chamber, where a little light leaked through the windows from the library across the court. He also knew well enough to move carefully, shuffling his feet so as not to trip over the stacks of books the wizard habitually and continually shifted from tables to divans to floor. He encountered two or three of these anyway, and once a low table undoubtedly rendered invisible by some spell. Two enormous pyramidal book racks loomed like mountains in the dark, the bullion threadwork and polished gems of the book covers glimmering like the phosphor that lay on the surface of the Lake of the Moon. "No, my boy, would that I could tell you that I were here," Soth went on, in a voice of great deliberation, as if the enunciation of each separate syllable were a matter of honor. "But the fact is I'm not. I have no idea who's here in my stead."

Soth's desk was beside the southern windows, and by the sound of his voice he was sitting at it. Oryn heard the alcohol in the slurred inflection and smelled *sherab,* the twice-distilled brandy of grapes, in the chilly, stuffy dark. Exasperation flashed through him—*Of all the times to pick to drown yourself in the bottle!*—replaced, a moment later, by pity, and shame at his own anger. He picked his careful way to the desk and said, "Perhaps you'll like him. I do."

"Kind of you."

Oryn's eyes were adjusting to the darkness. He picked out, by the dim ghost of the distant library lamps, the painted latticework doors of cupboards around the walls, open under the bulge of scrolls, codices, notes, tablets; the pale handbreadth of Soth's narrow, unshaven face. The wizard poured himself another cup of brandy—he was taking it in teacups, big as half oranges, rather than in the smaller vessels made for liquor—and unsteadily rose to fetch another for his guest.

There was a slithering clatter as Soth knocked over a pile of books; Oryn caught his arm. *All he'd need,* he thought, *was to tip over a lamp and soak everything in oil.*

"Thank you, dear boy." The wizard shook him off gently and fetched the cup with the dogged persistence of a drunkard. The unraveled braid of his hair made a tangled silky cloak to his hips. "But he's a paltry fellow, you know. Useless. Ask Lord Mohrvine. He'll tell you."

Oryn gritted his teeth. He'd been afraid his uncle's silky deference had hurt his former tutor worse than criticism would have.

"Your lovely lady will be of more use to you in your evening's quest."

Oryn accepted the cup held out to him but only pretended to drink. One thing he couldn't afford tonight was even the slightest possibility of misstep or misjudgment, and he recognized the vintage: laid down by his grandfather, twice distilled and aged thirty years. He wasn't sure that the smell alone wouldn't make him stagger as he left. "I'm sorry you won't be able to join us," he said, quite sincerely. "The last time I spoke to the djinni was twelve years ago, and even my memories of their summoning aren't what a trained wizard's would be. The Summer Concubine has performed it before, and watched you, of course, the time before last. But though you said she performed the rite perfectly last time, there is always something a man of experience sees and knows that doesn't get said. And she's never even seen the Beautiful Ones. Of the three of us, you're the only one who has actually summoned the djinni."

"She did the summoning perfectly last time." Soth groped his way back to the desk. The figured silk cushions of the divan sighed like a generation of disappointed parents as he sagged into them.

"They did not appear."

"My child, they're not servants." Soth blinked up at him, squinting to see in the nonexistent light. Or perhaps, thought Oryn sadly, merely struggling to focus his eyes. It had been years since Soth had read, as wizards do, in the dark. "They didn't answer my summoning a year ago, not that I was able even to summon so much as a dog by that time. But even when I had power, more frequently than not the djinni chose to ignore the call. They are unaccountable, my Peacock Prince. Creatures of magic, living in magical realms. They have no need of us nor of anything we can offer them. Particularly not now. We can only petition like hungry bankrupts at their invisible gates."

No, thought Oryn. He drew the great collar of his sable-fur cloak about him and left the dark pavilion behind the library, making his way by circuitous paths to the kitchen gate where the Summer Concubine waited for him with the horses. *There was a time when we could say, We can only do so much,* and if the djinni did not answer the call of whatever wizard tried to summon them, it was irritating but not fatal.

Now it could very well be fatal.

If anyone would know what was happening—to magic, to the rains, to the world—it would be the Beautiful Ones. The wild spirits who manifested themselves in the form men called djinni. Who lived, in their strange realms of crystalline light and magic, forever.

The Summer Concubine waited for him in the court behind the kitchen, where deliveries were brought in. She had a kind of slim neatness in her dark riding dress, like a little soldier. "You're not too tired?" he asked, helping her to the saddle, assistance she needed rather less than she needed help in feeding herself. "It may be a long night with nothing to show for it." He himself had slept, and spent a little time with his music, playing strange laments on an ivory zittern from the deep-desert oasis of Minh. The instrument was said to perfume the listener's dreams.

"I'll be all right."

She was a Pearl Woman, reflected Oryn with a mental headshake as he unbarred the gate and led his own mount through. No Pearl Woman on the face of the earth would admit that she was too tired, or unable to perform any task required of her. He closed the gate behind them, swung up onto his bay gelding, as tall and as bulky as himself. He felt a little silly as he wrapped a tribesman's scarf around the lower part of his face; there were few men in the palace of his opulent stature and surely the guards would recognize the horse, not to mention the sables. But perhaps the guards merely required that he fulfill the forms of incognito. They certainly made no comment as he showed them the pass he'd written for himself, only opened the outer gate.

The torchlight failed behind them. The full moon's light silvered the sterile furrows of the lakeside fields, the withe fences of market gardens as they struck out northward. As they passed close by the small houses clustering the base of the city walls,

Oryn heard the hum of day's-end commerce: the bray of asses being unhitched and the squeak of cart wheels. In every house in the city, women got up from their looms. Men and teyn left the bucket hoists that brought lake water to the fields. Somewhere on the margins of the lake a crocodile bellowed.

A woman's voice called to a child to fetch the turnips and be quick about it. A vendor sang about the finest-quality goose quills in the land.

The Citadel, looming high on their right, was silent and dark.

Dust stung Oryn's nostrils, gritted under his scarf. In spite of first-quality ointment his skin felt tight and dry. Ahead and to both sides the herds of House Jothek cattle lowed with thirst around dry water tanks. A rider whistled to his horse in the dark, and somewhere a dog barked.

This has to work.

The bluffs rose like a dark cloud on their right; the blanched light outlined Joshua trees and scrubby ocotillo.

We have to learn what's happening, and the djinni are the only ones who can tell us.

If they could be induced to tell.

Oryn had been six when first he'd seen the Beautiful Ones. He remembered the whirlwinds of gems far out in the desert, scintillant in their own light. Remembered the touch of wind that had flowed out from those brilliant beings, the scents that had filled the night. Wild, clean, delirious scents that he remembered with crystal exactness but had never encountered anywhere else, had never found words to compare them with. He'd struggled furiously against his father's iron grip, overcome with the need to run to them, to break out of the protective circle Hathmar had drawn. To absorb and be absorbed by those wild promises of love and unbelievable joy.

Meliangobet, who was Hathmar's friend among the spirits,

had looked down at the chubby, curly-haired child standing at the very edge of the circle, had smiled. For years Oryn had tried to capture in his music the wonder of that smile. The djinn's eyes were harder to describe, and tales differed about whether these spirits went naked or were clothed in robes of billowing silk dusted with jewels. About whether they flew themselves, or rode upon winged and nebulous things.

Only that they were beautiful, filled with magic and free.

This will be a king? the spirit had asked.

Hathmar had put his hand on Oryn's shoulder. "If he lives."

Oh, you will live, my lovely princeling. Meliangobet leaned down and extended a glowing hand. For a few moments only the hand was visible, emerging from a veil of light. *I see the years crowning you like a garland of summer flowers.*

And though Hathmar had warned him repeatedly against doing so, Oryn had stepped forward over the protective line. Both the Archmage and Greatsword lunged to pull him back; it wasn't safe for any mortal, let alone a child, to be unprotected around the djinni. But Meliangobet, and Naruansich, and the Bright-Fire Lady and Thuu the Eyeless had all laughed and drawn Oryn into their glittering circle, touching him with long, thin, cold fingers that trailed white flame.

He has no fear, had said Meliangobet. He'd been friend to Hathmar's master Gemmuz, ninety years ago in the days of the Akarian kings. According to the Citadel records, he—or it—had been friend to Gemmuz's master's master Wrotyn Rainlord before that. His appearances were attested to by records stretching back six hundred years.

Best you learn it, little prince, said Naruansich. In records he was described sometimes as a jeweled snake, or as a young boy; sometimes only as a burning light. Oryn remembered him as being white as lilies and fire. *You will need the lesson.*

Then they were gone. Looking back to the rock where

Hathmar had drawn the circle and made the summons, the child Oryn saw that he'd come much farther from it than he'd thought, two or three hundred feet. His father, running toward him over the rocky dust, was pale as a sick man, though of course once he had his son safe in hand again he grabbed his arm and struck him, leaving bruises that lasted weeks.

Returning to that same turtlebacked stone hillock with the Summer Concubine under the white, full midnight moon brought the memory back as if it had been yesterday. Amazement that no ill had befallen him. The lingering sweetness of Meliangobet's smile.

"Soth wasn't angry, was he?" The Summer Concubine slipped from her saddle, tied the rein to one of the palm stumps near the rock's foot. Oryn guessed there had been a water hole here once. The horses pawed and snuffed in vain. The flat miles stretched in all directions, the Lake of the Sun no more than a thread of silver, the city walls a dark rumple, like dropped velvet with a gold spangle or two still catching the light. The bluffs were black loaves, the cliffs of the true desert's edge a long black knife blade slitting the pale land. Jackals howled. "Angry that I'm able to do the summoning? When I tried it at the last full moon he seemed to accept."

"He isn't angry." Oryn helped her take from the saddlebags the things Hathmar had used for the summoning all those years ago, which had been brought down by the old man that morning before the council. In the past eight years, with the rains coming later and later, with the rumors of magic's fading blowing like poisoned dust through the marketplaces and alleys, Hathmar had come out here—and to other places in the wastelands—at least a dozen times, calling on the name of his friend. Or the spirit who he thought had been his friend, and his master's friend before. There had been no response.

"He isn't angry at you, anyway." He carried the implements

up onto the broad curved rock. They were beautiful things, old and mellow and sweet with years: lamps of gold whose light shone forth through circles of cabochon gems, water vessels carved of blue amber no bigger than thimbles, rough fragments of crystal woven round with silver wire and knots of iron containing the bones of hares. Each element, metal or jewel, was tuned to some unknown note of the secret harmonies of power. Each object held power of its own.

By moonlight bright as the glow of lamps, the Summer Concubine laid out the circle of power, drew hands of salt around the crystals and power rings around the candles and the frankincense, around the vessels of iron and gold. Powdered silver and animal bone, and three caged doves, to be killed for their blood. Other mages used other methods to summon other djinni—it was said the Eyeless One favored human blood, dribbled from the summoner's arms down onto the sand—but in eight years Oryn had not heard of a single mage whose attempt to speak to the djinni had succeeded.

Why?

The last time he had seen Meliangobet—to the best of his knowledge, almost the last time any mage had seen any of the spirits—had been twelve years ago. *You have lived to be a king, little prince,* that sweet voice had said into his mind. *And you have won by your patience the flower you sought.* Oryn was less surprised that the djinn knew about his love for the Summer Concubine, for the Beautiful Ones were popularly believed to be able to see into men's dreams, than that Meliangobet felt any concern about the matter.

There were more of them on that second occasion than on the first, a great convocation of the spirits of the night and the sand and the wind. Oryn had never been able to see more than two or three at a time, but he sensed the others all around, as if they stood behind curtains of blowing black gauze. Mocking a little, especially the strange ones like the Eyeless One, or the thing men called Smoke of Burning, as if they read something in his face that amused them, like adults who hear a child boast of subduing armies with a wooden sword. Most had merely studied him. A few, Oryn had thought, looked profoundly sad. That might only have been his imagination. Later Hathmar had said, "I've never seen so many come to see a new king."

Now, twelve years later, wrapped in his sable cloak and straining his eyes for the far-off glitter of their coming, Oryn wondered if they'd known.

Is that why they won't come? Because they know we're dying, and know we'll ask them about it?

A dozen feet from the protective circle she'd drawn around him, the Summer Concubine raised her arms, face wreathed with smoke, hair loosened and eyes shut in a trance.

Or was it just that, like men, the djinni didn't care for spells woven by womankind?

Oryn pressed his hands to his eyes, praying that when he opened them again it would be to see the far-off whirlwind of jeweled magic coming toward them across the endless sand, faster than a horse could run. *It can't be true that we're all going to die,* he told himself. *There has to be some way out of this.* Some way of buying time enough to finish the aqueduct—and others like it—before the lakes shriveled away and people began to starve.

He'd thought the tall, skinny sixteen-year-old girl who'd come to the College of the Sun Mages in boy's clothing a year and a half ago might be the answer, or *an* answer anyway. But so far she seemed to have lent nothing to the bringing of the rain. *Seven days,* he thought, aghast. And nowhere near enough grain in storage to last through a year like last year *and* provide seed.

The sweet scent of the candles, burning behind the crystals that magnified their light, seemed to fill the night. He thought of the other women who had come forward, shyly—whom the Summer Concubine had tracked down by rumor and gossip in the city, or who had come to her of their own accord, each as different and as fascinating as a new strain of rose. Oryn couldn't fathom how men could scorn women for age or unfashionably shaped noses when each woman was like an unread book: voice and hair and the color of her eyes.

Their power wasn't the same as that of the male wizards. They often couldn't make spells work, or couldn't make them work the same way. And of course they were completely untrained.

But they had power. And so many wizards didn't anymore.

Did Ahure the Blood Mage, who'd so condescendingly offered to add his spells to those of the college tonight?

Or Aktis, glancing around the council chamber with those bright, black cynical eyes?

Did Lord Sarn's brother Benno, who'd had to forswear his heritage as the Lord of House Sarn all those years ago when his powers had first been discovered?

Or even Lohar, the mad prophet of Nebekht of the Iron Girdle? A former Sun Mage who'd claimed to have been visited in dreams by the minor war god of his home village, whom he now alleged to have created the universe?

Oryn opened his eyes. Far away he thought he saw something like green flame, rags of whitish mist, among the shadows of the northern dunes. But he couldn't be sure. In any case, it was nothing like the wonder and glory of the djinni. Nothing like anything he'd heard of before at all. And that, too, was disconcerting. Things were not as they had been, and there was no way to know whether they would ever be so again.

And overhead he saw the moon riding in mid-heaven, surrounded now by thin streaks of gathering cloud.

SIX

"Who is it?" Shaldis sat up in the darkness, heart punching at her ribs. She pulled the blanket tight to her chin against the brittle cold.

Silence, and the thin skate of blown sand along the shutters of her window.

A dream.

She'd dreamed someone was calling her, calling for help.

The words skirled away down the corridor of sleep and were swallowed.

Shaldis lay back down. The rock-cut cubicle at the end of the novices' row was narrow. At any time of the day or night she could hear the smallest whisper in the passageway outside. Since last night's attack she'd put every spell of ward and guard she'd learned from the shadowmaster on the shutters and doors, not just the minor cantrips that sometimes kept the boys out and sometimes didn't. No one in the Citadel was supposed to use this type of spell. She'd felt guilty about placing them, as if she were betraying the order. But the malice that had searched for her last night had no business in the order either. No one had chided her so far. Could it be there was truly no one left in the college with the power to detect them?

Except the attacker, of course.

Why did he still have power, if no one else did? And if he had such power as she'd felt last night, why that bitter rage?

The worst of it was, she wasn't certain the ward spells would do any good. Certainly her earlier wards had only worked against the other novices about half the time, though she knew they had no power. The memory of her attacker's terrible strength came back to her, that crushing, alien cold.

All day, standing among the other novices in the Ring, exhausted from last night's terror, she had scanned the faces of the masters wondering about each man, *Is it him?*

Benno Sarn the rector, administrator of the Citadel? That broad, red face framed by the flowing hair pale and brittle as bleached straw, those cold blue eyes that always looked so angry at having been forced to enter the order when he had been firstborn of the House Sarn. Had his powers not manifested when he was ten, old enough to know himself the heir, he'd be a clan lord now instead of a mage.

Is it him?

Old Rachnis the shadowmaster, a white, fragile spider that has spun its webs in the dark too long, his pale eyes blinking as he swayed. He'd long ago ceased trying to demonstrate the illusions he taught. At the last new moon of summer, when Shaldis was the only novice able to conceal herself with the spells of the white cloak or the gray cloak, the only one who could conjure shadows into the semblance of cats and flowers and frogs, he had seen the faces of the boys in the class and declared that he would henceforth teach each novice separately.

Is it him?

Maybe Brakt the loremaster, who handed Shaldis the grimoires and list books in the library in such rigid, disapproving silence? At the conference concerning her admission, he had inquired whether the presence of her body alone—"female flesh," was how he'd put it—in the Citadel would shatter the essential magic of every spell wrought there and complete the ruin they hoped to avert.

What about Hathmar himself, standing at the center of the great loops and intersecting lines of power, calling out the chants while the great horns sounded against the golden cliffs?

Is it him?

And if it is him, to whom can I go for help?

Go to sleep, Shaldis told herself. *You can't do anything about this tonight.*

But she could not sleep. And as the wind groped at the shutters above her bed, she realized that she feared to sleep. There was magic somewhere. *Far off,* she thought, *wispy like smoke . . .* palpable as the dim jingling of shaken chains.

Terrible magic. Magic alive, and awake. Magic that listened for her. Magic of a kind she had felt at no other time but last night.

She must not go to sleep.

How long she lay awake between the dream and the first stealthy rattle at her window shutter she didn't know. Many hours, she thought. She had been taught to estimate the position of the stars, and of the sun beneath the earth, even when she could not see them, so that she could properly source their power. She had waked not more than an hour after full dark, and it was probably midnight when she realized that she could no longer see in the darkness of her room. If she had thought before of seeking help or comfort—*From whom?*—she shrank from it now, fearing what might be outside should she open the door. The window shutter rattled, though the wind had ceased an hour ago. Shaldis's breath jammed in her lungs and she drew away from the stout wooden slabs, but she dared not make so much as the noise of getting out of her bed.

Go away! she thought. *Go away!*

It was outside the window, pressing against the wood. In the back of her mind she heard a whisper: *Shaldis . . .*

The voice was that of her sister, Habnit's Second Daughter. Twosie they'd called her, like most second daughters. Shaldis pressed her hand to her mouth.

Shaldis . . . Big sister . . .

Silence, prolonging itself to the edge of sleep again. The weight of sleepiness on her mind, and beyond that sleepiness the dream of going to the window, of opening it and seeing her sister outside, smiling with love. Her father holding out his arms to welcome her. Just outside the window.

Shaldis pushed the dream, and the sleepiness, away from her mind. The hinges creaked, as if at weight so immense that the wood groaned and the bolts that held the lock squeaked as they pulled in the wood. The shutter was inches from the head of the bed and she didn't dare get up, didn't dare fly to the door, knowing that whatever it was, it might very well be outside the door waiting for her to do just that.

Eldest daughter . . . The nickname her father had had for her, and longing to see him again twisted around her heart. *Old One . . .*

No! she thought, almost weeping. *No, go away!*

She smelled his malice, like rancid smoke. Smelled sulfur and lightning and acrid cold. She spread her hands before her in the dark and called into them the power of the sun. It was hidden away now under the earth, but the light imbued the sand, the stone, the veins of iron and gold deep in the earth. She called that residual power from those, as she'd called upon it all day, to Summon the rains.

Drive away evil. Fill this man with dread.

She heard him curse and felt the jabbing wrench of his counterspell on her mind, like iron pincers clamped suddenly and twisted on her hand. *Bitch . . .*

Raeshaldis threw back the covers and got to her feet. Standing in the darkness, she faced the window, called spells of blazing light. Of cramps and migraine, spells that would stop the breath or trip the feet or dig at the belly. The counterspells jabbed at her again but she thought, *He has to be tired too. He's been at the Summoning all day, the same way I have.*

The knowledge that she might have stood next to him made her skin creep.

I won't let you drive me from this place. I won't surrender what I have. It's mine.

Bitch.

Thieving bitch.

Then he was gone.

Cautiously she probed at the night outside, but in fact he did seem to be gone. She could see in the darkness again, make out the shapes of the shutters. The wood all around the hinges and the bolt hasps was splintered where the blue scribbles of light that marked her spells flickered, deep within the wood. She saw again the small wooden chest at the bed's foot, the washstand with its vessels of ancient red pottery, the spare quilts folded on the shelf.

She sank down on the bed, trembling so violently she wondered if she'd be sick. She'd have to get up soon—it was only an hour short of first dawn—and face another day of Summoning.

Face another day of exhausted fasting, of the knowledge that she might be standing next to him.

Knowing what he was, but not who.

SEVEN

Torchlight transformed the kitchen gate to an oven mouth of ember-hued gold.

"Something's happened." The Summer Concubine nudged her mount to a hand gallop through the last stretch of road among the market gardens.

"Why am I not surprised?"

Cressets had been lit all around the walls of the kitchen's vast court. Huge shadows fluttered on the heavy stone archways of the laundries and the weaving rooms where the palace's silk was loomed, and on three stories of shuttered slave barracks above. Men clustered in the arch of light, mostly in the red livery of palace servants or the crimson cloaks of palace guards. Barún stood in the forefront, like a statue of a king, looking as solemn and noble as if he hadn't been blackmailed over sexual shenanigans by a succession of handsome beggar boys and cattle drovers for most of Oryn's reign. "I told everyone there was nothing to worry about," he called out as Oryn reined to a halt. "I can ride out there in the morning. I'm sure it's nothing."

"A band of teyn burned out the village of Dry Hill at sunset." Bax, the burly, dark-browed commander of the palace guard, stood at Barún's side. Under a single shelving brow his blue eyes struck one with surprising ferocity. *With eyes like that,* Oryn reflected, *one could scarcely help being commander of the guards.* "The runner said it was village teyn from the mine."

Dear gods. It's started. So soon . . .

"Which is ridiculous," said Barún, shaking his close-cropped, curly head. His eyes, hazel like Oryn's, were set close and gave him a look of stupid ferocity that was entirely justified. A close-clipped, soldierly beard concealed a weak rosebud mouth. "It has to be wild teyn."

"As my lord says." Bax's neutral tone almost shouted *Imbecile!* "Permission to take a squad and see what we can do."

"Granted. Yes. Of course." Panic and disorientation, or perhaps shortage of sleep and coffee, made Oryn feel slightly giddy. "And Bax . . ."

The commander had turned away, already calling out orders—he was armored, Oryn saw, and not in just the light leathers that men wore on teyn hunts, either—but he looked back with the combination of impatience and the respect owed grudgingly to Taras Greatsword's son.

The words *You'd best take Barún with you* died on Oryn's lips. Barún hadn't seen the cat sleeping on the village wall, wouldn't understand what he was seeing if he had. *Oh, I'm sure there's an explanation for it. . . .*

For a moment Oryn met those ice-bright, disdainful eyes and saw himself in them, with his immense cloak of sables and the barber's careful curls unraveling from his hair. "I should like to come with you, if I may," he heard himself saying. "Under your command, of course."

Bax's eyes couldn't have widened more if Oryn had asked him to come to bed with him. Never in his life had Oryn seen the commander bereft of speech. It was an interesting sight.

"I think that if a decision has to be made—er—about anything, it might be best if I was on hand rather than waiting for a messenger." And, when Bax still said nothing, he added, a little shyly, "I *can* ride, you know."

And to his absolute astonishment, Bax smiled. It changed his whole square, harsh face. "Yes, I know. I've watched you. D'you have armor?"

Are you joking? But even as he thought it, Oryn knew he should have had some made before this. His mind flirted momentarily with what his robe maker would say, and if he'd be able to get colors that matched his cloaks. "Can you fit me with some? Surely there's someone in the guards of my—er—kingly frame."

"Kiner, get His Majesty some plates," called the commander over his shoulder to a speechless aide. Barún, equally nonplussed, was looking from his brother to the commander like a dog watching a game of shuttlecocks, with the expression of one who knows he ought to contribute something but can't immediately think what. It was a common activity for Barún. "We can lace you up the sides. We need to go fast, though. The runner said they'd taken three children."

"Taken?" That didn't sound like wilding teyn, who simply laid hands on whatever foodstuffs they could carry. The wildings didn't even seem to understand the concept of water vessels, or at least never bore away water in them, a circumstance Oryn had always found curious. Lord Akarian, he supposed, would commend the completeness of their trust in Iron-Girdled Nebekht. In any case he couldn't imagine they'd be intelligent enough to reason out the need for hostages.

"Killed three men. Is Lord Soth . . . ?"

"I believe he's . . . unwell . . . this evening." His eyes met Bax's and he saw that the commander understood. Had probably understood for a long time.

"Let him sleep, then."

"Should I come with you?" Barún asked as if the idea had only just occurred to him, which it probably had. "I can be armed in minutes."

He could, too. It was one of Barún's great skills, one that Oryn—being laced between two plates of hammered steel over his blue velvet tunic by Bax and the breathless Kiner—had never fully appreciated before. Oryn looked around for the Summer Concubine, but she'd disappeared, something else Pearl Women were good at. Damn these conventions that would prevent him from kissing her good-bye.

"I should feel better knowing you were in charge of things here." He reached around Kiner's bent head to clasp Barún's hand. It was an absolute lie, of course—Barún wasn't capable of deciding whether to piss in a bucket or a hole—but since in his absence his brother would be in charge of the House of the Marvelous Tower anyway, he might as well make him feel better.

Gratitude warmed Barún's tawny eyes. "I'll try to be worthy."

Jethan, Iorradus, and Oryn's valet Geb appeared, Jethan still armored though he went off duty at sunset, Iorradus rumpled and buckling his belt. Geb was trailed by a servant who bore two duffels of things Geb knew Oryn considered indispensable to his own comfort—everything from mother-of-pearl table-ware to a selection of favorite nightshirts—and a small satchel of his own. "My lord," said Jethan, "you can't—"

"My dear boy, I'm the king," protested Oryn plaintively. "I can do whatever I want." Geb elbowed the aide Kiner out of the way and took over the task of lacing the too-small armor plates around Oryn's rotund form, muttering all the while about what the metal would do to the velvet.

Oryn turned to Bax. "Could you wait perhaps a half an hour for me?" he asked, and moved tentatively in the armor plate. It was made for a shorter man and incredibly uncomfortable. He felt like a tortoise and probably didn't look nearly so trim and graceful as one. "I think I may be able to cut some hours off our tracking time."

The commander's sharp glance rested on him, reevaluating. "As you say, my lord, you're the king," he said. "You can do whatever you want. We'll be ready. Kiner, get four of the biggest mounts you can for His Majesty. . . . Not the royal steeds but cavalry horses. No sense having them drop dead on us. Get rid of that stupid baggage, Geb—you think His Majesty's going to review troops out there?"

Oryn was already striding along the arcade that led to the Inner Court, his sables billowing about him.

The gardens that surrounded the Summer Pavilion were sweetly silent but for the occasional note of wind chimes and the rustle of a hunting cat. The beds were laid out by scent as well as by texture and color: On moonless summer nights Oryn could pick out where he was in their shady labyrinth by the jasmine, the sweet olive, the roses. Now in winter the only scent was that of turned earth and the sweetness of frankincense that lingered over the city from the Summoning.

And the scent of approaching rain itself, faint and ecstatic in a cloud-banded ebony sky.

Darutha, god of the rain, Koan, god of mages, thank you. . . .

Lamps of pierced bronze burned in the wall niches of the Summer Pavilion's lower floor. The flecked light showed him the big blackwood dining table, the musicians' dais, the Summer Concubine's lute and harp. In the room above, which opened onto an exquisite roof terrace, only a single lamp burned, and by its swimming glow he saw the Summer Concubine sitting cross-legged on the divan.

A shallow alabaster bowl rested on the table before her. As he came near, Oryn saw the glint of lamplight in water and in her gazing eyes. He took a seat on the divan where it cornered with the shape of the room, watched her heart-shaped face.

They called the gods pitiless. He supposed they were, or some of them were, and he couldn't imagine how one of them—he burned incense to them all, just in case—had decided to give him the woman he had believed would be denied him forever by his father's power. Every morning waking up at her side was a song.

And it was in this woman—this woman of all beloved women—that magic had bloomed.

A *woman-who-does-magic*. He shook his head: *We really must find a word for what is happening, whatever it is.* And how many mages—and others—still refused to believe that anything was happening at all?

Cycles of time, as Mohrvine had said?

Some vast cosmic testing, by Nebekht of the Iron Girdle or someone else?

A comprehensive and terrible counterspell, evolved by some great wizard somewhere for purposes that would later become distressingly clear?

He didn't like that one. Nine years ago Soth and Hathmar had investigated that possibility and had found nothing; only the intelligence that among the nomads, and in the towns beside the far-off ocean, it was the same. For centuries, mages in the Realm of the Seven Lakes had spoken by scrying crystals to black- or brown-skinned wizards in other lands, in realms no one had ever visited or heard of, who had never heard of them. Soth had had a friend thus, whose language he had laboriously learned as others had before him—who had told him of cities and magic and realms unimaginable. Soth's crystal, and those of all other scryers, had begun to fail ten years ago. One could only guess that elsewhere the fading was the same.

And for Oryn, it came back to that. To the Summer Concubine framed in the lapis-lazuli tiles of the Summer Pavilion, amber lamplight shining on her uncovered hair as she gazed into water to see things far away.

And succeeded at it.

Of course she'd succeed, he thought, as he'd thought when first she'd spoken to him of her dreams of power, and of how she had begun to call birds to her hand by thought alone. *She's a Pearl Woman. She was raised to be perfect.* He had almost not been surprised, having never seen her as other than marvelous.

"Did you see them?" he asked when she closed her eyes.

She pressed her palms to her forehead in exhaustion, nodded. "There are two rock chimneys, and a third farther off." She sketched the shape of what she had seen with her hands. "They're in a dry watercourse—the teyn are—near a red rock shaped like a kneeling camel. There's an old tomb there, closed with rubble. It has an eagle carved over its door."

"I'm sure Bax will know the place. The eagle was the badge of the Durshen Dynasty, and they were mostly buried south of the Lake of the Moon."

"They'll be gone when you get there. They have food from the village. The rain will cover their tracks."

"It may have been what they were waiting for. I should be composing hymns of thanks for it, I suppose. . . . Are the children all right?"

"I think so." Her eyes opened, filled with tears. "They're asleep. Their arms are bruised, their feet bleeding from running." Their son would have been four, had he lived. Oryn had always wondered whether the scorpion whose sting had ended the boy's life had come into his rooms via some malign wizard's machinations. That had been before they'd realized that the ward spells Soth taught the Summer Concubine didn't always work. "They'll move on the moment the rain starts."

"We'll get them." He got to his feet, awkward and puffing in his steel back-and-breast, and came to her side. Knelt to kiss her, tasting the dust of the night's ride still on her lips. "Are they village teyn or wildings?"

"Village," she said at once. "They're big and plump, and the hair's been shaved from their arms."

Dear gods. Oryn wondered if the village mage at Dry Hill—

Hobet, his name had been, or Hobekt, something like that—had survived the attack. He remembered making a mental note two years ago that the man should be replaced, but there had been no one to replace him. "And the djinni?"

The Summer Concubine shook her head. She was still in her riding dress, her gold-dust hair unfurled down her back in a shining coil. Oryn laid his cloak of sables around her shoulders, knowing how easily she chilled. More easily after she'd exerted her powers, as she had this weary and fruitless night.

Her fingers brushed his as she gathered the heavy fur around her. "Soth told me that one hears them, or feels them—like scented wind blowing, he said—before one sees them. There wasn't even that."

Her voice was dreamy with weariness, as if she already half slept. "He said the first time he didn't know what it was: He was seven or eight, and coming back from carrying lunch out to his uncle, who was painting a tomb in the Redbone Hills. It was about twilight, he said. He heard a kind of humming music, and felt the wind over his face from a direction the wind had not blown before. The air and earth opened up like a painted curtain, he said, and he saw a shining hall without a building around it, and a shining woman there who called his name. He ran away, he said."

"Good for him." Oryn shivered. Though no djinn would ever admit that he or she (or it) had ever had anything to do with such a thing, there were rumors and tales down through the centuries of children who had disappeared: children who had come back, some of them, a few days, or a week, or a month, later, with no memory of what had happened to them. Such children frequently dreamed dreams that rendered them in some curious way unfit ever after for life in the world of humankind. Other children simply did not come back at all.

But if this wasn't the first time teyn kidnapped children . . . ?

He shook his head, tucking away the information in the immense, ill-organized toy box of his mind. Pressing her hands, then her feet, between his palms, he found them icy: "I'll see Geb brings you some food." After the working of magic, the Summer Concubine was always ravenous for sweets, and this evening in particular she looked exhausted, as if haunted by some secret grief. He went downstairs and found Geb there already, bearing a wicker tray of dates and honey, hot barley tea and a syrup-saturated baba cake. The tubby eunuch glared up at him in motherly reproach as Oryn took the tray.

"What possesses you to abscond with a band of insolent soldiers I'll never know."

"Nor shall I, Geb, my little summer squash." Oryn carried the tray upstairs, followed by instructions about the ointment pots and how those barbarians in Bax's cavalry could *not* be trusted to care for Oryn's spare slippers properly.

Spare slippers? What else had Geb considered appropriate gear for a military campaign?

Coming into the darkened upper room, Oryn saw only a huddle of black fur on the divan and the long silken rope of her hair gleaming in the lamp's solitary light.

He set the tray down beside her, but she didn't wake. How comforting it would be to sit in the window embrasure and play songs while she slept, until the rain came. He could smell the water in the air, though ivory moonlight still glimmered on the bare-branched rose beds of the terrace garden. He was glad she'd wake to the rain, and hoped whatever had troubled her this afternoon had passed.

He shivered again, his mind returning to the present. When they overtook the teyn, he understood that he'd have to order them killed. He'd spent his boyhood deliberately misconstruing his father's demands—what had the man expected after he'd smashed Oryn's harp and burned his books?—but he knew that this was something that could not go unpunished. The news that the spells that had once held such power no longer operated could not be permitted to spread.

If the teyn who tilled the fields of every village, hauled the water at every well, swept the floors and ground the corn in nearly every house in the Realm of the Seven Lakes hadn't figured that out already.

It was to make whatever decisions needed to be made that he had asked to be taken along.

He stood for a time, gazing past the ornamental vines, the shrubs and trellises of the terrace, toward the eroded buttes and the dry ghosts of riverbeds. The thought of what he had to do sickened him, but he knew that the danger in which humankind stood from its erstwhile slaves was worse.

As he was turning away, movement caught his eye far out in the darkness. A flicker of light, like a greenish mist, near the mouth of what had to be an arroyo in the badlands that lay beyond the bluffs. He fetched a telescope from its cupboard and trained it on the place, but he saw nothing.

He folded the instrument and toggled it to his belt, and descended the stair to meet with Bax and do his duty as king.

Oryn, the Summer Concubine thought, *where is Oryn?*

Why was it so dark and so cold?

Sleep crushed her like stone blocks, as if she'd been buried in the foundation of a temple. The headache she'd taken from the calling of the djinni spread now to her bones, her muscles, her lungs and heart and brain.

Evil, there was something terribly evil happening, something she could prevent, if only she could wake up.

Someone was calling on her, crying her name desperately—

someone she knew, someone who trusted her—and she was too weary to respond.

Oryn . . .

The word wouldn't even pass her lips.

Maybe Geb? He was downstairs in the salon; she could see him silhouetted against the pierced bronze lamps in their niches, making a list of all her dresses grouped by color in an orgy of self-indulgent pleasure. He had to help her, wake her up so she could . . .

. . . so she could . . .

Someone was screaming her name.

And someone listened to those screams with a terrible thoughtful intentness, fingering a thing that moved and glittered in the darkness.

The Summer Concubine slid helplessly deeper into sleep.

Corn-Tassel Woman was asking her, "How did you know? When did you know?" They were sitting on the terrace in the thick heat of the summer night, the stars like smoky jeweled veils in a sky of profoundest indigo. "The first I can remember thinking *I'll use magic to do so-and-so* was when my son took sick of fever. We paid that Earth Wizard from the Grand Bazaar, Urnate Urla that used to work for Lord Sarn, to heal him, and he couldn't—he said the fever was too virulent. But looking at my boy I knew that wasn't so. I could feel it wasn't so. After the healer left I did all the things he'd done, putting my heart into them and my mind. . . . But it seemed like I'd known I could do it for a long time before that."

"Yes," the Summer Concubine said, recalling how she'd stuck little wards made of feathers, over which she'd sung certain songs, into the boughs around a dove's nest on the terrace, to send the cats away. "Yes." The mother dove had driven the young ones out of the nest and one had been killed by old Gray King anyway—even in the days of Taras Greatsword the big tom had been lord of the palace felines—but at least the baby birds had had their chance.

Someone was calling her, frantic, desperate, and in her dream she turned her head to look, frightened by some sound. When she looked back, Corn-Tassel Woman was gone, and the marble bench beside her was splattered with blood. The blood dripped down onto the terrace with a soft, deadly pattering, the smell of it mingling with that of the summer dust.

She woke, crying out, and for a moment heard the blood still dripping, dripping on the terrace stones. Shadow seemed to lean over her, listening. . . .

. . . then it dissolved away into the darkness of familiar things. She realized that the dripping she heard was the first patter of the rain.

Trembling, she gathered the robe of sables from the foot of the bed and wrapped it around her, went to the shutters to scent the wild, heartbreaking magic of desert rain. Though it was a smell she had all her life loved, as she stood there she could not rid her mind of the fear that what fell on her face was blood and not water.

The fear that someone—who?—would see her as she stood in the doorway against the glow of the lamps.

Oryn too, on the road to Dry Hill, would look up and curse the rain.

Like music over the palace's quiet, the Summer Concubine heard the horns and whistles in the city streets as men and women ran out of their houses to welcome the spring. "Darutha's blessing on you," they would say, naming the god of the rains.

"Darutha's blessing on you," she whispered, and shivered with the chill that she could not overcome.

The rain ceased an hour after first light. The clouds dispersed hastily, as if, an unwanted duty grudgingly accomplished, they had better things to do with the afternoon. It was customary for parties to be given during or after the first rain—in bad years, as last year and the one before had been, after every rain. By the time heavenly morsels and tea had been laid out in the Jasmine Gardens the sun was hot in an unbroken sky and the last of the puddles had steamed away.

A few of the guests commented on Oryn's absence, knowing how much the king adored festivities of any kind. "There was trouble out at the Dry Hill mines," Barún responded gravely, and fetched cups of mint tea for his guests with his own hands, dropping two. His wife, Blue Butterfly Woman, like a fair-haired doll in her seat of honor, rolled her eyes. When Lord Jamornid appeared with Ahure preening himself in his wake, the Summer Concubine made a point of thanking Ahure—who only looked down his nose at her—for the blessing of the rain, as if he'd been as personally responsible as he thought he was. Even more than Ahure, she implied with her glance above the pink gauze of her veils, was His Lordship to be thanked for his supreme wisdom in including the man in his court. It was a wonder Lord Jamornid didn't strut in a circle displaying like a cock pigeon. When Lord Sarn entered, with Hathmar and Sarn's brother Benno, the college rector, on his heels, she repeated the entire performance the moment she was sure Jamornid was out of earshot.

Which wasn't difficult, the Summer Concubine reflected as she moved from group to group of the guests with heavenly morsels, tea and sorbet. Jamornid was seldom aware of much beyond what he imagined people were saying about his nobility, his generosity and his general excellence. ". . . first heard of Ahure, no one else had at all," she overheard him saying to the rangeland sheikh Kan an Aket, who had undoubtedly heard the story before, "except just those few villages in the mountains west of the Great Lake. But I rode fifteen days just to see him, and when I saw him, I knew I had to bring him back here. An incredible man, incredible."

And Ahure, standing just far enough away to pretend not to hear, drew himself up a little taller, and gazed down his nose at the White Cat Concubine, who was offering him a piece of baba cake, and shook his head in scorn. "Offer not such poisons to me," he intoned. "I must preserve myself, that I may serve my lord again."

The White Cat Concubine, Barún's favorite this week, backed away, as well she might: Like most Blood Mages, Ahure never bandaged or treated the wounds by which he generated and focused his power. Last night's supreme efforts to Summon the rain had left his shaved scalp laced from brows to occipital bump with parallel slashes in which the blood had clotted thickly. Dried blood caked the pins he'd driven through his lower lip and nostrils, and made tracks from the cuts between his brows. *He has to retain some powers,* thought the Summer Concubine. *Else those wounds would have gone septic years ago.* His only concession to party manners was that he'd bandaged his left hand, the wrappings newly bloodstained over the stumps of his last two fingers. The right hand, mutilated similarly long ago, was as dirty as a kennel keeper's. Flies buzzed around the bandage but didn't alight.

The Summer Concubine fetched a cup of coffee and a fragile porcelain plate of opalescent moonjellies from the open supper room at the end of the garden and made her way to Hathmar, who sat quietly under the bare vine lattices of the pergola. "I trust you're all right?"

"Thank you, child. I'll be well." Behind the ground rock crystal of his spectacles his blue eyes had a sunken look, as if from long illness.

At the gate Barún was heartily greeting Mohrvine with ex-clamations of "Well, it looks like it's all turned out for the best after all," and slapping the mage Aktis on the shoulder with hearty familiarity. Aktis winced, and reached immediately for a blown-glass cup of wine that the Topaz Concubine held out to him on a tray. Sweat rolled down either side of his huge hooked nose, and the Summer Concubine saw that when he took up the cup his small hands shook.

She thought, *Ijnis.* And shivered.

Long before her introduction to the world of power—as a girl, training in the House of Dancing Water—her teachers had told her about *ijnis.* The essence brewed from that unpre-possessing, flannelly weed would magnify and strengthen a mage's powers temporarily, but it was said to be dangerously addictive, and the effects would gradually drive a wizard mad.

In those days one saw it seldom. But sometimes she'd be serving in the house's supper room and would see among the patrons a man in the brown or gray robes of an Earth Wizard whose desperate eyes would now and again flare wide at the sight of things others could not see. Whose hands would shake, or who pressed his fingers quickly to his own lips to smother sounds over which he had no control.

In the past ten years, she'd seen these symptoms more and more frequently among wizards whose strength had once been uncontested in the Realm of the Seven Lakes.

"I hear there was commotion here last night, lady."

The Summer Concubine rose from Hathmar's side and dipped a deep salaam to Lord Mohrvine. His simple dark robes were a variation of Greatsword's ostentatious militarism—*No nonsense about* me—though not many years ago he'd had the director of his silk-weaving rooms whipped by his private guards for producing a color that was no longer in fashion. Now he could barely be got to admit that there *was* such a thing as fashion, at least where anyone could hear him.

"Nothing compared to the later celebration for the first rain." She smiled and took in Aktis with her glance. "For which I understand you are partly to thank."

"I commanded Aktis to perform the Calling, as I understand others"—Mohrvine's pale green gaze flicked contemptuously to Ahure, who was lecturing a rather heavy-eyed Soth—"took it upon themselves to do as well. Whether that's the same as being 'responsible,' I don't know." His eyebrow lifted. "I understand my nephew actually roused himself to go out with the guards. It must have been a catastrophe indeed."

"A message arrived for my lord." The Summer Concubine touched two fingers to her lips, indicating that her lord's secrets were of course her secrets as well. She wondered who among those present in the kitchen court last night were in Mohrvine's pay.

In the rainy predawn darkness she had kindled the lamps in the pavilion again, had once more dipped water from the garden pool into her alabaster bowl and had sought sight of the escaping teyn. A messenger had been dispatched at once, with as detailed a description as she could manage of the countryside she had seen. She prayed it would give Bax some idea of which direction to take in the absence of tracks.

Then she'd eaten ravenously of the baba cake and dates she'd found on the wicker tray and sent a message to Geb ordering invitations sent out. Though her nightmare's nameless dread had whispered at her from the shadows, she'd known she couldn't afford not to sleep. And her sleep had been peaceful; whatever shadow watched and listened for her seemed to have dissipated into the rain.

She had barely waked in time to scry again, send another messenger to Oryn, wash, dress in pink gauze and garnets, make up her face to cover her weariness and present herself at the Jasmine Garden to watch Barún welcome Oryn's guests.

It was part of the training of a Pearl Woman not to consume so much as a morsel at any festivity she attended. She was like the flowers on the table, which she had also arranged: there to entertain, not to be entertained. The Summer Concubine would gladly have murdered any of the maids for the contents of her tray and cast a spell of sudden death on every person in the garden in order to be alone for a nap.

"Well, I trust he knows what he's doing," sighed Mohrvine in a voice that implied he didn't hold out much hope. "I suppose Bax has a large enough force to protect him from sudden attack? I understand nomad bands have invaded the Sarn and Jothek rangelands up on the White Lake and the Lake of Gazelles, and there's been trouble over nomad herds on croplands south of the Lake of the Moon. Or didn't that occur to him? Apparently not—nor to send for me? Or the other lords?"

"That I don't know, my lord." She gave him her luminous smile, certain that he knew exactly the size of the force Bax had taken. "Speaking entirely for myself, I'm only glad that you remained here in charge of the garrison forces, if there has been such a problem."

He tilted his head and considered her, only half a head shorter than he, and she kept her eyes modestly lowered. She had not yet picked up the wizard's trick of listening to all things and still carrying on a conversation, but she did hear, like the blinking reflection of fragmented glass, Barún say, "Maybe all that talk of an aqua-whatever was a storm in a fishpond, eh?" Lord Sarn stood between him and Blue Butterfly Woman, an avuncular arm around them both.

"And you, lady?" asked Mohrvine. "When all these several

Earth Wizards and Blood Mages were putting forth their power last night—setting shoulders to the wheel that the Sun Mages were not able to themselves turn—what of you? Did you put forth your power too?"

As if he were not informed of it, she thought, *every time Hathmar or Soth tries to teach me a spell that fails.* As if he were not the author of a hundred little broadsides and market songs about the fat king's woman-who-does-magic weaving her spells for the king in bed.

Mohrvine asking prying questions about Oryn was one thing. That was just policy, part of the chess game of being the old king's brother—one reason why almost half of the previous dynasty of Akarian kings had started their reigns with systematic fratricide. Asking about her abilities was another.

"Like everyone in the city," she replied, smiling and glancing again in the direction of Aktis, who was seated shivering on a bench, "I did what it is in me to do."

No council being called, the lords dispersed at noon. Mohrvine caught up with Lord Akarian and his two sons on the way out, draping an arm around the old man's stooped back and gesturing at the sky. The Summer Concubine heard Iron-Girdled Nebekht's holy name. The other concubines disappeared immediately, the White Cat Concubine on Barún's arm, leaving the servant women to clear off the tables and devour the remaining sugared pork, moonjellies and fried red-bean balls the moment they were out of sight. The Summer Concubine gathered a plateful and retired to the end of the garden, too exhausted for the moment even to consider walking back to the Summer Pavilion.

She'd have to scry again, she thought. And try once more to reach Turquoise Woman and Cattail Woman, though she wasn't sure what she could tell them—that she'd had bad dreams? She wondered if there was time to bathe, to sink her mind and body into the slow luxury of the successive chambers of steam, to give herself over to the renewing hands of the palace bath women. To rest on the cushions in the heated room afterward, wrapped in linen finer than silk, sipping tea while a servant combed her hair.

Or was it going to have to be another quick scrub in the pavilion's downstairs back room?

In the water bowl that morning she'd seen the teyn band moving. The slumped forms scurried warily along the stone floor of a deep canyon, far in the badlands now, shoving and pinching the three children they'd kidnapped whenever they stumbled or slowed. They were definitely village teyn, with shaved heads and arms.

Yet they moved as if they knew where they were going. And, she'd noticed—it was difficult to tell, seeing those shapes so tiny in the water bowl—they kept to the stony talus at the base of the canyon walls, where no tracks would show up in the loose sand near the dry wash in the center.

They're miners, she thought, and rubbed her tired eyes. *They can't have been more than fifty feet outside of their village in their lives.*

Why children?

"Lady?"

It was Lotus, one of the maids. Traditionally the palace maidservants were all called Flower ("Great gods, girl," Taras Greatsword had moaned, "you know how many of 'em there *are?*"), but with her elevation to the status of favorite, the Summer Concubine had asked each woman to choose her own name. Most had simply chosen the names of flowers: Lotus, Jasmine, Clematis. (One kitchen maid was now named Moon-jelly after her favorite sweet.)

Behind her stood that other girl who had chosen her own name, who had chosen a man's name.

Raeshaldis the Sun Mage.

The Summer Concubine got to her feet, held out her hands to the awkward, shy-looking adolescent. "My dear, I hardly recognized you! Please sit down. Lotus, would you please bring something for our friend. What would you like, lady?"

"Tea," said the girl, as if she weren't sure about that or anything else. "Maybe a little bread." She looked tired and ill, and no wonder, thought the Summer Concubine, studying the long, rectangular face, the too-large nose and deep-set brown eyes. The mages had worked, fasting, for seven days, to Summon that morning's rain. While Barún had gone from guest to guest with his hearty greetings of the rain god's bounty, the Summer Concubine had watched Hathmar's face and had seen in it the weariness of a man who understands that his job has not only not finished, but has barely begun.

The rain had been nothing. It had barely dampened the parched soil. After seven days' labor, that was a frightening thing to understand.

"What can I do for you, dear?" asked the Summer Concubine when Lotus had brought the bread and tea. "Do you have everything you need at the college?"

Raeshaldis's lips folded quickly in under her teeth and the Summer Concubine thought, Damn *them*.

They're hazing her.

She could see it in the way the girl's eyes flinched aside, in the wave of color that flared under those thin, sunburned cheeks.

Anger budded, swelled to an exploding sun under her breastbone. Anger that Pearl Women were never supposed to feel, let alone show on their well-schooled, smiling faces.

The male students were hazing her.

She had feared it when Hathmar first had come to her with news that a young girl had applied to the college. The talk among the men—Hathmar and Soth and Oryn—had been all about women's magic, grave consideration about whether proximity with the magic that seemed to be blossoming in certain women would disrupt the long-standing aura of power in the Citadel. Would a woman have the strength and discipline to master spells? Would Raeshaldis herself in fact draw her power from the sun, or perhaps she was more fitted to be trained by an Earth Wizard or a Blood Mage, supposing Aktis or Ahure or one of the leading Pyromancers could be talked into taking a female pupil.

Only afterward she had said to Oryn, *Will the men at the college accept her?*

And Oryn had seemed not quite to understand what she meant.

Everybody gets hazed, he'd said. He'd been sent for two years to the garrison far to the north, beyond Mud Lake, to "teach him to be a warrior," as his father had said—and to get him away from the concubine who, his father had suspected, had begun to trouble his dreams. *That's just a thing that boys do. One gets through it.*

That was all he'd say of that time; the Summer Concubine gathered the experience had been fairly brutal. And he'd added, *She may very well be the hope of the future. Of course they'll accept her.*

Eventually, yes, the favorite had thought. Once their own loss has been mourned—the loss that now isn't even recognized, let alone accepted. And in the meantime it is a different thing when a girl is being hazed by men.

Particularly men who feel themselves losing the thing that is now being given to her. The thing that has made them special, whose presence in their flesh has shaped their lives.

All this she saw in the way Raeshaldis's fingers shook when she set down the fragile celery-green bowl of tea.

The Summer Concubine was silent, waiting, her eyes on the girl's still face.

Raeshaldis took a breath, let it out and looked back at her as if they'd been talking for some minutes. "I didn't want to say anything the first time it happened," she said. "The boys . . . they just egg each other on. They're just being louts, you know? And I could really hurt them." She had big hands, and long knobbly fingers, and she used them when she talked. Her voice was low and a little husky; like a boy's, gruff and matter-of-fact.

"I mean, I know spells now that would do damage, and they—the boys—wouldn't have the magic to protect themselves. Because most of the boys—the novices, I mean—a lot of them don't have any magic at all. At least . . . sometimes I'll be walking along the south wall at night, or in the empty rooms in the vaults, and I'll see candlelight. That means somebody's reading who can't see in the dark and can't summon light to read by. I've gone back and found burnt tow, which means they had to light the candle, even, by flint and steel. No wonder they're mad."

"That's no excuse for ganging up on you," the Summer Concubine said. "Or damaging your things."

By the way Raeshaldis stiffened and glanced away again she knew that both these forms of torment had taken place. She'd once been the youngest girl at the House of Dancing Water, as every fledgling was. She knew all about that.

"But what happened last night was different." Raeshaldis took a deep breath, steeling herself to share something she didn't even want to think about. "It's why I decided to come to you. Last night . . . it has to be someone with some power."

The Summer Concubine was silent for a few moments, remembering her choice, to say nothing to Oryn and Hathmar, to let this most promising girl of all enter the training of a mage-born boy, something that was mostly out of the question for her small circle of women-who-do-magic.

Wondering if she'd done rightly.

"What happened last night?"

"Someone tried to break into my room." Raeshaldis picked at the bread on her plate, tore it into pieces and left them, pale brown hillocks on the pale green porcelain. "I think it was the same person who tried to grab me in the passageway outside my room the night before. When I finally went around to look outside the door and the window, it was nearly light and the rain had already started. If he left any tracks they were gone. But the . . . the *taste* of the spells he'd used to try to get the window open was still in the wood. You know what I mean?"

The Summer Concubine nodded again, familiar with the residue of magic that she felt when she touched some of Soth's books, or stood in that chamber of the old palace that had in centuries past seen the Rite of Obliteration performed upon a heretic king. She experienced it as a coldness or, in the books, as a gentle warmth under her fingertips. Turquoise Woman said she heard such residues in the form of sound, like faraway singing or cries. Pebble Girl described them as prickling, either stinging of nettles or the itching of a mild rash.

"I thought, it's one thing if it's just boys being stupid." Raeshaldis hesitated, seeing the Summer Concubine open her mouth to object, and then, when the favorite did not in fact speak, went on, "but it's another if it's a man, and a mage—probably a master— who should know better. I mean, if it's someone who should have something better to do. That's . . . that's more than stupid and loutish." She caught her gesturing hands together self-consciously.

"I didn't know if it was dangerous or just—just sick in the head. And I didn't know who else to tell. But I thought somebody ought to know."

I didn't know who else to tell. The girl had appeared, in boy's clothing, on the steps of the college one day the summer before last, asking to be admitted, refusing to tell her father's name. He had cast her out, she said. Told her that he would have no such shameless doings in his house. Later she'd told Hathmar her father's name—Habnit, a silk merchant in Sleeping Worms Street, and son of one of the merchant proctors who sat in judgment in the Grand Bazaar—and the Archmage had written him, but had received no reply. It occurred to the Summer Concubine to wonder who Raeshaldis talked to in the college, if anyone.

Or did she simply stay in her cell and read?

"Who do you think it was?" she asked, knowing how often instinct and feeling can work if surprised.

In this case she was disappointed of her goal, first by Raeshaldis's hesitation—the girl was clearly one who had learned never to speak an unconsidered word—and, a moment later, by Lotus wailing, "My lady . . ." and a man's harsh cry of "You thieving bitch!"

EIGHT

After eighteen months of grinding apprehension in the Citadel and the storm-black horror in last night's darkness, Shaldis's reaction was instant and automatic.

Even as the two men framed in the garden gateway thrust Lotus aside, the teapot she bore crashing to the worn paving bricks, Shaldis's hand moved. And when the men turned toward the bench where she sat with the Summer Concubine, she saw their faces change. Bafflement replaced fury as they stared at the bench, clearly unable to see anything but sun flecks dappling the marble. Then they both looked around at the pergola that stretched above its shallow, tiled pool.

"Where the hell is she?" The older man wheeled on Lotus, who was kneeling in horror by the wreckage of the teapot, which had been Durshen Dynasty celadon ware and almost priceless.

"They told us she was here, curse her!" shouted the younger. His red, square face was a slightly thicker duplicate of the other man's: same beard, same pug nose, same mousy brown hair. Same expression of harsh determination not to be made a fool of, though it was clear, thought Shaldis, that the son accomplished his goals by anger, and the father by craft. "I would have known it! Stinking rich with nothing better to do than lie to a poor man. . . ."

"If he's *that* poor, he stole that belt he's wearing," muttered Shaldis. The man's anger turned her hot inside, reminding her too clearly of her grandfather's shouting rage. "*And* those boots."

"They aren't armed." The Summer Concubine tilted her head consideringly as three guardsmen clattered through the garden's iron-studded gates. And as Shaldis released her hold on the cloak, a little embarrassed that her first reaction had been concealment, the Summer Concubine squeezed her hand and added, "But that was *very* good! Gentlemen . . ."

The men turned back, with double takes that would in other circumstances have been comical at the sight of the beautiful woman in pink standing only a yard or two from them where no woman had been before. Behind her the long, narrow garden lay around pergola and pond like a gracefully proportioned room, the walls screened with a light hedge of bamboo and barren of concealment: It wouldn't have sheltered a kit fox. "I beg your pardon." The Summer Concubine salaamed deeply and signed the guards back. "I haven't yet had the pleasure of your acquaintance."

"You've had the pleasure of my wife's!" bellowed the younger man, regaining his tongue after a moment's shocked silence. "You and those Ravens of yours!"

The raven was the only animal, Shaldis remembered from her childhood fables, whose female was attributed with magical powers. In the tales her grandmother used to tell—after her grandfather's little harem had closed its doors for the night and the women were alone—all ravens had magic, cocks and hens both. The word, "raven," was one of a handful of nouns that took the nearly obsolete intermediate article and case, unlike all other animals: bull and cow, horse and mare, tomcat and queen, teyn and jenny. Ravens were ravens were ravens—and ravens had magic. All of them.

"You have no right to be sheltering her." The older man motioned his son quiet. "You may be the king's woman, but even the king won't stand for it, for a woman to shelter a runaway wife." Even less than his son did he dress like a poor man. His coat was red and the shirts under it finely woven cotton—Shaldis recognized the costly lawn as the type most expensive in her grandfather's shop. His boots were new and latched with rosettes of silver. They were glassblowers, she gathered. The older man had to own a factory to afford clothes like that.

"Not to speak of losing a woman who had the best touch with a furnace in the whole of the street!" the younger man ranted. "I trained her for years, and yes, I'll even admit she had a better eye than I for the color of the fireback, to know when to mix in the frit! It's robbing a man to encourage a woman like her to think she can do magic, which is a crock—you understand me? A crock from under the board in the outhouse, and no one can tell me different! My woman, do magic? Corn-Tassel Woman? Shit, I say! First-grade, corn-fed, fish-liver-lubricated—"

"Shut up, Enak." The father turned his sharp dark eyes back to the Summer Concubine. "Pardon my son, lady. And pardon me for saying so, but shame on the woman that encourages a wife to leave her man. Nothing but pain can come of it, besides taking the bread from out of a man's mouth, not to speak of cheating his sons out of the care they need."

"Corn-Tassel Woman was an ideal wife—ideal!—until you got to her!" yelled Enak, disregarding his father's stricture as surely as his father and the Summer Concubine disregarded him. In the courtyard gateway the guardsmen lingered, arms folded in their crimson mail, faces inscrutable. Shaldis wondered if they agreed with Enak and his father.

"A woman like yourself, that hasn't a family nor responsibilities, I'm sure you do think you have power or something. But to call my son's wife away from her rightful work and fill her up with notions—"

"Your son's wife has left him, then, sir?"

"You think we'd have come all the way out here looking for her if she hadn't?" The elder glassblower glared at her as if confronted with willful stupidity. "I know she used to sneak away mornings and come here. She wasn't as clever as she thought she was being. And I know it was you she'd come to, and talk this magic codswallop that all these women are claiming."

"Corn-Tassel Woman comes here at my request, yes, sir." The Summer Concubine folded her small hands before the golden knots of her belt. Her voice remained low and sweet, as if these men were her husband's honored guests. Raeshaldis, in her position, would personally have spit in Enak's face and told the guards to put the pair of them in the street and be damned to the woman whose abilities they put beneath her usefulness at tending a furnace. Her grandfather . . .

"She's a woman of great ability, especially in healing," the Summer Concubine went on. "And a good friend. She's been invaluable to me in trying to find answers to what is happening to magic."

"Exactly fucking nothing is happening to magic!" shouted Enak. Raeshaldis wondered if Corn-Tassel Woman had been studying it with the intention of turning her husband into something small and squashable. "Except that people are getting themselves into a fucking panic over fucking nothing, and I'm fucking sick of hearing about it every fucking time I fucking turn around."

"That's as may be, lady." The father was watching her warily, as if wondering how much of the family business his daughter-in-law may have told this soft-voiced woman veiled in pink gauze. "Now, it's one thing for her to sneak away for an hour in the mornings. All women do it, to slang the neighbors behind their backs with each other in the baths—"

Like men don't spend half the evening "catching up on news" in the cafés, thought Shaldis.

"—just so long as she was back to make dinner and get the furnaces ready for the evening's work, I could deal with that. Women are like that. And whatever she may have told you about what happened yesterday, well, she flounced away in such a huff she didn't let Enak finish what he was saying. Hasty, she is. She may not have shown that side of herself to *you*, but you haven't seen her at home. What I'm saying is, we want her back."

"I'm sure I understand your feelings . . . Barbonak, I believe she told me your name was?" The Summer Concubine tilted her head a little, a characteristic gesture Shaldis would come to know well, and looked up at the burly man squared off against her. "If Corn-Tassel Woman fled your house last night, sir, she did not come here. Should she do so, I would of course ask her reasons for her departure before informing you of her whereabouts—and I would assuredly speak to the king concerning what she has told me over the past two years of your efforts not only to have her improve the quality of your glass with her 'touch,' as you put it, but to have her put words of ill on the furnaces of other glassblowers in Frit Street—"

"Now that's a complete lie!"

"She always lies!" stormed Enak, who didn't seem to have a lesser vocal range. "I never yet met a bitch who could tell a straight story!"

Not with you standing there ready to hit her for what she says, you pig-faced bastard.

"—which is, as you know," continued the Summer Concubine, in tones trained to carry over the noisiest supper party, "in direct contravention of all laws governing wizardry and is punishable by death. And what women do, sir," she added, *"is wizardry—even if it be performed by a woman."*

"That bitch never told—"

"Enak, I said shut up." Barbonak's voice was quiet now. "Lady," he cajoled, "I understand how you'd find my son's wife believable. She does have a reasonable way with her. Many and many's the time I've seen her tell the most amazing whoppers with the straightest face."

"I've heard my share of 'whoppers' in my time, sir," replied the Summer Concubine. "Told by the greatest nobles in the land, who are, believe me, far better talesmiths than Corn-Tassel Woman—or yourself, I might add. I promise you that you shall indeed be sent for if she comes here. Good day, sir."

And she sank another profound salaam, which would have left no one in doubt that the interview was ended even had the guardsmen not stepped forward—they had to be chosen for their size, thought Shaldis—and escorted the glassblowers, father and son, from the Jasmine Garden.

The Summer Concubine paused to make sure that Lotus hadn't been hurt by Enak's angry jostling, and to reassure her that the palace storerooms contained hundreds more Durshen teapots, before taking another half-full pot from the sideboards in the pavilion's open supper room—now nearly cleared of leftovers and dishes—and leading Raeshaldis with it down the length of the pergola to the cushioned marble bench at the back of the bare vine's lacework shade. She poured tea for them both, making a graceful show of it almost without thinking, as if after so long she couldn't do it any other way. Small yellow butterflies played about the favorite's brilliant hair.

"Damn him," she whispered, "*damn* him!" Even in her anger she moved gracefully, removing her veils and laying them aside so that they made a pleasing pattern of folds over the edge of the bench. Her hands did not shake with anger, nor did her expression contort, but Raeshaldis felt it come off her in waves, like the desert's summer heat.

"They fought yesterday—I don't know about what. When I spoke with her through the mirror she was bruised. Maybe it was only that."

A servant woman brought her a shawl, pink camel hair embroidered with pearls. "What was?" asked Shaldis.

"My feeling. The . . . the dread I felt. Three years ago I started seeking out those women the rumors were speaking of, women who had healing hands, or a 'touch' at keeping mice away from the family granary. This hasn't been easy."

"With husbands like Enak, I can understand that." And with fathers, and grandfathers, like her own.

"Some of them didn't want my . . . my interference, they called it. Some I simply never heard of again. Others became my friends. Corn-Tassel Woman and I made a sigil between us, a Sigil of Sisterhood, that our minds would touch as if we were twins. All yesterday I felt danger, uneasiness; last night I dreamed that she came to some dreadful grief."

She shook her head. Under rouge and rice powder transparently applied, Raeshaldis could see the marks of stress and fear—could see, too, that this beautiful woman was older than she'd at first thought, in her mid-thirties, though her body was slight as a child's.

"Now you tell me there was other evil abroad last night."

Silence fell on the garden again. In the deserted supper room, a big gray cat leaped up onto the sideboard and drank daintily from the remaining teacups, dipping with one soft, enormous paw.

"I don't know what it was," repeated Raeshaldis. It felt strange to talk about magic to another woman. To talk about magic at all, rather than simply to learn and absorb lectures and instructions, spells and lists. Endless lists of the names of things: all the different grasses, each type of pebble, birds, stars, djinni, formations of cloud. The true names that summoned them as Hathmar and the others sang for the rain.

She took a deep breath. "They don't talk about it, you know," she said. "At the college. Mostly they pretend it's not happening at all. But it is. There was a boy named Seb Dolek, Urnate Urla's apprentice originally, though he left him and came to the Citadel about a year before I arrived. All the masters praised him, the way everyone in the neighborhood always had: He was good-looking, and his family was rich, and he memorized all the spells and lists and was always first doing the exercises. But he couldn't make the spells work."

She rubbed her hands together on her thigh, as if she were cold, though the garden was pleasant. She remembered Seb Dolek in Rachnis the Shadowmaster's courtyard, struggling to perform the simplest of cantrips. Sweat had streamed down the young man's face as he'd stared at the steel sphere he was try-ing to make move. *Perhaps another time*, Rachnis had said at last, and Seb Dolek had screamed, No! *I'll do it!*

Then he'd looked up at Shaldis, blue eyes almost inhuman with hate. And he had whispered, *Get her out of here.* . . .

"It isn't just that magic is part of everything we do, healing and eating and keeping ourselves safe. All the mages in the college—all the mages everywhere, I suppose—have been raised and bred and lived their lives with the knowledge that they do this. It isn't merely a part of their lives, it's the whole of their lives, everything they are, like their manhood. I don't think anyone ever even asked themselves before this why it is that only men were born with these powers. Or why only a few men, out of all men born. And they built everything on it, not only for themselves, but for all the rest of us as well. We have only the most rudimentary ideas of what herbs will heal if they aren't imbued with spells."

The Summer Concubine nodded. "It's like the rains," she said. "You know, seven hundred years ago, in the time of the Durshen kings, the rains came of their own accord every spring, and for thousands of years before that."

"I know," said Shaldis, dipping a fragment of bread into the oil on her plate. "It's in the histories."

"So when they ceased coming, no one asked about why, or how to get water elsewhere. The mages just started calling them, and they came. It never occurred to them—or to us—that it would be any different. It's all become so much a part of everyone's life—the fact that magic was something men could do or might do. . . . Why are you laughing?" Her smile was bright and warm.

Shaldis chuckled. "I'm just remembering when the Nettle-flower Concubine—she was my grandfather's sole extrava-gance, and Grandmother always had a special tone of voice for when she spoke to her or of her—anyway, she was expecting a child. We brought in old Urnate Urla to lay his hands on her belly, the way people usually do, to see if the child would be a boy or a girl. This was seven years ago, when there was that long drought, and sales at the shop were so bad Grandfather was just *torn*—he wanted another son, but even more he wanted not to have to pay a healer to come in for the birth, so he was really hoping it would be a girl so we'd all just take care of it ourselves. I'm just remembering the look on his face."

Her grin faded as other memories of that red-faced old man came back to her: his rage when he'd learned her father was teaching her the elaborate characters of High Script as well as Scribble, the syllabary women used for shopping lists and horoscope almanacs and the romantic novels circulated among themselves. Remembered her father begging her not to practice her little spells. *I know it's fun, Old One, but word's going to get around.*

She'd tried to argue with him and had been puzzled by his stubborn refusal to accept her powers, until she'd realized: His father had told him to tell her all this. And he was afraid to go back and say to his father, *What's wrong if she does this?*

"I don't feel sorry for them," she said when she realized she'd been silent for some minutes. "I think they'd be just as angry if we started being able to do magic and their own powers *weren't* disappearing. The boys in the college—they'd still piss on my door."

And come rattling the window latches in the night?

"Are the others all right?" Shaldis asked hesitantly after a long silence during which the gray cat leaped down from the supper-room table and stretched itself out on the sun-warmed tile of the pool's brim. "The other Ravens?"

"I don't know." The Summer Concubine drew the softness of the shawl closer around her narrow shoulders. "I got word from Pebble Girl—whose father is a contractor in Woolpack Street—and from Cattail Woman, finally. She was one who would not enter the Sigil of Sisterhood with me. Turquoise Woman"—she shook her head—"I haven't heard from her, but sometimes I don't for days. She keeps her room down in the Slaughterhouse scry warded, for fear her husband will hire a mage to spy out where she's hiding."

"That isn't possible," stated Shaldis. "For a mage to scry another mage, I mean."

"I know. But she's terrified of him. He would hire her out to the neighbors, to put bug-ward spells on their windows or heal their servants, and pocket the cash. She found out later that he'd heard rumors of her powers, and that's why he asked for her hand—and paid her father twice the usual bride-price, to make sure he'd have her."

"Oh, feh!" said Shaldis, disgusted. She didn't think there was anything that could raise her opinion of her grandfather, but at least he hadn't peddled her to the neighbors for the most she'd bring.

Or maybe he'd wanted to. Maybe that's what he and her father had fought about the last day she'd been home.

"What about the other girl they were considering at the college at the same time as me?" she asked after a time. "I never said thank you, by the way, for getting them to let me into the college. I could tell when Hathmar talked to me that the other masters were only going to take one girl. . . . Did the other one come to you?"

Her voice stumbled a little over the words, remembering that beautiful girl with the amber eyes. On the single occasion she'd seen her, in the long visitors' room of the college, she'd desperately resented her, terrified that they'd take this other and not herself, knowing that she, Shaldis, had nowhere else to go. Now she felt guilty, wondering if that girl had been going back to something as bad as her own grandfather.

Or worse.

At the time, she remembered, she didn't think things *could* be worse than daily trying to negotiate the bizarre labyrinth of her grandfather's arbitrary rules and punishments. Worse than watching her father quietly drink himself into insensibility every night. Worse than falling asleep in her stuffy attic sanctum to the echoes of the old man's hysterical rage downstairs. The silence of the garden lay around her like a treasure; the ultimate luxury, Shaldis thought. Silence. Like the high silence of the Citadel, where for hours the only sound was the pure whisper of the wind. Prior to her admission to the college, the only silence she'd known had been in the small hours of the morning—and even then there'd be the growing clatter around the Grand Bazaar—and in those rare rides with her father out to the desert.

She remembered that desert silence, like balm on a wound. Others feared it: *If your horse breaks a leg, you will die. If you get lost, you will die. If you wander away and the noon sun catches you on these blank pavements of gray stone you will die.*

And still she'd loved it.

Her grandfather—one of the five proctors who judged weights and measures and standards of quality and conduct from their red-draped courtyard in the middle of the Grand Bazaar's sprawling maze—had had a little cubicle set at the far end of the main garden where he'd retire to be alone to read. But he never connected that rare peace with anyone else's need. *What woman likes silence?* he'd said dismissively. *Get one alone and she'll talk to the ants on the wall.*

"She was one of the ones I've never heard of again." The Summer Concubine's beautiful eyes darkened with concern. "I've tried several times to learn of her, because she had real power. But her father is one of the water bosses down in the Slaughterhouse District, one of the men who hire bullies to surround the public wells and fountains and charge the people there to draw water. The king has tried a dozen times to do something about the situation, but somehow the orders never quite get carried out. The water bosses are rich, and can buy off the constables, and the Slaughterhouse isn't under the control of any of the clans. Amber Girl was simply too great a risk to be taught the disciplines of real magic. I've tried since to find out what became of her, since her father was not one to let talent like that go to waste when he could use her."

She frowned, troubled, as well she should be, thought Shaldis. The thought of one of the big water bosses—Xolnax or Rumrum or Ebf—with magic in addition to his gang of toughs was not pleasant to contemplate.

She said, "And Turquoise Woman lives in the Slaughterhouse as well?"

The Summer Concubine nodded slowly. "I was going to send a page down there," she said. "But I think . . . you mentioned, I believe, when you entered the college that you used to go about the city dressed as a boy? Do you know the Slaughterhouse at all? Well enough to draw me a map to a place called Little Pig Alley? Because I'm not sure that I want to let anyone else know where she lives."

"You can't go down there yourself!" Shaldis tried to picture that flowerlike loveliness venturing through the tangle of dirt houses and reeking alleys that sprawled beyond the great green-tiled East Gate. Even in her adventurous childhood she hadn't often gone there, but on two occasions after she'd perfected her zin-zin spells, she'd explored the maze of tiny courts opening into still tinier courts, of cattle pens and hog shambles, of the barricades of the water bosses and the grubby, blood-spattered temples of the True Believers of Nebekht.

And had found there, instead of the exotic wholesale depravity she'd expected, only a lot of very poor people trying to make a living, some of them in very violent ways.

"Oh, I'll take a guard. And with a gray cloak I should be safe enough."

"*We'll* take a guard," Shaldis corrected her. "Provided one of your ladies can loan me a dress and some veils."

Honeysuckle Lady's screams brought the fledglings out of the kitchen on the run. In contrast to the girls' frugal breakfast of millet porridge and curds at dawn, the Blossom Ladies had wheat biscuits, honey and cream taken up to them mid-morning by a fledgling—it happened to be Foxfire Girl's turn today—after which the ladies who'd entertained at supper went down to the bathhouse. The ladies' chambers overlooked the sandy little kitchen court, so if the girls happened to be eating or snatching a quick scrub between lessons in the striped shade of the porch, they were frequently treated to the less genteel side of Honeysuckle Lady's vocabulary as she cursed at her maid or at Poppy Lady: The goldenly fair beauty had an impressive repertoire.

Now, however, no words came through the latticed paper of her projecting window, only shriek after shriek of horror, rage and disgust. The fledglings stared at one another in shock: Foxfire Girl had to clap her hands over her mouth to keep from whooping with laughter and triumph, and Opal Girl, next to her on the bench eating a hasty lunch between sessions with the literature master and the music master, stared at her with round dark eyes.

As one, all the other fledglings sprang to their feet and dashed across the yard, Cook and Gecko Woman hard on their heels. Only then could Foxfire Girl throw back her head, clench her fists and laugh out loud. "It worked!" She felt breathless, terrified, wondering. Felt as she'd never felt and never even imagined anyone *could* feel. As if she'd fallen from some great height and had not yet struck ground. As if she weren't at all sure that she wouldn't. "It worked!"

Opal Girl made a protective sign with her fingers. "Did you know it would?"

"Yes—no—I don't know." Foxfire Girl stared at her across the litter of dishes, aware that she was shaking all over. "Father's court wizard let me watch him make spells when I was little. He was funny—sweet. He said if you know something's true name you can call it with this little spell he showed me. He used to call butterflies into the garden and make them land on my hair. I thought it was wonderful. I tried it, over and over—he told me the true name for butterflies. Then I said, what's the true name for ants? Because my nurse had spanked me for teasing her cat or something and I wanted to call ants to her bed. And he looked at me with this twinkle in his eyes and said, *Wizards aren't supposed to do things like that.*"

She shrugged, and got to her feet, and made a quick check of the dishes the other girls had left behind. Wren Girl had left an untouched sugar dumpling, which Foxfire Girl took and divided with her awestruck friend. "I always thought, *What's the point of being a wizard if you can't get back at people who do bad things to you? Let's go,*" she added, dusting the sugar from her long fingers. "I want to see this."

Foxfire Girl's summoning had succeeded beyond her wildest hopes. Every ant in the Flowermarket District, it seemed, had descended on Honeysuckle Lady's room. Not just the little black grease-ants that invaded the kitchens, but marching lines of red cotton-field ants, big black canal ants that crawled in and out of the makeup jars, and even the knuckle-long brown-and-yellow bull ants, which brooded silently from posts high up the wall. Honeysuckle Lady stood in the corridor in her yellow-and-blue robe, hands over her mouth, screaming in horror—the whole floor was awash in skittering black bodies, and lines of insects trickled purposefully along the corridor out of every crack in the floor.

"Dear gods!" Chrysanthemum Lady, the former courtesan whose nominal husband Gorbas owned the house, came running, her long gray hair hanging down her back and her fingers inky from her morning's stint with the ledgers. "I've never seen field ants and kitchen ants together like that! Cook—"

"I've sent Flower out for pepper," promised the cook grimly. "That'll keep 'em away. But what we're to do about this . . .

"Boiling lye. Euh!" she added, jerking her foot back from a new line of scurrying invaders.

"It was Foxfire Girl who did it!" spat Honeysuckle Lady, turning with venom in her eye just as Foxfire Girl and Opal Girl mashed themselves into the rear of the clump of fascinated, horrified fledglings at the top of the winding stair. "Look at her face!"

"I . . ." Foxfire Girl hastily tried to assume an expression of wounded shock. "How could I have done it? You can check in there—there's no candy or syrup in there—"

"And how," asked Chrysanthemum Lady thinly, "would you know that, girl?" She stepped in fast, however, as the courtesan lunged at the girl, thrusting her back as she slashed, with real intent, at Foxfire Girl's eyes with her nails. "None of that!" She grabbed Honeysuckle Lady by the shoulders with hands strong as a man's, shoved her hard against the wall.

"Bitch!" the blond woman spat at Foxfire Girl. "Sow! Whore, making eyes at Iorradus . . ."

"Jealous?" Foxfire Girl lifted one eyebrow the way her father did.

"You . . ." She lunged again, and Chrysanthemum Lady thrust her against the wall.

"Enough of this! I won't have any catfights in my house and I won't have any sneaking around afterward, either! If Foxfire Girl ends up breaking out in a rash from bad cosmetics or puking from bad food I'm going to know who to talk to about it. And I might add," she went on in a lower voice, pinning the furious Honeysuckle Lady to the wall and bringing her face close to hers, "that the tuition her father pays for her instruction here—*and* her safety—is considerably more than *you* bring us in a dozen suppers."

In the hot shafts of the late-morning light, the ants milled confusedly on the floor; a couple of bull ants fell off the ceiling with audible plops, crept to the door and turned back, to be bitten to death by their swarming, tiny, infuriated cousins. A scorpion, baffled and covered with cream, emerged from one of the cosmetic pots on the dresser, leaving a smeary trail of white as it crawled across the lacquered surface.

"And as for you, miss . . ." Chrysanthemum Lady turned to Foxfire Girl. "You're to help Flower and Gecko Woman clean up the room."

"Me?" Foxfire Girl fell back a pace, revolted and alarmed. "How could I have had anything to do with it?"

"I didn't say you did." The mother regarded her with narrowed black eyes. "A Pearl Woman is equal to any situation, good or bad, dear. Sometimes one needs training in how to cope with the bad. Go to the kitchen now. Cook will show you what to do with the lye. But I suggest you stop in your room first and change your clothes."

Firmly taking Honeysuckle Lady's arm in hers, the mother frog-marched the infuriated courtesan away. The fledglings broke and scattered up the narrow unlit stairs to their own warren of cubicles on the floor above, or down to the kitchen yard to fill in the morning's duties in Cook's absence. All except Opal Girl avoided Foxfire Girl's proximity and eye.

Opal Girl regarded her friend with trepidation. "I'll ask if I can help you," she offered. "With two of us, and Flower and Gecko Woman, it won't be that bad."

"Oh, shut up!" Foxfire Girl pulled her arm away from the proffered gentle touch and stormed up the stairs to her room to find a short gown and sturdy shoes. In the squares of sunlight on the polished black-cedar floor, the ants crawled in puzzled circles until the humans came back and drowned and scalded them to death.

NINE

J ethan turned out to be a very large young man with the dusky complexion and bright blue eyes of those rangeland villages around Mud Lake who'd married for generations with the deep-desert merchants who came through to trade for sulfur and salt. It was a good thing, Shaldis reflected, that both she and the Summer Concubine cast a cloak about the three of them as they made their way down the broad Avenue of the Sun toward the eastern gate. Even in the knee-length baggy pantaloons and coarse shirt of a laborer, Jethan could not be mistaken for anything other than a soldier.

He kept fingering his hip, where a sword was supposed to be, and studied the crowd, the walls and each doorway or alley mouth they passed as if all the world were enemy territory and he the only soldier in it capable of defending against ambush.

His disapproval deepened profoundly when they passed through the dust-choked cavern of the East Gate and into the Slaughterhouse District itself. Despite the veils that would have rendered the two women completely anonymous had they been noticeable at all, he seemed to want to stand between the Summer Concubine and everything and anyone they met. And this, Shaldis reflected, was only because he could not hustle her bodily back to the palace and lock her in her pavilion, where she belonged.

"It isn't right that you should be here, lady," he said, halting to let a woman reel past, unveiled and almost undressed, incapably drunk on the arm of an equally inebriated pimp. "What my lord would say—"

"My lord," replied the Summer Concubine, gazing around her with enormous interest, "would commend you for your obedience—is that candy that man's selling?"

"In a manner of speaking." Raeshaldis forced herself to remember that, first, she was hidden by veils and, second, by spells: Old Grapot wouldn't recognize in the veiled woman the soft-voiced boy who'd come around exploring a few years ago. Maybe he wouldn't even have known her had she been in her brother's clothing again. He looked pretty flown on his own merchandise today. "It's mixed with hashish. He didn't used to sell it to children," she added, feeling she had to apologize for the rheumy-eyed vendor as he handed a bolus of fig paste and nuts to a boy of about eleven.

The child, to be honest, was probably an accomplished housebreaker already. Most of the urchins hereabouts were—if they survived infancy.

Still, reflected Shaldis, the Slaughterhouse was a lot safer than Jethan seemed to think it was, if you kept your wits about you and didn't do anything stupid.

The Slaughterhouse District was one of the poorest of the

city, a tumbledown brangle of shacks, shambles, tenements and taverns that had grown up between the caravansaries of the city's Eastern Gate and the villas of the Salt-Pan Quarter, which had been a small oasis owned by various connections of the Sarn at the foot of the Citadel bluff. The wells of those pleasant dwellings had long since run dry. Those nearer the city, Shaldis knew, weren't bringing up much that was drinkable these days, but the poor who worked in the slaughterhouses, or who cured hides or boiled glue or simply lived out there because it was cheaper than the city rents, were willing to pay what the water bosses charged to draw from them, to avoid the walk into the city. A lot of the residents of the Slaughterhouse were wanted by the city guards anyway, for picking pockets or petty thievery, and had no choice in the matter.

The reek of boiling bones, of rotting hides and untended cesspits, extended for about ten miles into the open rangeland beyond. The lowing of thirsty and terrified cows, the bleat of sheep, the screams of pigs as they were clubbed to death hung thick in the dirty air, along with vendors' cries for everything from cheap veils to fried locusts.

It was a place where neither the great houses nor any of the temples held jurisdiction, as they did in the city; a place where the big merchant guilds disdained either to sell wares or send proctors. It was the place where the wells ran dry first in bad years, the place where plagues broke out in the stinking streets, where thieves ran to hide in the daytime and from which they sneaked back into the city just before the closing of the gates.

Vultures circled constantly overhead or invigilated the passing crowds from the edges of every roof.

"Now, that is outside of enough!" cried the Summer Concubine indignantly as they passed through the narrow right-of-way that snaked around the side of a mostly barricaded public square. She craned her neck to look back through the stout fence that had been built around the well head, where two of Warfin Xolnax's bullyboys were shoving an old woman with a yoke of buckets away from the well.

"It was five coppers *yesterday*, Granny," one of the thugs was saying. "It's a silver bit today. If five coppers is all you got, you shoulda come yesterday. . . ."

A trough had been built next to the well extending back to the nearby shambles where sheep, goats, pigs and a few steers were penned. The woman fought against their grip, struggling to get to the water and cursing like a stevedore. "This is outrageous!" When one of the men threw the woman's yoke and buckets into the street, the Summer Concubine showed signs of thrusting her way through the gate to confront them, but Shaldis and Jethan both stepped in her path. Shaldis rather nervously thickened the spells of inconspicuousness about them until another market woman nearly walked slap into them, unseeing.

"It's done all over the Slaughterhouse," said Shaldis, gently herding the indignant favorite away. "You're never going to get anybody to testify before the king about it. Not if they want to use that well, or any other hereabouts, again. And since nobody here owes allegiance to a house or a clan, there's no order. All the water bosses are friends, when they're not fighting. And they've got damn long memories."

Between the tenements—either tall, rickety warrens of bleaching wattle raised on the foundations of crumbling villas or rambling heaps of half-decayed adobe and rubble that had been the painted temples of gods—the noon heat condensed, breathless and sickening with the fetor of garbage and pigs. As she'd changed into the cheap cotton dress the Summer Concubine had sent one of her maids to fetch, Shaldis had advised also that they take pomander boxes, strong-smelling herbs and camphor held up under the veils to combat some of the worst fumes. These worked in most of the poor districts of the city, but in the Slaughterhouse it only served to make one sick. She could barely get the words out as she further explained, "Everybody else in the city—inside the walls, I mean—has catch jars on their roofs because it's handier than going to the wells. But here it's to put off dealing with the water bosses until the end of the season. Right now Xolnax is making a killing. This is Pig Alley," she added, turning down a still narrower way between a squalid café and two of the biggest slaughter-houses of the quarter. The stench of blood was nearly suffocating. Under ramadas of pine poles and palm fronds pigs complained ear-piercingly. Under others, head-high clay jars swarmed with flies in the shade: blood to be sold for puddings. "This used to be called the Avenue of Niam, for the big Temple of Niam down at the end. The priests left when the temple wells went dry. Then for a long time it was empty, until Lohar and the True Believers took it over. A family of thieves was living in it, and a brothel set up under a tent in the court-yard—"

"Cutpurse! Cutpurse!" shrieked someone in a tenement courtyard that seemed also to be set up as a market, though what it was selling was difficult to determine. A youth crashed past them, followed by an angry swarm of men waving fists and sticks. Jethan's hand went to his bare side in search of a weapon that wasn't there.

"You see?" he said accusingly, as if Shaldis should have been more careful.

Pig Alley joined Chicken Lane in a sort of irregular square in front of the temple, which like all of Niam's houses was spartanly plain—in keeping with the god of wealth's known stinginess—and built like a fortress. Down a dogleg of Chicken Lane men were lined up by a side gate into the temple's narrow yard, some bearing yoke poles with buckets, others carrying baskets or pots. A young man with his hair half shaved in the manner of the True Believers sat in the gateway like a porter in a rich man's lodge. In the high-walled courtyard beyond, a man's voice could be heard, snatches of oratory echoing shrilly but with the formal intonation of a Sun Mage.

"Lohar must have dug one of the wells deeper and hit water again." Shaldis angled her head, curious, trying to see past the jostling backs. A man came out past them, flies buzzing around the hunk of raw meat he carried. His hair, too, had been hacked and shaved in the pattern prescribed by the Mouth of Nebekht. "It's cheaper than paying Xolnax's prices, I suppose. How long has Turquoise Woman lived here, did you say?"

"Six months," said the Summer Concubine softly. "Making her living as a healer, mostly."

I bet she gets lots of customers, reflected Shaldis wryly. Between territorial fights among the water bosses, fights of the inhabitants with the bosses' bullyboys over the cost of drawing water, drunken brawls in the cafés and taverns that decorated nearly every intersection of the winding street and the number of children attacked by jackals among the middens, there was probably as much human blood shed here as there was animal.

"She can't do much, for fear word will get to her husband. If this water boss Xolnax chose to kidnap her—hold her prisoner, or even blackmail her with the threat of returning her to her husband—I'm not sure she'd have the strength to fight him, particularly not if his daughter is Raven-wise herself. The king is trying to get the laws changed, about both women-who-have-power and women in general, but at the moment almost no one will admit that women *have* these powers—or the right to live by themselves. And so many women themselves are raised to believe . . . Here!" she cried suddenly at two unveiled slatterns emerging from an alleyway barely wider than a door. "That dress belongs to Turquoise Woman!"

She stepped forward—to Jethan's protesting gargle—and seized the first, taller, woman by the arm. "Where did you get that dress?"

The woman, big and stringy and nearly toothless from childbearing, grabbed the favorite's wrist and twisted her hand free. "You a pal of hers, baba cake?" She glanced past the Summer Concubine at Jethan—the concubine's activity had effectively swept away any spell of concealment—and smiled ingratiatingly. "Told me herself, she did. She says, 'Rosemallow Woman,' she says, 'if ever I be gone for more than three days, you come on in and take what you like, for it'll mean some ill has befallen me, and I ain't comin' back.' Now, how can a poor woman like me tell . . . ?"

"Three days?" Raeshaldis interposed herself in front of the other woman, who though short and swarthy had bleached her elaborately dressed hair a virulent reddish blond.

"Well, it's five now. And we weren't the only ones that took her things," added the girl self-righteously. "That old drunkard Zarb that lives across the court, and Grapot the candy seller, they were in there the very first night she didn't come home, helping 'emselfs to the larder and sayin' as how it was for money she owed 'em."

"Me and Melon Girl," provided the older woman with the air of one martyred to friendship, "we watched Preket and those sons of his just about clean the place out. And the folks from Nebekht's Temple messed up the place bad. Lohar, he hated Turquoise Woman like poison, and he'd never see her on the street but that he'd spit at her. 'Course, he done that with lots of folks. Where he gets all that spit from I don't know."

"What happened?" asked the Summer Concubine. "To Turquoise Woman, I mean." A man driving a herd of goats

down Chicken Lane yelled "Outa the way, sluts!" and everyone crowded back into the mouth of Little Pig Alley except
Jethan, who tried to stride over and take the man to task and
was nearly trampled by goats for his trouble.

"Done a bunk, bet me," said Melon Girl, and unselfcon-
sciously scratched her bottom. "Preket—he's the landlord for
all those little rooms on Greasy Yard—he charged her somethin' cruel for that stinkin' chicken coop he rented her, and
she never would get her hands dirty." She jerked her head toward a red-painted arch about halfway down the alley, which
had clearly once been the kitchen gate into a villa whose
front, larger half had since burned. The remains of the
kitchens, laundry and stables had been, Shaldis guessed, parti-
tioned into rooms and let for whatever they'd bring. "I talked
to her the night she left. . . . What night was it, Rosemallow
Woman? Five nights ago? Six nights?"

"Five," said her friend. "Xolnax did his hog-slaughterin' that
night. Usually it quiets down here after dark, but you could
hear 'em squealin' all over the district 'til damn near moonset."

"That's right." Melon Girl nodded briskly. "Turquoise
Woman had some kind of run-in with Lohar; she was standin'
in the gate there tryin' to clean herself up. That very dress
Rosemallow Woman's wearing now," she added, cocking a
bright eye at her friend. "Which as you can see is too short on
her and not her color."

"Not yours, either," returned Rosemallow Woman. "And it's
good linen."

"You look like a cow in it."

"A damn well-dressed cow, and better'n you."

"Did Lohar make any threats?" asked the Summer Concubine, since the two women showed signs of escalating into
physical combat over the garment.

Melon Girl shrugged her plump shoulders dismissively.

"The holy Mouth of Nebekht always threatened her. Called her a she-demon and a trans-passer on the laws of the gods."

"Transgressor?"

"That's what I said. But that's what he says about everybody that does magic, for all he used to be a wizard himself. Poor Turquoise Woman was cryin' over it—she cries a lot, though—and scared, 'cause he said righteousness would rise up and destroy those who went against the will of Nebekht. I said, *Get a grip, girl! It's all talk, talk and shit.* But she went on into her room and shot the bolt."

"How do you know she shot the bolt?" asked Shaldis. The four women had turned down the alley, picking their way single file along the walls to avoid the marsh of garbage and slops in the center of the way, with Jethan glowering in their wake as if he wanted to attack and slay the smells with his sword for daring to inconvenience his king's dear friend.

" 'Cause she always did."

"I can't think why," muttered Jethan sarcastically.

"You shut up," said Rosemallow Woman. And to the Summer Concubine, "I think she was afraid Lohar would tell her husband where she was. Three!" she yelled as a little brown-haired girl came darting out of the courtyard at a run, a broken doll in her hand. "You give that back to Little Sister! I swear—" And she strode off in pursuit.

Melon Girl shook her head. "My man'd beat the daylights out of me if I went around latchin' myself in my room." She shrugged again. "And he'll beat the daylights out of me if I'm out loiterin' much longer." She led the way into the court, where half a dozen children played with chips of adobe brick in the dust. For the rest, it was pretty much as Shaldis had guessed: In the open door of what had probably been a tack room a couple of men sat sharing a gourd bottle of *sherab*, talking in the long, pointless, drunken spiral of men who had long ago said to each other whatever they had to say. "Big Sister," Melon Girl called to the oldest of the children, "get me my shawl, and tell your mama I had to get going. . . . You tell Turquoise Woman we've got all her stuff safe," she added self-righteously to the Summer Concubine. "But if you're lookin' for her, I'd go check with that husband of hers. Fergit, his name is—he's in the Weavers Quarter."

"But don't tell him where she was," put in Rosemallow Woman, coming into the court with Number Three Daughter gripped hard by an unwilling arm. "She said he'd kill her if he found her. And she'd never hurt a fly, poor thing. . . ."

"Would Xolnax have taken her?" Raeshaldis asked, and Rosemallow Woman looked first startled, then thoughtful, then finally shook her head.

"What would be the sense of it?" she returned. "This whole street's his territory. He could pay her for whatever little this-and-that he wanted, not that he ever has—has proper wizard friends of his own, I expect. None of Rumrum's boys dare come this far, and even if they did, poor Turquoise Woman knew enough to know not to do favors for no other boss unless she was willing to move out. And I know she didn't do that."

No, thought Shaldis, considering the purple linen dress—which, as Melon Girl had stated, was both too short and the wrong color for her informant.

"Myself . . ." Rosemallow Woman's voice sank as she trailed Shaldis across the sand and garbage of the courtyard to the door of what had once been a storeroom, "I think she bolted. That last day she was nervous as a rabbit, barely coming out to use the privies. . . ." She gestured at the shed in the corner of the yard, quite unnecessarily, for they would have been easily identifiable as privies by the smell in complete darkness at the distance of a mile.

"Nervous of what?" asked the Summer Concubine, turning in the door of what had been Turquoise Woman's room.

Rosemallow Woman shrugged. "Don't know. Maybe she didn't either, since she didn't seem to know which way to look when she did come out. But I know fear when I see it. And she was afraid."

"Wouldn't she have told you?" asked Shaldis as Rosemallow Woman strode off across the court hauling her daughter by the arm, leaving the Summer Concubine, Shaldis and Jethan alone.

"I'm not sure she could have." The Summer Concubine looked around the tiny chamber, stripped now even of its bedstead. Scrapes in the dirt floor and marks in the crumbling plaster showed where the bed had been; more scuffs marked where a table and chair had crowded for space near the hearth under the room's sole window. The open shutters revealed an alley even narrower and more noisome than Little Pig.

DEMON HAG DIE had been chalked on the wall—properly spelled, Shaldis noticed.

"Turquoise Woman did not have a particularly strong power," the Summer Concubine went on, walking slowly around the room, her fingers trailing lightly along the filthy wall. "Sometimes she could not sense it when I tried to call her to a mirror to scry, or to water or fire. Sometimes she would try to call on me, and I would not hear, not even after we made a Sigil of Sisterhood between us. I worried about her."

Shaldis walked to the window. The bolts on the shutters were intact. They'd been written over with wards: Shaldis could feel them in the wood. The Summer Concubine was right: The woman who had written those marks of protection had not had a great deal of power, and had not learned to focus what she had.

But she could feel, through those uncertain sigils, the love

Turquoise Woman had had for animals and birds; the residue of spells to call sparrows to her hand was still resonant in the wood, spells to heal them of their strange ills and fevers and mites. She felt her love of cooking, and of flowers—amid the debris the looters had left there were flower petals strewn all along the base of the wall, scraggy lupine and squash flowers and the poppies that sprouted in the cracks of broken walls. Somehow Shaldis knew the woman had had a garden in her husband's house.

She felt the woman's loneliness. Even after her grandfather's tyranny and the anxiety of the college, Shaldis found the thought of living completely alone for six months unnerving.

She moved along the wall, passing her hands over the plaster, probing into it with her mind. Outside, Rosemallow Woman's children shrieked at one another and one of the two men drinking in the other doorway screamed at them to shut up. In the mud brick—mixed with layered confusions of other people's tears and giggles and fright and lust over a dozen generations—Shaldis thought she sensed the sound of this single young woman's weeping, alone in this strange place.

The sense of her was like a perfume. She probed deeper.

A light foot scrunched on the dirt floor behind her. "What is it, dear?"

"I don't know. Sometimes you can sense what's gone on in a place, especially a place where magic is worked. There are rooms in the Citadel where great spells were done that have had to be shut up for hundreds of years. You go in them and you hear voices muttering in the air." Her eyes slipped closed. It was like trying to distinguish a tune through a wall, or to follow conversation in the market on market day.

"But there's something here," she said softly, softly as the darkness whispered to her out of the plaster and mud of the wall. A whisper . . . or screaming, heard a long distance away. "Something happened here. Something . . . something cold."

"Did she have books, lady?" Jethan knelt by the hearth, rummeled the ashes with a stick.

The shadow, the darkness—the far-off echoes of terror— vanished with the sound of his voice, and if the room hadn't been comprehensively stripped, Shaldis would have thrown something at him in sheer annoyance.

"Some." The Summer Concubine looked down at the crude brick shelf with an expression of pain and regret. "And she was making notes for me. I taught her the spells Soth taught me, to protect them. . . ."

"They must have worked." Shaldis came to stand by her. "That ash is mostly wood and charcoal, not paper ash. And I don't see any wax, which there would be if note tablets were burned. That doesn't mean they didn't get burned elsewhere, or that the neighbors didn't take them for kindling."

A voice shouted in the courtyard, "Demon sluts!" and a rain of brick fragments and dog excreta rattled against the wall.

"Curse," said the Summer Concubine, and Shaldis made a remark considerably stronger: "It's the Mouth of Nebekht."

"Sluts! Devils! Transgressors upon the will and the patience of Nebekht, commander of the universe! You pitiful fool"—he was now addressing Jethan, who had gone to loom in the doorway, fists doubled, mostly filling the narrow space—"deluded by wicked women! I marvel that such as they would even trouble themselves with a man's countenance at all!"

Past Jethan's shoulder, Shaldis could see the Mouth of the god. She'd seen him around the marketplaces and in the Grand Bazaar in her days of boy's disguise, and had always despised him, partly because he never failed to jeer at wizards— he was one of the first to shout that they were losing their powers—and partly because he also seldom missed a chance to jeer at any woman he saw, veiled or unveiled. He was a sturdy little man with a round, red pug face, balding—*No wonder he requires the True Believers to cut their hair*—and dirty as a Blood Mage in his sleeveless brown laborer's tunic and bare legs.

"Do they walk barefaced, bare breasted maybe, to visit their barefaced friend?" Lohar's trained, powerful tenor was heavy with sarcasm. A number of his followers had trailed him into the court, and more were coming. Mostly, Shaldis guessed, because in a district where work was scarce and beggars numerous, it didn't take much to get up a crowd. "I saw them standing like harlots before the porch of the temple, staring as if they had never seen holiness before! Don't think I didn't! Veiling themselves in their evil glamours, demons in disguise, assuming only the outer form of women in order to deceive!"

"That's one I haven't heard," murmured Shaldis.

"No," returned the Summer Concubine softly. "And it doesn't sound promising. How powerful a mage was he?"

"One of the best, according to Hathmar. He was herbmaster of the college, and a powerful healer. But his were among the first powers to fade. Hathmar says he didn't used to be like this at all. He started drinking *ijnis*—brewing it up in his rooms— and of course that's something you can't hide for very long." The marks of it showed in his face as he harangued his True Believers: the frenzied sparkle in his bulging brown eyes, as if he were being eaten from inside by something he could not control. The way his voice scaled up and down like a crazily played flute. The way his wide mouth grimaced and stretched.

"The masters of the college were still trying to figure out what to do with him—he'd already started having fits, and his spells, when they worked at all, were getting unreliable— when he started having visions of the god Nebekht."

"Why do you think every basin and bucket on your roofs stands empty?" Lohar ranted. "Why do you think you have to deal with Xolnax and Rumrum? Why do you have to walk halfway across the city to be jeered at and driven away by the rich folks' guards? The Lord of the Iron Girdle is angry, my friends, *angry!* Furious at these hussies, these impudent tramps! For a thousand years he has forborne. . . ."

Shaldis explained, "He says—I've heard him preach it about two hundred times in the bazaar—that Nebekht directed him to a tomb in the Redbone Hills, to find his statue: Nebekht is the war god they worship up near the White Lake, where he's from. I don't even know if what's in the temple—what he found in the tomb—is actually a statue of the real Nebekht or some other god. He has long conversations with it, supposedly. It tells him how the world's supposed to be run."

"And the running of the world appears to involve killing large numbers of animals," the Summer Concubine commented. "Phew, can you smell the blood on him? I think getting out of here looks like a good idea."

"Bring the hussies out of there, the demon sluts! Let's show them how the *true* servants of *true* gods treat those who persist in defying their commands!" The men around him cheered and another volley of rocks and dung hit the wall.

"Lose yourself in the crowd." The Summer Concubine brushed Jethan's shoulders with her fingertips. "We passed a café in the plaza just outside the East Gate. Meet us there."

"Lady," protested the young man, "only common women sit in cafés! You can't—"

"We'll all have a better chance of getting away if we separate." And when Jethan opened his mouth to object, she added wearily, "I command it."

His mouth set and his nostrils flared with a thousand unspoken words about willful women who wouldn't do what was obviously best for them.

"I'll put a cloak over you. . . ."

The men had crowded up to the door, Lohar staying prudently in the rear. Two or three of them leaped at Jethan when he lunged out; he seized the nearest and wrenched the billet of wood from his hand, swung it at the others. The beggars, laborers, farmers out of work were armed mostly with clubs and sticks, but a few had knives, or axes from the slaughtering pens. Shaldis knew from experience how much damage could be done simply with chunks of adobe brick.

"Can you distract them?" whispered the Summer Concubine. "I can put a cloak over him, but not while everyone's looking."

The two women sidled to the doorway. Shaldis counted over the men in the mob with her eye, naming them: Bald Guy, Squinty, Big Nose, Blue Tunic, Food-Stains . . . weaving those names into a Wyrd of Quarrels, which she cast like a net into the square. Then, stooping, she picked up one of the thrown rocks and flung it at Tall Guy in the middle of the mob.

Years of running with the boys in the markets had made her good.

"Watch the hell what you're doing!" Tall Guy yelled, whirling, and grabbed a skinny dark-skinned man behind him by his beggar's rags.

"Bugger you!"

"Whoreson!"

"Who're you shoving?" This from the two men into whom Bugger You had hurled Whoreson, jostling them into others still.

"I don't take that kind of talk from any goddam thief. . . ."

"Who you calling a thief?"

"I'm calling a thief the whoreson who sells bread that's half sawdust is who I'm calling a thief."

Lohar whipped around, shouting for order—as a former mage himself he must have guessed what was going on. The moment his eyes were off Jethan, the Summer Concubine swept a gesture with her long fingers and Raeshaldis yelled over the din, "Jethan, *run!*"

The young man stared around him for a second, making Shaldis want to hit him, then bolted. Shaldis herself kept hold of the Summer Concubine's hand, the two women dodging through the crowd, which by now had dissolved into a dozen knots of struggling, cursing, shoving men. Someone grabbed at her dress, others yelled—obviously their own cloaks left something to be desired—but they managed to dart through the gate of Greasy Yard, feet slipping in the muck of Little Pig Alley outside. They turned several corners, crossed a court where a stringy old man was taking down the shutters from a tavern, hurried along an alley permanently mud-sodden from blood oozing from the slaughter yards and stinking to the gods in heaven.

From the tops of the walls, the vultures watched them sardonically as they fled.

They met Jethan a few minutes later at the Hospitality of BoSaa café on BoSaa's Square, just outside the East Gate. The Temple of BoSaa, god of cattle and farmers, for whom the broad plaza had been named, had long ago been swallowed up in the maze of caravansaries and markets that had little by little encroached on its grounds. From the table where they sat—in the curtained corner where other veiled women sipped coffee with each other and unveiled ones chatted with men—Shaldis could just see its gate pylons peeking over the jumble of low domes and tiled roofs, painted statues faded and sand scrubbed and what was left of the electrum of their cornices flashing patchily in the afternoon light.

"Wait a little and go back there," instructed the Summer Concubine. "Find Preket the landlord and rent that room. I'll send a page tomorrow with money for you." She turned to Shaldis. "If you had more time in that room, would you be able to listen into the wood the way you were doing and tell what happened to Turquoise Woman? Of who may have come, and where she might be, and if she's all right?"

Her voice sounded desperate. Above the veil Shaldis met her eyes, and the Summer Concubine looked away, as if not wanting to admit the fear already strong in her heart.

"I don't know." Shaldis lifted her veil awkwardly to sip her coffee—she'd never been graceful, and years of drinking coffee like a boy hadn't given her much practice in the ladylike handling of veils and cups in public. "The first thing to do would be to check at her husband's house, wouldn't it?"

"If I thought he'd tell the truth about it, yes." The Summer Concubine's voice turned bitter. "I'll send there and make inquiries this afternoon. But whatever he tells me I'd like to compare with whatever you can learn—can sense—in that room. In the meantime Jethan can go back there now."

"Lady!" protested the young guardsman. "First let me return you to the palace!"

"Don't be silly," said Shaldis. "By the time we walk back and you pack up whatever you think you'll need, the city gates'll be shut and by tomorrow that room may be rented out for a whorehouse. I'm surprised it hasn't been already."

Jethan's back stiffened at the reference. "I am very sorry my lady was ever brought into contact with the disorderly women who haunt that district," he said. "But to let you return to the palace without an escort . . ."

"I'll be with her," pointed out Shaldis.

Jethan's upper lip seemed to get longer. "That isn't the point. It's only women of the common classes who walk around together without a manservant." And he glanced speakingly at the other women at the tables nearby. One of them was Melon Girl, with a potbellied man in red who looked like a senior bullyboy: She caught Shaldis's eye and waved.

"Of course." The Summer Concubine clasped her small

hands and smiled at Jethan, without meeting his eyes but with ready, warm sympathy in her gaze. "But we *are* dressed as women of the common classes, you know, and properly veiled. And in an emergency we can always rely on a gray cloak."

Jethan looked as if he wanted to say that neither protection nor appearances were at issue, but rather the inherent right-ness of things, and moreover in *his* hometown there wouldn't even *be* a section of a public café for women, but the Summer Concubine went on: "And the Lady Raeshaldis is quite right about the room being rented out again. We must learn what happened, and where she is . . . if she can be helped." Her fair brows drew together under the coarse yellow cotton of her veil; pain shadowed the depths of those blue eyes. "Please help us. There's clearly something going on, something evil."

"As you wish, my lady. But it isn't right that—" He lowered his voice at the furiously hissed insistence of both women; already men in the main section of the café were beginning to look. Disgruntled but quieter, Jethan went on, "It isn't right that you should return to the palace alone."

And then, to the bemused stares of everyone in the café, he executed a deep salaam and vanished into the jostling crowds.

TEN

B ax and his riders pursued the fugitive teyn through the whole of the day.

Rain had washed the tracks of the teyn from the canyon that the Summer Concubine had described—as Oryn had

thought he might, Bax identified it instantly from her description—but they found evidence of the band's concealment
nevertheless. Bax's scouts were still casting about for the trail
when the Summer Concubine's messenger arrived with a description of her second vision in the water bowl. The commander recognized that place, too: She had seen a cave that
was barely more than a longitudinal slit in the rocks, beneath
a huge dust-colored overhang of stone above an open hillside.
"Headed southeast, it sounds like. I wonder if they're making
for the Singing World?"

"They wouldn't know about it, surely?" Oryn followed the
commander back toward the horses, nonchalantly trying not to
limp. It is one thing to be a competent rider—which Oryn was,
mostly because as a fat child he had had a horror of looking silly
on a horse. It is another to ride for almost six hours when one
is not accustomed to doing so. Oryn was already debating
whether he should spend one week or two in the hot room of
the palace baths, drinking soothing tisanes and being massaged.

"You ever been there?"

Oryn shook his head. Few people had, of those who made
their homes in the farmlands along the lakes. He'd heard
about that vast, lumpy platform of twisted rock—twenty miles
long by some five wide—like a tawny island above the gray
gravel pavement of the desert beyond the Dead Hills. But he
doubted even his father had gone there in the wars that had
brought House Jothek to the rulership forty years ago. There
was no reason to visit the place. Nothing grew in the Singing
World, nothing could be mined there, no water had ever been
detected in its bare, wind-smoothed ridges. Only the crooning
wind, muttering with near-human groans around the rocks.
Hermits had dwelled there once, devotees of Kush, god of the
desert wind. What had become of them no one knew.

"It's a perfect place to hide," Bax said. "Once you get among those rocks you don't leave a print, and your pursuers haven't more than a few feet of vision in any direction." The flicker of morning winds showed up the silver in the commander's coarse, dark hair under the edge of his helmet. Though this red-walled canyon—Camel Rock Canyon, it was called, of course—was still in what was called the near ranges, meaning that paloverde grew among the rocks and in the open land stands of cactus and sagebrush occasionally broke the brown monotony of the earth, it was close enough to the outer limits of the king's authority that there was danger from the bandits who haunted the nearer wastes and the nomads who had grown bolder with the desperation of thirst. All the guardsmen who waited for them at the canyon's mouth wore full armor, back-and-breasts, greaves, helmets, mailed skirts.

Head aching from the helmet's weight and knees chafed from the greave straps, Oryn felt considerable sympathy for them. The mantlings that protected the back of his neck from the sun seemed determined to creep down his collar and whipped him in the eyes every time he turned his head, and the somewhat short-waisted cuirass gripped his bottom ribs like a torturer's iron clamp. On those occasions when his father would insist that he ride out in armor on some training expedition designed to "make a man of him," Oryn had regarded it as a point of honor to play the fool, wearing his gaudiest eye paint and covering himself in perfumed ointment. He recalled once constructing a crest of crimson wildflowers for his helmet and discoursing on aesthetics to his disgusted parent and half a regiment of baffled palace guards. No wonder Bax had looked surprised when he'd asked to come.

It had been quite polite of him, Oryn thought, not to look either alarmed or appalled as well.

But this was no longer matter for play. He wiped his dripping forehead and tried to loop back his hair out of his eyes. The lives

of three children were at stake and, more than that, the lives of
perhaps many more in the villages that relied on the labor of
supposedly domesticated teyn. Bax had a job to do and the last
thing he needed was an amateur getting in his way, particularly
one he couldn't just shove aside.

So Oryn's voice was diffident as he said, "Yes, but according
to my lady, these are village teyn. They wouldn't know the
Singing World, would they?"

"They've got to have wildings among 'em." Bax rubbed his
chin, where beard stubble lay like granite dust: Oryn was wishing he'd had Geb shave him too, but that had been out of the
question in terms of time. "Though you're right—I haven't
seen a handprint all through the canyon, and it's the wildings
that run bent and push off with their hands." He shook his
head and strode down to where the horses waited, remounts
saddled while the men hunted for signs. "I'll be curious what
we find when we find 'em."

Oryn gritted his teeth as discreetly as he possibly could,
waved away a sergeant's offer of aid, prayed very briefly for the
dignity of success to Oan Echis the guardian god of the Jothek
house and got his foot up into the stirrup. Oan Echis was in a
good mood that morning and Oryn made it to the saddle unas-
sisted. *New robes for all your priests, first-quality silk. . . .*

"Do they communicate?" he asked as the cavalcade rode out
through the harsh midmorning light. The clouds were gone as
if they had never been. Rain pocks made a thousand tiny
craters in the thin desert dust, like the false promises of young
lovers. The hooves obliterated this evidence of the wizards'
Song. Dust settled in their place. "You've ridden patrols for
thirty years. We've taught the village teyn to understand us
and even to speak a bit. . . . Have you ever heard a wilding
teyn speak to another teyn? Do they *have* a language? Or make
any noise once they're past infancy?"

"We only see 'em when we're hunting 'em," pointed out Bax, his eyes always moving, always scanning each slight hollow of the land. "They may discourse natural philosophy back in their caves for all I know, my lord. Yes, I think they communicate somehow, from the way the bands will move to avoid patrols. But I've never seen or heard a thing, nor has anyone I've ever spoke to, not even the nomads."

"Have you ever known them to steal children?"

Bax didn't answer for a time. The gray-brown emptiness rose to chewed-looking ridges of stone, then fell away again. Even the cactus was sparse here, small and squat and farther and farther apart. Once Oryn saw a snake coiled in the black puddle of a rock's shade. Once he saw a rabbit far away, bounding over the heat-paled dust. In all the world there seemed no other life.

There was poetry here, he thought, but it was a music he did not understand. Maybe the nomads did, who wandered the wastelands from oasis to oasis, living on the edge of the winds.

And there were limits beyond which even the nomads would not go.

"There's always children that disappear from the rangeland villages, my lord," the commander said at last. "Not often, but regularly. Not taken by jackals, I mean—you'll usually see vultures and a body—but just disappear. The djinni get the blame for it, and it may be the djinni, though myself I've never figured what the Beautiful Ones would want with a squalling brat. They could have had all four of my brothers for the asking, I'll tell you that." He shaded his eyes against the white glare of the southern sky.

Oryn opened his mouth to ask what he sought, then thought about it and didn't. So far only a single vulture could be descried, like a dust mote in the brilliant air.

"Curse it." Bax froze, looking out to the southwest, then reined his horse and groped for the spyglass that hung at his belt. Oryn unfurled his own and trained it toward what the commander had seen first: a long, low whisper of dust on the southwestern horizon.

Good gods, how many of them are there? he thought in shock, putting the glass to his eye, and a moment later was glad he hadn't said anything. "Nomads?"

There was a confused suggestion of movement all through the dust cloud, a bobbing that had to be beasts, and then the tall upright necks of camels.

"They'll have to be Rai an-Ariban's tribe." Bax stood in the stirrups, sun flashing from the brass mountings of his telescope. "Best we be moving. An-Ariban would kill a dozen men, if he thought he could get away with it, to keep his advance on the lakes quiet until it was too late for us to marshal a force against him. Only reason he wouldn't is if he thought we had a mage watching over us back in the city, as was done for years with patrols. And it may be the nomads know as well as we do that that isn't done anymore. Kiner . . ."

The corporal spurred up to his commander's side.

"Get back to the city, fast as you can go. Watch your back— the nomads will have patrols out ahead of them. Let Lord Barún know we've got nomads moving in our direction, start him marshaling a patrol. One thing that brother of yours knows how to do, it's put together warriors," added Bax as the guardsman caught up a couple of remounts from the cavvy and headed back toward the city in a very small cloud of saffron dust. "We've plenty of time. There should be no trouble."

"No," said Oryn quietly, troubled nevertheless by this first evidence that the nomads were starting to move in toward the arable land along the lakes. "No, he's quite good at that. My father always said he'd make a better king than I. But then again, my father seemed to think that the average camel driv-er would make a better king than I."

"If all we needed of a king was patrols along the rangelands and fathering more kings, I'd agree."

"Oh, so would I," said Oryn, quite earnestly. "Only my feelings in the matter are complicated by the fact that since I *am* the elder, sooner or later Barún would have to kill me. . . . It's just what's done, you know, in our social circles."

And Bax laughed.

In the cave beneath the overhanging cliff they found where the teyn had clustered: scuffed concentric rings of knee and buttock marks, deepened at the sides where they'd swayed. Three little zigzag scrapes in the dry sand at the side of the cave showed where the captives had lain.

"The hoot knelt here in the middle of the rings." Bax held low the torch that one of the men had kindled for him. Oryn came to his side, trying to disturb the tracks as little as possible. "You ever seen teyn cluster?"

"Oh, yes." Oryn squatted to study the marks, wondering if he'd be able to straighten his knees again to rise and deciding to deal with that challenge when the time came. With the restless orange glow supplementing the wan daylight from the front of the cave he could pick out the crooked little toe prints, the heel marks and traces where fingers had stirred the silk-fine dust. "Village teyn, that is. I used to sneak away from the palace at night when I was a child and climb a tree near the compound wall. A lot of lords have their minders break them up when they cluster, but I never saw the harm of it. They just sit in those circles and sway together. . . . I've seen them carry on for most of the night, then return to the fields in the morning, without even benefit of coffee. Can't imagine how they do that. Do the wildings cluster?"

Oryn stood up—without even crying out in pain, on which he congratulated himself.

"Again, you've got me." Bax moved back, stooping lower

and lower with the shelving of the roof, to hold the torch into that thin crack of ultimate darkness. Myriad furious rattling sounded in the crack, though the torchlight only showed more than a dozen tortoises—some of them the size of shields—plodding patiently away from the light.

By the tracks, as far as Oryn could see, none of the teyn had ventured anywhere near the crack. But again, how would they know? Most of them had never been away from their village and the Dry Hill diggings in their lives. Even if teyn *did* speak to one another, how would they have learned the language of the wildings to understand information about the desert?

"Soth have anything to say about it?" Bax asked.

Oryn remembered the reek of *sherab*, the stuffy dark of the study, the drawling, wretched voice of the man who had taught him to love the life of the mind even above the swooning delights of the senses. He felt the same grief he'd felt watching his father burn his books of poetry and tales. As if something beautiful were disappearing out of the world.

He still had a patch of red flesh on the side of his right hand where he'd tried to snatch *The Song of the Moon Prince* out of the blaze. Stupid, of course; it had earned him nothing but a whipping. He would gladly take another whipping—and the pain of the burn—if some god would show him what blaze it was that was consuming his friend's soul.

But he only said, "Only that he'd never heard of teyn stealing children either. Surely they would have realized that taking children would guarantee pursuit?"

"Their escape has guaranteed pursuit." Bax led the way out of the cave and thrust the torch into the thick sand at its mouth to kill the flame. Milk vetch and dandelion grew there. Oryn could see where the stalks and leaves had been freshly plucked, but nowhere in or around the cave had he seen the broken pieces. "And if they don't know that, it's a lesson all the others will have to learn." He glanced down the hillside at the men regrouping by the horses near the trail of scuffs and scratches that marked the teyns' retreat southeast again.

His blue eyes met the king's, studying him. Knowing, Oryn thought unhappily, that he, Oryn, was a keeper of cats and finches, who had had a servant beaten for sticking halved walnut shells on Black Princess's paws and setting her on a slick tile floor to watch her slither and slip. That he had a reputation for softheartedness, and poems about roses and moonlight. Gauging him.

Oryn sighed, understanding that he was right and hating it. Hating being king.

"I shall rely on your judgment," he said, in an almost inaudible voice.

They saw the vultures circling above the Singing World shortly before the fall of the early winter darkness on the land.

The Singing World itself was astonishing enough on first sight, and Oryn would have laughed aloud with amazement at the delicate spires and domes, the layered swirls of color, the smooth curved holes, bridges, tunnels—if he hadn't been seeing things now with the eyes of a tracker, a father, a king. He thought, *Bax will never find the teyn. And now the light's going.*

His heart ached at what the buzzards told him they *would* find.

The dark birds wheeled around a rock promontory near the north end. As the riders approached across the featureless desert, Oryn could hear the birds' cries. They left the horses where the rocks first rose in a wall the color of ripe peaches, scrambled up the wind-smoothed cliff and then among the maze of faults and crevices for perhaps another mile. When they finally climbed the eroded golden dome, the highest in the whole huge formation, Oryn saw where the rocks had been marked, circles and crosses daubed with mud, plant sap or blood.

As they neared the top there was a great deal of blood.

The rock knob where the children lay commanded the desert like a watchtower. Even as Oryn stood, panting and light-headed, over the three mangled little corpses someone shouted, "Down there! I saw 'em move!" and the men went scrambling in pursuit. Oryn signed to two of them to remain.

"Wrap them in blankets. Treat them gently. They'll want to burn them decently in the village when we get back."

"The girl too, sir?"

"The girl too."

The buzzards screamed, flapped their dark wings and hopped off the rock, swooping and veering as the guardsmen gathered up those three small bodies. Though the children had been crudely butchered with knives taken from the raided village, Oryn noted how calm their faces were. As if they'd been deeply asleep when the cutting started and simply had not waked. He prayed this was the case.

Sprigs of milk vetch and dandelion had been scattered around and over them, and stuck in the cracks of the rocks. Wilted—they'd been carried for many miles from the cave where they'd grown. Circles and Xs were scratched on the rock, in rude approximation, he thought, of the marks wizards made around the villages to control the thoughts and fears of the teyn. The scratches looked fresh.

"Have you ever seen anything like that before?"

The commander shook his head; his heavy-lipped mouth shut hard.

Men were calling out now that they could see the teyn fleeing. On this god walk above all the aisles and crevices of the Singing World, Oryn saw them clearly, like roaches darting along cracks in a wall. Saw the men pursuing them, through the rocks and over the twelve-foot golden wall, down to the gray desert floor.

He knew he couldn't hope to keep up with either the pursuers or the quarry, so he took his tablets from the satchel Geb had packed for him and in the slanting mellow light meticulously copied everything he saw: the position of the bodies, every twig and stem of the plant sprigs and where they lay, each rude symbol and dribbled line of blood. Scarcely the activity a bold hero king would undertake, he supposed with a sigh. On the other hand, at least Bax wouldn't have to worry about guarding him through all those caves and gullies.

Soth should know this, he thought.

He wouldn't even articulate to himself that it might be useful to have notes of the first occurrence, should there be a second.

Wouldn't let himself look at their faces. One boy was four, Illyth's age when he'd died. Another looked about eight. The girl was probably five or six. He'd have to tell their parents. He couldn't imagine handing the job to some palace official.

Two soldiers, bows in hand, remained beside him, and whatever they thought of what they saw they kept to themselves.

Some of the teyn reached open ground, began to run. Here they showed themselves for the novices they were, without skill at cover or experience in evading pursuit. The men rode them down, then dismounted to butcher them like sheep. The smell of the blood came to Oryn in his high place, from the open desert and from the rocks where the men massacred the cornered teyn in every crevice and hole.

"Weird." Bax clambered up the rocks to him, sword in hand. "Did you have a look at the blood of those kids? At the bodies? Ants had got to them already; that blood was dried almost black. They were killed hours ago, midafternoon. Yet the teyn were still here."

Oryn looked at the blood again. To him, blood was blood,

something to be avoided if possible and washed out of linen with cold water before the stain set. Geb had told him that. He supposed his father, like Bax, would have been able to classify it in terms of wetness, stickiness, slickness, dryness. That was a warrior's job, a warrior's knowledge. "They had to know we were on their trail," he said at last. "From up here they must have seen us miles away."

At the fringe of the Singing World, a dark cluster of movement marked where men and horses were reassembling, preparing for the ride back to Dry Hill. Torches were lit, pale as fireflies in the final light. The dead teyn made shapeless dark blots on the sand. Blood spattered Bax's boots and pantaloons as if he'd splashed through puddles of it.

"What were they waiting for?"

The commander shook his head. "Best we get out of here," he said. "There's light up here, but it'll be full dark by the time we get to the horses and dark isn't when you want to be down in the cracks of this land." He was clearly still thinking about the nomads. Oryn had some concerns in that direction himself.

At Bax's command, the men cut up the carcasses of the teyn and scattered the pieces. They were all village teyn: boars, jennies and pips. Oryn supposed that if they had been joined by wildings in their flight, the desert dwellers would have been the ones to escape. But somehow he didn't think that had been the case.

Could they communicate with the wildings in the hills?

Was that what they were doing—somehow—when they "clustered"? When they sat in rings around one of their hoots, patted the earth, their thighs, one another's hands, softly and rhythmically while they swayed? Soth—and other mages— had assured him repeatedly that there was no magic involved. And surely, Oryn thought, if the hoots—the cluster leaders—

had been able to generate magic, they'd have used it to escape before this.

So what *were* they doing?

Why children?

Why remain beside the bodies while the pursuit drew near?

Come morning that little corner of the Singing World would be a horror of ants and flies and vultures. Already Oryn could hear the skitter of foxes in the rocks, the yik of jackals creeping close. The rocks flung back the day's heat around him, a tall fat man in rumpled blue velvet and borrowed armor that was gouging him mercilessly in the ribs, watching the vultures gather in the dimming sky.

Far to the east, miles distant across the darkening infinities of sand, Oryn could see, as he had last night, a distant flicker of greenish flame.

If he rode out to the place, he wondered, would it be there still when he arrived?

And would that be a fortunate thing for him, or not?

He ached in every bone, and almost stumbled down the bare, yellow knob of rock to the horses, wondering what it meant—and what he or anyone would do if this happened again.

ELEVEN

I'd like to go back." Raeshaldis propped herself on one elbow and reached languidly for her glass of hot mint tea. "Something happened in that room, I know it." She moved languidly because after being massaged and oiled and scraped in the hot room of the Baths of Mastra'ar—and returning the favor upon the Summer Concubine, beside whose skill she felt hopelessly inept—and a half hour sweating in the steam room, there was no other way to move. The sugared tea, she suspected, would revive her only long enough for her to walk back to the Citadel and collapse.

She felt supremely at rest and at peace.

After Jethan's departure, the two women finished their coffee and betook themselves to the nearest bath, for the mud of the Slaughterhouse clung to their clothing and the stink of dung and rotten vegetables to their hair. It had been eighteen months since Shaldis had truly bathed, as opposed to washed in a tub of water lugged from the kitchen to her rooms. She hadn't even been aware of how badly she'd missed it. Not just the sensual warmth of the heated chambers, the aching relaxation of every muscle and tendon under a stinging scrub and massage; the Summer Concubine was a lot stronger than she looked. She had missed the camaraderie of soft chatter—the only time she'd been able to relax with Twosie and her cousins—as they worked on each other with sponges, scrapers and oil, as much as the timeless enervation of the steam. The Baths of Mastra'ar were not luxurious; it was an ordinary well-kept bathhouse of the Flowermarket District. The Summer Concubine had had to pay extra for the best-quality tea and for clean sheets on the couches. But Shaldis felt reborn.

Reborn into the world of women after eighteen months of trying to live among the Sun Mages and be what she wasn't . . . not quite.

"The first attack on me was the night of the full moon," she said, propping herself up on her elbows and looking across at the Summer Concubine, who lay on the next couch. She sipped her tea, sweet and soothing; across the room a foursome of shopkeepers' wives giggled over gossip and combed each other's hair. "The night before last. It was early in the night, probably less than two hours after sunset. Last night's was much later, close to dawn. I was still awake when the rain began. Something woke me up just after midnight, a dream. . . ."

She shook her head, trying to remember more about it. Someone calling her name? Calling for help? "I remember lying awake for hours before it . . . it came."

The Summer Concubine whispered, "Yes. It was in the deep of the night that I dreamed."

"Your friend—Corn-Tassel Woman—couldn't have disappeared much before the third hour of the night because the household would have been awake. And Turquoise Woman has been missing for five days."

They braided each other's hair and donned their clothing, which they'd paid to have brushed while they bathed, and walked back toward the House of the Marvelous Tower through the late afternoon hush. "Shaldis," said the Summer Concubine, as they jostled through the crowds in the square before the Temple of Rohar, god of women, anonymous in their veils. "Will you do something for me? With me?"

At this hour the whole district was changing its complexion and character, waking up, as it were—even as the high-class courtesans who dwelled in its tall, rambling houses were doing, putting up its hair and donning its nighttime paint.

"Of course." Though she still felt in awe of the older woman's poise and beauty, Shaldis spoke with the unthinking promptness of friendship. "What is it?"

"Will you make a Sigil of Sisterhood with me? Soth showed me how the master wizards form sigils to unite their minds with those of their apprentices in order to teach them. . . ." She paused to let a charcoal seller and his donkey pass; late sunlight through the awnings that covered the narrow street dyed her face pink and her veils the orange of raw flame. "We—Corn-Tassel Woman, and Turquoise Woman, and Pebble Girl, and I—formed with our blood, our minds, our hearts, a sigil made of the runes of twin sisters. Put a piece of ourselves into one another's souls. I hoped—we all hoped—that if something happened to one or the other of us—and I was mostly thinking of Turquoise Woman's husband, frankly—at least I would sense that something was wrong." She passed her hand wearily over the small breadth of white brow between eyebrows and veil. "Obviously that didn't happen."

"Have you tried redrawing the sigil and meditating in a power circle with it? That's how the master wizards touch the sigil to find out if something's happened to their apprentices," she added, when the Summer Concubine shook her head. "Or how they access their power over their apprentices when they want to keep them in line, though they're not supposed to do that. Sigils like that—Sigils of Mastery—give a mage access to . . . to the mind and the magic of another."

"I'll do as you suggest as soon as I'm back at the pavilion," said the Summer Concubine, and Shaldis heard again the uneasiness in her voice. "And if I . . . if I can't feel their presence, their thoughts—Corn-Tassel Woman or Turquoise Woman— would that mean that . . . that something has happened to them?"

A surge of voices from where the Street of the Goldsmiths ran into Rohar's Square made both women turn their heads. Shaldis saw Lord Mohrvine, the king's uncle, riding in the direction of the Eastern Gate, unguarded as he usually was and bending from the saddle to greet this person or that with his easy friendliness. At his side rode Aktis, whom Shaldis had watched with envious admiration back in the days when she'd still been running around the markets dressed as a boy. Though he'd been Mohrvine's court mage for many years, he'd still come to her grandfather's house, and to other houses in the district, to write mouse wards on the walls or lay healing hands on the sick. Like his master, he was now greeted from all sides—by laborers who came out of the cafés, and beggars who propped their crutches against the nearest wall to stroll over and say hello, and though in the glare of the late-afternoon sun he looked exhausted, Shaldis could see he smiled.

"It *might* mean something has happened to them," Shaldis replied after the riders had gone by; she felt the gray cloak that the Summer Concubine called about herself, subtly, to shield herself from Mohrvine's eyes. *Good thing Jethan isn't here: You couldn't miss him, crowd or no crowd.* "It could also just mean the spell wasn't working. There are a lot of spells that either I can't make work or that work sometimes and don't work others. I can feel the magic there," she added, frustration creeping into her voice. "I just can't . . . can't grasp it. Can't grip it."

"I know exactly what you mean. That happens to me all the time." The favorite sounded relieved. Was she relieved to know she wasn't the only one that happened to? Or to have some other reason, if she couldn't touch the minds of her friends, than that they were dead?

They turned along Slippermaker Alley, a shortcut away from the noise and pickpockets around the markets. Lamps were being lit behind the projecting latticed window guards. Cats prowled insouciantly above dog level on the tops of courtyard walls.

"Would you like to come and stay at the palace tonight, dearest?" the Summer Concubine asked. "Would you feel safer? You could still go up to the Citadel in the morning." She glanced up at the dove-blue sky, clear and hard as metal. Shaldis guessed that at supper that night Hathmar would announce that the Summoning would recommence at dawn.

It was tempting. The thought of the darkness of her narrow

room, not to mention the debilitating wariness of just being around the other novices, made Shaldis cringe inside. But after a moment she said, "I don't think so. For one thing, if it *is* the person who attacked me who has something to do with your friends' disappearance, I'd like him to go on thinking that *I* think this is all just hazing. For another . . ."

She hesitated, wondering if she sounded like a fool or a stubborn boy. "I worked hard to get into the college. I don't want to give anyone a reason to come to me and say, *Oh, I think you're not working out here.* Besides," she added quickly, making her voice light as she saw the look of worry on her new friend's face, "after the Song is over tomorrow I'm going to spend some time in the library going through spell books to see if I can come up with other spells of deep listening.

"The magic I felt when I was attacked—the energy it generated—felt . . . strange. Alien. Like nothing I've encountered or read about. Cold and . . . and shaking, as if I were trying to push through a room filled with chains . . . it's hard to describe. But I'd know it again if I felt it. And I want to see if it's the same that I'd feel in that room."

"Would that be an effect of *ijnis?*"

"It could be. The only time I was near someone using *ijnis* either I didn't have power or he didn't. I'm not even completely sure Redbeard was using it, but looking back I think so. He was acting pretty strangely by that time. I wish there were someone at the Citadel I could ask, but since it could be anyone there who attacked me . . ."

They had reached the Gate of Kings, which opened into the Golden Court, the semipublic square that actually comprised the outer compound of the House of the Marvelous Tower. It was the hour of sunset, and a hundred sweet-tongued bells were ringing within the Temple of Oan Echis; the daily procession of white-robed priests crossed through the crowd of vendors and strollers to make sacrifices for the realm. Flower sellers under the arcade that surrounded the court were packing up their wares; vendors of lemonade called out to the two women, urging them to buy. Those who'd remain into the evening were lighting cressets and lamps, so that the whole arcade glowed like a luminous flower bed in the clear indigo dusk. Not a puddle of the morning's rain remained. A few shredded streamers and trampled flower petals from the morning's celebration made a bright-hued mockery in the dust.

They traced the sigil on the tiled space before the terrace garden's shallow pool. The rising moonlight cast soft, strange shadows among the bare vines, and the gray cat watched gravely from the balustrade. Shaldis wasn't sure, as she and the Summer Concubine drew out the power circles and the curving lines of limitation, balance and strength, whether the magic they wrought would in fact help or protect either of them against the evil she had felt. Her own power, and that which she felt in the favorite, seemed small things before the vile hugeness of that storm of icy hatred. Even linking the strength of the vanished sun into the sigil didn't feel like adequate protection against what had been outside her window last night.

But it *had* gone away, she thought. She *had* stood against it. And as the glowing lines of her name and the favorite's hung in the air above the circles, she thought, *At least I won't be alone. Neither of us will be alone.*

And that, she thought, as she walked back by herself—again in her novice's white, cloaked against the stares of passersby in the intersecting alleyways of her private shortcut—was a joy to be treasured in itself, whatever came after.

Torchlight again in the arch of the gateway, the color of marigolds. Oryn made himself sit straight on his horse and adjusted the hang of his cloak to cover the handspan of gap where extra lacings held together his borrowed armor across an embarrassingly wide gap of blue velvet tunic. The cut of the armor in his side was agony, and he prayed he'd be able to walk when he dismounted. He had never, ever been so sore in his life, and Geb would die of humiliation when he saw the state of his master's sunburned nose and sadly uncurled hair.

"Would it create much of a scandal if I had four of your warriors carry me to the baths?" he inquired of Bax, and the old warrior shot him his sidelong grin.

"I thought your aim was to create scandal, my lord. It'd make your father turn in his tomb, that's for sure."

"Ah, then start picking which of your men we'll ask."

"You'll do, you know." Bax drew rein to let the guards at the city gate open the huge panels of bronze-faced cypress wood. Torches flared against the green tile of the passageway, the smell of the smoke thick and choking. The clatter of hooves echoed skull-piercingly, voices shouted, "The king . . . the king . . ." like the sickening clamor of a dream.

It was nearly dawn. Beyond the gate the Yellow City lay silent. The Southern Gate would be open shortly, to admit market gardeners and the sellers of milk and fish. For the moment the air was clean of dust and smelled of sewage and the dung burned by the poor who could afford neither charcoal nor wood. In a very short time the horns of the Citadel would begin again, as would the bleating and screaming of the beasts in the Slaughterhouse District. Bits of flowers and paper banners lay crumpled by the walls, the reminiscence of the day's celebrations of the rain.

Oryn experienced a deep but momentary regret for the party he had missed. The thought *I would kill for a gazelle-horn pastry* drifted through his mind, but the recollection of the blood on the stones of the Singing World washed that flippancy from his mind. He wondered what things he truly *would* kill for, and couldn't think of many.

"I watched you through the day," Bax said as they urged their horses on into the Avenue of the Sun. "You've got a brain in your head—which can't be said of your brother—and an eye for what's important. You did well."

"Er . . . thank you," said Oryn, surprised and a little touched.

"I don't envy you what you're going through."

"I assure you I don't envy myself. I don't think anyone does."

"That's where you're wrong, my lord."

Oryn glanced sideways at the saturnine face, the ice-pale eyes.

"I think there's some—with less brain that you, but more cunning—who envy you the rule of this realm. Who'd take it from you. And I'd be sorry to see it, for I think you're right. Magic is fading—the light is fading—and if we're to live in the night that's coming we'd better live differently than we do now. You're one of the few that sees that. I'd hate to see you go the way of the last four Akarian kings and any number before them, put out of the way because some blockhead liked the sight of other men bowing to him."

In the torchlight the lined, dark face was harsh with bitter memory.

"But if you're to survive you'll need to know how to use a sword and you'll need to know how to use a knife. Maybe other things as well."

Oryn winced at the very thought of physical training. "Surely at my time of life . . ." He then realized Bax was probably twenty years his senior and said, "I'm grateful for your protection. . . ."

"You're a scholar, lord." The cold blue eyes pricked him like knives. "You've studied all the old chronicles. How many of the Akarian kings, or the Durshens before them, were killed when they were where they could call their guards?"

"Oh," said Oryn. "Well . . . er . . ."

"You wouldn't be a warrior for your father," said Bax. "And I understand that, because I wouldn't be a farmer for mine. But I'm telling you this: You're a smart man, and I think you have what can save us. But get you alone and come at you with a knife and you're like a turtle on its back. Will you come to the guards' court tomorrow and let me teach you how to use a sword and a knife?"

Oryn shivered, all sleepiness, all weariness, sponged away by the memory of Lord Sarn warning him his uncle Mohrvine posed a danger—was it only yesterday morning?—saying, *You'll have to have him killed. . . .*

Cressets flared in the Gate of Kings. Guards and grooms came to take the spent horses, to help companions unpack gear. Iorradus strode across the Golden Court like the hero of a ballad, with Geb fussing along at his heels. No sign of Barún, but other household officers swarmed like the vultures above the Singing World, big with news about nomads, Sun Mages, aqueducts, bucket hoists and silk production, determined to be delivered of their business now or die.

"I will come, yes," Oryn said, turning again to Bax in that enclave of stillness that yet remained about them. "Er . . . not this morning but tomorrow. I seriously don't think I'll be able to acquit myself at all creditably. But I will come. And I thank you."

Bax touched the edge of his dented black helmet. "My plea-sure."

Oryn gritted his teeth and swung down from the saddle—it was every bit as agonizing as he'd feared it would be. A dozen voices around him said, "My lord . . . my lord . . ." And by the time he looked back to speak to Bax again, the commander of the guards was gone.

Someone was calling her name.

Pomegranate Woman's eyes snapped open in the darkness. She felt the clothing and blankets piled up on top of her shift as Pontifer Pig clambered over them; in the darkness she could see every detail of the stone-flagged stillroom behind what had once been the villa of the Tarshab-Jamornids, cousins to the present lord of that name. Saw the places where the plaster had crumbled from the brick, the long marble counter where servants of the house had brewed syllabubs and dried garden herbs. Her daughters and granddaughter in the city, when she talked to them, seemed to think that with all the empty villas of the old oasis to choose from, she'd naturally spread her blankets in the marble-floored pavilions where the lords had slept, or in the garden kiosks of the favored ladies.

But when the walls whisper tales to you of the things they've seen, and the voices of people long dead murmur about old loves and old sorrows in the shadow zone between waking and sleep, you pick carefully the places in which you lie down. The rooms where lords lay turning in fear of their own sons and grandsons, or where their women dreamed of those they'd rather have wed had they been free to choose, do not make for easy sleeping.

Better to lie here and smell the scents of the herbs dried two generations ago, and touch with her mind those sweet, simple kisses of servants and gardeners.

Someone, somewhere, was in pain, in pain and terror.

Like her dream of the Citadel Ring, but more distant now. She could smell the blood and the lightning, but could see nothing of the woman. But she could hear her scream, as if when she closed her eyes she stood at one end of a long dark passageway. . . .

And when she opened her eyes, silence, and the moonlight blanching the marble of the old counters and tracing on them the thin patterns of the desiccated vines.

I have to tell someone this, she thought. *I have to save her.*

It might even be someone she knew, someone she'd spoken to in the market or the street. But who would believe her? Everyone in the Slaughterhouse knew she'd gone mad. Everyone had heard of her, curled day after day in the back room of the little house she'd shared with Deem, unbathed, uncombed, neither eating nor drinking, only holding on to the shirt he'd had on when he'd fallen off the ladder in Lord Nahul-Sarn's garden. Who was going to accept as truth a story about a black cloud with a blue light in it that killed women?

And by the time day dawned and she was able to seek help, the woman would be dead.

Pomegranate Woman wrapped her arms around her skinny knees and sat up, her back propped against the corner in which she slept—as she'd slept in a different villa last night, not daring to return to her own house for fear she'd find the darkness waiting for her there. Pontifer crept to her lap, as if he trusted that she could defend him against the horror that moved, somewhere, in the night.

Would that I could, my child, she whispered, stroking the little white head. *Would that I could.*

It was a long time until dawn.

TWELVE

R aeshaldis." Even after eighteen months Benno Sarn pronounced the name as if thinking it should by all rights still be Habnit's Eldest Daughter.

Shaldis had seen him making his way through the lamplit gloom of the refectory toward the novices' table but assumed he had words for the clutch of boys at the other end. After months of occasionally disgusting and unbelievably petty conflict, Soral Brûl, who'd inherited Seb Dolek's mantle as the chief instigator of the mockery, had finally responded to Hathmar's command that he neither speak to nor go near Shaldis. But the stocky, dark-browed boy never let a morning go by without some stage-whispered remark to his friends. After eighteen months Raeshaldis still ate alone, and ate warily.

She looked up now from the list she'd been studying—forms of clouds, this one, and the names of the wind's twelve quarters. The rector stood with hands folded, his usual expression of angry peevishness overlying the haggard look of too little sleep. How this could be during the days of the Summoning, when everyone fasted and stood from before first light until the final glimmers had died from the sky, Shaldis couldn't imagine, but she'd heard that many of the mages in fact slept poorly in these dragging, exhausting, fruitless days.

She also couldn't imagine how anyone could feel resentment at being mage-born. How could anyone choose the position of clan lord, even clan lord of one of the greatest houses, over the powers of a mage?

Unless of course those powers disappeared. And you were too proud to admit they had.

She rolled shut her scroll of notes. "Yes sir?"

"You're to work in the scrying chamber today." The rector kept his narrow lips in a neutral expression, but spiteful satisfaction glimmered in his pale blue eyes. "It has been eight days since anyone was there; too long for it to go unwatched."

Shaldis felt herself go pale; first cold, then scalded with a flush of anger. At the other end of the table the boys exchanged glances and grins, and she fought to keep from reacting, from staring at Benno Sarn, from leaping to her feet and shouting, *What?*

"I told you," she heard Soral Brûl say to Minktat. "Took them long enough to figure out that's why the rains haven't come. With a bitch up there at the ring, sucking up everything we can do?"

And Mekwa said, "We'll get it now."

"If the scrying chamber's far enough away."

They didn't even bother to lower their voices. Benno Sarn must have heard them, but he only watched Shaldis, waiting for her to speak.

She took a deep breath and forced her voice to steady friendliness, like the Summer Concubine speaking to Barbonak the Glassblower. "Yes sir. You understand that my languages aren't very good yet, not even Shore dialect."

"I understand." The rector's voice had a patronizing note to it, as if there weren't masters in the college who had no more idea of how to speak the tongue of the folk beyond the distant mountains—let alone the strange languages of the Otherwhere wizards—than Shaldis had. "If images arise in any of the crystals or mirrors, any images at all, take careful notes of them and report them to Yanrid at the end of the day."

He sounded like he didn't think her capable of even that, and the heat that burned beneath her sternum flamed hotter. She had to lower her eyes in order to say, "Yes sir." She was almost shaking with anger.

"Good girl." Benno Sarn went back to the masters' table at the other end of the low-arched chamber, its walls half cut from the living sandstone of the bluff, melon pink in the lamplight. For a moment Shaldis sat very still, not trusting herself to move. The muted murmur of voices seemed to roar in her ears with the clink of pottery vessels, the scents of coffee and couscous, yogurt and fruit. Braziers burned among the tables, the smoke of the charcoal adding to the lamplight haze; it was the cold hour before first light and the room was freezing.

"Hey, you think it was something real simple, like she's on her period or something and that's why the magic hasn't been working?"

Shaldis stood up, all appetite for breakfast gone. "I think most wizards' magic is a little stronger than that," she said. "But you'd know best about yours." She walked out of the lighted refectory into the night's blue cold.

The scrying chamber! Indignation and betrayal almost took her breath away. *Like a shepherd, like a child!* "Good girl" indeed! *"Take careful notes. . . ."* Did he think she'd be too lazy to write down every detail if some image were to appear—after all these years!—in any of the scrying crystals, the mirrors of silver or gold or quicksilver, the bowls of fresh water, in which for years the Sun Mages had spoken with those other wizards who inhabited other parts of the world?

There had been no flicker of life in those devices, no sign, for close to eight years.

Eight years ago, when Hathmar's sight had failed and it was clear that something was terribly amiss, the king had sent messengers with the trading caravans to the scattered towns that clung to the waterless rock mountains in the west. There were mages on that barren coast who for lifetimes had been in communication with the great population centers around the Seven Lakes: a little colony of Sun Mages in a town called the Sun Above Fog, a line of Earth Wizards in the village of Black Giants, who passed from master to pupil the wisdom they'd learned through the scrying crystals from the mages of the Yellow City. It was a journey of three months going and three coming, and when the messengers returned it was with the word that the mages of the coastal villages were losing their powers too.

Whether women in that place were finding those powers, Shaldis had not heard.

She paused in the little courtyard before the scrying chamber, cloak wrapped tight around her, shivering in the cold. The library bulked above her, and the domed head of the Citadel bluff above that. Between the House of the Adepts and the rector's house—where robes, bedding, papyrus paper and parchment for copying were stored—the Lake of the Sun was visible over the domes and roof tiles of the city. She couldn't see the orchards or fields from here, but dawn stillness carried their scent to her, and the rising creak of a thousand bucket hoists, laboriously raising one measure of water at a time to the thirsty fields. Her breath hung in puffs of diamond. She listened, straining her senses, to pick up some whisper of her former attacker. But there was nothing. Only the chitter of rock sparrows waking and calling their territories before first light, the dim hum of bees.

Market carts, coming into the city below. The smell of fires kindled, where women woke early to make breakfast for men.

The voices of the Sun Mages as they emerged from the refectory climbed the twisting stairs from the refectory to the lookouts, from the lookouts to the Ring. Rachnis, and Brakt the loremaster, and Yanrid the crystalmaster had spent the freezing hours since midnight laying out anew the power circles, the limitations, the lines and the sigils to draw up the power of the sun.

They're only doing what they can, Shaldis thought, her anger rebuked by that patient willingness. *They're trying everything they know.*

In the small, round scrying chamber, crystals and mirrors seemed to wink at her in the darkness. She thought of them, those unimaginable mages she'd never seen but had heard described, or read of in accounts that went back centuries. Black-skinned naked wizards with jewels braided in their thick black hair. Brown-skinned men with huge disks of gold in their ears and plugs of jade in their lips. Men whose round faces were entirely covered with red or brown or pale yellow hair, like teyn, so that only their bright, black eyes gleamed through. Men who wore thick furs even within the small rooms of cut stone where they seemed to dwell. Laboriously, the Sun Mages of centuries past had learned the languages of these men, and had spoken to them: of the sky, of the earth, of magic, of the djinni—whom they also knew by other names and who apparently existed in the mountains of the brown men, and in the icy wastes. Of where their cities were and of their empires and their kings.

No expedition, no matter how well supplied, had ever found these lands or these mages. Most had not come back at all.

There were men in the Citadel who still mourned the friends to whom they'd spoken for so many years. Teg the windmaster, who up until the Song had begun had spent most of his days here, searching for the dark-skinned Reb-Nak in the mirror that had been silent for years. Rual, who would still sometimes speak of his red-furred friend Nyan-Nyan: "His wife was about to give birth—I gave him advice, but whether she lived . . . the child would be able to run, now. I never said good-bye. . . ."

Two of the scryers had since died, though the languages they'd so carefully learned continued to be taught in the college, in the hopes that somehow, some way, the communications could be revived.

From the scrying-chamber door, Shaldis turned and ran up the pink sandstone steps to the library. The door was barred and written over with spells to keep novices out, but it was long since those spells had had power in them. Shaldis had learned how to work even a spelled bar from the other side through the wood of the door. This wasn't the first time she'd come into the library when Brakt and his assistant were gone.

They'd both spend the day in the Ring, at the vortex of the summoned power.

Meaning, Shaldis knew, they'd never miss a book if it were returned by evening.

She knew exactly what she wanted and went straight to it, choosing among the great shelves of codices that lined the walls of the high stone room. Windows circled the lower edges of the long chamber's three whitewashed domes, in daylight filling the room with a soft, diffuse light. Lately, as everywhere in the Citadel, lamps had been set up, so that no one wizard would have to admit it if he could no longer see in the dark. During the night hours the light shone forth like necklets of topaz around the dark outlines of the domes.

Shaldis took three of the signacons—the books of sigils— and a syllabary of the High Script glyphs whose study was part of the education of all upper-class boys. After days of training in meditation, of practice in the weaving of spells and illusion, of lectures and lessons in the properties and preparation of herbs and the anatomy and taxonomy of disease, Shaldis spent several hours each evening in remedial study and memorization, trying to make sense of the runes that formed the sigils.

Most men only learned a few thousand glyphs of the High Script, enough to carry on commerce day to day, study their horoscopes and read the simpler classics. Scribble, though far less beautiful and connotative of philosophical truth, consisted of only twenty letters and anyone could grasp it in a few months.

As she slipped through the library doors again, Shaldis tried to picture a recipe for baba cake in High Script, and the effort to keep from giggling aloud restored her good humor completely. She thought, *I'll have to tell the Summer Concubine that,* and the memory of the friendship was like touching an amulet, dispelling all Soral Brûl's dirty remarks.

She pressed her hands to the door of the scrying chamber, listening within—anyone in the refectory could have heard Benno announcing to all and sundry where she would be found today. As far as she could tell, the room was empty.

She pushed open the door. Fortunately, the scrying chamber was a solitary building, barely a dozen feet in diameter and topped by a dome as perfect as a blue-and-gold soap bubble; there was no place in the tiled room where anyone could hide. The crystals on their stands of carved mesquite wood, the mirrors in their frames of iron or silver, all stood on a single table in the center of the room. The bowls—two alabaster, two onyx, two jade—had been emptied and dried. She took two or three deep breaths to calm her mind and soul. Then she filled the water ewer at the fountain near the library steps and came back to pour three bowls full with water. While she was grinding ink for the other three she felt, through her skin, through her heart, through some part of her that had no physical existence, the rising glitter of magic in the air. Felt it before the first whiff of frankincense spiraled down like a luminous ribbon from the Ring. Felt it before she heard Hathmar's pure, powerful tenor speak the Praise of the Sun with which all rites of Sun Magic opened:

Heart of all warmth, Source of all light, Life of all life . . .
Needing no praise and asking no reciprocation in thought, word, or deed.
The shining hand held out to us all.

Tears of anger and betrayal burned her eyes. The magic flowed up through her, rising from the ground and saturating the air, strong as the light itself that was just beginning to dilute the cobalt of the sky.

The voices of the mages lifted into that first-touched magic sky, calling on the name of the Bird Sun, the Coming Sun, the sun that was promise and relief and hope. She felt the power triangulate, place the hour of the day with the day and month in the earth's turning, as she knew the lines written on the Ring's pavement changed a little with each day to align precisely with the changed position of the sun in the sky.

The horns spoke, eerie and not like music at all.

They're trying everything they know.

She wiped her tears aside and went back to grinding her ink. *And I'm trying what I know,* she thought. *And what I know is to find some spell in the lore of this order that will let me read the name of the mage who attacked me: the mage who may well be behind the disappearances of the Summer Concubine's friends. The mage whose hate for women-who-do-magic is like lightning and storm.*

His magic has to have lingered in the places he's touched. And from his magic, I can follow him.

"Why children?" The wizard Soth handed Oryn his small crystal-glass cup of mint tea in its silver holder; the king groaned piteously as he settled again on the blue silk cushions of the Summer Pavilion's divan. "Aside from the obvious an-swer that they're human beings who are too small to fight ef-fectively, and can be easily carried?"

The rear downstairs chamber opened into a private garden, redolent, in summer, of wax-white gardenias. A small bath was half hidden among the pepper trees and jasmine vines; Oryn had spent a good part of the morning there slowly regaining his ability to walk. It was nearly noon now. Wrapped in a robe of bloodred velvet, he had decided against a nap and had sent for heavenly morsels, tea and Soth. Blinking with the dazed weariness of what had to be a merciless hangover, Soth sipped strongly brandied coffee.

"But why carry them away at all?" Oryn asked. The calm faces of the dead children were still visible to him, as if yester-day's evening sun had etched them onto the backs of his eye-lids. Exhausted as he had been for the remaining hour or so of last night, it had been hard to sleep. "Even the wildings never carry captives away when they raid a village. Not to kill or for any other purpose."

"No one's ever heard of a woman working magic, either," pointed out the librarian simply. "No one's ever heard of one wizard, let alone dozens, suddenly being unable to perform even the most elementary of spells that they've been perform-ing all their lives. No one's ever heard of a god choosing a man to speak to humankind directly for him, to say nothing of tak-ing the opportunity to announce that contrary to every scrip-ture, he, not Ean, was the creator and is the lord of the universe, and we'd all jolly well better toe the line, do as his sacred Mouth instructs, and donate lots of money, land and sacrificial beasts to his temple."

Soth pushed up his spectacles to rub the bridge of his nose, wincing. The Summer Concubine, veiled with the thin silks that wealthy women wore indoors in the *seryak* portions of their husbands' houses, added more coffee to the wizard's shallow alabaster cup and returned to sitting at Oryn's feet.

"Could it have something to do with the stories about the djinni taking children?" she asked.

"Even the djinni don't butcher them," protested Soth, and the Summer Concubine replied, "How do we know?"

"We've made slaves of the teyn for a thousand years," said Oryn thoughtfully, and selected a date ball from the plate before him. "We've captured them in battle, bred them, chosen which boar will cover which jenny . . . chosen the docile boars and cut the throats of the intractable ones as casually as we castrate steers. We've taught them to speak to us—a few simple words about the work we give them—so we know they *can* speak. For all that thousand years there have been mages who've attempted to learn if they *do* speak with one another; who have tried to figure out exactly what they're doing when they cluster, and whether they dream. . . ."

He shook his head, even that small movement making him flinch. The Summer Concubine was an accomplished bath mistress and had done much to loosen up muscles cramped and stiffened and agonizingly painful after nearly twenty-four hours in the saddle, but he was still earnestly regretting his decision to actually investigate something of what was going on instead of lounging back on his cushions and writing another poem. His nose, insufficiently anointed during yesterday's ride, had turned an embarrassingly unfashionable shade of red.

As he'd feared, Geb wasn't speaking to him as a result.

"Remember how Hathmar went to live up in that teyn village on the Lake of Reeds? How he'd go out into the fields with them and pick Lord Sarn's cotton, gods help him? Three years, and all he got were calluses on his fingers and a sunburn he was another three years getting rid of, and he came away not one whit wiser about the teyn."

In the garden, Pome the gardener moved carefully from rose tree to rose tree, dippering each its ration of water. The teyn he'd trained for years followed after him with the buckets. Salt and Sugar, he'd named them—the gods knew if they had names among themselves. Like the irruption of bright birds into sunlight, Pome's two grandchildren bounded out from among the pools of papyrus, the shaded beds of lilies; Oryn started to spring up, with reflexive dread, and sank with a yelp back onto the divan as the stiffened muscles of groin and thighs and back jabbed him with pain as if a dragon had seized him in its mouth.

The two teyn patted the children, smiling—or were they only baring their tusks?—and touching their fair hair.

"What do they think?" he asked softly.

"What does Black Princess think?" Soth nodded toward the graceful little cat, curled asleep in a spot of sunlight on the blue-and-crimson carpets of the pavilion floor. "I've shared a house, and a bed, and an infinite number of cups of tea with her, drat her impudence, and I've no more idea what goes on in her mind than I have of where the rain clouds have got to. Maybe the teyn have gotten a new religion, a new god of their own. Just because they've never worshiped any god before—unless the clusterings are a form of worship—doesn't mean Nebekht hasn't revealed himself to a teyn Mouth as well as a human one."

"Oh, *please!*" The Summer Concubine shuddered. "Whatever you do, *please* don't mention *that* where one of the True Believers is likely to hear it."

"Lord King!" Young Iorradus appeared among the roses. Oryn wondered idly whether Barún had made the young man an offer and whether he ought to speak to his handsome brother about the inadvisability of taking up with a nephew of

Lord Akarian—he had no idea what the young guard's tastes were—or if Barún had enough sense to see that for himself.

Better not count on it.

In any case, Barún would be at the stronghold of the Brodag-Jothek subclan by this time, in the foothills of the Mountains of the Moon, gathering levies to meet Rai an-Ariban and his tribe.

Something in the handsome young face, as Iorradus strode up the garden path, made Oryn reflect, *I should have taken that nap.*

"Lord King, there's bad news from the aqueduct."

Sigil of Deep Awareness. Meditate ten breaths. Sigil of Whispers, linked at the Bird Sun and the Sun at His Prayers. Runes of Shin, Olor, Hobe. Pursue the sounds downward into the fiber of wood and follow the line of the grain inward. Repeat in infinite breath.

Sigil of Whispers? Shaldis frowned. Was that another name for the glyph whose stem was *The Sound of Wind Crossing Deep Sand?*

She flipped open the signacon and scanned the charts of radicals.

The Hero Sun of midmorning was moving into the King Sun of noon. The smell of incense blessed the air. Shaldis's anger at the mages came and went, accompanied by shallow evanescent schemes to quit the college entirely or, alternatively, to put forth a massive counterspell to keep the rains away long enough to convince the masters that it hadn't been her presence that had kept them away before.

She shook her head, amazed at the selfishness of the fantasy. *Come on, Old One,* she told herself, *if your counterspell could work, so would your help in the Summoning and you wouldn't be having this problem.* She reread the passage on the Spell of Deep Awareness, and noted it down on her tablets with the others that had seemed promising. Then she pushed the signacon aside, touched tongue to fingertip and sketched the Sigil of Deep Awareness on the waxed oak of the tabletop, taking care to orient it along the path of the sun.

At the two sun-points on the sigil, she linked it with the Sigil of Whispers (*Deep Sand or Thin Sand?* she wondered— they were different words—*Well, I'll try it both ways*), and wove in the three runes of Shin, Olor, and Hobe: Shin the Ear, Olor the Tree, Hobe the Voice of the Living. Closing her eyes, Shaldis laid her hand over it, palm spread—there were some who read best with the backs of their knuckles or their finger-tips, but Shaldis had found that the spread palm worked best.

Beeswax and dents. Dryness and age. Student elbows and the scents of leather and papyrus . . . Teg the windmaster's voice speaking in a language she didn't understand.

Then the smell of magic smote her as if she'd thrust her nose into the kitchen spice box and inhaled. Blinding, chok-ing, impossible to distinguish one mage's thoughts or personal-ity from another's. Shaldis gasped, literally rocked back on her seat and for a moment clung to the edge of the table fighting not to throw up.

And thanking every god in the universe that there was no-body in the scrying chamber but herself.

Well, it works, anyway, she thought when she got her breath again. That was more than could be said of three-quarters of the sigils and spells she'd copied and tried that day.

She unmade the sigil, and made it again a foot or so to her left. Touched it lightly, light as a feather. It was still like stick-ing her head into a bushel of spices and trying to distinguish pepper from mace.

It's like trying to learn to dance from a book, she thought. Maybe you can walk through the pattern, book in hand, hum-ming to yourself and looking like a fool. Maybe—if you were already a dancer—you could remember to keep your elbows curved and your shoulders down, and to rise and drop and bend your knees at just the proper places. But what you really need is someone to take you through it, at least once.

And there was no one in the Citadel she trusted to do that.

A sharp tap of cold, as if someone had touched her shoulder, made her sweep the signacons and her tablets into her satchel and slide it under her cloak, which was folded beside her on the floor. She cast her hearing into the little plaza before the scry-ing chamber and picked out footsteps—Benno Sarn's, she thought, though all mages were taught to walk so lightly that it took an extremely high master to distinguish between their footfalls, as wizards routinely identified the footsteps of indi-vidual *kyne*. It had to be Benno Sarn, she knew, because the rector was the only mage in the Citadel not at the Song.

And how, she wondered, did that make him feel?

She herself at least had the comfort of knowing she *did* have magic. That she was being wronged not by some unaccount-able alteration in the rules of the universe, but by something simple like prejudice and desperate fear. That her exclusion, if unfair, was understandable.

Or did he tell himself that it was just part of his duty as rec-tor to patrol the Citadel during the Summoning and let it go at that? Shaldis knew from her own experience how enormous was the temptation to perform unsupervised experiments—and how devastatingly spells, or combinations of spells, whose effects seemed clever and hilarious could backfire.

Great as was the need for every mage, every voice in the Song of Rain, the masters had learned years ago that at least one of them had better be roving around to make sure no novice was laying badly made curses on seniors who'd hazed him, or setting little summoning spells to call mosquitoes or fleas or roaches to some master's room. That no servant was prying into matters too dangerous for untrained concern.

But no footfalls approached. Shaldis got to her feet—carefully, since she didn't know how much Benno Sarn could still cast his senses into the rooms and passageways about him—and glided to the scrying chamber's vestibule, cracking open its outer door enough for her to look out. Sure enough, she saw the square, powerful form of the rector in his blue robe of mastery standing just beside the fountain at the foot of the library stairs. The hot, gold noon sun—the King Sun—beat on his bare head, showing up how much gray there was in his long, straw-colored locks. He was too far off for her to see his expression, but she saw that his hands were clenched into fists at his sides, and he looked not toward the scrying chamber, but up the narrow stair to the North Lookout, and from there to the hidden rim of the Ring itself.

He stood for a long time gazing up like that, listening to the singing of the mages. Looking at the hard, dry blue of the empty sky.

Then he brought up his hands and clasped one fist in the other meaty palm, a gesture of anger—or despair.

He turned and was gone.

THIRTEEN

There was nothing wrong with the scaffolding, lord." The man who'd ridden in from the aqueduct's base camp rubbed a hand over his dusty face. The rough dressing around his forehead was powdered dun like the rest of him. "I'm fore-man of the gang working on the forward section, and I checked every inch of it this morning, same as always. Scaf-folding, hoists, the lot."

Two men dead, thought Oryn, settling back on the divan. *Thirty injured, ten of them critically.* Fifteen teyn killed outright when the framework of timber and bamboo, tall as an apart-ment block, suddenly collapsed, without warning and appar-ently without previous damage.

"And the witnesses . . . ?"

"There was twenty witnesses, my lord, and they all say the same. None of the beams broke. It was the ropes holding 'em that let go, all in a moment. Sure, the beams broke when they hit the ground, but I'll swear Ean's Oath it wasn't a beam breaking that started the fall. It was too sudden for that, and too silent."

The man glanced at Soth, possibly recognizing him as the royal court mage whose recollections of information from the mages of Otherwhere had given birth to the aqueduct in the first place. "The True Believers on the crew say as how it's that god of theirs showing how he thinks the aqueduct's a poor idea. Myself, I think it looks more like a wizard's curse."

Oryn hadn't the smallest experience with construction—he'd always preferred those tales where obliging djinni set up everything from the foundation stones to the selection of din-ner wines in a night—but the man's reasoning made sense. He signed a servant girl—Freesia, if he remembered, she called herself—to refill the messenger's wine cup. Beside the pavil-ion's garden door Iorradus gazed into the garden: The boy was the proverbial deaf-mute one always heard about decadent Durshen kings possessing. The Summer Concubine, behind her screen of lattice, would be listening. Geb, also listening, his ear glued to the keyhole of the vestibule door as usual, would be wringing his hands in mortification that Oryn had taken no more time to dress than he had, slipping out of his crimson bathrobe and into whatever was handiest, an orange-and-yellow tunic, robe, and trousers of silk velvet that didn't match his earrings and made him look like a colossal tiger lily. *Really, if I keep taking these matters of state seriously, my reputation as an arbiter of taste will never recover.*

"Have you had occasion to think there might be a curse before this?"

By the alteration in the man's face, he saw he'd touched a nerve. "It's the first time this much has happened, my lord." Possibly because Oryn hadn't said *I'll have someone look into it*—or maybe merely the way he leaned forward again to listen to the answer—the way he said "my lord" was different. The foreman's tone was no longer the awe proper to a king, but the worried respect a workman would use if speaking to a landchief who knew the meaning of what he was hearing.

"Fact of the matter is, I was having the horse saddled up to ride back here when the scaffold gave way. There's been . . . odd things." The clever, dark, worried eyes went from Oryn to Soth to the screen of carved lattice and jade, as if he knew perfectly well who was listening behind it.

"There was a dozen teyn down sick this morning in that front section gang. Maybe as many in each gang through the whole of the camp. Not just from a single thing, which you'd get if the food had gone bad or something. Some had belly cramps, others had swollen feet or light blindness or toothache . . . different things. The men, too. There was ten, twelve different accidents this morning. All of it stupid things, like harness breaking, or ropes slipping, or some fool dropping a pot and cutting his foot to the bone stepping on the pieces. That kind of thing. But everywhere. Like as if the shadow of the laughing god fell over the whole camp. Now, I've heard tell of such things. . . ."

"Yes," agreed Oryn, when the little foreman fell uneasily silent again. "Though one hesitates to point fingers, of course." The librarian met his eyes across the inlaid table, then looked away.

"Do you have family here in the city—Ykem, I think you said your name was? Or would you accept hospitality here in the palace until morning? I think we need to ride out and have a look at this, my court mage and I."

"I'd appreciate it, my lord." The foreman looked hugely relieved. "I left word that none of the broken scaffolding was to be touched."

"Did you? Good man!" Oryn got to his feet and, when the foreman did also, clapped him warmly on the back. Even the king's worst detractors allowed that he had great charm, and a genuine friendliness that made the caricatures of him dissolve from the minds of those who met him. "Can you be ready to ride at the second hour? That should get us to the camp by noon.

"What do you think?" he asked, as soon as Iorradus had conducted the man out of earshot and the Summer Concubine emerged from behind her screen. "Geb, make yourself useful and fetch more coffee," he added, raising his voice. "You go help him, if you would, Freesia my dear."

"It isn't what I think," said Soth, looking into the dregs of his coffee cup as if expecting to see the name of the culprit form up in the grounds—a method, Oryn supposed, that had been tried at times. "But whom I suspect."

"I'd say it's Mohrvine," added the Summer Concubine, settling herself at the foot of Oryn's divan again, "except that I sincerely doubt Aktis has that power anymore. He's taking a great deal of *ijnis* these days."

"I thought *ijnis* was supposed to give you power."

"Up to a point it does." Soth straightened up and sat tailor fashion on his divan. Behind the ground-crystal lenses his blue eyes had lost their bloodshot look and he ran a self-conscious hand over his unshaven cheeks. "After a point, instead of increasing it, what it mostly does is make it erratic. Spells don't work the way you think they will. A death spell might have the effect of making the subject fall madly in love with the wizard casting the spell, for instance. Luck spells may simply bring on painful rashes."

"I see we have a great deal to look forward to as magic continues to fade," remarked the Summer Concubine dryly.

Soth shook his head. "As magic continues to fade, all the *ijnis* in the world won't help," he said. "And each dose unhinges the mind a little more. As for Aktis, he may very well be able to lay quite an effective curse, on a good day—and on another he might not even be capable of getting into the camp unobserved."

"Not something I'd want to rely on, were I Mohrvine. . . ."

"If Mohrvine knows."

"Could Benno Sarn do it?"

Soth and the Summer Concubine traded glances.

"He could have ridden out there yesterday when the Sun Mages all rested," Oryn went on. "I assume a major spell like this has to be cast on-site, rather than from a distance?"

"Oh, yes," said Soth promptly. "There are few spells that can be cast out of sight of the victim. And even those are greatly increased in power by having the victim, or the victim's property, physically marked. And a hex of this scope and scale would absolutely require the mage's presence."

"Which means," said Oryn, "that we need to ascertain who *could* have gone out there."

"Benno Sarn was at the rain feast in the morning," said the Summer Concubine. "Afterward I don't know, but maybe Raeshaldis can find out."

"The young lady who spoke to you about being attacked," said Oryn thoughtfully. "And who is, incidentally, absolved from complicity."

"But it leads me to wonder"—Soth cast an apologetic glance at the Summer Concubine—"if you will forgive my saying so, my dear, whether the perpetrator of this hex was a trained mage at all."

"No," said the concubine, "no, if women want credit for having power we must accept with it the suspicion of misusing that power. And the gods know enough women are misusing power in small matters all over the city."

Her winged eyebrows drew down under the seed-pearled mists of her veils. "For that matter, Raeshaldis and I parted company shortly after full dark. It's conceivable she could have gotten a horse and made it out to the aqueduct camp to set a hex in the night, though I can't imagine why she would have."

"That's the point," said Oryn. "Because of the rain yesterday morning, almost anyone would have felt justified in trying to put a halt to the aqueduct. I know it's a terrible burden in terms of taxes. I know there isn't a lord who likes having his herds and his teyn confiscated for what appears to everyone in the Seven Lakes to be a folly. They can't see—"

He broke off, aware that one big, soft hand had bunched into an angry fist on his knee.

Anger at their obtuseness.

Anger born of fear.

He opened his hand, for a moment fixing his eyes on the crimson gems of his rings before raising them to his friends again. "Would you be able to tell who set the hex by looking at the marks in the camp?"

"Oh, easily." Soth's breath expelled in a rueful chuckle. "There are few enough of any line or school who can work magic anymore. If it's an Earth Wizard sign it will almost certainly be Aktis. I don't know any other Earth Wizard—including myself—who still has the smallest vestige of power. If it's a sun sign it will be Sarn—or possibly Lohar."

Oryn widened his eyes. "I thought Lohar decided to surrender his magic to Nebekht when he discovered he couldn't do it anymore."

"It's what Lohar says," agreed Soth, raising an eyebrow.

"Ah. Yes. I should know better than to confuse the appearance of imbecility with sincerity." Oryn shook his head. "And presumably a blood sign would indicate Ahure, in spite of Lord Jamornid's ostensible support of me in the council. Geb, my darling, thank you." He took the coffee tray from the eunuch's indignant hands. A box beside the sugar dish contained rings and earrings of topaz and citrine, a broad hint to repair the incoordination of his ensemble. He must have sent a page to fetch them while Oryn conversed with the foreman Ykem.

"Would you be a spirit of light and make arrangements for me to ride out to the aqueduct camp tomorrow at the second hour? Horses, tent—we may spend the night there, I think, Soth? Suitable wardrobe . . . what color goes with sand, Geb? I think the pale yellow silk and that gold and violet ensemble. . . . And horses to match, of course." He poured coffee for Soth, for himself and the Summer Concubine, and passed around a plate of fresh coconut candies, pink and white. "Do you still have a valet, Soth? I don't know what I'm going to do with you. . . . Geb, darling, before you leave, would you just . . . ?" He held out a hand, and with a long-suffering sigh the chamberlain grasped it, and helped him, groaning, to his feet.

"And I suppose now I'll have to send word to Barún, and make arrangements with Bax and the guards. . . ." Oryn shook his head regretfully and put an arm around the Summer Concubine's thin shoulders the moment Geb and Soth were out of the room. "Will you be seeing your girl Raeshaldis tomorrow, beloved?"

"We hadn't spoken of it," said the Summer Concubine. "I could send for her."

"Do. See what she knows about Benno Sarn's whereabouts yesterday—and about others in the college who might still have the power to accomplish a hex like that. I suppose he— or she—would use a cloak spell to get into the camp. . . . Would someone be able to set up hex marks and keep a cloak about them at the same time?"

"They'd have to, wouldn't they?" said the Summer Concubine thoughtfully. "That would rule out any woman I know, probably even Raeshaldis. I don't know of any woman with the mental training to make two spells work consistently at the same time."

"And what about the women you don't know?"

She glanced up at him, blue eyes meeting hazel.

All she said was "Hmn."

"Just a thought." Oryn tightened his arm around her, comforted by the scent of her, by that light, slim shape, like a gazelle or a miniature greyhound. The thought of spending several hours riding out to the aqueduct camp in the morning made him shudder.

"If I'm going to be gone tomorrow I suppose I need to send for Sarn today instead of tomorrow as planned—and I'll have to put forward the meeting with the lord proctor of the Grand Bazaar, drat it, which means reading his report on the water bosses. . . . And Stagweth . . ." He named the supervisor of the royal silk weavers—a not inconsiderable source of the House Jothek's revenues—who had also required an audience. "I can't imagine how the heroes in ballads get on the road five minutes after receiving the bad news. 'He called for his horse . . .' which was presumably stabled somewhere and had to be saddled, 'and leaped to the saddle,' without lunch—or smoothing down the feathers of those who thought they'd have a council that afternoon, or making sure someone was going to feed his birds in his absence—and where did the hero plan to sleep that night, if he didn't pack a tent? I can only conclude," sighed Oryn, "that this is the reason that the heroes of ballads are so seldom actual reigning kings."

Honey-colored sunlight stroked Shaldis's hair like a warming hand as she hurried down the library steps. Even had she not heard the pulse and groan of the horns, the call and echo of the responses, she would have been able to tell at what point the Song stood: For eighteen months she had lived by the slightest alterations of the sunlight, until she knew within her bones how much of the day remained.

It was the time the masters called the Time of the Sun of Judgment, the harsh, hot burning sun of midafternoon, weighing the desert down like inexorable law. The time under the rule of Ka-Ashkar, god of the afternoon sun, whose images were made of brass and kept heated smoking hot.

In other words, she thought, she still had plenty of time.

Through the hours she had been in the scrying chamber, she had seen not the slightest flicker within the mirrors or the crystals or the bowls. Between her studies of the Sigils of Listening, her practice of the High Script and her perusal of her lists (the true name of the long-eared leaping rat of the deep desert was *Gurantes;* its short-eared golden cousin was called *Bronas;* the little red burrowing rodents of the water holes at the feet of the Dead Hills were called *Corms* for the purposes of magic), she had considered those empty devices, and remembered the tales the grieving scryers had told.

What *had* happened to Ru'hak Boh of the City of the Gods (though not the same gods that were worshiped in the Realm of the Seven Lakes)? To Dik-sjan whose chamber windows looked out onto night, when Yanrid the crystalmaster would speak to him at the tenth hour of the day? To Nyan-Nyan with his dogs and his tales of his mother-in-law's iniquities?

All gone.

Dead?

Shaldis wondered if anyone would ever know.

At the ninth hour of the day she had rinsed out and dried the water and ink bowls, and returned the signacon to its place in the library. Walking about the Citadel afterward in the hot slanting light still felt dreamlike. Her footfalls, trained to be as unobtrusive as the breath of a sleeping kitten, still scraped loud on the pink and gold sandstone pavements, her shadow ran long and blue on the walls. She encountered no one.

The Song, though it still stirred resentment and hurt pride in her breast, comforted her as it echoed in these empty walkways, these silent buildings. At least, she thought, she knew where her attacker had to be, in any case until it was too dark to see. Unless of course her attacker was Benno Sarn. Less than an armspan wide, the passageway by the novices' dormitory still made her shiver, filling already with shadow. In it she felt trapped, and she looked back over her shoulder constantly.

She wondered if she'd ever be able to think of it as anything but a trap again.

Her own small door, and the air shaft by the wall onto which her window looked, seemed tiny and distant as she approached them. She hugged the wall, kept her hand wrapped around the straps of her satchel, ready to swing. Her thoughts probed at the three doorways into the novices' rooms to her right. Halfway down the passageway she stopped, retraced her steps and at its entrance sketched a ward sign like the one she'd put by the foot of the library steps, an invisible mark that would cry out to her should anyone pass. She put it low on the wall, almost at its base, knowing that the man she feared would be capable of seeing it—might very well, in spite of her limitations, feel it as he passed.

Finally she crept into the entryway and drew a Sigil of Listening on the first of the dormitory doors.

She tried several without results of any kind. Even the ones that had reacted on her so strongly in the scrying chamber were mute. This was something she'd gotten used to: that spells sometimes worked and sometimes didn't. When she was able to follow her thought down into the fibers of the wood, she sensed only a confusion of little half-formed magics, a sense of things very old and very strong. Fading odors of power. Layer upon layer upon layer of personalities, all of them male. Bright and dark and flashing, cold and hot.

Little that could be clearly identified at all.

She drew her mind back, concentrated closer to the surface.

Better. A few personalities she could recognize, like the sound of voices or the eyes of women friends glimpsed between veils. She was aware of clever Minktat, and of that dark gruff boy whatever his name was—Kylin—who refused to participate in the hazing, and of the strong, furious personality she recognized as Seb Dolek.

Seb Dolek, she thought. Of course, he'd been here for several years and she could feel no magic connected with him. Still . . .

The rest was only dim scuffings, faint and without power. Most of the novices, she realized then, had no magic at all. No more than if they'd been born *kyne*—common Empties, powerless as teyn.

And some of them were already taking *ijnis*. Its dark echo seemed to stain the whole door, as if she'd sniffed rotten meat.

Saddened and repelled, she drew her hand away. Her anger at them—even at Soral Brûl—mingled now with a pity that she wasn't sure wouldn't show in her face when she looked at them. And if it did, would they hate her more for it?

She licked her finger again and unmade the sigil. Then— because she'd only had a glimpse of the dormitory room once, on her first tour around the college—she pushed open the door and looked in. No door in the Citadel was supposed to be locked or warded; she felt obscurely afraid of what the masters would say when and if they discovered her spells of guard on her own door. The room itself was as she'd seen it that first time: bare stone walls, three beds, goat-hide chests at their feet, unlocked and, it was assumed, unspelled. It crossed her mind to search for the *ijnis* bottle, or the bundle of dried leaves, just for her own curiosity—and maybe to have something over them, in case she needed it—but she put that thought away too and closed the door.

She went to the end of the corridor and drew the sigil again on her own door, near the lock.

And perceived in the wood nothing that she hadn't perceived on the door of the other dormitory.

No spell of malice and danger. None of the terrifying sense she'd had of the nearness of storm. Nothing of the cold column of darkness, of the unexplained trailing flicker of bluish light. Of the hoarse voice whispering *Bitch* . . .

No sense that anyone had worked a spell to undo this latch at all.

Raeshaldis muttered a marketplace curse and dug in her satchel for another tablet, to try another spell.

She tried a Sigil of the Retrieval of Dreams.

She tried a Summoning of Lost Voices.

She tried a Glyph of Resonance.

She tried the doubled sigils of summons and night—*Why night?* She puzzled over the instructions . . . in the instant before hate hit her, vile and sudden as a blow in the face.

Nausea cramped her belly as she jerked her hand from the wood. Hate and anger and a disgorged vileness, like a vulture spewing its carrion, a loathing so personal, so contemptuous, that she had to step back, her breath short in her lungs.

And something else. Cold, alien magic that burned the air, like the far-off jangling of a universe of chains.

She thought, *Is it like* that?

She wanted to reach out her hand, touch the wood again, and couldn't. It felt fouled, as if with a physical stickiness that would come away on her fingers and eat at the flesh.

She hadn't understood, she thought, shaking all over with shock, that hate was like *that*. *Could* be like that.

And there was power in it. Power unlike any she'd felt in the library, any she'd felt in the door of the boys' room. As if she'd been comparing the flavors of bread and fruits and cheese and then someone had struck her over the head with an ax.

She stood for a long time, sick and shocked, a sinking chill gripping her in the blue cold of the passageway. Behind her the horns sounded, the chants lifted to the unsympathetic sky.

That *is up there in the Ring, calling the rain.*

And they send me *away because I'm a* woman?

Everything in her screamed against doing so, but she took a deep breath, stretched forth her hand and touched the wood again.

And there was nothing there at all.

Nothing she could feel. Nothing she could see or smell or taste.

It was still there, though. She knew it. Feared it.

She went around to the air shaft and tried every spell in her notes—starting with the double sigils of summons and night—on the shutters of the windows where his malice had nearly broken the hinges two nights before. Nothing, not even the shambly murmur of everyday touch. *Damn it, where are you?* She shivered at the memory of the latch rattling sharply in the dark.

She was obviously doing something wrong, but she didn't know what.

Or was it just that she wasn't all that anxious to feel that hideous hate, that spitting contempt, again?

She heard someone coming in the same instant that the rune at the end of the passageway called out her name. The next instant Benno Sarn's voice snapped, "Raeshaldis," and she thought, *He wouldn't have called my name if he meant to assault me.*

She sprang down out of the air shaft and gathered up her tablets, thrusting them into the satchel.

"I trust you have nothing to report concerning the scrying chamber?"

"No sir." She wondered if he'd gone there first, looking for her—or checking up on her. "I thought, before getting some supper, sir, that I'd do a little practice." She gestured back at the window. "Try to figure out why the unlatching spells Rachnis taught me only work some of the time, even though I do them the same way."

The slight perpetual downward curve of the rector's too-small mouth didn't alter, but the line of it seemed to darken as his lips pinched. Looking into his blue eyes, Shaldis saw irritation that a woman would not drop her gaze before his.

Only this wasn't something masters could say to novices.

Instead he said, "You only think you do them the same way. A curve that isn't perfectly round"—his stubby finger traced the glyph of focus in the air—"feeding lines that aren't properly connected, a rune misaligned . . ."

He shook his graying head. He should not, properly speaking, have been appointed rector of the college—the masters were usually very careful to keep the near kin of the clan lords away from anything that smacked of rulership—but Shaldis suspected that the appointment had been maneuvered in those first few years of consternation about the lengthening labor of calling the rains that refused to come.

"You need to be more diligent at your practice, girl," Benno Sarn went on. "Everyone wants to work spells, and a girl more than others, I suppose." Shaldis had to press her lips hard together and look away from his face to keep from retorting. *Does he think I practice glamours to make the adepts fall in love with me?* "But ordinary, common runes, simple exercises, like calligraphy, to make sure that each spell is perfect each time. To concentrate the mind and discipline the thoughts. That's what the problem is," he went on, "and not all this absurdity about magic failing or dying or whatever people say it's doing. What's failing or dying is the discipline that novices are willing to put into their craft."

"Yes sir." Shaldis's eyes returned to his.

"Before you try to mess about with spells you'd best learn the sigils more thoroughly." His voice grew harsh. "And before you can make a proper sigil you need the basic runes."

"Yes sir."

"And if that isn't the answer," added Benno Sarn, "it might pay us to look into whether you belong with the Sun Mages at all. I understand the king's desire"—his small blue eyes flicked her up and down—"to have you taught, I suppose. But you were never properly tested. Hathmar was overeager, there, to impress the king. That's understandable. But you may not be capable of sourcing your power from the sun at all. It may be you should study with an Earth Wizard, or a Pyromancer for that matter." He sniffed, as if to make it clear that only the custom that forbade mages of one order from speaking ill of those of another kept him from voicing his contempt for such persons. "But that's typical. For the time being I'll just say you need more practice."

And he stepped aside, a silent injunction for her to pass and return to more public venues of the college.

Shaldis collected her satchel and preceded him along the passageway. Despite the fact that if he meant her ill he would have already done it, the nape of her neck prickled at the presence of that cobalt-robed form so close at her back in the empty quiet of the spell-wrapped Citadel.

She remembered the hate imbued in the wood of the door. *Is* that *what they feel about me? Is that what* he *feels?*

Someone does.

Had that someone also been responsible for the disappearance of Turquoise Woman? Of Corn-Tassel Woman, missing now two days?

And if that were so, whom would he seek out next?

FOURTEEN

F ew prettier sights existed, reflected Mohrvine, than a supper room perfectly dressed for a party. It was an art practiced by fewer and fewer women in these days, this art of being a hostess. To know that a thing was simple, and perfect in its simplicity, and then to let it go; to let events flow where they would—that was the art of it, and the separation point between the truly noble houses like the Jothek and the parvenus whom he despised.

He had selected the House of the Six Willows because Chrysanthemum Lady, whoever had been her parents, had been trained in the understanding of the right way of doing things, and she passed this understanding to the women she instructed. It might cost the price of a good first-quality robe to host a supper here with one of the courtesans of the house, but, he thought, it would be worth it.

The men met in the gate lodge of the house, a pink-stuccoed building tucked away on a quiet street of the Flower-market District. No footman, no banners, no bell, just an anonymous door in a rose-colored wall. Even the ward spells against vermin and insects, which formed a frieze of stylized glyphs and sigils around every window and door in the city, were pleasingly proportioned, drawn by a master. The old marks had been scrubbed away or pink-washed over before the latest set was put on. As Mohrvine stepped down from his litter and straightened his cloak, the door opened for him—naturally, the gesture implied, you are a known and awaited friend—and Chrysanthemum Lady herself was there to greet him in the lodge. One of the elderly females who served in the house brought sweet mint tea and another offered towels wrung in warmed rosewater to clean his face and hands while he chatted with the gray-coiffed mother.

Having come here many times before as both host and guest of parties, Mohrvine knew that a second lodge existed on the next street; a second supper room stood in its own garden in the labyrinthine little complex, equally spacious, equally pretty. A student of human interactions, Mohrvine had observed Chrysanthemum Lady for years, trying to determine how the mother arranged it that one party of guests would arrive later than the other so that she could personally greet each man. Certainly she had never suggested to him or anyone ahead of time at what hour they should assemble.

Yet she always was there when the first guest arrived, and she never left the lodge until the last appeared. At that time she would personally conduct the party through the lamplit gardens to the supper pavilion. And she never glanced at a water clock—Mohrvine had never seen such a thing in any Blossom House he'd ever visited—or seemed to be aware that another party would be going on more or less at the same time.

Some in the Yellow City accused Chrysanthemum Lady of being twins. Others, like his overmuscled elder brother King Taras Greatsword, didn't even notice such niceties, accepting them as their god-ordained due. But graciousness like this impressed men, and it was the mark of the great houses, and so it interested Mohrvine. It had been a long time since a king had dared take a formal consort—ten generations of Akarian kings had been the sons of concubines and thus the grandsons of camel drivers and weavers and anyone else short a few pieces of silver in a bad year—but among the clan lords, marriage alliances were still the rule. His own mother had been the daughter of a nomad hunter, something for which he'd never forgiven his father, King Oryn I. His sons, he'd made certain, had wed into the families of the Jothek-allied houses and would pass this care for the right way of doing things along to their sons. His daughter . . .

"I trust the cook obtained the meat for the supper from the Temple of Nebekht?" twittered Lord Akarian as he came through the door. "I wouldn't wish to feel that any beast perished unwillingly to provide us with a feast."

"My dear lord, how could I look you in the face were it otherwise?" cried Chrysanthemum Lady with every evidence of genuine distress. "I sent my servants this morning to the temple to obtain food that is lawful for you."

Which was not, reflected Mohrvine, with a shudder at the thought of the hacked fragments of limbs and bones that were daily handed out to the True Believers, *by any means the same as saying yes*. From the water boss Xolnax he knew all about the complicated process of local blackmail among the shambles keepers that provided the huge numbers of sacrificial animals killed each morning in the Temple of Nebekht and permitted Lohar to feed them to any worshiper who came to the gates. The meat, Xolnax reported, was generally tough or old; there were gods who, according to their priests, demanded only tender, succulent and unblemished animals for sacrifice, but Nebekht wasn't one of them. Volume counted more than quality by all accounts, and the sacrificial killing—all done by Lohar himself—seemed to be the work of a lunatic with an ax. But Lohar reported that the animals themselves went willingly, even happily, to sacrifice, and being individually and personally blessed by himself were therefore lawful eating among his followers.

At the moment, the other butchers in the district weren't sure how to deal with this novel mode of competition. Mohrvine had a private bet with his daughter—an intelligent girl, if far too saucy for her own good or anyone else's—as to how long it would be before pieces of prime real estate belonging to the more influential of the True Believers started making it known to Lohar, through the medium of Nebekht, that they would be happier belonging to the temple too.

He glanced across now at Proath and Whorb Akarian as they entered, stern young men with their father's prominent chin and slightly mismatched, narrow-set eyes, and wondered what they felt about this latest in the long line of their father's answers to the great question of life. Both, he saw, had clipped their hair short and shaved the twin bands of novitiate across the crowns of their heads. "One could feel the presence of Nebekht in the room during the prayers," Proath was saying in a reverent voice to the somewhat glassy-eyed Chrysanthemum Lady. "It baffles me—truly baffles me!—how so many can still put their trust in wizardry when Nebekht has quite clearly revealed that such foolishness must and will be destroyed."

"The very fact that the temple wells have not run dry should prove beyond a shadow of doubt that he speaks the truth," added his brother. "But do people believe?"

"Is it true, then?" Mohrvine tilted his head inquiringly. He'd heard rumor to that effect from Xolnax and the two or three other minor water bosses in his pay: Every other well in the Slaughterhouse was bringing up mud. Xolnax had been buying water from him, surreptitiously, for weeks.

"It is, my lord." Proath dipped a clumsy salute. "Nebekht's followers do not lack for what they need, neither meat nor drink. Nor do rats and mice spoil the granaries there."

The door opened again, admitting Verth Marsent-Jothek and Chalath Wildstorm, sheikh of the Riders of the Stone Forest, a thin, hard-faced man whose simple white robe and burnoose showed up startlingly against the brilliant golds and purples of Lord Akarian's clothing, the bullion embroidery that crusted the sleeves of the younger of the Akarian sons.

"Lohar was a Sun Mage, wasn't he?" asked Mohrvine, and Whorb Akarian looked profoundly shocked.

"Lohar, the Mouth of Nebekht, voluntarily surrendered his powers," he said, "when the commander of the universe appeared to him in a vision and told him that this was what he must do." His tone implied that Mohrvine should have known all this—Mohrvine certainly had heard the tale. "And it takes more power than any wizard ever possessed to bring water to the dry wells. That he would flout Nebekht's expressed will to . . . to hocus granary walls is unthinkable!"

"My dear sir, of course it is unthinkable, nor do I think it." Mohrvine threw into his voice precisely the note and inflection Chrysanthemum Lady had used when assuaging the elder Akarian's anxieties about supper.

"Sorry I'm late—damn silly of me." Iorradus Akarian breezed in, handsome in the crimson tunic and cloak of the Guards of the Marvelous Tower, his wheat-colored curls like gold on broad shoulders. "Velvet Mare foaled and I simply couldn't leave until I made sure she was safe. A breech presentation, you know, and her dam always had trouble. . . . Finally killed her, poor thing, Sunrise Mare, I mean, not Velvet Mare. Velvet Mare is fine." He salaamed deeply to Lord Akarian. "I abase myself, Uncle. And as for the lovely Chrysanthemum Lady, if she made me sit in the corner and eat millet and water I shouldn't blame her."

"Nonsense!" exclaimed Marsent-Jothek, clapping the young man heartily on the arm as the smiling Chrysanthemum Lady opened the garden door for them all. "I remember the time Sunrise Mare birthed War Captain. That was a breech presentation too."

Mohrvine sighed inwardly and rolled his eyes. The stable-yard conversation bubbled behind him as if the men were loitering in their home courts rather than walking through one of the most exquisite gardens in the realm. Candles touched here and there the feathery leaves of the pepper and jacaranda trees, picked out shaggy-textured bark like an artist's brush in gold. An unseen fountain murmured; the green, cool smell of moss and water was succeeded by the sweeter song of jasmine, the musky breath of exotic lilies. He'd invited the personable young nephew of the Akarian clan precisely to be company for the horse-minded Marsent-Jothek—whose support Mohrvine had been seducing away from his nephew for months—so it was possibly all to the best, but he still wished for more entertaining company. It was going to be a long evening.

Lamplight through leaves, amber in cobalt. Fiddles and flutes gentle after the daylong wailing of the far-off Citadel horns. The men mounted the three rustic steps, Chrysanthemum Lady bowing them to the low tables. The divans were cushioned in plain gray-and-black striped silk, the tables

wrought of cedar, simply formed and without ornament beyond the grain of the oiled antique wood and their own graceful shape. On the other side of the lattice-and-paper partition,
the damsels played songs from the latest plays. The woman
Honeysuckle Lady, waiting by the door, performed perfectly the
most complicated of the twenty salaams appropriate to women,
then rose and greeted each man so adeptly, asked so knowl-
edgeably about his interests, that it was barely noticeable when
Chrysanthemum Lady excused herself and disappeared.

Three serving girls brought in the heavenly morsels, kneeling to offer the lacquered willow-work trays to Honeysuckle
Lady, who placed the plates before Akarian, his sons, his
nephew, the other guests, their host in exact and effortless
order of precedence. They might be the daughters of whores,
or farmers, or nomads, reflected Mohrvine, watching those
earnest, sweet faces, the precise grace of their movements.
And they might be destined for marriage, or a position as a
courtesan in some house like this one. . . .

But wherever they went, they would always be ladies of the
Blossom Houses.

His eye slipped slantwise to Lord Akarian, who was staring
at the trio of fledglings with a greedy intensity and absent-
mindedly fingering the front of his pantaloons. Honeysuckle
Lady came and engaged him in chat—as much as one could
refer to a sermon about the true nature of Iron-Girdled
Nebekht as "chat"—but the old man's attention clearly kept
straying to the young girls. When the dancers came out, he
watched the serving girls still: sweet, serious, virgin children in
robes of cherry red, and butterfly blue, and one girl in simple
white and black.

The dark-haired girl came to Iorradus with a cup of sweet
mint tea, offered it to him timidly, her face schooled but ado-
ration in her jade-green eyes. Mohrvine sighed, well aware of

the effect of the young man's good looks on any and every girl whose path he crossed—and evidently on Honeysuckle Lady too, for as the handsome guardsman smiled at the girl in black, the courtesan turned, with every appearance of naturalness, from her applause of Chalath Wildstorm's story about the mouse and the hippopotamus and intercepted the cup from the child's hands. She took it as if to hand it to Iorradus herself, then glanced down into the cup, pursed her lips just slightly and made some kind of laughing remark—and a little moue of disgust—to Iorradus, as if she'd found a hair floating in the tea, or a drowned mosquito. She put the fragile vessel down on the table and leaned to pour him out another cup. The dark-haired girl made no change in expression, but if looks could kill, thought Mohrvine, deeply entertained, Honeysuckle Lady would have left the chamber on a plank.

"How can you tell if a stallion is going to be a prizewinner, so soon after he's foaled?" Honeysuckle Lady inquired of Iorradus with every appearance of deep fascination, and the question served to pull his eyes from the girl in black, and to plunge him into a detailed explanation of his private system for gauging a colt's speed, conformation and heart, apparently while still in the womb.

For a moment the serving girl stood back, her face still sweetly smiling. That, Mohrvine had heard, was another skill they taught in the Blossom Houses. How to smile through nearly anything, no matter what they felt inside. A skill worth learning indeed, more than all the years of poetry, cosmetics and twenty different salaams.

Honeysuckle Lady had it, he thought, watching her. Gorgeous in her stiffly pleated golden overdress and her emeralds, gems twinkling in her lacquered hair. Beside her, the girl in black was only a girl, lovely as a lily in the way only a fourteen-year-old girl can be who has known nothing evil in her life.

Only a girl, and spitting mad, oblivious to Lord Akarian's devouring gaze.

"My lord." Mohrvine leaned closer to the elderly clan lord and spoke beneath the music, beneath the soft patter of talk and the shadowy perfection of the dancers who drew the other men's eyes. "We conversed the other day concerning the True God, the great Nebekht of the Iron Girdle—and I've been giving some thought to what you said. Uncomfortable thought, I'll admit—thoughts about the nature of truth, the nature of the universe, that I've never allowed myself to see in my heart before." He made his face earnest, molded his features into the expression of a man who has had a profound spiritual experience—much as Honeysuckle Lady, he reflected, was molding hers into the expression of a woman who would love nothing better than to hear graphic details of every foaling experienced by Velvet Mare, and her dam, Sunrise Mare, through the previous two decades.

"Open your heart, then!" urged Lord Akarian, seizing Mohrvine's hands. "Your heart is the wisest guide you can have, my lord. Are you willing, now, to see that Nebekht is not simply the war god everyone thought him, but in truth the commander, the ruler, the giver of law for all the universe?"

Mohrvine said gravely, "I am."

Not only were few actual reigning kings the heroes of ballads, reflected the Summer Concubine the following morning, but the companions of those who *were* heroes generally seemed to be people without griefs, terrors and ills of their own. This did not, alas, seem to be the case with Oryn.

She stood in the doorway of the Wisteria Pavilion behind the library, between the sharp morning sunlight of the Green

Court behind her and the gloom of the curtained study, the fug of stale brandy an unmistakable reek in her nostrils. The door had been open when she'd passed the place on her way back from bidding Oryn farewell in the shadow of the Marvelous Tower. It had crossed her mind that Soth might be late getting his things together, for she hadn't seen him among the riders, guards and baggage wagons assembling in the Golden Court.

It had also crossed her mind that she might find here exactly what was visible through the still gloomier curtained door of the inner room, where Oryn's friend and tutor lay heavily asleep, still dressed as he had been the afternoon before. The cat Gray King sat on the table beside the bed, dipping his paw into the dregs of the librarian's wine cup and licking the potent date wine from his toes.

The Summer Concubine took the cup and poured it out onto the grass beside the outer door—*Rohar only knows what it will do to the flowers,* she thought—and, looking up, saw Oryn walking along the path from the Marvelous Tower in his robes of scarlet and flame like an immense persimmon in the sunlight.

He sighed. "Oh, dear." The fact that he'd come back alone told her that he, too, was not surprised by what he found.

"The ride out would probably sober him," she remarked as he came to stand in the doorway at her side.

"Judging the quantity he's taken by the smell, it would likelier kill him." He stepped over a stack of books and around an overset stool, and made his way to the round, tiled hearth, stone cold and heaped with warm ashes; shed his outer robe and gingerly scraped the mess aside. Somewhere he'd learned how to arrange a fire—the Summer Concubine reached out with her mind and touched the kindling with flame, and Oryn half turned on his heels, the gold light warm in his hazel eyes.

"Thank you, my Summer Child. With luck this will last

until he wakes. . . . Oh, good, he has beans roasted." Straightening, Oryn opened the inlaid lattice of a cupboard and lifted the lid of one of Soth's coffee canisters. "Is there water? Well, one out of two isn't bad. Don't blame him," he added, turning back to the doorway with the water jug in his hand.

She shook her head. "My uncle Uzuk would do this," she said. "I've told you about Uncle Uzuk, haven't I?"

"The one with all the hats?"

She smiled. Ordinarily no Blossom Lady—let alone a Pearl Woman—would speak to any man about her family once she'd left the house where she was born, though she had known Blossom Ladies to make up eccentric families for the purpose of telling amusing stories about them to patrons. But from the first Oryn had been like a brother to her as well as a lover.

"Drink was like a shadow that followed poor Uzuk. It would seize him without warning, no matter what my father or my mother would do. I can understand that Soth would not wish to ride out to the camp and hear them whisper, if only in his mind, *There goes the man who was once a mage and who is nothing now.*"

She took the water jar from Oryn's hands and carried it to the end of the courtyard path, to the thick-twined arbor gate that set off the library grounds from the rest of the Green Court. She left it there for the palace water bearers to fill when they came by. When she returned to the pavilion Oryn was in the inner room, gently pulling off Soth's slippers and covering him with a blanket.

"Do you think you could find a hex mark?"

The Summer Concubine hesitated. Last night the page she'd sent out to the Weavers Yard had returned with the information that according to the neighbors, Fergit the Weaver's missing wife had not, in fact, returned. She'd scried repeatedly for Corn-Tassel Woman, reaching her mind into the Sigil of

Sisterhood from within the strongest power-circle she could make. She had felt nothing, had gotten no reply.

And had waked gasping from nightmares that folded themselves away to nothingness, leaving her weeping in Oryn's arms.

She was aware of Oryn watching her now, worry in his eyes.

"I will try, of course," she said slowly. "But by your leave, I'd like to return here tomorrow. Corn-Tassel Woman . . ."

"You've heard nothing of her still?" Generally the Summer Concubine had met her friends alone, but on one occasion Oryn had happened to arrive while Corn-Tassel Woman was there and had thoroughly charmed the usually unflappable glassblower's wife. He had offered what help he could in finding her, but at the moment there was very little he could do.

The Summer Concubine shook her head. "I don't know what help I can be to her, or to Turquoise Woman—or to whoever else this peril will touch—by remaining here until I hear from Raeshaldis. But like you riding after the teyn—or indeed to the aqueduct today—I would feel better were I here."

"Of course." Oryn put his hands on her shoulders, looked gravely down into her eyes. The Green Court being *seryak*, the public area of a house, she had worn veils to walk with him to the tower. He bent now and kissed the two fingers of brow above her eyes that was the only part of her face exposed. "And I thank you for riding out with me today. I shall tell Bax to have one of his men bring Soth out to the camp this afternoon as soon as he's able to crawl into a litter. I would have the guards bring you back tonight, if it weren't so far."

She shook her head again. "No, tomorrow morning is as well. I'll have Pepper and Lupine get my things together. We won't be but a few minutes."

"Nonsense, my darling, Geb assures me that even for

overnight it requires a minimum of a week to prepare properly."

She smiled beneath the concealment of her veils and, reaching up, touched Oryn gently on his sunburned nose. "I'm sure for Geb it does."

Watching the slim, straight little form walk away through the Green Court's sunlight, Oryn thought, *She should be the hero of the ballad, not I.*

Then, *Quite possibly she is.*

"Gone?" Raeshaldis looked at the maid Lotus in alarm.

"It isn't anything amiss, I don't think." The stout girl's eye flickered to the Golden Gate's head porter. The Golden Court was basically a public square; to enter the Green Court beyond, one had to be escorted by someone from the palace, or be known to the porter. Shaldis wondered how Enak and Barbonak had managed. And, almost certainly because she recognized Shaldis from her meeting with the Summer Concubine in the Jasmine Court, she added, "They rode out with tents and baggage and guards and all, about two hours ago."

"Oh." Shaldis relaxed. After what she had felt through the wood of the doorways yesterday evening, she had feared desperately that she would come here and find the Summer Concubine dead—or missing.

Through the wide windows of the porter's lodge Shaldis could see into the room where the palace pages waited, young boys all clothed in red and gold. She thought, *How could anyone get in to take her?*

And then, *He's a mage. He could get in.*

She shivered, just the memory bringing panic to her breast. She had dreamed last night of her father.

Dreamed of coming home from the marketplace, climbing the ladder up the rear of the house to her attic sanctum, stripping off her brother's clothes as she went. The hot smells of dust and mice. The sweat on her face and the noise of two of the maids chattering as they sewed in their little dormitory. The sight of the floorboards in her attic torn up, the concealing mattress tossed to the floor. The panic, fury and despair in her throat as she scrambled down the ladder again, all those worn, fat oaken rungs shaking under her feet, to find her grandfather on his knees by the kitchen hearth, feeding the last of her books into the fire.

Her father had been in the kitchen too. Bigger than her grandfather, burly where the old man was wiry, but burly with a curious gentleness, like a big dog whom none of the other dogs will fight. His father had had the flat-eared malign intensity of a terrier killing rats. Auburn and freckled, like she was, like her grandfather, like Second Sister and brother Tulik, whom Grandfather had early taken to be his heir.

And as she saw herself screaming at them both, grabbing at the fragments of her notes—the pages and scrolls that she'd copied so laboriously by hand—it had occurred to her sleeping self to wonder if her father was in the kitchen because he'd tried to talk his father out of burning the books.

At the time she hadn't asked; had only stormed out of the house, weeping.

It was the last time she'd seen either of the two men.

Or been in her grandfather's house.

In her dream the street outside hadn't been drenched in hot yellow summer light as it had been on that day eighteen months ago. It had been dark, wintery and cold under the mad, staring eye of the full moon, and the air had jangled like softly shaken chains. Someone waited for her at the end of the street, someone she couldn't see. Wreathed in the smell of lightning, haloed by blue light that illuminated nothing. Holding something small and glittering to his breast. Something that moved.

"If you'd care to leave a message, miss?" The head porter cast a quelling glance at the maid, who looked as if she might have added something else: He obviously didn't approve of servants telling more than they absolutely had to about the movements of their betters. He scrupulously used the form of address appropriate for a child, or for a well-born man's unmarried daughter.

"What about Lord Soth?" asked Shaldis. "Would you tell him that Raeshaldis of the Sun Mages is here. . . ."

"It's my understanding," said the porter stonily, "that Lord Soth is unwell, and not able to see anyone."

"Thank you," said Shaldis, and turned from the gate, not certain what she should do. A line of white-robed priests crossed the court behind her, jingling sistrums and striking triangles, to burn Oan Echis's daily ration of incense in the god's small shrine. The scent of it was sweet against the day's rising dust and the smell of cut flowers and frying sausage from the vendors in the court.

She had asked leave of Hathmar that morning to let her visit the Summer Concubine for a few hours instead of watching in the scrying chamber again, but in fact her intent had been to ask for an introduction to Soth, the king's librarian and a former Earth Wizard. She'd met that tall, quiet-faced man briefly during the nerve-racking process admitting her to the college, but they had never spoken alone.

But he would know spells beyond those the Earth Wizards taught. Spells of Deep Listening, spells to probe more surely into the walls than those she had already tried. She sensed that Benno Sarn might be right: There was certainly something askew with the way she was learning, though the Summer Concubine had said she had the same problems making spells work. There had to be something that would work for her every time, or at least more frequently than the spells she'd gotten from the Sun Mages' signacon.

Now she stood in the hot sunlight of the Golden Court, listening to the fig sellers' cries, her arms folded around her satchel.

Whoever it is, she thought, *it's someone with a great deal of power. And it's only a matter of time before he strikes again.*

And possibly, she thought, very little time.

She found herself hoping that the king was keeping a close eye on the Summer Concubine. That he was taking proper care of her out there at the aqueduct.

She could, of course, go back to the Citadel and sit in the scrying chamber all day.

But Soth, she thought, was not the only mage in the city who might help her.

She turned and hurried the length of the Golden Court, her white robes billowing about her in the dust. Crossed through the shadows of its many-pillared arcade to the outer gate and plunged into the city.

FIFTEEN

The whisper of magic was everywhere.

It was very faint, a kind of all-pervasive ugliness. The Summer Concubine had hoped to sense something of its origin—earth, sun, blood, fire, wind—and thus have a better chance to guess who had set the curse. But all she could feel, as she clambered over the ruin of broken scaffolding, was malice, like an itching in her skin. The scaffolding itself had been hauled a little distance out into the desert, to leave room for the new framework already under construction. The men at work on this grumbled about having to bring in virgin materials—huge quantities of mature bamboo needed to be shipped in from the lowland forests that fringed the Lake of Reeds, a journey of almost three weeks—but the two foremen, Grobat and Ykem, were cautious about using any materials that might be either still tainted with a curse or damaged from a fall.

They were right, the Summer Concubine thought, running her fingertips along the woody yellow tubes, the narrow boards still stained with workmen's blood. Everywhere she touched, the hex seemed to stick to her fingers like slime.

"It's here, all right," she said when Oryn—who'd been conversing animatedly with the scaffold foremen while she searched—picked his way through the jumbled scatter of rubble to where she sat on the broken heap. Amid the constant dust cloud of the construction zone he looked like a giant orchid, unbelievably incongruous in his coat and tunic and trousers of violet and gold, a servant trailing faithfully with a gold-tasseled violet sunshade. "It feels diffuse, like . . . like glue mixed with water. It's all spreading out from a mark somewhere." She gestured around her to the tangled riggings, the broken hoist beam, the lashed frameworks that covered nearly the area of a wealthy man's house.

"Are you sure?" Oryn squatted beside her, and the maid Lupine, whose job it was to hold a sunshade over the Summer Concubine's head, stepped closer to Oryn's parasol bearer to form a long rectangle of shade to cover them both. "According to our friend foreman Ykem the scaffolding's been guarded not by one guard, or two, who might have been touched by a sleep spell while the mark was drawn, but by half a dozen."

"A mage wouldn't have to make the mark on the scaffold itself, you know." The Summer Concubine flexed her aching shoulders. "The mark could have been written some distance away on an amulet, or a talisman. If a mage put the proper limitations on the hex he could come up under a cloak, hang the talisman eye on a beam and slip away again. It would spread out from there, infecting the whole structure."

"I'll have a couple of the men start looking for—how big would it be? No larger than your palm, I suppose, or it would have been seen."

"Not necessarily. And it could have been written on paper and pasted on, or on a ribbon and tied."

"Well, if it was hung it might have fallen off—or been taken away once the damage was done," he added grimly. "I'll have Ykem put men to searching." He offered her his silver flask of lemon water to drink, the gingery tang stinging on her tongue, and opened the small container of ointment he carried—violet jade set in gold—to tenderly daub the bridge of her nose above the line of her veil. "Can I send for anything for you?" he asked. "A willow tree perhaps to shade you? Musicians? A small shower of rain?"

Around them, under the bright, brittle glare of the desert afternoon, the camp jostled and clamored. Teyn filed in and out of the three walled enclosures where they were kept, enclosures guarded now, as well as written with runes of obedience and subservience and fear. The silent half-human faces were flat and expressionless under the thin, silky bristle of their shaved hair. Now and then a guard or minder would ask one of them something to be replied to in simple grunting words, but they never spoke to one another. Only now that Oryn had spoken of it to her, the Summer Concubine noticed that they *were* always reaching out to touch one another, the touch passing down the stoop-backed lines. Comfort? Communication? How could one tell?

She smiled into Oryn's worried eyes. "I'm well cared for, thank you."

"You let me know."

"I will."

Other teyn, watched by their minders, dragged cut stone in from the East Road, where the king's cavalcade had all that morning passed the steady stream of low, wheeled sledges on its way to the camp. The line stretched back through the desert, through the arid rangeland to the fields and orchards by the lakefront. At landing stages just south of the wharves of the fishermen, barges brought in rough-hewn blocks floated down from the quarries in the mountains that bordered the Great Lake's western shore, via the Sun Canal. By this hour of the afternoon the air was impenetrable with golden dust.

I'm coming to hate this aqueduct as much as the lords do, the Summer Concubine reflected as Oryn clambered away to speak to the foremen about assigning men to investigate the wreckage. She surveyed the mass of debris before her and reflected that this was something people didn't generally hear about wizardry: How occasionally wearisome it was to be the one person in hundreds, or even thousands, who was able to effect change in a situation and to be therefore obliged to do so.

With a sigh she lifted her gaze to the stockpiles of stone blocks, around the advancing end of the aqueduct, the half-raised pillars, the arches that would support the artificial river's bed once it came down off the desert's cliffs and had to be carried to the city across the low, flat lands between.

Madness, the clan lords said—and the priests of many other gods besides Nebekht. But according to Soth such devices worked, to channel water from far away, and the Summer Concubine could see no reason why it should not.

And beyond the aqueduct, sprawling south between the building site and the road, the shuffling gangs of teyn, the masses of penned sheep, nearly hidden in a fog of wheat-colored dust. Workers' tents, mess tables, depots of food, butts of water . . . all of this had to come from somewhere. And in all of it, hidden somewhere, was a clue, a trace of magic, that only she could find.

Before the camp the cliffs loomed, the rough drop-off from the still more barren desert tableland, a jagged zone of badlands called the Dead Hills. Beyond that, the oasis of Koshlar—fifteen days by camel, if all went well.

If the rains never come, she thought, *we will die anyway, long before we reach Koshlar.*

They must come. She closed her eyes in brief prayer to Darutha, lord of rain. This year, and next year, and the year after . . . Just enough to let this be accomplished.

Two hundred miles. And it was only the first they'd have to build if the cities around the drying lakes were to survive. The aqueduct now stretched just over twelve miles, and in another three would climb through the Dead Hills to the tablelands of the deep desert beyond. There, according to the surveyors Oryn had sent out five years ago, the aqueduct would be cut into the earth, a canal roofed over with stone to prevent evaporation, lined with stone to cheat the dry earth's baking heat. The springs of Koshlar were bountiful, filling a deep lake in the heart of burning salt-white wastes and overflowing into acres of marsh. Mohrvine was right, she thought. The nomad tribes wouldn't let that water be tapped without a fight.

Two hundred miles. And in between, bleak flats of gray rock; bleached miles of pea-sized gravel without so much as a cactus to relieve the endless lifelessness of the landscape. More miles of sand, where white dunes two hundred feet high crept with the slow, wind-driven inexorability of predators. Decayed ridges of saffron rock—black canyons where rivers had flowed so long ago that even the bare stones had forgotten. The Durshen kings had had their tombs carved in the Dead Hills, under the assumption that no robber would find his way through the harsh maze of the badlands; there were rumors of necropoli still farther out in the wastes.

And beyond all that, more wasteland still. The first three surveying parties sent out had not returned, nor had any sign of their end ever been found. It was not known whether the nomads had taken exception to their trespass—or guessed their ultimate intent—or whether they had simply been led astray and destroyed by the djinni.

Squads of teyn were already at work cutting the notch of the canal on the far side of the badlands.

From here the Summer Concubine could see the rising cloud of their dust glimmering in the dry, burning light. Now and then a mirror would flash, a tiny blink of light as one engineer signaled another.

Two hundred miles. And how many dry years, before the lakes themselves sank away in their beds?

She turned her attention back to the broken planks, the tangled ropes crusted with the blood of those who'd just happened to be in the wrong place at the wrong time. Trying to align the dim, prickly ugliness she felt in the wood with a sense, a feeling, of the amulets Soth had brought her, talismans ensorcelled years ago by Ahure, Aktis, Isna Faran, Urnate Urla. But of course talismans lost their strength over the passage of time. And when those talismans had been imbued with spells, had Aktis and Isna Faran already begun to lose their powers?

Or was this hex the work of some mage she'd never heard

of? Some nomad sorcerer trying to keep the aqueduct from the oasis? Or a mage from far away? One of the wizards who'd healed or cast love spells or laid wards of obedience on the teyn in a village in the north somewhere, or in Ith or the City of White Walls or the City of Reeds—maybe even from the faraway coast?

She couldn't tell.

And as she concentrated, the images of Corn-Tassel Woman and Turquoise Woman kept returning to her, breaking her concentration. *No wonder I can't find anything familiar here.*

Don't let them be dead, she prayed to Rohar, god of women, the gentle protector whose small chapel and flower-draped image could be found in every harem from the Lake of the Moon up to the scraggle of drying mudflats beyond the Lake of Gazelles. *Please guard them, keep them, wherever they are. . . .*

Her fingers brushed another section of planking, another bunch of rope, and the recollection of last night's horrible dream breathed upon her like the halitus of the grave. She felt again the awful grief in her heart, as if a twin sister had died.

Grief—and dread. Dread that whatever it was knew *her* name as well. Dust gritted in her eyes and beneath her veils, and in spite of the protecting gauze, her nostrils and throat felt like a sandpit. Lupine moved over, the parasol's shade shifting with the sun—Lupine herself wore a double-crowned straw hat more substantial than the roof of a poor man's house.

Keep Shaldis, too, she prayed. *Hold her in the palm of your hand.*

"I'll see if he's receiving company." Mohrvine's porter, a fat man with the sloppy accent of a longtime resident of the Circus District, waved Raeshaldis to a bench. She'd gone to the bronze-strapped gates of the old House Jothek in Great Giraffe Street with heavily beating heart, expecting the usual sidelong looks at her novice's robe and unveiled face, but the man barely gave her a glance. If he'd been raised in the Circus, she reflected, watching him as he whistled through his fingers for a page, this wasn't a surprise. People in the Circus were used to just about anything.

Mohrvine's house—the house the Jothek clan had owned long before they'd become high kings—stood in the Circus District, rowdier and smellier than the more fashionable purlieus of the Flowermarket, where most of the other clan lords had their compounds. Shaldis had been, naturally, forbidden to walk these streets as a child and had, naturally, disobeyed whenever she thought she could get away with it. Even today, the men who played dominoes in the cafés in their short, bright-hued tunics, and the bare-faced women in their jangling jewelry, gaudy dresses and gaudier hair, stared at her less than did passersby in other parts of town.

Upon reflection, Shaldis supposed it was an improvement that her novice's robes and unveiled face classed her with the girl acrobats and female rope dancers rather than marking her as simply a disobedient member of some man's family.

"Ain't you supposed to be up with the rest of 'em bringing the rain?" As a little yellow-clad page scampered away across the high-walled, narrow expanse of the brick-paved court on his errand, the porter turned back and dipped her out a cup of water from the jar in his minuscule kiosk beside the lodge. At the court's far end, over a wall of plastered brick that could have stood repainting, poplars and sycamores displayed brilliant, healthy leaves in a silent boast of water to spare. Tiled roofs heaped behind them: crimson, yellow, blue, ornamented with sand-scored gilt. A couple of teyn patiently swept the courtyard bricks, backs bent under the glare of the sun.

"Special message." Shaldis patted her satchel as if it contained something of importance. In fact it contained all the tablets on which she'd written her Spells of Deep Listening, whether they worked or not; she had meant to ask Soth about them.

Was there some rule, she wondered, about mages from one discipline helping those of another? She'd never heard of it being done, but then, prior to this it had never *had* to be done.

The porter grunted. Both the dripping cup and the jar he dipped it from were painted ware a hundred years old, simple and delicate as anything Shaldis had seen in the Marvelous Tower. She remembered what her grandfather had always said about Mohrvine being a "true gentleman"—true gentlemen being those who held to ancient traditions and didn't wear pointed-toed shoes. The noise from the street grew louder for a moment as the boar teyn who was sweeping the courtyard bricks opened the gate to brush the dust through and into the thoroughfare. *To be tracked back in tomorrow, belike,* thought Shaldis, exasperated. The flat, round faces of the teyn under their clipped white beards were inexpressive; sweat trickled down the boar's back and shoulders, stained dark the jenny's rough brown dress. Their eyes were blue, and startlingly human. Shaldis wondered if they felt heat the way people did.

The page came running back and traded a word with the porter, who came to Shaldis with a bow. "He'll see you, miss." He used a more respectful pronoun than before.

"Thank you." Shaldis tipped him—out of a very slender reserve of savings—and followed the page out into the court, to three tall brick steps and a gate that let onto a covered walk. Morning sunlight glared from the pink-washed walls, splashed the grubby white and brown palimpsests of overlaid door and window wards, gilded the scrim of dust in the air. As she passed the teyn the boar glanced sidelong at her, and for a moment she had the disconcerting sense of seeing calculation in those bright blue eyes.

Aktis waited for her in the small courtyard that Mohrvine allotted his court mage, thin and lined and a little stooped, with a nose like a medium-sized yam and eyes dark and wise and twinkling under a gray shelf of brow. A trellis and vine had once circled the walled enclosure, shading the line of chambers and open workrooms that looked into it on three sides. Most of the vine had been pulled down and replaced by an apparatus of pulleys and mirrors. The basin of what had been the courtyard pool stood empty, its tiles smudged with smears of red and white chalk.

The Earth Wizard listened to her account of being hazed by the other novices—and possibly adepts as well—at the college, of having the ward signs that defended her room violated, of her attempts to locate the perpetrators through the residue of their spells left in the wood. "I copied every spell I could find from the library, but I can't make most of them work," she finished. "Even the ones that are straightforward. Ben— One of the masters I spoke to said it may be something simple, that I'm not drawing the sigil precisely enough. But I do practice, and I have successfully made sigils on the air, not once but many times. Sometimes these work perfectly. And other times"—she spread her hands, baffled—"other times they don't."

Thoughtfully, Aktis turned over the spell tablets in his pale, ink-boltered hands. When she'd made up her mind to go to the Sun Mages, Shaldis had resolved that if they wouldn't take her, she'd seek out Aktis, whom she'd seen many times in the Bazaar. He was reputed to be both a strong mage and a man willing to help even those who could not pay—something not all Earth Wizards would do. With no overriding authority and no single Archmage—their informal council met only a few times a decade—the Earth Wizards had a reputation for being much more everyday than the Sun Mages, living in houses and shopping in the market. But because they had to buy their own bread instead of being supported by a college that over the years had been given farms, city rentals, cattle herds and the cash to found a substantial moneylending business, they and the Pyromancers were reputed to be more mercenary than the Sun Mages, and far more variable in quality. The Sun Mages trained those who could source power from the sun and tested them rigorously. Earth Wizards drew strength from the ground beneath their feet, from the gold and silver and hidden lodes of water in the soil: They and the Pyromancers, and others of the smaller orders, simply apprenticed likely lads, the way a potter or a carpenter or a goldsmith would.

Yet even after Aktis was pledged to Mohrvine and had no more need to earn his living, Shaldis had seen him heal a beggar child's foot of a camel bite in the marketplace. Had seen him go into the shabby huts in the Slaughterhouse District to spell their pitiful cupboards against mice, their windows against the incursions of the mosquitoes that came whining in clouds from the borders of the lake. Urnate Urla and Khitan Redbeard had muttered about people taking away their business, but one didn't mutter too loudly against Lord Mohrvine Jothek's court mage. The beggars called out blessings on him when he passed, and on Lord Mohrvine as well.

"Trace out this sigil on the table." Aktis selected one of the tablets. "Just as if you were going to scry the wood."

He watched as she obeyed, eyes following the track of her finger on the coarse peasant bench. He hadn't said to put the focus of her power on it, so Shaldis didn't, and as a result she couldn't see the glowing line that sometimes appeared under her finger as she made a sigil in a spell. Still, when she'd completed the sign he nodded, said, "Stand up and close your eyes and spin around three times. . . . I can see you must have been a champion at blindman's bluff. Now trace it again, exactly over the first. That looks good," he finished when she repeated the invisible sign. The simple bench was in keeping with the plain furnishings of the rooms that she could see through the wide-open windows that faced onto it: a few cupboards, an adobe divan scattered with cushions of pink-and-blue country-work. The teapot and cups he brought out were plain green-glazed work from the papyrus forests and fishing villages around the far north end of the Lake of Reeds. A black glass idol, of the kind found in very old Hosh tombs, stared bleakly from its niche in the wall. "That's very good. You have a good inner eye. I don't think practice is what is lacking.

"Everyone needs practice," he added, his fleet grin suddenly lightening a face gouged with the marks of weariness. "If you plan to follow the path of power, child, you'd better learn to love practice and memorization, because you're going to be doing a lot of them. But it doesn't look as if that's the problem. And your orientation to the sun is certainly accurate."

"Then what's wrong?" asked Shaldis, frustrated. "Why can I make spells work sometimes and other times they just . . . they just turn into lines and words?"

Aktis sighed and rubbed his eyes. He was, Shaldis reckoned, a good twenty years younger than Hathmar, yet something about the way he tried to straighten his back, the way he shifted his shoulders, reminded her of the old Archmage. His hair, which had been coal black and thick only a few years ago, was thin now, limp and the color of cave mud.

"I do have power," Shaldis went on, more softly. She stared down into her teacup, the strong burnt-honey smell of the steam rising around her face. "Some things—spells of conceal-ment, and illusion—I can do . . . oh, as if I were born knowing how to do them. Just shaping the illusions with my mind. The power is there."

Aktis opened his mouth as if he would speak what was in his thoughts. Then he seemed to change his mind and only shook his head. "Where does it come from, child?" he asked. "This power."

Shaldis hesitated, casting into her mind, into her dreams. "It's—It's inside me. In my chest, I think."

"But when you focus it, channel it," went on Aktis, "where does it flow from? I know you've been taught to source from the sun, and every spell and sigil you know has reference to it." His expressive fingers played above the tablets, scattered on the bench between them. "Have you studied the sigils the Earth Wizards use? Seen them at all?"

"I've seen them." They were very different, odd-looking and shaped to a completely different geometry, as different from the signs of the Sun Mages as formal High Script was from Scribble, or as the classic sun glyphs of men's horoscopes were from the complicated, ever-altering lunar women's signs.

"Are you so sure," said Aktis, "that you are a Sun Mage at all?"

Benno Sarn had said the same thing. Raeshaldis shook her head, uncertain and feeling a kind of despair.

"Have you ever been tested?"

"By the Sun Mages, yes."

"Hmm." Aktis's mouth twisted and he tugged at his pigtail, winding its thin gray strands around thin fingers. "Hathmar hasn't had a new novice at the college for three years. I expect he'd have taken anyone with any sign of power and not asked about source." His dark-circled eyes returned to her, searching her face.

"Would you teach me?" asked Shaldis. "Write out for me the runes and sigils I'd need to—to feel, to see, who this was? *What* this was?"

The thick brows quirked upward, but Aktis only looked

down at the table, at the spot where Shaldis had traced the sig-ils, invisible on the wood. He said nothing for a time, and sipped his tea in deepening silence while the noises of the house, and of the streets outside, clashed on the high pink walls. Looms thudded in the workshops somewhere near; a groom cursed a teyn. A woman in the street outside called, "Hot bright gingerbread—a dequin for a cake!" "Anybody anybody, chairs to mend?" wailed a male voice, and a camel groaned. Irritating contrast, Shaldis realized, with the absolute restful silence of the Summer Concubine's terrace gardens.

"You mean," said Aktis at length, "that you want me to go against the Sun Mages with an Earth Wizard's spells?"

His dark eyes flicked inquiringly to her, and Shaldis under-stood what he implied.

"It's just one spell."

"And no one would know?" The brows went up again. Then he sighed. "Child, you don't remember what happens when the orders of wizardry fight one another. I barely remember the last time it happened—I couldn't have been seven years old—and that was a small spat, a stupid squabble between a Wind Singer who worked for the House Sarn and some of old Lord Akarian's court mages—Earth Wizards, I'm ashamed to say.

"People are always saying how wizards are useless—how they'll never do the things you most want them to. And this is why: Because we have learned, over the years, to watch how we use our power. Five or six days ago a man came to me com-plaining of vomiting, of paralyzing pain in his hands. It turned out his wife had paid one of these new—these new women-who-do-magic to make him stop spending his money on drink, and this was the best way this woman could think of to make him do what made *her* most comfortable. Not knowing, of course, that no spell has ever been found to cure a man of drugs, or drink, or gambling."

He shook his head in genuine distress. "If you're being taught by the Sun Mages you must have learned about the limitations that must be on any spell, the boundaries to keep ill luck from spreading everywhere in the world, to keep a simple spell of bellyache or migraine from spreading and duplicating itself until half a village is puking itself to death.

"In that last quarrel the Order of the Wind Singers came to an end, except for a few hermits in the desert west of the Eanit. What you're asking is forbidden. And for good reason. For the best of reasons."

Shaldis looked down for a time at the tablets, at the grain of the table. At her own hands, long and white and skinny, lying in the knotted shade of the naked vine.

"The Sun Mages won't help me," she said at last, glad that she'd decided not to mention the disappearance of a couple of freelance spell weavers like Corn-Tassel Woman and Turquoise Woman. Not that she would have done so in any case, given Aktis's position in Lord Mohrvine's household.

"Then you should leave them."

She looked up, startled.

"I can't do what you ask—simply hand you spells like a street-corner peddler passing out two-penny mouse wards. For one thing, I doubt you'd be able to use them." He pushed over a couple of tablets that lay beyond her reach, and she saw his fingers trembled a little with a kind of constant, unsteady vibration. "You certainly wouldn't be able to use them safely. But I *can* teach you. In fact I'd rather do that, and make sure you learned your limitations properly. I promise you—"

"My lord." The page reappeared in the gateway of the court, a chubby boy whose long old-fashioned curls reminded Shaldis of the streetwalkers outside. "My lord Mohrvine would see you. Now, sir, he says—please, right away." The boy glanced at Shaldis with a combination of apology and fascination, the kind of stare she got often in the streets from young boys un-used to seeing a woman's face uncovered in public.

Aktis glanced at the angle of the sun on the table and his mouth tightened. Shaldis got to her feet and gathered up her tablets, counting to make sure she had them all.

"I won't keep you, sir," she said. "Thank you for your time, for your help and advice."

He stood also, reached a hand as hesitant as a cat's paw to touch her sleeve. "Child," he said, "don't do anything foolish. If the spells of the Sun Mages won't work—spells that you've been taught to bound and limit properly—don't endanger yourself or anyone else by tampering with other types of spells. You don't—"

The page glanced over his shoulder through the gate, as if he expected to see the greatest and most dangerous of the clan lords storming down the walkway at his heels, and cleared his throat. "My lord wizard, my lord said as how it was . . . That is, he told me to tell you—"

"That he wants me right away." Aktis's voice was very quiet, touched with pain. With anger, too, thought Shaldis, and no wonder: that even the lord of one of the great houses would command a mage to come, like a servant. "Of course he does. Come back to me tomorrow, child. Promise me that you will. We need to talk more of this. And between now and then, be careful. Don't tamper with what you don't understand. I assure you, only dreadful grief will come of it."

"No sir." Shaldis stepped back under the trellis, waiting to be taken back to the gate, as Aktis went into one of the sev-eral small rooms that surrounded the court. The page followed him to the door, having doubtless received instructions to make sure he didn't delay. She heard the man say, "Just give me a moment, boy," his voice muffled by the curtain that cov-ered the door. Turning her head, she saw him through the window of what had to be the next room taking something from a locked cupboard in the corner opposite the window.

He opened the cupboard with a key, and she thought, *He doesn't use a ward sign.*

What he took out was a black clay bottle, which he stood looking at for a moment. The late sunlight coming through the window stood clear on the sweat on his face.

He wet his lips, made as if to put the bottle back—then brought it to his mouth and took a small, a very small, sip.

And shuddered, with a look of such desperation on his face that Shaldis's heart seemed to twist in her breast.

He put the bottle back, closed the cupboard.

Then opened it again fast, and took one more desperate gulp, as if fearing that he would be observed. Past his shoulder Shaldis could see into the cupboard—saw a big gourd, stained dark and surrounded by dead roaches; saw a bundle of dried *ijnis* leaves and a porcelain mortar likewise stained; a small retort for distilling and a golden bottle, wrapped in three strands of iron and sealed with a crystal stopper. She knew he was going to look around and turned away, moved behind the post of the trellis and gazed across the garden, feeling shaken and sick.

Aktis reemerged from his door with a brisk stride and pulled it closed behind him. The page stepped respectfully aside as the Earth Wizard traced signs on the door with one finger: "One can't be too careful, my child," he said with forced heartiness. "Topeck will show you out, won't you, Topeck? Good lad. Tomorrow?" he said, laying a hand on Shaldis's shoulder.

She nodded. When he turned to go through the gate of the courtyard ahead of her, she reached out casually and brushed the door with her fingers, seeking the ward mark he had left.

She felt nothing. She could have gone in and helped herself to his supper—or his *ijnis*—for all the mark would do to keep her out.

The curly-haired page was waiting, with no very good grace. She slung her satchel up on her shoulder again and followed him through the gate and into the slatted shade of the covered walk, heading back toward the main court. For a few minutes Aktis's stooped, black-clothed shoulders bobbed ahead of them under the flicking bars of shade. Then he turned down another walkway, ascended a flight of tiled steps to pass through a door.

Just because he's taking ijnis, thought Shaldis, *doesn't mean he can't teach me.*

Or does it?

How soon did the drug begin to affect the mind? Immediately, everyone said, and far quicker for some than for others. He'd seemed perfectly in control except for the trembling of his hands. But if his spells weren't to be trusted anymore—as they obviously weren't, if he'd used a key rather than a ward spell on his cupboard—did that mean . . . ?

And as clear as a bell, sweet and strong as if she'd walked past a rosebush in full scent, she felt magic.

And turning, saw the fugitive glimmer of a freshly drawn rune of ward on the corner of a wall.

SIXTEEN

There were spells Shaldis had used when she was a child—like the zin-zin spells of *I'm not here*—to make the servants in the kitchen yard think everything was going along as it usually did, while she slipped through and out the gate in her brother's clothes. They weren't exactly cloak spells be-cause if someone was really looking for her they could see her easily, but she thought of them as blinkers: It was a blinker that rose most easily to her mind now and she whispered it into the already preoccupied thoughts of the curly-haired page.

She's right behind you all the way to the gate, Topeck.

As the boy strolled jauntily down the narrow passageway between courtyard walls, Shaldis slipped into the turning where the ward was written and ran her hand exploringly over the pink-washed wall.

It was definitely a ward sign and definitely not one of Aktis's. She'd sensed Aktis's ward sign, blurred with the pas-sage of time, on the wall at the far end of this walkway. His was an earth sign and nothing like this one. When the page turned the corner, Shaldis hurried along the uneven brick pavement to the place to run her hand over the invisible mark to be sure.

Then she went back to the turning.

There was definitely another wizard in House Jothek.

It was a Pyromancer sign, she thought, but made by an am-ateur. Something someone learned somewhere and had enough strength to make work. The walkway beyond it was narrow and unused looking, the worn old bricks pitted, unswept and in places covered with sand. The stucco behind the torch sconces was deeply stained with soot. Still a narrow trace through the sand showed that people did go this way, and through the open gate at the end Shaldis could see greenery.

There was another ward sign on the arch of that red-tiled gate, the same kind.

The garden there—more an agglomeration of vines, orange trees and plants whose pots and tubs had been crammed into the tiny paved space at random rather than an organized gar-den—was watered but not well trimmed. An old woman stood on a wooden stool to feed finches in one of the dozen cages that hung from every limb big enough to support them. Shaldis took in almost unconsciously the brilliance and new-ness of her black-and-red silk robes, the complex rolls and jew-els in her white hair, and the soft, well-cared-for hands.

A member of the Jothek household, and an important one.

The old woman turned around and gave a start at the sight of her: "Who are you?" And then, taking a closer look: "Ah. You must be the Raven girl my bath woman was telling me about. Come to see my son?"

"I . . ." Shaldis put two and two together in her mind and made a deep salaam. "No, my lady. That is, I didn't come to see Lord Mohrvine, but Lord Aktis."

"*Lord.*" The woman sniffed. "*Lord* for a fisherman's son? For a boy born in a hut on a marsh? Who I'm told can't so much as ward mosquitoes away these days . . . can he?" Her eyes were sharp under beautifully shaped white brows, a clear, light hue like very green turquoises.

"I don't know, lady."

The old woman studied her a moment more at the distance of a few feet—the courtyard itself, even without the tubbed or-ange trees and statues half hidden in cloaks of vine, was barely the size of a medium-sized bedroom. Then she hobbled closer and took Shaldis's arm. She'd lost many of her teeth, but those that remained looked white and strong, and her flesh smelled of the mild aromatics of very fine ointment. "Help me inside, child," she said. "Do you know who I am?"

As they passed through the open door of a beautifully ap-pointed wine room, a servant woman hurried to relieve Shaldis of the slight burden of the old woman's weight; the old woman waved her impatiently aside. "Fetch us tea, if you'd be of any use," she commanded. And, when the servant bowed herself back through the curtain of embroidered black wool, the old woman said, "I don't trust a one of them." She lowered her voice. "It's true, then, that women can do magic now? Some women? It's not market prattle?"

"It's true." Shaldis felt uneasy under the scrutiny of those wise, calculating eyes. She helped the old woman to sit on a divan of plain black cushions, and was herself gestured to a stool covered in a sheepskin dyed red after the fashion of the nomad sheikhs. But before she could draw away, the old woman's hand tightened on her arm.

"I think one of them's that way." The old lady's voice sank to a whisper, and her huge green eyes darted toward the door. "One of the servants, I mean."

"You mean mage-born?" It was a word that had application only to a male birth; there was no similar term that applied to a female child. Shaldis sank down onto the sheepskin stool.

"I'm called the Red Silk Lady," said her hostess, and Shaldis's eyes widened: She'd heard the name. Now that she thought about it, she did remember that Mohrvine was the son of the Red Silk Lady by Oryn Jothek I, the old generalissimo's final passion after he'd defeated the last of the Akarian kings and taken the throne for himself. The daughter of a deep-desert hunter—though sometimes she claimed a sheikh for a father—the woman had been notorious in her own right for her extravagance, her intrigues and the stubbornness her lover had shown in keeping her by him in the face of all his advisers' exasperated urging. The old grandmother of her grandfather's cook had been full of such tales, and Shaldis, fascinated, had been the only one in the household to listen to her.

"Yes, I see you stare. It's good to know one's name has survived—though I'm not what I was, I can tell you that, girl. But I've seen a thing or two, and I swear one of the girls here—and I don't know which—is working magic." She shook her head, the rubies in her lacquered hair twinkling. "And I won't speak of it, either, to my son. Nor must you, nor to any."

"Why not?" The darkness of her room at the Citadel came back to her, the whisper of her name at the window.

The servant "girl" came back bearing a wicker tray with tea things. In contrast to Aktis's strong, black honey-flavored smoke tea, this was the finest green leaf tip from the hills to the northwest of the Lake of Reeds, light as rosewater to the taste. One did not, Shaldis knew, pollute such delicacy with honey, and none was offered. On her knees the servant, who was probably old enough to be Shaldis's mother, offered first Shaldis, then her mistress, a plate of flat crisp vanilla cakes, then a bowl of figs and nuts.

Only when the woman was gone did the Red Silk Lady say, "And put her into my son's hands? It's not a fate I'd wish on even the silly sluts he sends to wait on me. Tell me if those cakes aren't to your liking." Her tone held a world of grief for the cook if Shaldis so much as grimaced, and in fact they were excellent. "He uses everyone, my son. Everyone who comes to his hand. As that fat custard Oryn is using that skinny concubine what's-her-name, the one Greatsword paid too much for . . . and as he means to use you, if you'll let him."

"I owe the king . . ." Shaldis hesitated, remembering the afternoon heat as she'd stumbled through the streets with the tears of grief and rage still on her face, wondering what she'd do if the mages at the college didn't take her. Wondering where she could go that wasn't back to her grandfather's house. She remembered looking at the prostitutes as she passed them, bored, young, unveiled faces in the open windows, lolling limbs in tight-fitting dresses of yellow and red. Remembered wondering how one became a prostitute and whether it would be worse than going back.

Even the echo of that despair was like the breath of the abyss blowing over her face.

"I owe the king everything."

"You think Hathmar wouldn't have jumped to take you on without Oryn's say-so?"

Aktis had said much the same. But they hadn't taken Xolnax's amber-eyed daughter, and the Summer Concubine had said she was good.

She said, "I don't know."

Finches fluttered in from the garden, black and white and red. The Red Silk Lady chased them away from the crumbs with a wave.

"Don't let yourself be used, child," said the lady. "That's all I'm saying. Don't let Oryn—or the Summer Concubine, who can charm the birds off the trees—make you think that you owe either of them one solitary thing for sending you to be trained in arts that will make you into a more effective weapon for them. Watch out for yourself, think for yourself. The favorite—is it true what I've heard, that she has power too?"

Shaldis nodded.

"Is she any good?"

"I don't know, lady. Are you any good?"

"What? At what?"

"At staying alive in the desert. At climbing a tree. At keeping out of sight of . . . of someone who wants to kill you." (A *black shadow in darkness—a burning in the air like the jangling of chains.*) "I don't think she knows how good she is, any more than any of us do, until we have to find it out."

The Red Silk Lady sank back onto her cushions again and sipped her tea. "You're saying you won't tell me."

"I'm saying I don't know." Shaldis set her tea aside, with the feeling that Mohrvine wasn't the only person in the House Jothek who used everyone who came to hand. She hesitated a moment, wondering whether she should speak of matters that might be the Summer Concubine's secrets in the House of Mohrvine, but she knew instinctively that the concubine would be horrified if she did not. "Thank you very much for the tea, lady. Tell your servants—tell all of them—to watch out. There's someone—and we don't know who—who seems to be attacking women-who-do-magic, carrying them off."

The old lady startled, then leaned back almost at once. "Are you sure?"

And Shaldis thought, *It's her.*

She's the one who made the ward sign.

She's the one who has power.

She knew it. Yet she hadn't told her son . . . and Aktis's powers must be shrunken to nothing if he didn't know to tell Mohrvine, either. Her heart beating hard, she said, "Two women so far that we know about have been taken, and there have been two attempts on me."

The green eyes narrowed, and the Red Silk Lady folded her big hands, with their rings of ruby and gold. Calculation fleeted behind her veiled glance. For a time she sat so still that the jewels in her snowy hair held the light in steady reflection and did not gleam. "And you have no idea of who this is?"

Raeshaldis shook her head and stood. "No. Nor why. But it's filled with hatred and rage, and I fear the women who've disappeared were . . . were killed. I tell you this in confidence, lady, so that you may guard yourself—"

"I'll tell my girls to guard themselves, yes." In the dimness of the curtained wine room the old woman's face was still as ivory. "Whichever of them is indeed the Raven's wife. Flower!" She clapped her hands and the servant woman appeared again. "Show Habnit's Eldest Daughter to the gate."

It wasn't until she was nearly to the forecourt of the house that Shaldis realized what it meant, that the Red Silk Lady knew her original name.

She's had me watched, she thought. *Probably from the moment I arrived at the college saying I could do magic.*

She looked back over her shoulder at the passageway among the high red walls, the cramped courtyards, of Mohrvine's house. But they'd already turned a corner, and when she checked her stride even a half pace the servant woman glanced over her shoulder, as if to make sure she didn't wander off again.

Neither hex mark nor amulet could be found on the scaffolding. The sun burned orange and hot above the dust cloud that hid the road. The Summer Concubine's fingers ached from passing across broken bits of framework and rope and she was coming earnestly to hate the sight of bamboo.

It has to be in the camp somewhere, she thought. *Spreading by touch from a center nearby.*

She looked across at where Soth knelt among the debris, patiently touching, probing, turning over fragments of rope and wood and bamboo in his hands. He moved slowly and she guessed the former wizard was able to ascertain nothing—certainly nothing through the channels of the magic he had once had. But like a good scholar he was reexamining everything anyway, hoping to see something that in the light of his theoretical knowledge might tell them something, anything, of who had set this hex.

The same man who had attacked Shaldis?

Could there be two wizards who had somehow retained their powers in force when all around them was fading?

The Summer Concubine didn't know.

Quietly she said, "Lupine, go see if my lord Soth needs any-thing, would you, please." And when the young woman propped her parasol amid the wreckage and picked her way through the debris in the wizard's direction, the Summer Con-cubine got to her feet, wrapped herself in the thickest cloak she could summon and moved off through the camp.

Listening as Soth had taught her to listen. Focusing her mind in the search for whatever trace of magic she might find. Breathing in the scents of the dust and the mortar, the out-houses and the cooking smoke, unraveling those great tangled knots of sensation with the patience of womankind.

Camels and teyn and engineers. Guy ropes creaking. Jackals rustling in the arroyos, waiting for darkness and the garbage of supper. Shrill voices: A young man in the rough tunic and ragged haircut of the True Believers was haranguing a work gang, whose members had downed tools to listen. "... will of Iron-Girdled Nebekht ... Trust in the care of the commander of the universe. ... The king has transgressed against his will, taken the part of the devil-hags, the wives of the Raven! Nebekht says to you, Such a man can lead you only to ill!"

Nebekht says that, does he? Her eyes narrowed. It was one thing to preach the god's hatred for certain groups, or certain policies of the king. It was quite another to preach against the king himself.

The wives of the Raven. Devil-hags. The Summer Concubine remembered the words scribbled on the wall of Turquoise Woman's room.

Was that what this attacker, this stalker, called them?

She closed her eyes, seeing the little room again, looted and stripped. Seeing, too, Turquoise Woman, swarthy and neat-featured like the countrywomen but with lovely blue-green eyes. So young—only a few years older than the girl Raeshaldis—and so uncertain of herself, feeling her strength and afraid of it, as she had been taught to be afraid.

Don't let her be dead, whispered the Summer Concubine to Rohar, god of women. *Bring her back. We can't spare her, any of us.*

But she had been missing for a week now, and in her heart the Summer Concubine knew that her friend was dead.

A few yards away a teyn slipped on the uneven ground, dropped the load of bricks he carried. With a curse the guard stepped in, struck the stooped, silvery creature a sharp blow across the shoulders with his staff. "Get that picked up, you! Pick up!" And he pointed to the bricks.

The teyn picked up one brick: adobe, a foot square, and weighing several pounds. He stood unmoving, short and pale furred and bandy legged, naked as a pony, the way all the teyn on the work site worked. Silent, with a silence that seemed to spread. The Summer Concubine saw the other teyn in the moving line stop, turn, look with those flat, slit-pupiled, in-scrutable eyes.

They know, she thought. *They know that the magic of hu-mankind no longer has power over them.*

If they rose up now—if they attacked the guards, or tried to flee—she, the Summer Concubine, would have to use the spells, twist their minds to subservience again. The way women had been twisted to subservience all those thousands of years.

She stood unseen, a shadow in the blowing dust, waiting for the attack and wondering what she would do.

Cast fire at them? Fling spells of fear into their hearts, or spells of pain into their bodies: belly cramps, headaches, weak-ness in their muscles? Soth was beginning to teach her these spells, to cripple and to shock, to bring down an opponent and leave him incapacitated on the ground. Was teaching her, too, the counterspells, so that she could not be brought down—if her magic was stronger than that of her attacker.

The thought of using them against beings that had no magic, that had no defense, made her sick.

Slowly, glowering, the teyn dropped the brick onto its pallet, began to load on the others. The others of its kind stirred again and moved on, resuming their labors on the aqueduct; the Summer Concubine had the sensation of seeing birds or fishes that had moved in the unity of a flock or school break apart, each going its own way again.

Wondering what she would do when someone—Bax, or Oryn, or one of the clan lords—came to her saying, *I need a spell to keep the teyn in line.*

And without the slightest idea of what she would do or say.

SEVENTEEN

B e so good as to let Lord Ahure know that it would please me if he would see this young lady." Lord Jamornid waited until the overdressed page had scampered away for a second time down the long, rather gloomy passageway that led to the Blood Mage's private court, then inclined his head apologetically to Raeshaldis. "Lord Ahure's meditations—the exercises he does to keep his spirit fit for the terrible burden of power they must bear—fill a great deal of his day and are of the first importance to him. And to us all, of course."

"Of course," agreed Raeshaldis. When Ahure had sent back the page who had announced her at the gate with word that he would see no one, Shaldis had given considerable thought to the wording of the note she'd then sent to Lord Jamornid. A week ago she would probably simply have retreated, too proud and too angry to try to work her way around a snub. Having watched the Summer Concubine in action, however, she had begun to realize that the use of levers to make work easier is not a principle limited to engineering; nor is the use of oil on recalcitrant machines.

Her note to Lord Jamornid had simply begged him to use his influence with the great mage whose opinion she sought, those of her own preceptors having proven unequal to the complexity of her problem with magic.

The implication that he, and only he, could be of help to her because he was so important and so gracious had worked better than any charm she'd learned in the College of the Sun Mages. The lord of the wide acres that circled the White Lake—the owner of most of the silver mines in the Mountains of the Moon—had hastened to the porter's lodge fairly glowing with graciousness. Raeshaldis had been careful to execute her deepest and most womanly salaam.

"It's his meditations, and his exercises, you know," Lord Jamornid went on now, signing one of the troop of pages who had followed his cushioned litter to bring him a crystal candy bowl. "They keep his own powers strong while so many others have flagged in this difficult time." Two more pages plied enormous fans of ostrich feathers, though the afternoon's heat, so oppressive a few hours earlier among the high-walled passageways of House Jothek, was already fading. With Lord Jamornid's arrival Shaldis had been immediately conducted from the porter's lodge by the gate to a separate, inner chamber obviously furnished for more important visitors. Shaldis shook her head inwardly over the tufted silk rugs, the bright-colored hangings, the gilt-and-porphyry statuary and the elaborate tile work of the walls. Even the House of the Marvelous Tower lacked appointments like these.

Yet at the same time she wondered what he wanted. She was, when all was said and done, a merchant's daughter and the newest novice in the College of the Sun Mages. Why the attempt to impress her? Which he was clearly trying to do.

"That's what he says, at any rate." His lordship's weak brown eyes took on a glow of shallow sincerity. "But I think it has to be something more, don't you? Some inner might, some depth of soul, like a . . . like a well deeper than others, going straight down into the rock. Have they found anything at the Citadel—among the researchers in their library, I mean—concerning why this is happening? Please, dear girl, have some apricot paste. My own workshops make it from trees that grow only in my gardens. It's a variety unknown in the rest of the Realm of the Seven Lakes. My great-grandfather discovered it."

"It's delicious."

He beamed as if he'd actually had something to do with the production of the confection himself, and straightened the sleeves of a robe sewn with bullion like an idol's altar cloth. "Everyone tells me how excellent it is—it's all due to the fruit, you understand, and of course to my chefs. Now, I've had scholars searching my library here—which has fully as many volumes as that in the Citadel, five hundred more than even the palace library—for references concerning the relative strength of magic over time. Did you know I operate a school for youths from my lands? There are two or three who have come up through it who are true geniuses, and they've been seeking anything that will help others—those not so fortunate as Ahure, whose powers remain intact."

"My lady—miss . . ." The page seemed a little at a loss as to how to speak to an unveiled woman clothed in the robes of a scholar. "My lord wizard says please come."

Raeshaldis knew enough to take time for effusive thanks to Lord Jamornid before she followed the boy up the narrow sloping way to Ahure's gate.

When she'd returned to the Marvelous Tower after leaving House Jothek, she'd been told that Soth, too, had gone. She knew of Ahure by reputation, having only seen him at a distance. As a rule she, like most Sun Mages, found the Blood Mages rather disgusting. Moreover, she had heard that Ahure was as proud as his patron, and difficult to approach.

But her encounter with the Red Silk Lady had sharpened her sense of urgency about learning as much as she could—as quickly as she could—about the man or creature that had assaulted her. If there was one Raven sister in the city whom even the Summer Concubine had never suspected, there would be others, and their danger would be all the greater.

In stark contrast to the opulence of the House Jamornid—the intricate mosaics that covered the walls of the porter's lodge, the gilded marble of the fountain there, the embroidered carpets—the passageway that led from the outer court to Ahure's quarters was starkly plain, and led between high unbroken walls of dark stone. The corridor was so narrow as to be in perpetual gloom, but the narrowness collected heat, even in wintertime. By this late in the afternoon it was stifling. Shaldis wondered that Ahure would have chosen the place. That he *had* chosen it was clear to her from even a few minutes' conversation with Lord Jamornid—the lord would quite clearly have provided any sort of residence the Blood Mage demanded, if for no other reason than to display to the world his own consequence at possessing the best.

On the other hand, she reflected, licking the last of the stickiness from her fingers, the apricot paste *was* delicious. So there was something to be said for ostentation after all.

The smell of sandalwood reached her nostrils long before

she arrived at the tall blackwood gate at the passage's end. Sandalwood and musk, incompletely covering the stink of old blood. The page who guided her had slowed his steps. He was only a very small boy and clearly afraid of the court mage. "You can wait here for me," Shaldis said as the child pressed open the gate. To do him credit, the boy made one halfhearted offer· to accompany her across the vast, bone-bare courtyard to the wizard's door, but when Shaldis shook her head again he stepped back with relieved alacrity, leaving her to go on alone.

This close to sunset, the courtyard's high walls had already put it into deep shadow. The wizard's house stood at the far end of almost two hundred feet of unbroken sand, a single small rectangular building like a temple of Niam, and absolutely plain. The walls were probably the only ones in the House Jamornid that didn't bear both painting and statuary, but there was something curiously ostentatious about them in spite of that fact. Stone, not stuccoed brick, thought Shaldis, trudging across the enormous, featureless yard. Brought down from the quarries on the Great Lake at the gods only knew what cost, polished, seamlessly cut and fitted. Windowless— there wasn't even a porch before its bronze doors, such as Niam had, to provide shade.

He's got to have another house on the other side of that rear courtyard wall, Shaldis thought, suddenly amused. *He can't actually live in this place.*

The door opened before her in eerie silence. The smell within was of bad things: blood, charred hair, burned flesh, incompletely mingled with incense. Standing before that darkness, Shaldis shivered with a sudden chill. A bare, dark chamber, windowless and stark as the courtyard outside, its walls smeared with years' accumulations of bloody handprints. A second door, without handle or lock, opening soundlessly to reveal a second chamber. More cold, and the stink of blood and frankincense.

"You bear a message from Hathmar?" Ahure's slow, harsh voice was beautiful in its way, speaking out of the gloom as a third door opened in line with the first two. On either side of her as she passed through the second chamber Shaldis was aware of smudged lines and circles of power on the floor, of piles of ash, and dribbled blood long dried. No furniture. *And this,* thought Shaldis suddenly, *in a palace crammed with every sort of expensive table and pedestal and cabinet that could be wrought of bloodwood and purple heart, of nacre and ebony.*

Where does he go to the privy in this place?

And as the irreverent thought flicked through her mind, she heard, with the keen, preternatural senses of the mageborn, the faint, grinding scritch of machinery somewhere, and the moist hiss of steam as the doors behind her closed. Extending her senses as she had been taught, she smelled other things beneath the overpowering blood and incense: charcoal smoke and hot metal, damp goat leather and straw. Somewhere she heard the tiny drip of water, and identified the wan wheeze of bellows behind hidden slits in the wall as cold air was blown across her once again, producing that shivering sense of chill.

Pity stabbed her, and disgust. Aktis at least was still trying to be what he had been, trying to call from his emptied flesh the fire that had once illuminated his life.

Ahure only wanted the credit for doing what he could no longer do.

"No, my lord." She salaamed deeply, fighting her first instinct to snap at him *Your magic doors need oiling* and stalk out. "I came of my own accord, to ask your help, if you would be so good."

The Blood Mage sat in the third chamber; it was smaller

than the first two, which wasn't saying much. Given what city land cost in the Flowermarket District, the expanse of the two outer rooms—end to end they must have stretched nearly seventy feet, and the immense courtyard added still more distance—the waste of space sheerly for effect shocked her. A blue glow of mage light—or of wax candles concealed behind blue glass—silhouetted him in a raised black wooden chair like a king's throne or the sort of thing men sat on in the north. The floor of the third room was arranged in a series of steps or risers, obliging a visitor to enter the room only so far and no farther, and to stand in a specific spot. Shaldis wondered what the setup would look like from another angle.

"You may be seated." Under the Blood Mage's booming voice Shaldis heard the faint, grinding whir of machinery. She turned and saw a low stool behind her. That startled her, for she hadn't seen him move. The black cloak that swathed his narrow shoulders covered his right hand; his left lay still as that of a wax image on his knee. *It probably is a wax image*, thought Shaldis. *Leaving him both hands to work levers in the arms of the chair.*

A table stood beside her stool. The mint tea in the cup was still vibrating. The cup, Shaldis noticed, stuck ever so slightly to the surface of the table, and when she nudged the table with her toe she found it was fixed to the black stone of the floor.

"And how may I help Habnit's Eldest Daughter?" There was an edge of sarcasm in his voice. "Am I given to understand that these powers that make you such a treasure to the Sun Mages are perhaps not as useful to you as you would wish?"

You should talk, she thought, and almost said so, but she remembered again the Summer Concubine's gracious tact. "I'm only a novice, sir, and you are a master." And that was true, she told herself. Whatever he was now, he had learned more spells when he actually had power than she'd probably even seen so far. Hathmar was always telling her that the first principle of magic was not cultivation of power, but keeping an open mind. "I've been attacked in the Citadel, by someone who's clearly a mage." Which was all he needed to know about the situation. "I have to find a Spell of Deep Listening that works for me in order to learn who he is. And I need to know why so many don't work for me, or don't work all the time. This is something I can't ask them at the college, because anyone there might be the one who's sought to do me harm."

"So there are still some at the college with the power to attack you?"

Shaldis had turned away from him to pick up her cup of tea, and when she looked back he had put off the concealing cloak and was standing beside her. *He moved very fast,* she reflected, startled. *And his timing must be like a dancer's.* Close up he smelled, not just of the old blood of the scabbed cuts on his head, but of plain dirt in his unwashed robes. The thought of drinking any tea that he'd brewed—she could see the dirt under his uncut fingernails now, and dried blood in the creases of his palms—made Shaldis queasy, but she couldn't think of how to avoid it. Being mage-born—and able to see in the dark—had decided disadvantages, she thought, watching a roach slip under an almost-hidden door at the rear of the chamber and walk unconcernedly up the wall. Among other smells in this third room she could detect the nearby presence of kitchen garbage and an untended privy.

Blood Mages were notoriously filthy, forbidden by the disciplines of their order to bathe or wash their clothing, though they did, thank the gods, keep their heads shaved. Beneath the stinks of dirt and old blood, he smelled very slightly of alcohol and slippery elm. He was doctoring his cuts, she realized, as well as rigging his doorways. Goodness knew what he was doing to keep himself from feeling pain.

Or maybe pain was what he wanted to feel.

"There appears to be, yes. Someone who can brush aside the ward spells I've put on my rooms. Someone who can hide in darkness I can't see through."

He studied her for a moment with those deep-set, hooded eyes. Looking across at him—on level ground they were nearly of a height—she saw in them bitterness and suspicion, ingrained wariness and anger so deep as to have long ago devoured his heart. "What did you speak of with Lord Jamornid?" he asked abruptly.

"Apricot paste," she said, and smiled.

His mouth curled in an expression of both distaste and disbelief. Had he been from the Bazaar he'd have said *Yeah, you right*. "Show me the spells you've been trying to use," he said. "And drink your tea, child. It grows cold."

It had arrived cold; he'd clearly made it up and set it on the table the moment he'd gotten Lord Jamornid's message that he'd be obliged to see her after all. Another use for those endless outer chambers. But she drank it obediently, trying not to think about the kitchen where it had originated. It couldn't be any worse than some of the lake water being used in the city these days. While she did so, Ahure examined the spell tablets, quite frankly copying most of them: "These differ from the volumes in my own study," he said. "I must compare them, you understand."

He then gave her a grave lecture on the sourcing of power—similar to Benno Sarn's yesterday afternoon—which told her nothing and occupied nearly an hour. By the time the beribboned page led her along the dark, hot passageway back to the main court, night had fallen, and lamps and torches burned both within the House Jamornid and in the streets of the Flowermarket District round about. "My lord left word for you to wait upon him tomorrow or the next day," the porter told

Shaldis as he opened the outer gates for her. "He's gone out to supper now, or he'd have asked you to stay and dine with him." He sounded impressed, and bowed deeply to her as she stepped through the gate and into the street.

It crossed Shaldis's mind to wonder whether the lord of the House Jamornid was beginning to have suspicions about his court mage himself, and might be shopping for another.

It might pay her, she thought, to go back to him, if not for outright patronage, at least for information. She'd have to speak to the Summer Concubine first. The older woman would understand the possible pitfalls of the situation better than she. *He uses everyone who comes to his hand*, the Red Silk Lady had said of her own son Mohrvine and of King Oryn as well. As magic changed, the patterns of power would change.

Hurrying through the gaudy streets, sweet with the scent of the drying flowers, Shaldis felt very conscious of her youth and her ignorance of the politics of the Realm of the Seven Lakes.

She paused in the colored lamplight of the Spice Court, one of the wider covered markets of the district, and leaned against the marble pillar of a fashionable café, trying to remember when or if she'd had anything more substantial to eat than a few dainty sweets. Her head ached and she felt breathless, and she wondered if this café—or any of the hundreds that made up the Flowermarket District—would serve a woman alone and unveiled.

But the thought of eating made her ill.

She walked on, leaving the wider streets to wind her way more quickly toward the Citadel gates via Slippermaker Alley again. Over the tops of high walls soft lights glowed, piercing to her tired eyes. The scents of cypress groves, of jasmine and moss and water, from the Blossom Houses went into her sinuses like chisels. She missed her way, could not seem to find where the ground rose toward the bluff. Twice she paused, certain that she heard someone following her, but, turning, saw only the jostle of the evening streets: water sellers, whores and women hawking silk handkerchiefs and pornographic gingerbread. Her head throbbed and she found herself thinking more and more of just sitting on a bench somewhere and dozing for a little, just until she felt better.

Out in the open? For anyone to come along and pick your pocket or carry you off to the nearest brothel?

Even before she'd been attacked in her own chamber at the college she'd never have even considered such behavior.

She blinked, dizzy, trying to identify where she was. Only the recollection of the hate she'd felt through the shutters of her room, the vile, alien malice of that power, kept her moving. Her heart began to thud with fear. She emerged from a gaily lanterned street of cafés and found herself looking at the Temple of Oan Echis, which wasn't anywhere near the Citadel, or Slippermaker Alley, for that matter.

I'll never make it in time for supper. She leaned against the corner of a wall, fighting to get her breath.

At this rate I'll have to counterspell the wards on the gates to get in.

And then, *If I could do that, why am I so sure my attacker was from the Citadel? The gods know the wards on the gate have no strength in them anymore, and Shrem the gatemaster can barely keep awake at his post even without the assistance of a sleep spell.*

It could be anyone.

Anyone I've talked to today.

She walked on, shaking her head against a gray buzzing that seemed to fill her ears. The flower sellers who normally lined the arcades of the district by day were gone. Away from the wide streets, the cafés and Blossom Houses, the chill air was redolent of drying leaves and petals spread on flat roofs. From the underground taverns—half buried beneath houses to keep the wine cool—came the clack of dominoes, the rattle of dice, the chatter of men's voices and the smell of wine. *Tomorrow I'll have to speak to the Summer Concubine. She has to be back by then. Or Soth. I have to tell her . . . tell her . . .*

Did someone call my name?

There seemed to be more fire around her than even the torches on the housefronts could account for, white flecks of it falling through the indigo darkness. The noise of the cafés mingled into a kind of chiming roar in her skull, like a swarm of metal bees.

She thought, *I've been poisoned.*

EIGHTEEN

The serving girl at the café where Shaldis ordered rice gruel mixed with oil and cayenne pepper stared at her. The owner, wise with the cynicism of longtime contact with the public, only cocked an eye at her and said, "Watch the steps going up to the privies. It's dark back in the yard." His gaze flicked over her dust-blotched white robe, her haggard face, inscrutable, but she was past caring. She supposed she could have come up with an illusion to make him think the customer demanding this standard hangover cathartic of her uncle's was a camel driver or one of the neighborhood sluts, but her mind felt blunted, fogged, incapable already of any spell of defense. She couldn't even figure out a circuitous route back to the Citadel gate from the Oan Echis Temple, much less deal with the thousand small details that made up such a spell.

After throwing up in the yard she felt better. But the night seemed to her to be alive with the whisper of that jangling magic. Everywhere she turned she thought she saw the creeping ghost of blue flame.

He'll be waiting for me, she thought. *In the darkness, in the alleys between here and the Citadel. . . .*

The tavern's rear yard was barely ten feet by twenty, stinking of kitchen waste. Rats scuffled in the darkness as Shaldis climbed on a rain barrel, then to the top of the privy shed to look over the wall. There was another yard back there that smelled of soap and cheap starch; Shaldis swung over the wall, crossed the hard-packed dirt, muzziness clawing at her mind.

Tea? she thought. *Apricot paste? Vanilla cakes?* Again she saw the Red Silk Lady's turquoise eye cocked at her under the grizzled brow, saw big, soft hands chasing the finches away from the crumbs. The dark around her seemed to be getting thicker, as if she walked in fog. Magic shivered in the air.

Waiting for her? Listening for her? She scrambled over the gate, dropped into a narrow street that stank of camel dung, tried to get her bearings. The walls were high, hemming her in. She couldn't see the shape of the bluffs above them, though she knew she had to be close. Lamplight made wavering patterns behind latticed windows. Straight overhead she picked out the constellation of the Weeping Ladies, the burning red gypsy star. Left would lead her to the Citadel.

And toward the darkness that waited for her.

He's a mage. He'll know the city as well as I—better, if he's a man and has been able to rove its ways all his life.

Drink your tea, she heard Ahure whisper in her thoughts, *before it gets cold.*

The taste of red pepper and vomit still in her throat at least served to keep her head clear, but she blundered against the wall as she turned right.

Darkness among the alleys. The smoky blare of torches and

music, the long tangle of the Night Market between the Baths of Ragonis and the Circus walls: booths of coarse-dyed camel hair hung with flowers, cheap brass statues and pitchers, a woman selling shoes. A man offered attar of roses in painted pots and another carried trays of teacups slung from his hips, serving tea out of an urn on his back. Bullyboys in leather body armor smoked kif and called out to her, laughing, grabbing at her as she passed. Darkness again, alleys and yards and the reek of greasy cooking. Frankincense in a temple court no wider than a tall man's arms. A god's statue watched her from a niche. A cat yowled. A woman hastened up an empty covered street trailed by a white pig. Two girls dipped water from a nearly dry well—one of them had the face of Shaldis's sister Twosie, but that might only have been a dream.

Somewhere in the night, someone was calling her name.

Seeking her, smiling and harmless, with an acid-blue crown of invisible fire wickering somewhere behind his back.

"Do you think you could keep the teyn in line?" asked Oryn. "If you had to?"

"That depends on what you mean by 'had to.'" The Summer Concubine was a shadow against the enormous half-quenched glow of the camp, an outline backed by the creeping worms of red, distant firelight. The bitter smell of dust flowed over them with the wind off the desert, and Oryn felt a twinge of gladness that the horns of the Citadel had ceased. In the silence out here they would have been dimly audible, a weight on his shoulders, a reminder of the desperation of their plight.

He felt guilty about his gladness, as if his longing for silence were disloyal to his friend Hathmar, and to all the adepts and masters of the college. They were doing their best.

Maybe Akarian was right. Maybe all he needed was more faith.

"If I had to defend myself, or you, or Rainsong Girl from immediate attack by teyn, yes, I think I could. If I'd been in Dry Hill the night of the attack, yes, I would have done all I could to keep those children from being taken, the men from being killed."

"But you wouldn't put fear spells on the walls of the compounds to keep them in at night?"

She said nothing for a time.

A guard's horse snuffled, made uneasy by the scent of the jackals in the hills. Though the tombs of the Durshen kings clustered farther back up the dry wadis of the Dead Hills, nobles and merchants centuries dead had paid to have their own resting places carved out—or erected in granite and basalt—in these lower sandhills, the ragged foothills of those fanged heights. The old fears that clung around the realms of the dead seemed to breathe up out of the ground. Oryn skirted the bulk of this middle-class suburb of the royal necropolis, turned his big gelding Sunchaser's nose toward the open desert to the south.

At length she said, "I don't know if I could. My spells . . . don't seem to work that way. Sometimes a spell will work perfectly well and three hours later the exact words, the exact placement of power, will yield nothing. Every one of the women says the same, except Cattail Woman, of course, who won't admit that there's anything her spells can't do. Even Raeshaldis, who's had formal training. Soth doesn't understand it any more than we do. I would hesitate to put any reliance on any spell I might use to . . . to dominate the teyn or any other creature, simply because it might not hold."

Curious, Oryn asked her, "What if you knew it would hold? Would you place such spells then?"

Her silence was her answer, opening before him disturbing vistas of choice and responsibility and possibilities that he didn't want to think about: What if Sarn, or Mohrvine, or Jamornid allied themselves with a Raven who could, and would, keep the teyn enslaved? He hadn't the slightest idea what he'd do in such a case.

He was the king. It was his job to decide.

It was his job to save his people, even the ones he didn't like. Even the ones who hadn't any table manners and thought it was a good idea to drape their rooms in cloth-of-gold.

Even at the cost of the love that was the heartbeat of his blood.

Dear gods, don't let it come to that.

"Why couldn't I have just continued to be a disgrace to my family and the dynasty?" he asked aloud with a sigh. "I was quite happy as a disgrace. I even had a name picked out for my-self, to be remembered by posterity: the Peacock King—which I suppose is better than being known as Oryn the Fat. I gave good parties; I treated my concubines well and kept the gar-dens up to date. I didn't do harm to anyone. If I'd been my fa-ther's younger son I'd have frittered away hundreds of thousands of gold pieces and not have had to be followed everywhere by guards to keep me from being murdered by irate clan lords or rebelling teyn. Would you have loved me less?"

In the dark cloud of her veils she was only a moving shadow. But the smile in her voice thanked him for not pressing the issue; for saying, *We shall deal with that when we have to and not before.* Lord Akarian was not the only one, Oryn reflected, to trust in the gods. "I would have drunk pearls dissolved in vine-gar at your side, O Peacock King," she said. "And so we will one day, when this is done."

"I shall hold you to that promise, my dear Summer Child."

If the Yellow City doesn't rise in outright revolt. If Lord Sarn doesn't have me murdered over the next rise in taxes, or Lord Akarian doesn't convince himself that the Iron-Girdled Nebekht— *Why iron-girdled? It sounds horribly uncomfortable, not to speak of unfashionable—really wants* him to be king and not me . . .

If the rains come.

The guards formed a rough square around the circular dip in the ground where, three hundred years ago, a mage named Goan Bluecheek had met regularly with the djinn the records called Bright-Fire Lady. The Summer Concubine drew out the five sigils and linked them with loops and strings of runes, with chalked patterns of magic, with lines of iron and ocher and silver dust. The smell of incense mingled with that of desert dust, and the whisper of her spells misted away into the desert stillness. The candles burned, small ensorcelled stars in endless night, and while Oryn sat quiet in his own protective circle she sang the names of the djinni, some of which appeared over and over in the lore of the mages and some of which marked only a single appearance: Thuu the Eyeless, Naruansich, Great Ba, Meliangobet, Smoke of Burning. . . .

Someone, anyone, come.

Someone, anyone, tell us what is happening. Tell us what we can do, must do, to live.

The moon edged the eastern sky in silver, above the dead goblin hills. Then showed itself, gibbous and gold. The Weeping Ladies walked down the sky in pursuit of the gypsy star. A cat watched them from the top of a half-crumbled tomb, casual indifference in its yellow eyes. Southward, endless infinities away, Oryn saw again the wavering mist of greenish light, but it disappeared as soon as he was sure it was real.

What is that?

Where are you?

Why don't you come?

Nothing else stirred.

Candles and incense burned away to nothing, as they had three nights ago on the turtleback rock where Oryn had seen the djinni as a child. Stumbling with weariness, the Summer Concubine collected her wide-flung magics, or disarmed them as Soth had taught her so that they could not float abroad and do harm. She gathered the vessels of water and fire, now equally cold, and eradicated every line of power from the earth. She said nothing as they rejoined the chilled and weary guards and rode back across the flat, harsh plain the two miles to camp, where Soth slumbered in his brandied sleep. Geb had honeyed figs, bread and tea ready for them, and though the Summer Concubine ate, it was clear to Oryn that she had no awareness of what she was eating.

An hour or so before dawn she cried herself to sleep in his arms.

A *girl?* said the voice of a gray-robed adept, passing down the tiled corridor that ran behind the Citadel lodge. *Please tell me you're joking.*

Gods help us, I think Hathmar's serious.

Gods help us indeed.

Shaldis had forgotten that overheard scrap of conversation. It came back to her now, with the heat that had been thick as yellow cheese in the lodge, and the scrape of her brother's shirt against the cut on her arm that she'd earned going over the wall of her grandfather's house the day before. There was another girl in the lodge, as there had been on that day, a pretty girl a few years older than herself, as far as she could judge.

The girl—Xolnax the water boss's daughter—was veiled, but she held herself as the pretty girls did. The girls who knew they'd be wanted and sought after no matter what they did.

Why am I back here? Shaldis wondered, her stomach clenching in panic. *Please, please, don't let the past eighteen months have been all a dream!*

Fear flashed through her, fear that she'd wake up and find herself in her grandfather's house again after all. In her grandfather's house, listening to them talking about whether to marry her to Forpen Gamert, the harness maker's son, or to one of the merchant proctors who could give the family better placement in the market stalls.

Fear that she had dreamed it all: the Citadel, and magic, and learning.

Xolnax's daughter glanced at her over the green gauze of her veil. Golden eyes, like mountain wine. Just seeing her made Raeshaldis feel sticky and awkward and out of place, in her brother's clothing with her hair braided up under a cap. They'd both been sitting for hours, since Hathmar had spoken to them and left. The veiled girl showed no signs of impatience, only now and then stretched out one hand and conjured little illusions in her palm: once a pile of jewels, another time colored fire that danced. Shaldis had wondered then—and still wondered—if she thought they were being observed and wished to show possible watchers just what she could do.

Hathmar had only asked them each to kindle fire without touching the wood, and to make a pebble move.

They'll take her, thought Shaldis in panic. *They'll take her and not me.*

The thought turned her sick.

Don't send me back, she thought. *Don't make me go back to Grandfather's house, to marry Forpen*—whose silent, pliant father was her grandfather's best friend and whose mother was a bossy horror dreaded by every woman in the district. *Let me stay here and sweep the courtyards, just so I can read in the library, so I don't have to go home.*

Footfalls outside the door. The golden-eyed girl got to her

feet, readying a salaam of deepest respect while Shaldis scrambled awkwardly from her cushion as well. It would be Hathmar and Benno Sarn, Shaldis knew—and Benno Sarn was angry at her because she'd talked back to him the day before yesterday outside her room. *But that happened later than this*, she thought foggily, *maybe he won't remember*.

But it was a very tall, grim-faced young man with brilliant blue eyes under a heavy bar of brow, a young man whom Shaldis knew she ought to recognize, clothed in a laborer's baggy yellow trousers and coarse tunic, his black hair gathered back and lacquered into a severe soldierly knot. "Are you all right?" he asked.

Shaldis opened her eyes. Harsh light from the single window gouged her brain. Someone was murdering children somewhere close by. She hoped the murderer would finish quickly; the noise of their screaming was agony to her aching head. The air stank to heaven of blood, dung and garbage, so there was no question about where she was. "Don't send me home."

"Don't be silly," said Jethan.

(*Of course it's Jethan.*)

"I've been waiting for you since yesterday," he said, as if he suspected she'd spent the intervening time lolling at the baths eating candy. "What happened to you?"

"Long story." She drew a couple of deep breaths. Her lungs felt stronger than they had last night. She had a dim recollection of stumbling through the alleys of the Slaughterhouse last night—none whatever of how she'd gotten through the East Gate. The confusion was gone from her mind, but she felt bone tired and drained of strength. "Somebody poisoned me."

A miscalculated dose? she wondered. A sufficiently speedy application of oil, cayenne and a finger down her throat? Her mouth tasted as if she'd supped on badly prepared and extremely spicy garbage.

Or did someone want her incapacitated in some alley some-where, but not dead?

She opened her eyes again, noted by the light, which came in through the room's open door from Greasy Yard, that it was midmorning. The horns sounded over the city. If she listened as a wizard listens, she could hear Hathmar's voice lifted in the sun's brave song.

"I need a place to hide for a time, at least until I get some idea of who did it, and why."

"You can't stay *here*." He sounded as horrified as if Rae-shaldis had proposed matrimony.

"I have to get word to the Summer Concubine. Don't you have any furniture here?"

"What's furniture got to do with anything?" asked Jethan.

Shaldis closed her eyes again, to take a momentary rest be-fore answering him, and didn't wake again until the middle of the afternoon.

Hands folded on the white knots of her student belt, glancing now and then to the left and right to observe the budding wis-teria in the House of Six Willows' tiny garden as she walked, Foxfire Girl was conscious of appearing supremely unhurried. Every girl in the class had been aware of it when Chrysanthe-mum Lady herself had appeared in the dance pavilion, watch-ing the girls at an hour when she was usually arguing with the grocer. When she'd laid a hand on Foxfire Girl's sleeve as the girls were coming off the floor, all the others had crowded around the door, just out of her sight, to listen.

"Someone is here to see you."

She felt their eyes: Opal Girl and Wren Girl and Blue Flower Girl and the others. Felt too the stabbing glare of the

Honeysuckle Lady as she passed her by the baths, and smiled inside. Of course the girls were not supposed to have visitors and of course they sometimes did—men who glimpsed them in the supper rooms, who asked discreetly, *Who is that girl? The tall one in the black?*

That morning old Gecko Woman had slipped a note under the bowl of barley she'd given her at breakfast: *Know that Iorradus dreamed all night of you.*

And I of you, she thought, exhilarated, ablaze. Not only that he'd dreamed of her, but that he'd been willing to pay the exorbitant price Gecko Woman usually charged men to sneak notes to the girls. *And I of you.*

Today's horoscope promised "a blossoming of the roses of desire." She'd sent Gecko Woman to the Flowermarket early and wore in her black hair the two scandalously expensive red hothouse roses the old woman had bought at her command.

They'd all known of that, too. At least half of them bought Starbright Woman's horoscopes—they were by far the most accurate—and everyone in the fledglings' attics read the daily predictions for everyone else. She'd heard—felt—the whispers go around, had seen Opal Girl's widened eyes. Opal Girl had been with her when she'd sat up two nights ago, after the supper party when that cow Honeysuckle Woman had kept her from giving her special, ensorcelled tea to Iorradus. But she'd been clever. She'd watched the bowls as they were cleared away, had taken the fragments of the food he'd left, the tea dregs from his cup. Had stayed up half the night weaving spells of her own devising with the sun glyphs of his name.

Know that Iorradus dreamed all night of you.

There was a little pavilion off one of the gate lodges where the women of the House of Willows could speak to admirers who came in the day to visit. As she crossed the moss-stained stepping-stones and approached the delicate paper screens,

Foxfire Girl heard Chrysanthemum Lady's voice. "Here she comes, my lord." The screen slid open.

The man on the divan was Foxfire Girl's father.

"Papa!" All pretense of being a Pearl Woman, a damsel of the House of Blossoms, a worthy pupil of the arts of civilized joy, dissolved, and Foxfire Girl caught up her parakeet-colored gauze skirts and threw herself into her father's arms.

"Child, I'm very sure this isn't how your preceptors have instructed you." Her father's narrow face was wreathed in joy. He hugged her close; she felt his strong arms under the gray-and-black-striped linen of his simple jacket.

"Stand straight, child," added Chrysanthemum Lady in her cool, melodious voice. "Let your father see that your manners at his special supper the other night weren't mere show for company."

"When I came into the supper room and saw you there, it was everything I could do not to smile at you," said Foxfire Girl breathlessly, straightening up and holding her head high. She'd dislodged two of her long jade hairpins in the embrace but knew that to readjust her coiffure in a man's presence was worse than having it disordered. A Pearl Woman's perfection lies, in part, in her sureness of it no matter what her hair looks like. She met her father's eyes—bright, cool, glimmering jade, like her own and her grandmother's—and smiled.

"My Lord Mohrvine." Chrysanthemum Lady swayed down in a deep salaam. "The calligraphy master teaches the girls at the third hour. Shall I give warning in time for that?"

"Do." Foxfire Girl's father nodded genially, and the woman slipped shut the screen behind her, closing them into the sunlit room with the clatter of the noise from the street. "There is a time to smile at those we love," he added, turning his eyes back to his daughter, "and a time to keep our minds on business. I'm glad you're learning the difference, child."

"Well, since you placed me here and talked to Chrysanthemum Lady about me, I knew you had to understand." Foxfire Girl looked around her, saw that a plate of dates and goat cheese had already been brought, and a teapot of silver and glass. "May I pour you out tea, Father? I see Chrysanthemum Lady has already cheated me out of serving you."

"And here's the girl who wouldn't put her own hairpins in a dish! You may pour me out a little more tea. That cup is for you." It stood already poured out, on the side of the table nearest her; larger and deeper than the minute glass vessels that were all a Blossom Lady could consume in public, and musky smelling. Mint tea was drunk in the evenings, green tea in the day. This was smoke-cured tea, of the kind generally consumed first thing in the morning, when her father preferred coffee. "Chrysanthemum Lady tells me you do well in your studies here, and I saw the other night that she spoke the truth."

"I have marvelous teachers." She salaamed a little as she said it, to cover up the glow of unmaidenly delight at the praise.

"Did you have a chance, in the course of your excellent service the other night, to observe anything of the men you served? They observed you."

She felt the color surge to her face and knew that the light dusting of rice powder didn't hide it. A Pearl Woman would have praised the damsels whose dancing was supposed to be the main attraction of the evening, the lady whose graceful conversation had kept the room aglow. But she could think only of Iorradus touching her hand.

She whispered, "I know."

"Do you now?"

She peeped at him under her lashes; he was smiling.

"So what do you think of House Akarian?"

Her cheeks warmed still further. She wanted to say, *That*

they have the most beautiful man in the world as one of their own, but knew she couldn't: "That if Lord Akarian truly accepts the principles of Iron-Girdled Nebekht, they'd probably better have a skilled cook."

He flung back his head with that flashing silent smile that for him was a shout of laughter; she'd never seen him do so with anyone else. "They're binding that lunatic Lohar to them; winning his loyalty, and with it that of all his followers. The old man's already in the inner circle of the temple. I've heard he's grooming the younger son to be initiated as a priest."

"Are the followers of Nebekht really that powerful, for Akarian to do that?" Mischievously, she added, "Perhaps you'd better call back Sormaddin from up north and have him cut his hair like that." She named her least favorite brother, and her father gave her a reprovingly lifted eyebrow and no reply.

"I wouldn't have said so," he said instead, and sipped his tea. "But Akarian isn't thinking like a clan lord about them. I believe he really thinks what Lohar says Nebekht wants is true: that mankind should follow his word, regardless of their other responsibilities. And last night, I'm told, there was trouble in the Slaughterhouse, so bad that the city proctors called the watch out: a hundred people or more gathering to stone the house of some clerk Lohar had it in for, enough to fill three streets. I didn't know Lohar could call so many, so quickly."

"But aren't they just laborers and layabouts?" As a child she would have said, *They're just laborers and layabouts,* but Chrysanthemum Lady had impressed upon her that every remark addressed to a man had to be in the form of a question that he could answer, information that he could impart, and it had grown to be a habit with her. And a little to her surprise, her father warmed toward her as men did toward Honeysuckle Lady; even her father, she thought with an inward smile, couldn't resist being a pedagogue.

"Not anymore, obviously, if the uppermost lords of the House Akarian have become members. And don't speak ill of laborers and layabouts, child," he added. "They have their uses. Particularly as the wells run low, and that imbecile nephew of mine makes new demands for a project that will cripple every house from highest to lowest, and bind every man to his service if it succeeds. Tell me, child. Would you object to a husband from the House Akarian?"

She blushed again, and turned her face away. *I knew it,* she thought, *I knew it,* and felt again Iorradus's warm, virile touch on her fingertips. Saw his face as she'd conjured it in her dreams, bending over hers. . . .

The blossoming of the roses of desire.

She'd seen Iorradus's face in the few minutes she'd snatched that morning, between her own scrub and that of Opal Girl, when she'd taken a mirror, as wizards were supposed to be able to do, and had gazed into it in the semidark of their attic room.

He'd been ankle deep in the straw of a stable, feeding an apple to a black mare while his groom stood smiling by. A long-legged colt, black like the mare, wobbled about in the straw, nuzzling the young man's pockets for treats. The sight had startled her; unexpected, tiny, distant, like a miniature painted in glass. But the fact of the vision itself didn't surprise her. It was like something she had dreamed about. Something she had always known. Looking back on it now, a few hours later, she wasn't entirely sure it hadn't been a dream.

Except that never in her life had she heard a ballad that involved a wizard calling someone's image in a crystal and seeing him in his stable feeding a horse.

Iorradus had looked unutterably dear, with the first slant of the early sunlight haloing his head in fire. His linen tunic had been open at the throat, the points of his collarbone visible, his sleeves turned up over tanned forearms.

Know that Iorradus dreamed all night of you.

The roses of desire . . .

She felt her face pinken again.

Maybe it was only a dream. Maybe the little conjurations she'd started to do were only dreams: the powder she'd prepared, and put into his tea at the supper, that Honeysuckle Lady, the hag, had intercepted; the incense and sigil and ashes she'd burned, to put herself in his dreams. The ants in Honeysuckle Lady's room. They didn't let wizards marry. If she spoke of any of this to her father it would put paid to any hope of being Iorradus's wife, not to mention that if her father was courting Nebekht's prophet he probably wouldn't welcome the news that his daughter was trying to see her beloved's face in mirrors.

It probably was only a dream. And the ants only an accident. She had used honey in making the marks, after all.

"No," she murmured, barely audibly—not as a Pearl Woman should speak, she knew, but she was not able to say more. "No, I wouldn't object."

"Good," purred her father. "Excellent. Tomorrow night there will be a supper for Lord Akarian—and some of his guests—at House Jothek. I think it would be appropriate if you waited upon us there. Call it a test of your training." He smiled. "Now drink your tea."

NINETEEN

"What's furniture got to do with anything?" asked Jethan again when Shaldis finally opened her eyes.

It was evening. The whole world smelled of dust and greasy cooking.

The children outside were still screaming, but a voice Shaldis recognized as Rosemallow Woman's was yelling at them to shut up.

"To make it look like you're not just staying here for a few days on somebody's orders." Shaldis sat up, waited for the room to stop swaying, then fished in her satchel for her spell tablets. There were still twenty-five of them. Her hands shook but she felt better, and ravenously hungry. "What did you tell the landlord?"

"Preket? I didn't tell him anything. I told him I wanted to rent the room. The Summer Concubine isn't back from the aqueduct yet, by the way; I sent one of the children to ask around the market whether the king's procession had returned."

"Curse." Shaldis looked around her. The room was more barren than any cell in a barracks. There wasn't even a lamp: just the water jar, the gourd cup, the pillowless blanket and a broom. The broom was typical of Jethan. The dirt floor was spotless, the hearth clean as a bridal chamber. "And the people in the court didn't ask questions?"

"What business is it of theirs?" He looked surprised at the thought that they'd even take notice of a new neighbor.

Shaldis rolled her eyes. "What business is it of theirs that Turquoise Woman bolted her door during the day? What business is it who Rosemallow Woman is sleeping with, or what names Preket's wife calls him when they fight?" She'd heard both of these topics discussed outside in the yard—even with the door shut voices carried like plague in the summer—during the hours she'd lain between sleep and waking. "In a court like this everybody knows everybody's business. You might as well just hang a sign on the door saying, I'm Just Staying Here for a Purpose. New bedding, new water jar, no apparent work. Of course everybody here knows you're working for someone."

"So?" Jethan settled himself cross-legged on the floor in the corner farthest from the bed, his back straight as if on parade. Shaldis wondered what he'd done here for the past three days other than sweep the floor.

"So people talk about anything that seems unusual to them. And it's not going to take long for our friend, whoever he is, to learn that the Summer Concubine is asking questions, especially if he isn't a Sun Mage after all. From her to me isn't a big leap, which means that as a hiding place this is about as secretive as my room in the Citadel." She finished sorting the tablets into which sigils she could make work and which she couldn't, and pulled up her spattered and filthy outer robe— which had doubled as a blanket over an immensely proportioned and very dirty cotton nightdress—around her shoulders. "Don't you have any coffee here?"

"I don't drink it." The young guardsman's tone implied that neither should women who were proper women.

"That explains a lot about you. Can you make yourself useful and get me some from the café near the Temple of Phon south of the road? Get me some food, too, if you would." She found her belt and purse on the heap of her robe beside the mattress and dug in the purse for money, which Sun Mages weren't supposed to carry. There wasn't much left of the little hoard of dequins she'd had in her pockets when she'd fled her grandfather's house. In addition to nightlong nausea on top of a day without anything to eat except a few vanilla wafers, some apricot paste, and a lot of tea—poisoned, at that—she had worked more magic yesterday than she had ever done continuously outside the Summoning of the Rain, and as usual felt that if she couldn't get sweets she would die. Women weren't supposed to wear purses, either; a respectable woman was to look to her husband for money, as Sun Mages were to look to the college. It always gave Shaldis a sense of exhilaration to handle money like a man. "On the way back could you stop at that slop-shop on the corner of Hot Pillow Lane and get me a dress and some veils? I can't keep a cloak over myself the whole time I'm here."

"I thought you could do any sort of magic you chose," retorted Jethan, and took his departure before she could reply, pointedly ignoring the handful of copper and silver she held out to him.

Beyond the room's shut door she heard Melon Girl call out, "'Morning, Excellency," in a languid voice, with a dip in it as inviting as if she'd pulled up her dress—which Shaldis reflected she might very well have also done, for all the good it was likely to do her. His footfalls neither paused nor altered stride as Shaldis's mage-born hearing traced them across the yard:

"Xolnax's boys never heard of him," she heard the prostitute remark quietly as the young guardsman's tread lost itself in the yammer of the street.

"You stupid sow—Xolnax would never give one of his goons money for a new blanket," retorted Rosemallow Woman. "I think he's got to be from out of town."

"You mean Udon's gang from Reeds, or one of the boys from over the White Walls?" She lowered her voice still further. "Why send a man here? You think they'd try for a takeover?"

"Well, if the wells over there are drying quicker than they are here . . ."

Shaldis grinned to herself, wrapped Jethan's red cloak around her shoulders and strolled to the door with the hem of it dragging. Rosemallow Woman sat next to her door spinning wool with a simple weight and distaff, while Melon Girl sat next to her painting her fingernails, neither woman veiled and neither of them taking the slightest heed of Zarb and his friend Vorm drinking in Zarb's doorway and talking about cockfights, as they appeared to have been doing for decades. Melon Girl looked up and called out to her, "Hey," and Shaldis idled over, doing her best to walk like the girls in the market.

"Hey," she replied. "Thanks for the loan of the dress." She flipped the sleeve of the nightdress, which she'd deduced had to belong to the short, plump Melon Girl. The young harlot's round and extremely pink painted face broke into a lazy smile.

"I asked your boyfriend what you wanted a dress for. You all right now? He said you were sick, and cold with it. . . ."

"Honey, I thought I'd shiver to death." Shaldis propped a shoulder companionably against the wall. "You probably saved my life. I'd have paid money to see Jethan borrowing it, though," she added, with a giggle she hoped was flirtatious. "I mean, he's a sweet boy, but wherever he's from, they raise 'em strict there."

The other women laughed. Shaldis supposed she should have realized that the neighbors would jump to the conclusion not that Jethan was a guardsman, but that Jethan—obviously trained in war, obviously well fed, obviously doing nothing to earn his own living—was a bullyboy for one of the city's gang leaders staking out the district.

I'll have to tell him, she thought. And then, *Maybe I'd better not. Whatever unconvincing story he'll come up with if anyone asks will sound a whole lot more like a genuine lie if he's not trying to make himself sound like a thug at the same time.*

"You from town, sweetheart?" asked Melon Girl. "We thought you'd be back, seeing you here with old Stone-Face Jethan the other day."

Shaldis shrugged. "Over by the Bazaar," she said. She was tempted to claim origin outside the city—White Lake or the Lake of Reeds—but wasn't sure she could get the accent right.

Besides, she didn't know enough of the intervillage affairs out-side the Yellow City, and to pretend knowledge was simply asking to be tripped up. She ran a self-conscious hand over the straggling lacquered snags of her undone hair, added, "Boy, did I have a night last night. . . . I know it's asking a lot, but could one of you lend me a mirror? I feel like such a teyn. . . ."

"Sweetheart, don't we all have mornings like this?" It was at least five hours past noon, but Shaldis groaned and nodded in agreement, and Melon Girl heaved herself to her feet and trotted to her own room, which was next to that of Rosemallow Woman. Shaldis extemporized a name for herself—Golden Eagle Girl—and a brief and fictitious history of meeting Jethan at the Hospi-tality of BoSaa Café, and listened to Rosemallow Woman's account of Preket the landlord's iniquities and what a nuisance it was to live so close to the Temple of Nebekht, with lunatics com-ing and going all night and the absolute stink of the animals they were always killing there, and Lohar rampaging through every few days to throw stones at Turquoise Woman's door.

"The poor girl never did anybody any harm! Not like that Corn-Tassel Woman, who was always claiming she could do this or that with her magic. She all but killed Normac's poor dog, putting a spell on it to shut it up from barking just because a friend of hers asked her to. Then Normac's house was robbed because the poor thing couldn't make a sound besides just a lit-tle hoarse wheeze, and it broke my heart to hear it try to bark. She couldn't take the spell off it, either, after that."

"Cattail Woman is worse." Melon Girl emerged with a cheap brass mirror, which she held out to Shaldis. "She lives over in the Fishmarket, and she's always doing things 'for your own good,' like making her friends' husbands impotent after they've had a fight—"

"Like *that's* going to make them friendlier," put in Rosemal-low Woman.

"—or putting ward spells on the whole neighborhood that are supposed to drive away rats but that make everybody's chickens lay out and their pigs stray as well. Sometimes I think old Lohar has a point about women doing magic bringing nothing but trouble. At least wizards don't do anything much besides healing and spell warding."

Shaldis returned with the mirror to Jethan's room, and settled herself once again on his blanket. On the two or three occasions that she'd been instructed in scrying, it had been with a crystal specially ensorcelled to show her faraway scenes. She'd never attempted to communicate with another mage through it. But before all else, the Summer Concubine had to be told of yesterday's events. She was still trying to summon the concubine's image in the mirror when Jethan returned, bearing a round wicker basket of bread, fruit, and soft goat-milk cheese, a little sack of coffee beans, and a mortar, pestle, pan and coffeepot all wrapped together in a netted string shopping bag. He also had a horrifying green-and-yellow-striped dress.

"It was the only thing they had," he said into Shaldis's appalled silence. He frowned at her expression in the dense gloom of advancing evening. "What's wrong with it?"

"Nothing, if I needed money in a hurry." She held the thin, tight, low-cut bosom to her shallow breasts, inspected the grimy golden bows on the front, the clinging petticoats and ostentatious, front-fastening girdle.

"I got you veils." He held them out. They were pink and almost transparent. "I think it's pretty," he added, and under his defensive tone she detected chagrin that she didn't approve of his choice.

"You're supposed to."

Shaldis changed clothes while Jethan resolutely looked at the wall. "I'll have to go out later and buy some paint, I suppose," she said, settling once more on the floor and picking up the mirror again. She had no idea how such a thing was applied—her veils looked like laundry on a wash line. "By the way, I told the neighbors that I'm your girlfriend. Golden Eagle Girl."

"*Golden Eagle Girl?*" She didn't know whether he was more disgusted by the name or by the idea.

"Why can't a woman be named after something splendid?"

"Eagles eat carrion," pointed out Jethan. "And no woman should be able to—"

"Devil spawn!" roared a piercing voice from the street beyond the court. "Transgressor! It is your stubbornness, your wicked willfulness, that has brought down drought and the wrath of Nebekht on us all!"

"Not again," groaned Jethan. "This happened last night too. If I hear Lohar one more time about wizards . . ."

"Wait a minute—who's he calling a wizard?" Shaldis yanked the larger of the two pink veils back over her hair, wrapped the smaller around her face as she pulled open the door and strode across the dusty stink of the court. The children were already streaming through the gate to watch the fun, the men who'd been drinking in the doorway ambling after.

Most of the people gathered in Little Pig Alley were of the same type: loafers, or the lowest type of artisans taking a break from their work. A couple of men from the slaughterhouse were with them, flies circling the blood on their hands and clothing; the women who did the flensing tagged along with their knives still in hand. Lohar marched ahead, managing to keep up his tirade even while he bent and picked up rocks, dog filth, and broken bottles from the roadway to pelt his target, a stooped, balding man whose tight-screwed little face was gouged with bitter wrinkles of resentment and hate.

". . . have not repented, have not seen *even yet* the sin of your blindness, the sin which draws the righteous punishment of Nebekht upon the whole of the Valley of the Lakes!"

"You bastards think I asked to give up my power?" screamed back the little man. His voice was old and cracked, his movements stiff, and something about him snagged at Shaldis's memory, as if she knew him. "You think I like writing Xolnax's letters for him? You think I like living in a stinking hovel?"

"Still you seek to regain what was rightfully taken from you, Earth Wizard! Dirt wizard! Dung wizard! *This* is your blindness! *This* is your sin!"

"Damned right it's my sin and if I still had it in me I'd put a wyrd on your bowels that'd have you praying day and night to Nebekht for relief!" The man called Earth Wizard turned at bay before his house, jabbed a skinny finger at Lohar and his followers, who had swelled, Shaldis was disconcerted to see, into a crowd that blocked the whole of the street. "You're a crazy man, you know that? I know you, Lohar! Listen to me, all of you! This man started drinking *ijnis* ten years ago, he was so afraid he'd lose his powers!"

"Lies! All lies!" Lohar had a voice like storm wind in the Eastern Cliffs. He flung up his arms, face distorted in a pop-eyed grimace of passion. "In his house he still keeps the devil books, the vile books of spells, seeking to regain that which the great Nebekht rightfully took away."

"And how rightfully did your great Iron-Dicked One take it away from you, pal?" The little man ducked, flinched as a rain of rocks and bottles shattered on the wall around him, bloodying his face and upraised arms. He dropped the satchel he carried, record tablets and scrolls tumbling into the dirt of the street, fumbled with a latchkey at the door. The mob, encouraged, began to fling half bricks and chunks of adobe and tiles. "I'm watching you! I'm watching you all!" screamed the former Earth Wizard. "Just wait until one of you wants to borrow money from my master, or buy water—damn it!" He slipped through the door of the little house, and Shaldis, stretching out mage-born senses, heard the scrape of a bar over the door, the scratching of furniture shoved against it.

The mob closed around the house, hammering the door and window shutters, cursing and screaming and pelting the walls with garbage. Others gleefully tore up the papers their quarry had dropped, or hurled the tablets into the air. Jethan drew Shaldis aside.

"He's all right," he said.

Footfalls thudded in the narrow street; someone shouted, "Here, what's all this, then?" and people began to disperse, fast, in the face of the constables of the watch.

"Who is he?"

Jethan shrugged.

"Xolnax's clerk." Melon Girl appeared behind them in the narrow street, what appeared to be an entire garden of silk flowers flourishing tipsily in her garish curls. "Urla, he calls himself, Urnate Urla."

Shaldis startled, remembering the face now, remembering the blue eyes. He'd had a beard in those days, and the long pig-tail Earth Wizards generally wore. His hair had been black then, too. She recalled him as a soft-voiced man, always ready to lay a mouse ward on a kitchen or mosquito spells on windows. He'd been very well off then, and a good wizard.

"I remember him when I was a little girl coming into Mama's kitchen to witch it against rats." Rosemallow Woman joined them as they walked back around the twisting alley to Greasy Yard, one of her little girls—Five-Fish, a delicate, fair child—on her hip. Her mouth twisted a little at the sound of his name. "He slipped a candy to me when I was fourteen that gave me dreams of him—what dreams!—for weeks, and when I'd see him I couldn't hardly help myself, wanting him to kiss me . . . ugh!" She flinched, and hugged Five-Fish tight. "Later on I found out I wasn't the only girl in the neighborhood he'd lay those spells on, either."

Shaldis looked over her shoulder at the shut door of the house, the closed shutters. It was true, she thought, that he'd always been giving candies to children. She'd only thought he was kindly at the time.

Maybe Jethan wasn't the only naive one.

"Serves him right." Melon Girl cast a speculative glance up and down Jethan's strapping form. "Preket's like that, you know, our landlord—not a wizard, I don't mean, but if I had a little boy I'd move. I guess just because a man's a wizard doesn't mean he's a decent man. Now old Pomegranate Woman, she's crazy as a bedbug, and she can write mouse wards that really work and do a little healing. . . . She fixed my cat's broken foot, anyway."

"Like Murder Girl's foot wouldn't have healed up anyway?" demanded Rosemallow Woman with good-natured sarcasm. "Pomegranate Woman claims she can make rocks and bricks and pieces of old glass talk to her too." She turned to Shaldis. "Pomegranate Woman lives out in the ruins, and she has this imaginary pig—she used to have a real pig, but he got run over by a cart about five years ago, so now she has an imaginary one. Old Urla, he'd always act so meek, but you could tell he thought it gave him rights over everyone, just because he could do healing. Like it was something he'd done, instead of something the gods gave him just for coming out of his mother's belly like everybody else. And now there he is, working for a couple pennies a week for a crocodile like Xolnax."

She glanced back in the direction of the shut door, the mud-spattered house, hidden now by the turn of the walls. Lohar could still be heard shouting alternately at the constables and at Urnate Urla behind his enclosing walls: "Not until the king bows to Nebekht will Nebekht open the skies to the people! Not until Nebekht is acknowledged in all his greatness, his infinite greatness, will the rains return. . . ."

Melon Girl sniffed. "The gods only know how he's getting laid these days," and ducked into her room to get herself ready for business.

"I wonder," said Shaldis softly.

She spent the remainder of the evening alternately sitting before the little brass mirror, staring into her reflection—staring past her reflection—and meditating on the Sigil of Sisterhood, and writing Sigil after Sigil of Deep Listening on the walls. But her concentration kept sliding away, broken by bouts of dizziness. At last she gave up trying to scry the events within the room and concentrated on conjuring the Summer Concubine's name and image. Trying to summon her, to warn her—trying at the same time to put from her mind all the things that tugged it away: the foul memory of the spells that whispered in the door of her Citadel room, the glowing ward sign on the peeling stucco wall of House Jothek, and the sharp wary eyes of the Red Silk Lady. *He'll use you as he uses everyone . . . as Oryn will use you.*

Tried to put aside the resentment that pulled at her heart with every groan of the Citadel's horns, with every whisper of chanting that the desert wind brought down from the bluff.

The red God Sun, as it was called—the sun's final name—seemed to swell and flatten as it touched the waters of the lake, slipped away out of sight and gave way to cloudless night.

"The Red Silk Lady is a Raven, like us."

"Good heavens!" The Summer Concubine sat, a little numbly, on the leather cushion before her dressing table and stared in surprise into the depths of the mirror where she saw reflected not her own face, but that of Raeshaldis of the Sun Mages. "My dear, are you all right?" she asked, seeing in the next moment—the light where the girl sat was not at all good; the tiny glimmer of a tallow-soaked reed, it looked like—how haggard her face was, how hollow her eyes and cheeks. "Have you been ill?"

"Not exactly ill. I was poisoned; I've been trying to reach you all day."

"Poisoned?" Having found, at last, the small talismans marked with a jumble of Earth Wizard signs that had been buried beneath the scaffolding, she and Soth had spent the day riding with a small detachment of guards through the Dead Hills searching for the place where the talismans had been en-sorcelled. Her body ached now from the hours spent in the saddle, and she thought with longing of the baths in the Summer Pavilion, and of her horoscope for the day: *You will yearn for that which is far away.*

The horoscope had added the admonition that rose pink was a lucky color for water-influenced Five-Rabbits—which the Summer Concubine was—to wear.

"It might have been Ahure," said Shaldis. "Lord Jamornid may be thinking of hiring me—I don't know how he knows I've been having trouble in the Citadel, but something made him think I might be looking for a new job. And Ahure knows he's damn well not going to be able to convince anyone of his powers once he's out of that fake lair of his. And it could have been Aktis, acting under orders from Lord Mohrvine, who'll do just about anything to undercut the king's power. And it might have been Red Silk Lady, who apparently hasn't told Mohrvine about her powers and isn't going to."

"Did she tell you this?"

"Not in so many words. *Someone* in her household definitely has magic. There are ward signs at her gate, and in the walkway leading there. She claims to 'suspect' one of the servants, as if a woman like her wouldn't have found out the moment she 'suspected.' She said that Mohrvine uses everyone who comes to his hand, and I got the impression she wasn't about to be used. She may have poisoned me simply because she thought I suspected. She hides in a run-down courtyard at the far end of the compound, which I don't think would be the case if Mohrvine was using her powers. As far as I could tell, the court-yard isn't guarded. And the ward signs she used to protect it are Pyromancer signs—and badly distorted ones at that—instead of the earth signs Aktis would have taught her."

"The Red Silk Lady," the Summer Concubine murmured, and ran her hands through her dusty hair. All her fears and ap-prehensions—everything Oryn had said to her about the deli-cate balance of power with Mohrvine and the other clan lords, based on the enslavement of the teyn—came back to her, turning her cold and ill.

"I sent Jethan out to the aqueduct camp with a message, in case I couldn't get through to you at all," Raeshaldis went on. "I wrote it in blood on a brass circle and then wiped it away— the spellmaster at the college once told me that was the easi-est kind of message for a mage to summon back. He should get to you sometime tonight."

Just in time to wake me up urgently, thought the Summer Concubine with an inward sigh. Jethan was such a desperately conscientious young man that telling him tactfully that his message could wait until morning might not work.

"Did you learn anything of Turquoise Woman?" she asked after a time. "Did you find anything with your scrying?"

"Not yet. I'll try again in the morning—I think the poison is still interfering with my ability to work. But it's got to be the same person who attacked me. I can't imagine a woman with power being carried away by someone who had none. It isn't necessarily someone from the college, either. Anyone with power could have gotten past the Citadel's gates. And another thing: According to Rosemallow Woman, there's another Raven who lives in the ruins out beyond the Slaughterhouse, someone named Pomegranate Woman. I think I need to find her, warn her . . . and warn Xolnax's daughter Amber Girl as well, though the gods know how I'm going to get to Amber Girl. Xolnax apparently keeps her pretty close."

"Have you heard anything about her working magic?"

Shaldis shook her head. "I haven't had much time to ask, but I think if anyone in the district knew about it, they'd have said. It stands to reason he'd keep it a secret, with the True Believers so strong around here. What did you find out about the aqueduct? Did you sense a power that's . . . kind of cold and jangly feeling? Prickly, like the smell of the air before a storm?"

The Summer Concubine shook her head. The smell of lamb stew and fresh breads filled the tent, mingling with that of steam and scented oil. Blessed rest, blessed quiet, save for Jasmine and Lupine giggling together as they set out the wash things in the tent's opulent silk-curtained bath cubicle. Oryn would sup with Bax and Ykem again. All the Summer Concubine wanted to do was sleep, but she knew he'd be in late and would need, like Raeshaldis, to know what she'd found.

"The marks I found were indistinct, only conduits, Soth said, for power that was raised elsewhere, with a circle of some sort. That way the mage had only to place the talismans—the hex marks were written on copper dequin coins—without having to divert his attention from the cloak that kept him safe from the guards. We searched for such a thing among the tombs of the Dead Hills. There was one, a Hosh Dynasty tomb, the only south-facing tomb on the hills, that looks out over the desert. Every time we passed its entrance we both felt there was some power there, but we couldn't find a way in.

We'll go back there tomorrow. Where are you now, dearest? Are you somewhere safe?"

"Where's safe?" returned Shaldis. "Whoever it is who's after me, he knows to look in the Citadel. I'm in Turquoise Woman's room." She gestured behind her. The Summer Concubine saw that the chamber, tiny as it was, had been further divided by muslin sheets hung on a rope, like crude curtains, which when drawn across would officially separate the room into *seryak* and harem. "I'm with Jethan, except I sent him with the message to you. Who let him in the guards, anyway? He should be a nursemaid!"

The Summer Concubine smiled in spite of the day's weariness and anxiety. "Will you be all right there? You could go to the palace if you don't feel safe in the Citadel."

"If you can figure out a way to keep my presence unknown to the servants, that might be a good idea, but offhand, without you there, I'd be afraid to try it. At least down here I'm known as someone else—I'm supposed to be Jethan's girlfriend Golden Eagle Girl—and nobody knows I'm a Raven instead of a golden eagle."

That explained, thought the Summer Concubine with another, inner, smile, the too-pink stains of cochineal on Raeshaldis's thin cheeks, and the fact that her long brown hair, formerly slicked back into the tight knot demanded by Sun Mage austerity, now lay in loose heavy waves over her shoulders. She'd changed clothes, too, into a startling green-and-gold dress that revealed curves and softness unguessed in her rangy body.

"I'll try again tomorrow to see what I can see here, after I've had time to sleep and let the last of the poison work out of my system. I told Rosemallow Woman I had a former boyfriend who might be looking for me, and she's got a couple of her children recruited to keep an eye on the place through the night. I don't know how safe that'll make me, but I don't know how safe *anywhere* is. I've put every ward and wyrd I can think of on the door and window bolts, but all I can do is hope for the best."

Looking at the smudges under Shaldis's eyes, the Summer Concubine would not have bet a worn hairpin on the girl's being able to stay awake for more than a few minutes after she put aside her scrying mirror. Shaldis was right: Trying to install her anywhere in the House of the Marvelous Tower, now that the gates were shut for the night, would be risky, and there was no way to keep servants from talking. So she only said, "Speak to me through the mirror tomorrow at"—she was about to say dawn, then took another look at the girl's exhausted face and amended it—"noon. Just so that I know you're all right. Do you need a message sent to the Citadel?"

Shaldis sighed and shook her head. "Until I know who's after me," she said, "I have to assume that it could be anyone, in the Citadel or outside. Anyone who has power. The gods know what Hathmar's thinking: I only had a few hours' leave yesterday to speak to you. I may not even be welcome there when I go back." She spoke casually, but the Summer Concubine heard the strain in her voice.

She is isolated, and terrified, she thought, *cut off from the Sun Mages for whom she traded her family. Divorced from family and friends.*

She wondered where she got her strength.

"Whatever happens," the Summer Concubine said firmly, "I—or the king—will deal with Hathmar. You won't lose your place in the college over what you're doing. So sleep well, dearest. We'll speak in the morning, and all will come out right."

Shaldis smiled, like marble melting into life. "Thank you."

The mirror went dark.

TWENTY

Through the following day—from dawn when, in spite of her exhaustion, she woke as all Sun Mages wake with the coming of the light, until the horns of the Citadel ceased with darkness—Raeshaldis examined every inch of wall and floor in Turquoise Woman's room. Examined them with not just one spell, not just one set of instructions and sigils and alignments of power, but with all twenty-five, even those that she hadn't been able to make work at the Citadel.

And found nothing.

"It's maddening," she said to the Summer Concubine when at noon she settled into the coolest corner of the room with oranges, bread and oil, and the mirror she'd gone out to the Grand Bazaar to buy as soon as the day grew light. "I know he put spells on the latch. But I can't get a thing. I nearly burned the place down calling fire to make sure the poison was out of my system. Were you able to ask Soth about spells I might use?"

"I did. He said he'd write them up today—he was barely awake when I spoke to him this morning, poor man, and green with headache—and send them to you by way of Jethan. Jethan orders you to go back to the Citadel at once. . . ."

"Of course he does."

"And he was horrified that you'd spent the night in Turquoise Woman's rooms without protection. I take it all was well?"

Shaldis nodded, though her dreams had been foul. She'd waked again and again, sweating and trembling, the buzzing horror of remembered evil scalding her, only to find the darkness peaceful, or as peaceful as it ever got in the Slaughter-house.

"Did you find a way into the Hosh tomb yet?" she asked, for she saw that the Summer Concubine sat, dressed and veiled for riding, in the narrow shade of a wadi somewhere. The concubine shook her head.

"I understand many of these old tombs are connected by grave robbers' tunnels, but we haven't made much headway. It is . . . a fearful place. Most of the old magic that was laid on the tombs—the curses, and wards, and those strange old spell glyphs against what seem to be local spirits that the Hosh believed in—most of that's dead now. But we're going carefully all the same. Soth told me last night what he remembered of protective wyrds, but I should hate to find he's forgotten something important."

After the concubine's image faded from the mirror, Shaldis sat still for a time, gazing around her at the stubbornly uncommunicative walls. Her head ached and she felt exhausted, though it was barely past noon. Her shoulders were stiff from the repeated gestures of passing her hands over every square inch of wall surface, and her palms were rough and black with transferred dirt.

I need to get out of here for a while, she thought. *I need to rest.*

At a guess it would be long after dark before Jethan returned, and then it would be all to do again with whatever sigils Soth sent.

Voices in the yard. Looking out into the harsh sunlight, Shaldis saw Melon Girl and Rosemallow Woman emerge from the doorway opposite, bundles under their arms made of towels, scrapers and gourds of oil, ointment and soap. Shaldis snatched up her own veils and the bath supplies she'd purchased at the same time as the mirror that morning, and caught up with the two women—without the slightest appearance of hurry—as they were going out the gate.

"I swear I don't know what men think women are," she said, falling into step with them as they stepped into the street. "Or doesn't 'come with me and I'll take care of you' mean 'I'll let you know if I'm going to disappear some night'? Here's your mirror back—I can't tell you how grateful I am for the loan. Are you on your way to the baths? Can I go with you? I have no idea where things are in this neighborhood."

As they massaged and oiled and scraped and scrubbed each other in an exceedingly grubby establishment just inside the Eastern Gate, Shaldis picked up whatever gossip she hadn't managed to glean just by leaving the door open yesterday—more, in fact, than she'd heard since her days of roving the marketplaces as a child. For eighteen months she had been relatively immured, hearing little except those things that affected the Sun Mages. Even of that she hadn't heard much, since she ate alone and spent most of her spare hours in the library or reading in her rooms. She had heard the masters say things like *The people are grumbling because of the drought;* now she felt the hot wind of rebellion breathe on the back of her neck.

"Of course the rich'll take it all. . . ."

"The king's a fool—Greatsword would never have let things get this bad. . . ."

"I think Lohar's crazy, but he has a point. Why should we be the ones to suffer when it's the king's rich friends who're causing the problem?"

Shaldis listened uneasily, contributing only as much as would keep the pot stirring as they basked in the breathless heat of the tiny steam chamber ("They're only using about half the water they used to, and dirty water, too"). Wondering if the king, or any of the clan lords, truly understood how deep the current of blame was that trickled through the poorer districts of town.

"Of course the Sun Mages are the king's pets. That's why he's not letting other wizards bring the rain."

"They could do it if they wanted. They did, didn't they, right after the full moon. One pissy little shower, and that not enough to get the streets wet hardly. . . ."

"I swear I thought all our troubles were over. . . ."

"Well, what do you expect? If this aquaduck brings in water, they'll quit calling rain completely. Why give people free rain when you can sell water from an aquaduck?"

"My husband says Greatsword was in full health and lively as you or me the night before he was struck dead without a mark on him. . . ."

He died of a stroke, Shaldis wanted to shout at her; *what does your idiot husband know about anything?*

"Vorm says they're going to tax where you live: Pay it or they put you in the street and brick up the door. . . ."

"I'd like to see 'em try with Preket. . . ."

Hanging around her grandfather's kitchen in her girlhood, Shaldis had heard grumbling before. But it had been mostly neighborhood gossip, the usual complaints about husbands and in-laws and the high cost of water and fuel. Even during the bad years, the women had still been mostly concerned with the day-to-day annoyances of their lives.

"I bet old Xolnax will take his bite of whatever money we pay," she remarked casually as she rebraided Melon Girl's fanciful Tree of Life coiffure. "You'd never see that stuck-up daughter of his around here, I'll bet." She had no idea whether Amber Girl was stuck up or not: The one time they'd been in the same room she'd been so sick with apprehension herself she hadn't been able to speak a word. But by her companions' derisive whinnies, she guessed she'd hit the mark.

"You won't see her much of anywhere," jeered Rosemallow Woman, pulling on her much-stained purple linen dress. "Two nights before the full moon she ran off with some man, which should go to show old Xolnax what comes of keeping a girl that age locked up, fancy tutors or no fancy tutors."

"Tutors?" So the Summer Concubine's fears might have been justified, thought Shaldis. Xolnax evidently had had his daughter taught.

"Wanted her to learn to read the stars," provided Melon Girl. "Corner the market on horoscopes, I'll bet. He had Starbright Woman teach her."

"Starbright Woman's an idiot," opined Rosemallow Woman. "And her horoscopes are crap."

"She is not." Melon Girl bristled. "She said two nights after the full moon was a night for bringing fortune if Metal Butterflies sought the sweetness of flowers—I'm a Metal Butterfly with a secondary trine—and I wore real flowers in my hair that night, and got a whole silver piece for just a hand job."

As they walked back to Greasy Yard, Shaldis was at some trouble to draw the conversation back from the various merits of the several women's astrologers working in the district—and the comparative costs of hand jobs, stand-ups, "kneeling in prayer" and other chargeable acts—to the subject of Xolnax's daughter again. "Urnate Urla taught her, I know that," said Melon Girl, who seemed to be on tolerably close terms with a number of the water bosses' "boys." "There were others, scholars and even a wizard, but it all turned out for nothing. She ran off with some man she met in the Bazaar, she said in her note, just like any poor man's daughter. They say after all the money he spent on her Xolnax is spitting blood."

As well he might, thought Shaldis. Were she a water boss, if she even suspected a rival had a daughter learning the arts

of power, she'd waste not a moment in sending the most personable of her lieutenants to seduce the girl into running away.

But it was equally possible that Xolnax's daughter had met
some darker fate. The coincidence of her disappearance at the
time of the full moon was simply too strong to be ignored.

The women stopped at the market in BoSaa's Square for
cheese and sausage; competition with the free handouts from
Nebekht's Temple had kept prices down but did nothing for
the quality. Walking back to Greasy Yard, Shaldis was conscious of how much anger there was in the voices she heard in
the street, how much desperate fear. The streets teemed with
men who had nothing to do. They congregated in the cross-
ings, muttering and falling silent when any man better dressed
than they walked by. How many men were armed, not just the
bullyboys of the water bosses, but common men carrying sticks
and knives. How few men rallied when a shopkeeper cried,
"Thief!" How most only looked and shrugged.

After a lunch of sausage, cheese and rather gritty cold couscous, Shaldis returned to work refreshed. But the walls remained impervious to her efforts. She recalled the Summer
Concubine telling her that Turquoise Woman had scry warded
the whole room from fear of her husband.

The bar of sunlight that had blinded her that morning,
falling like hot brass through the door, disappeared. The wash
of burning gold that had soaked the opposite wall of Greasy
Yard slowly climbed the dirty stucco, then faded from gold to
ocher to pink. The horns of the Citadel, slow as a dying man's
breath, continued to pulse, but Shaldis knew without even
consciously listening that they sang to the Wise Sun, the
Philosopher Sun, sinking red over the waters of the lakes.
Voices rose louder from the Temple of Nebekht, where the
True Believers gathered to be handed the smelly, torn-up meat
of the morning's blood sacrifices.

Damn *these spells!*

She returned to her corner and peeled the last of the oranges.

The day before yesterday Aktis had said, *Come back.* But even though she was fairly certain that the little man hadn't the power to shift a door bolt, let alone drown her mind in searing alien magic, she was massively unwilling to present herself at the door of any compound where the Red Silk Lady dwelled. *Someone* had poisoned her.

So there was nothing to do, she supposed, but wait for Jethan.

Yet the thought of spending another wakeful night in this room set her teeth on edge. And as fatigue tightened its grip on her, the thought of sleeping heavily—so heavily that she might not wake at a sound—frightened her still more.

Xolnax's daughter, as well as Turquoise Woman and Corn-Tassel Woman. How long before he found someone else? Before he found her?

Yelling in the street. The yapping of men who have nothing to do all day, who will attack just to vent their own frustration: Seb Dolek's voice boomed impressively, "Wizard! Scorpion! It is you who bring down this evil on us, you and your foul, grasping lord!" and Shaldis guessed Urnate Urla was coming home again from work. She wondered where Lohar was this evening. Having dinner with the Iron-Girdled One?

"Lackey! Bloodsucker!"

The crash of bricks on shutters. The fast pat-pat-pat of running feet, the slam of a door.

"Tell your vile master that even so long as he harbors the spawn of iniquity the skies will be as brass, the land will be as stone!"

Shaldis thought, *He has books.* At a guess, he was the one who'd sneaked in here and secured whatever volumes and notes Turquoise Woman had collected. Shaldis had asked Melon Girl about them and she recalled there had been some, but not where they'd gone.

And if he had the smallest trace of power, much less the magic I felt in the Citadel, he'd use it to cloak himself instead of putting up with this.

She glanced at the color of the fading light in the sky, estimating how long it would be until dark and what she could promise—how much money the Summer Concubine could come up with at her request—to win the former wizard's help.

"Well, child." Mohrvine stretched his hand to pour another cup of wine. "What do you think?"

The supper tables of the House Jothek's largest dining chamber had been cleared. The guests, a slightly smaller party but in most respects the same as had dined at the House of Six Willows two nights before, had been seen to the gate with the old-fashioned hospitality that few lords practiced anymore, not that any of his guests deserved it of him, reflected Mohrvine. But they'd all seemed impressed that he hadn't relegated the task to the usual gentleman usher. Their gratification was worth remembering.

Lohar in particular had seemed to bask in the honor of being invited to the House Jothek, preening as Mohrvine had opened the gate for him with his own hands while Lord Akarian watched approvingly from beside his litter, and his lordship's sons and nephew had held their peace.

Catch them looking that way at my precious nephew, thought Mohrvine. *When he returns from his little investigation at the aqueduct he'll have a surprise indeed, to hear of my daughter's be-*

trothal. His rule won't last long in the face of an alternate prince backed by both Akarian and Nebekht.

Returning to the supper pavilion, Mohrvine had found his daughter there, still in the devastatingly tasteful white gown and robe she'd worn to serve the head table. The white was a subtle boast. Not a stain, not a droplet, not so much as a fleck of oil smirched its gauzy pleats. At the end of the evening it was still as it had been at the beginning, spotless as the pearls and jasmine in her thick-piled raven hair.

"I think Nebekht's Mouth could do with a bath." She came to kneel on the cushion beside Mohrvine's divan, where she'd knelt to hand him his wine cup and to offer the best cuts to Lord Akarian, who had shared the divan as his most honored guest.

Mohrvine laughed and tugged at one of her curls. "He lives among the poor, my blossom. Any man who washes too frequently in the Slaughterhouse is looked upon as a whoremaster. You should hear what they say about our friend Xolnax. The Mouth has his uses."

"Well, I couldn't tell who Lord Akarian fawned on the most, him, or you for inviting him to your own house, like a lord." She filled a cup with the tail end of the wine jar, tepid and strong. "With Lohar's manners, I could see why he doesn't get out much."

"Don't mock at him, child." He dipped his amulet of toadstone into the cup, wondering as always how long Aktis's powers could be trusted to renew the device's efficacy against poisons. "At least not where anyone can hear. He's a man who needs above all to be valued, to be perceived as special, as more important than those around him. Hence his unwillingness to let the topic of conversation stray to anything upon which he is not the most informed person present—that is, anything but the god's personal revelations to him. I suppose if one spends one's days hacking up pigs in a stone-walled room one doesn't learn much of the talk of the markets. But he wields great power, and he has many spies. Hundreds of people will spring to do his bidding—thousands, maybe. More than I'd counted on." He was silent, turning the wine cup in his fingers. Turning over in his mind all that Lohar had told him that evening—sifting through the preening and the fiery images of madness—and matching it with what Xolnax's reports said about the temper of the people in the streets.

"Is Nebekht really the greatest of the gods?"

"My child, that I do not know." Mohrvine shrugged. "I don't pretend to know more about the gods than is discernible with my eyes and ears. Who and how many of them there are and what they want of humankind are mysteries to me. They may think no more of us than we do of the bats that teem in the desert caves. Should you object to pretending that he is?"

She tilted her head a little, considering the matter with the saucy judiciousness that had been characteristic of her since childhood. "You mean in front of Lord Akarian?"

"That is precisely what I mean, my pet. If you're going to become a lady of the House Akarian . . ."

She'd been all cool impudence, peeling a tangerine with delicate fingers; now suddenly she was all child, eyes blazing with passionate delight. *So much for my concerns about the toad-stone*, he thought, amused at the intensity of her yearning. *And so much for my concerns about her calf-love for Iorradus. Good thing I thought to have Aktis brew a love philter to slip in her tea yesterday. If this is any indication of his power—getting this kind of reaction to such an unpromising specimen as Lord Akarian—I see I need have no fears. In fact I should ask him to mix the next one more lightly. No sense having her become willing to the extent that she puts her husband's interests before her father's.*

"Will I?" she whispered, as if she hardly dared speak.

"Does it please you?" Aktis had assured him that it would. But then, reflected Mohrvine dryly, he could hardly have said otherwise to his patron.

"Does it . . . ?" She sipped air, breathed a light little breath, her whole face singing. "Lord Akarian agreed?"

"That's why he was here tonight, child."

She looked as she did when she was little, when she'd be so excited that she'd leap to her feet and dance. Her mother had been like that, he thought, remembering that fragile and beautiful girl with a terrible stab of regret that never seemed to lessen with the passage of time. "It's all right with him?"

"My child," said Mohrvine, "a child as lovely as yourself, as perfect . . ."

"I never hoped," she stammered, her blush visible even in the dim glow of the supper room's few remaining lamps. "I never dreamed that you'd say it was all right. I dreamed of him last night. . . ."

I'll just bet you did. The thought of a fourteen-year-old girl having wildly erotic dreams about the shuffling and querulous old lord made him smile: *She'll have him wrapped around her little finger by the first morning. Him, and with him the whole cult of Nebekht.*

My dear nephew, thought Mohrvine, the smile hardening on his lips, *you may have your spell-weaving ladies, but I'll have the people of your city in the hollow of my hand. We'll see who wins.*

"You're sure Lord Akarian says it's all right?" Her fingers trembled as she arranged the slices of tangerine on a tiny yellow plate. "When you brought them all to the House of Willows, I was so afraid you wanted me to marry one of his sons."

"My dearest." Mohrvine smiled. "What man could see you offered to one of his sons and not want you for himself?"

Plate and tangerine crashed to the tiled floor. She stared at him for a moment aghast, uncomprehending—or trying to convince herself she didn't comprehend. *"Himself?"* All the instruction and precepts at five hundred gold pieces a year whirled away like a gust of chaff in autumn wind. "That smelly old *grandpa?"* She sprang to her feet, scrambling backward with the old coltish limberness of her childhood. "You don't mean— Papa, he *smells!* He's got hardly any teeth and he picked his nose all through dinner! He thinks Lohar is the most marvelous man alive!"

"A man's friends aren't any of his wife's concern."

"They are if he doesn't talk about anything else!"

"And," added Mohrvine grimly, "that doesn't matter anyway. Whom did you think you were going to marry? That blockheaded pretty-boy Iorradus?"

"He isn't a blockhead!" cried Foxfire Girl with such vehemence that Mohrvine understood at once. She saw the change in his eyes and added hastily, "I didn't . . . I didn't mean anyone particularly."

"The devil you didn't, girl—don't lie to me." Mohrvine was on his feet too, striding to take her by the arm. "I saw you playing little games at the supper with that Honeysuckle bitch, trying to get him to drink some potion you'd bought from gods know who. I don't think I need remind you, child, that marriage to Lord Akarian is the greatest service you can render to this house—that, and refraining from deceiving your new husband with members of his own family! It isn't simply that I would repudiate you—House Jothek cannot be seen to tender faulty goods. Certainly not to—"

"I'm not a bale of silk!" She pulled her arm free of his grip. "I'm not a—a mare who has to be warranted not to bite or pull! Papa, please . . ." She was crying, tears of anger and revulsion tracking lines through the white and pink of cosmetics. "Papa, don't! He's disgusting! He kept trying to touch me."

"That's because he had been assured, by me, that you would be his wife."

Seeing the face she made, seeing the shaken anger, the tears rolling down her face, Mohrvine bit back his next words and put his big hands gently on the girl's shoulders. "Child," he said, "you'll feel differently about this when you've had a chance to think."

"I won't!" She looked appalled. "What's wrong with Iorradus? He's a member of the House Akarian."

"Iorradus is the younger son of a second cousin and hasn't so much as a home of his own," snapped Mohrvine impatiently. "He's a palace guardsman who lives in a barracks. If he was a woman he wouldn't even have the status to rank as a secondary wife to whoever they could find to marry him."

"That's all you can think of."

"As head of this branch of the House Jothek," said Mohrvine, "yes, as a matter of fact, that *is* all I can think of. And you must think of it too. Or do we need to go to your grandmother with this?"

"No!" Foxfire Girl pulled free of his grip, stumbled a few paces backward, her white robe making her seem to shine like a lily in the candlelight. "No, please . . . I won't marry him! If I can't marry Iorradus I don't want to marry anyone."

And, turning, she fled from the room, scattering tangerine peels like the torn-off petals of a brilliant rose on the black tile floor.

So much, thought Mohrvine grimly, *for the spell of passion that Aktis swore would have her dreaming of him as of a young prince*. He looked around him and struck the gong that would summon the servants, then followed his daughter down the cedar-smelling stair to the tiny garden in which the dining pavilion stood. But instead of pursuing her to her own court-yard—to the rooms that she'd had as a child before the House of Willows—he turned in the other direction. Torch flame sent his shadow veering over the stucco walls as he made his way toward Aktis's courtyard to have a word with his court mage on the subject of love spells and Nebekht's will.

TWENTY-ONE

Seb Dolek, once he had his audience, continued to expound his own version of the will of Nebekht until darkness had well and truly settled on the lane. He spoke with startling authority for one so young—as a Sun Mage he had already been one of the most prized singers of the rain, and his voice had been trained to be both carrying and pleasing. He spoke, moreover, pleasantly and reasonably, not shouting but conversing, man to man. Those who'd gathered to receive the Iron-Girdled One's bounty of hacked gobbets of meat and clean, sparkling water from the temple well choked Little Pig Alley almost from end to end, forcing Raeshaldis to stay where she was in the doorway of Greasy Yard.

"You ask why a god who commands all the universe, who could send the rains at any moment, withholds water from mankind? You ask how he could do this? But haven't each and every one of you done the same, when your child grew to an age to be willful and would not surrender a plaything that was bright, that was shiny, that held his fancy but that you knew would hurt him? Wouldn't each man of you threaten *Unless you put that knife down you'll have no sweets?*"

He's good, thought Shaldis unwillingly. And he had, in

some fashion, slightly altered the tonsure of the True Believers so that it didn't make him look ridiculous. She wondered how quickly he would rise in the temple ranks. Long after it had become obvious to everyone at the college that he had no power whatsoever, all the masters had continued to treat him almost as a son.

"Nebekht wants—Nebekht demands—that you acknowledge him now for what he is, the true commander of the universe's truth."

And your master as his prophet. Shaldis wondered if the crowd would ever clear.

Or you, maybe, if you can manage to edge Lohar out of the way.

Little Pig Alley was barely an armspan wide. She dared not emerge from the gate until the young man finished and went back into the temple and the crowd of listeners dispersed. When she and the Summer Concubine had first looked into the long yard that ran along the side of Nebekht's Temple, Lohar had claimed to see them. Whether this was true or not she didn't know, but it wasn't a risk she wanted to run. Seb Dolek was, as far as she knew, empty of power. But if her cloak should happen to fail as other spells sometimes failed, she feared what would happen. She hadn't forgotten the glare of hate in his eyes, the twisted, tight voice whispering, *Get her out of here.* . . .

Even draped in her silly pink veils she did not feel safe.

So she waited in the growing darkness, wondering just how she was going to get the former mage to unbolt his door. The sheer quantity of smears, scrawled curses and dents in the barred shutters bore eloquent testimony to Urnate Urla's understandable unwillingness to respond once he was closed in his fortress for the night. She wondered, too, what she'd do if he asked a reward that she didn't think the Summer Concubine or the king would pay.

Her apprehension turned out to be completely for naught,

like most apprehensions. Hardly had the last True Believer vanished into the darkness than the wizard's door opened and a shuttered beam of lantern light floated in the dark like a hooded eye.

His head poked out. His eyes gleamed as he looked cautiously up and down the street.

Shaldis heard a tiny, whimpering groan.

The door opened wider. Urnate Urla emerged, a rawhide satchel over one shoulder and in the other hand the end of a braided rawhide rope by which he led a three-year-old teyn child.

Shaldis recalled distastefully what Rosemallow Woman had said of the former wizard's proclivities, and almost turned back to her own room in disgust. *I'll wait for Jethan, thanks very much.*

But a moment later she thought, *If he wanted to abuse the poor thing he'd do it in his own house.* She could see from the shadows where she hid that the pip was gagged, its hands bound behind it. It wouldn't have made outcry.

So what was he doing with it? In the narrow alley's absolute blackness the little creature's downy white fur seemed to shine. Almost nobody bought teyn that age. Like the human five-year-olds they resembled, they were too small and weak to do heavy labor and were not old enough to be trained in anything skilled. Most people would let the mother's owner keep and feed the pip until it could be taught to do some actual work.

And what would Xolnax's clerk want with a teyn anyway?

Instead of speaking, Shaldis simply stood back and let him pass. When he was about twenty feet ahead of her she ghosted from the shadows, flitting in his wake through the tangled passages of the Slaughterhouse, far from the lights that burned on the city's walls. In the icy night, the smells of blood and dung grew stronger as they passed among the holding pens. Then rot, and garbage, and the scuffle of jackals as they crossed through the zone of middens that straggled away south of the tenements and corrals. The parched smell of the ranges took the place of the scent of the lake and the farms. Distantly a hippopotamus lifted its curious whuffling grunt, but no other sound came from the direction of the muddy shallows.

Only the rattle of wind in the sagebrush, and the scrunch of Urnate Urla's boots as he led his little prisoner along. A funeral had passed along this track before them in the afternoon, bound for the tombs in the Redbone Hills south of the city. As she wove a robe of starlight and dust to conceal herself, Shaldis felt in the air the echoes of the funeral songs, saw by the roadside the dropped flowers and boughs that mourners had carried, and fragments of funeral cakes.

Among the hills that rose before them, jackals lifted a thin howling. Shaldis shivered in her thin cloak, remembering all the tales she'd heard as a child of the djinni that haunted the wastelands. At the college she'd read tales of other spirits, older still, that had supposedly haunted the Redbone Hills in the days of the first kings when all the dry lakes and marsh flats to the north had been a single great sheet of water. Things whose names the Sun Mages didn't even know. Now and then one would still see, in very ancient tombs, glyphs of protection against them.

She half expected Urnate Urla to turn aside before he reached the hills, but he didn't. Against the dark jumble of shadows, tombs gleamed white, weathered like the bones they contained. The great houses had never favored the Redbones as a place of burial: They lay too close to the city and its robbers. Artisans of her father's order, however, raised sepulchers there by the thousands. Faceless and crumbling, the stone statues of the warrior guardians flanked the road where it turned aside into the hills: She felt, as she passed them, the whisper of their eroded wards against things no longer recalled.

A scraggy path led up either side of a rock-strewn gorge. Like little huts of whitewashed brick, tombs ranged along the lip of the ground above. Farther along, the eroding sandstone had collapsed, dumping bricks, bones, memories down into the brush. Urnate Urla followed the right-hand track, the rough climb still marked by fresh footmarks, broken flowers, here and there a mourning cake dropped into the sand by some child. Shaldis bent and picked up one of these bird-pecked confections, superstitiously fearing that it would be marked with the High Rune H, for her father's name.

G. Who had G been, she wondered, turning over the palm-sized fragment of bean paste and cornmeal in her hand, and what had he done with the years the Good God gave him?

Urnate Urla picked up the teyn pip and set it on the plastered brick of a tomb. Standing behind a three-level brick tomb some forty feet away, Shaldis could see now it was a jenny. On this, the southern side of the wash, the dead were mostly covered with stone slabs to keep the jackals from digging them up, or rectangles of brick inscribed with the names of the men whose bones they covered. Occasionally newer patches showed in the stucco, where wives or unmarried daughters had been buried later. Slips of thick paper, or sometimes ivory, stuck out between cracks where requests to the souls of the dead had been thrust, giving some of the tombs the look of enormous pinfish with their bristling fins.

But it was a risky business, this petitioning of the dead. In ancient times, when the great houses themselves had been little more than sheikhs and nomads, there had been orders of mages who sourced power from death itself, from blood and bones, horror and grief, and from the life force that flowed out of the soul in death. That magic still whispered in places in the ground. Shaldis couldn't imagine anyone coming up here alone for any reason, particularly not once the sun had set.

Jackals cried again, nearer. Urnate Urla was taking things out of his satchel: red chalk, a small bag of something heavy that settled like sand. A golden lamp whose lid caught the moonlight on crystalline facets when he ran his fingers around the black wires that wrapped it tight. A disk that flashed silver in the starlight, which he set on the sand before the tomb where the teyn child sat. Around this disk, and around the tomb, he drew a power circle, its lines radiating away into the dust after the fashion of earth magic. He fumbled at the bag, his hands unsteady; Shaldis, behind the tomb, watched closely the circles he drew, unable to guess his purpose from the unfamiliar patterns but making note of them anyway.

The power circle was standard. The second circle he drew had the shape of the gate circles wizards sometimes used to conjure simple elemental spirits. She didn't understand that one completely, but she imprinted it in her mind. A pentagram within a circle; a triangle within that. A square, a hexagon, an octagon, smaller and smaller within the sourcing circle of power, beside the crumbling tomb.

She had no idea what the silver disk was, but it was clearly important to him. He ringed it with runes: Hoeg, Akag, and a third Earth-Wizard sign she didn't recognize. Hoeg, the Sand; Akag, Fire Falling through the Air—simpler than Sun-Mage glyphs. She felt no magic in the night, but he went through the motions as one long trained. He sighted on the peaks of the hills to orient himself to the energy flows of the earth, and in relation to them drew a defensive square, still within the power circle, with the silver disk between the square and the gate circle. He left a door in the square—an opening in the lines.

He's going to summon something, thought Shaldis. A ghost? She'd heard of it being done, but it was a horribly dangerous procedure that often had totally unexpected results. Not some-thing she'd have wanted to try with all magic in its currently unstable state.

The teyn child watched, too, from within the circle, sound-less, eyes glinting like stars beneath the moon-white snarl of hair.

The circle was finished at moonrise. Urnate Urla took a bottle from his satchel, unstoppered it and drank. Shaldis saw him flinch and shudder, and heard the involuntary gasp; she guessed it contained *ijnis*. The former wizard looked around him, scanning the toothy black semicircle of the hills where wealthier men than those buried nearby had had their tombs dug. In the thin bluish light all the world was colorless save for the warm spot of lantern glow at the foot of the tomb, the dim luminescence of the small candles.

Urnate Urla swallowed another gulp of *ijnis*, pulled a knife from his satchel and with one abrupt movement grabbed the teyn child and cut her throat.

Shaldis, forty feet away, saw the blade-flash and smelled the blood in the same instant, and clamped her hand over her mouth to stop herself from crying out in horror, protest, rage. *Pig*, she thought, *pig*, wanting to scream at him, but the pip was already dead, slumping back onto the tomb, whose lid trickled with a thin black line of blood.

Urnate Urla laid down the still jerking body and set the golden lamp within the gate circle. He opened the lamp's crys-tal lid, catching a handful of the steaming blood, poured it in as if it were lamp oil. The whole night smelled of it. Jackals scrabbled, restless and hungry, in the ravine.

Then the former mage stepped back into his defensive square and closed the "gate" with a long, looped sigil drawn in the blood.

And waited.

The thornbush rustled among the tombs. Extending her senses, Shaldis smelled the feral musk of jackals on the other side of the gorge, scratching around the cairn of bricks erected over the unknown G's new-made grave. Now she heard the pad and scuffle of feet, the soft whine of breath, coming close. . . .

Stopping.

She reached out her perceptions, found each animal with her ears and her nose and her mind. Heard what no Empty would have been able to detect, the low chorus of growls in the darkness.

Then the growls turned to whines of fear. The thornbush told of their going, leaving silence behind.

Silence terrible, filled with the stinging whisper of magic.

Alien magic. Not human at all, terrifying in its familiarity, tingling and prickling on her skin.

A rolling blast of graveyard stink. A slow scuff of stumbling feet.

A kind of glitter in the air, like falling fire.

Is it him? Is it the same? Is he—it—in league with Urnate Urla? The magic didn't feel identical; was it only the darkness and open air that made it seem different? That made it seem so similar? Shaldis didn't know. She hadn't smelled rot when she'd been attacked. . . . For a few moments, before the dead man appeared, her mind groped in panic, trying to tell.

The man who staggered out of the darkness had been dead, Shaldis judged through a haze of shock, for probably less than two days. That was the usual time it took to organize a funeral at this season of the year. His square, rather handsome face had the purplish lividity of death; his unseeing eyes, sunken and flattened, still seemed firm in their sockets. His mouth hung open, the loose jaw swinging back and forth as he walked.

She pressed her hands to her own mouth, her breath

jammed in her throat. The air burned around her not with a sense of storm, but with one of decay.

Brightness shimmered about the dead man, a foul corpse glow magnified, coming off him like mist. It was hard to look at him, hard to see details.

He groped toward the tomb, pawing the air with hands shredded from tearing apart the tomb bricks that had held him in. Urnate Urla crept forward within his defensive square, lips parted, staring as the dead thing passed its hands fumblingly over the dead teyn child's bloodied face.

"*Meliangobet.*" Urnate Urla's voice was hoarse, desperate with something close to unholy passion. He lifted his hands and the corpse stumbled, staggered back with the pip's fresh blood on his hands. "*Meliangobet, annana dermos ha'ram, dermos ha'ram.*" Shaldis recognized the spell words, the True Names studied by all the mage-born: *dermos*—crystal. *Ha'ram*, the secret name for fire-cleansed gold. The former mage's lined face twisted with strain, his thin voice trembled. It seemed to Shaldis that light flickered around the open top of the blood-smeared golden lamp.

Urnate Urla reached out his hands as if it was all he could do not to leap over the protective lines, to seize the thing that stood swaying with tomb mold and blood and filth all dripping from its hands. The corpse backed away, stumbled and fell. Still it attempted to crawl, but it could not seem to leave the power circle. It crept around the tomb, crawling helplessly among the trampled thorns. Urnate Urla rose to his feet, swaying with his hands raised before him. *Annana dermos ha'ram. Drinata*, he said, and this Shaldis knew was the name of a sigil—she could see it in her mind, the glyphs of bondage and sanctuary linked, an unpleasant concept Hathmar had once urged her to meditate on: the image of a servant cleaning out stables, sheltered while lightning leaps from cloud to earth outside. What *mellian-gobet* was she did not know.

The corpse reared to its knees, and around it the air burned more fiercely, though it gave neither heat nor light. Out of its open mouth fire spattered, orange and blue in the inky darkness, piercing brightness that illuminated nothing, and blue lightning leaped from its wildly thrashing hands. But the lightning grounded, burning, into the silver sigil on the earth before Urnate Urla. *It draws the spells to it,* Shaldis thought, sickened, fascinated, shocked. *Pulls the power into it, renders it harmless.*

Within the gate circle, the facets of the golden lamp's crystal lid caught the snap and brilliance of the light. The corpse heaved to its feet, staggered toward the tomb again, weaving, flailing, like a drunkard fighting to escape a net. Its mouth worked, shouting words Shaldis could not hear. And Urnate Urla went on singing, his face rigid, almost expressionless, but his dark eyes stretched and blazing. The thin voice soared up and down the scale as he repeated the name of the sigil, the words for crystal and for gold, and the gold and crystal of the iron-bound lamp glowed like flame. Sweat glittered on his face and ran down his cheeks, and he swayed as if he were going to fall: *Meliangobet,* he sang, *drinata . . . drinata . . . drinata.*

The corpse began to scream. Something came out of its mouth: long, wriggling threads of white light. They writhed and whipped like tent ropes in a sandstorm, pulled toward the lamp. Urnate Urla's mouth gaped, laboring to form words. He fell to his knees, eyes locked to the corpse, as if he dared not look away, and indeed Shaldis couldn't imagine anyone in that situation daring to take his eyes from whatever it was that burned and flared and glowed around the corpse's head. The corpse fell forward, almost across the body of the teyn pip on its bier. Urnate Urla's hands stretched out, clawing at the air. The corpse pulled back, fell again, shrieked—

—and the white light that seemed to flow from its mouth veered suddenly away from the lamp, ran like lightning down the black trail of the blood, splitting into finer and finer fingerlets of flame that vanished into the earth and died.

"No!" Urnate Urla screamed, and ran forward, breaking from his protective square. He snatched up the lamp, shook it, spattering blood. Pressed it, bloody, to his face, then fell upon the corpse, seizing its stained grave cloths and shaking it about.

"Don't you dare!" he screamed. "Don't you *dare!* You're nothing, nothing! Dead!"

The blinding glamour was gone. The thin singing noise that had seemed to go through Shaldis's head was gone too, leaving behind not even a memory of exactly what it had sounded like. The silence seemed leaden in the wake of its end.

Urnate Urla clung to the corpse, clung to the lamp, doubled over like a sick man, sobbing, "Come back! You don't understand!"

Sickened, Shaldis pulled her thin yellow-striped cloak around her and watched him while he wept. Watched him when he dug handfuls of dirt and threw it about him, when he threw stones, his lamp, the corpse of the pip in all directions into the dark. *Ijnis,* she thought as the rage grew into madness and he flung his body back and forth, now weeping, now screaming, now tearing chips of marble and brick from the tomb and smashing them into his own forehead and chest.

But she had to be sure. She stayed where she was, sitting on the ground behind the tall tomb, and watched that wretched man through the night, even after he passed out weeping and shaking the golden lamp. Watched him until the ravens began to caw, harsh voices claiming their territories once more among the lizard-gray hills where the dead lay, and to circle the corpses of the pip and the dead man who had walked. In the predawn iciness Urnate Urla woke and pawed the lamp, then looked at the corpse once more with empty and despairing eyes. The dead pip he did not even regard. Vultures hopped angrily away, opened their mouths and squawked.

Ants had begun to trail up out of the ground, through the cracks of the blood-smeared tomb.

Urnate Urla crawled to his feet, gathered up his equipment from where he'd hurled it about: red chalk, iron filings, and candles. The knife with which he'd cut the pip's throat. He paused twice to throw up. Then he crept back down into the wash, and returned along the graveyard road to town, to take up again his work as clerk for a slick, hardfisted man.

And behind her tomb, Shaldis held her breath until he was out of sight, her eyes on the spot where the silver disk lay, covered with the dust he'd kicked over it in his frenzy.

Only when he was out of sight down the wadi did she dare slip from hiding, clutching it up into her hand like the most starving beggar in the Slaughterhouse. It bore the runes he'd written on the sand around it, Akag and Hoeg and the one she didn't know—Mem, maybe? Even now, after the freezing night, it felt hot in her palm.

Whatever it was, she thought, it had power in it, spelled to draw the lightning bolts of malice. Out of all his power, all his implements of magic, Urnate Urla had kept only this. What he'd wanted with the corpse, and the iron-circled lamp of gold and crystal, she had no idea. She'd neither read nor heard of any such ceremony as she had seen last night, nor of any being that walked abroad in the corpses of the dead.

What was *that?* she wondered, shocked and sick now with what she had seen. *What was he trying to do?*

You're dead, he'd cried, as if that fact had somehow escaped G's corpse in all the excitement of the funeral.

Morning was high in the sky and Little Pig Alley jammed once more with beasts being driven to the temple for sacrifice when Shaldis finally reached her room. There was no sign that Jethan had been there, and his absence, rather surprisingly, sent a stab of disappointment and grief through her. She'd hoped . . .

Well, of course, she told herself, *he has Soth's spells*.

But it wasn't only that. Gruff and straitlaced and arrogant as he was, she had sensed in him a sturdy comfort, and longed, in her weariness, for at least a few hours in which she wouldn't be so utterly alone.

Who can I ask about what I saw last night? she wondered, as she crept shivering into her chilly bed. *Was that some piece of hidden knowledge that Hathmar would have? Some secret of the Earth Wizards?*

Her last thought before dropping into nightmare-ridden sleep was *Aktis would know*.

But why she was so certain of this slipped from her into the dark.

"Come on, you lazy little cow, I haven't got all morning." Honeysuckle Lady shrugged free of her gauzy outer gown, started pulling the pins from the flaxen oceans of her hair and dropping them behind her, sharp tinkling brightness on the waxed black-cedar floors. "God of Women, I thought that lout would never have his fill."

She stretched, rolled her head gently, then snapped, "Come over here and rub my neck." Opal Girl, bending to gather the dropped hairpins before anyone could step on one, hurried to the gilded leather cushion where the courtesan sat, dumping the three hairpins she'd managed to find onto the corner of the dressing table. Cold dawn filtered through the oiled paper of the windows. Ordinarily, the fledglings who waited on the Blossom Ladies were instructed by them in the mysteries of the inner room at such times. Giggling reminiscences, questions asked and answered as hair was brushed, robes were folded, jewelry was put away. Opal Girl couldn't imagine asking this tall, lovely, hard-eyed woman anything, certainly not about what a man expected and wanted of a girl. The only time Honeysuckle Lady had spoken of the inner room to her, it had been to tell tales of disgusting requests and callous treatment. "They're all pigs," she had said. "They rut like donkeys."

Despite all the romances she read—and Foxfire Girl was very good about sharing with her those she bought with her candy money and hid under the floorboards of their room—she couldn't get those brutal images out of her mind.

"She only does that to scare you," Foxfire Girl had said yesterday when Opal Girl had been called on to wait up for the Honeysuckle. "She knows you're going to be a Blossom Lady, and prettier than her, and she wants you to be afraid." She'd shrugged, secure in her own prospects for matrimony. Secure too in the spells Opal Girl had watched her weave these past few days, to draw the handsome Iorradus to her. She had given her friend a careless hug. "I'll fix her for that, too."

That had been just before the cushioned litter had arrived to carry Foxfire Girl to the house of her cultured and terrifying father. Since the note Iorradus had sent her, Foxfire Girl had grown more confident of those fragmentary spells she'd learned from this or that astrologer and servant in her childhood. She wove into them fragments of her dreams, omens she'd seen during the day, the appropriate colors and flowers recommended by Starbright Woman's almanac for that day and symbols the moon seemed to show her. In the gardens she sat patiently, calling the butterflies to dance around her the way, she said, her father's court mage Aktis did. The night before last, still stinging with rage and ant bites, she'd written Honeysuckle Lady's name on a piece of paper and inscribed marks of cursing all around it. Had burned it in the kitchen brazier with whispered incantations of ill.

"You watch while I'm gone," Foxfire Girl had said as she'd packed up her things to go to her father's house. "You tell me if anything awful happens to her. Let me know what it is."

Nothing had happened yet. Opal Girl wondered if, after the incident with the ants, Honeysuckle Lady had gone to another wizard for a counterspell.

She hoped something would happen. It would serve her right.

"Not that way, you imbecile! My gods, what do they teach you little sluts?" Honeysuckle Lady pulled away impatiently. "Go make sure the water's hot for my bath. And put some charcoal on the fire. It's freezing in here."

That was unjust—the courtesan's bedroom was considerably warmer than the attics that the fledglings shared—but Opal Girl knelt to tong a big piece of charcoal from the pierced brass can into the brazier beside the bed.

Later in the day, Chrysanthemum Lady explained to Opal Girl's owner that she'd probably slipped on a hairpin that had rolled neglected into the shadow under the brazier. On polished floors, that kind of thing happened all the time. Honeysuckle Lady, whose entire wardrobe—thousands of gold pieces' worth—perished in the fire, said that the girl had lost her balance getting up, had pitched into the brazier, scattering its flaming contents across the bed. Springing back, her dress already in flames, the girl had blundered into the flaming bed itself.

Stumbling, staggering, escaping from the burning room herself, Honeysuckle Lady's own trailing dress had caught fire and she'd ripped it off, sustaining a painful burn on her buttocks and the back of one thigh.

It was a curse, she fumed to Chrysanthemum Lady as the healer later spread sheep's-milk ointment on the burns before going up to look at the drugged, moaning, blistered thing that had been Opal Girl. A damned, filthy, bad-luck curse.

TWENTY-TWO

Raeshaldis half expected Jethan to be sitting patiently outside in the noon glare of Greasy Yard when she shot open the door bolts a few hours later, but there was no one there but Rosemallow Woman grinding corn in her doorway as usual, Zarb and Vorm drinking in Zarb's doorway as usual and a gaggle of the local urchins playing ball. To her question, Rosemallow Woman replied that no one had come asking for her; an attempt, back in the dusty blue shade of her room, to contact the Summer Concubine through the mirror yielded nothing but a headache.

Her own exhaustion? she wondered. The Summer Concubine's, after another day of searching the hills?

She set the mirror aside and sat for a time, staring at the silver disk that she'd taken from beneath her pillow, remembering what she'd seen last night.

The energy had felt familiar, the burning, jangling of the air. Not exactly the same—was that because Urnate Urla was an Earth Wizard and her attacker was not? But she didn't know that her attacker was not. The spirit of the dead thing . . . what had that been? Would Hathmar know? Would he tell her if he did?

What in the name of all the gods had happened to Jethan?

She waited an hour, then combed her hair, put on her veils, and slung the silver disk in a little bag around her neck.

"If Jethan comes, tell him to wait for me," she told Rose-mallow Woman, who merely nodded. Then she set out for the green towers of the Eastern Gate.

RATS KILLED
HIRE MY MOUSER—BETTER THAN POISON
RAT SPELLS HERE

The chalked sign caught her eye as she turned down Goat Street.

MOSQUITO HERBS
SMUDGES—NO BUGS

Under the dirty awnings of Chickenplucker Alley she heard a man say, "Why doesn't the king do somethin' about it instead of taxing the hell out of us?"

"It's a curse on the whole land, I tell you, a curse been put on the rain."

Extending her senses, she picked up the muttering all around her, like bees in swarm: "One bit of a drizzle—what's that? My son tinkles more against the courtyard wall!"

"Nomads coming in from the north now, all along the ranges by the White Lake. . . ."

"The hell I'll go if they start drafting men for the damn bucket lines. Work all day in the goddam sun . . . ?"

"Bucket lines? They're saying at the café that they're gonna draft for the aqueduct. . . ."

"If *he* doesn't know what to do about it, I say, let's get somebody who does. . . ."

Men crowded outside the guarded barricades around fountains that should have been free. Angry men, shoving each other, eyeing each other, counting the people ahead of them in line. Estimating how much water had been in the well last night, and how many buckets and pitchers and jars would be filled before theirs reached the front. Others trudged, sweaty and weary, up from the lake, the water in their buckets muddied from the cattle and goats and smelling of the whole town's waste.

Shaldis quickened her pace. On the temple porch Lohar, arms and legs sticky with sacrificial blood, shouted to passersby: "Those who cling to the old ways are fools, yes, and worse than fools! In holding to the course Nebekht hates, *they* condemn you and your children to death!"

A blue sky like arched metal above the city walls. The dark gloom of the tunnel of the Eastern Gate, and above the smell of camels and goats, the smell of rats.

Meliangobet. Annana dermos ha'ram . . .

Dead fingers caressing a bloodied little face.

She shivered, wanting to put last night from her mind and knowing she couldn't. The energies she'd felt were too similar to those of her attacker.

Where had Urnate Urla been on the night of the full moon? Yet she could swear he had no magic.

Where had any of them been? Aktis, Ahure, the Red Silk Lady? Benno Sarn or Lohar?

Small odds of finding out the truth about that, anyway. It was clear Ahure could simply close his steam-driven iron gates and claim communion with the majesty of his own power and nobody would ask whether he was actually in his obscure private quarters or not. Who among Lohar's followers wouldn't swear that they'd seen the Mouth of the Iron-Girdled One wherever he said he was? And who among the Red Silk Lady's servants would dare whisper a word about her movements even if she weren't capable of covering her tracks with illusion?

Meliangobet. She'd read the name in a list, she knew she had—one of those endless lines of memorized names.

She fingered on her neck, beneath her dress and veils, the silver disk she'd taken from the dust. *Crystal and fire-cleansed gold . . .* A golden lamp with a cap of crystal, five candles of white wax. Sand and fire.

Shaldis hastened on under the cold, green-tiled shade of the East Gate. Last night she'd dreamed someone was calling her, someone who was imprisoned in darkness far away and barely audible. Xolnax's daughter missing. A crazy woman living in ruins who'd healed a cat's hurt foot.

We have to find them, she thought. *There are so few of us, and the need of the land is so great.*

Had that been the favorite's voice she'd heard, calling wordlessly in the darkness?

No, she begged the god of mages, *no. . . .*

She turned down the Lane of Blue Walls and the smells of smoke, charcoal and cut wood stung her nose from the Glassblowers Quarter. Wide gates revealed hot bare yards, brick furnaces, piles of sand and harsh-glittering frit. Half-naked men and women moved about in the white heat that roared from the oven doors, while teyn carried charcoal from long sheds roofed in desiccated pine poles. Shaldis asked a ragpicker where Barbonak the master blower had his factory and circled around it to the back. A kitchen court opened onto an alley, as it had at her grandfather's. Rabbit hutches clustered on one wall. A young

unveiled woman in the head clout of a maidservant was bargaining with a woman selling chickens:

"What, three dequins for Grandma there? Looks like she's
been tanned alive, she has. . . ."

"Bah, this chicken isn't but a twelvemonth old. . . ."

"Oh, you right. And I'm the Queen of the Harvest, too."

When the sale was concluded and the bird in question
handed over ("You're robbing a poor woman and starving her
children, you're that heartless, but since it's the first sale of the
day I can't turn you aside"), Shaldis approached the gate. "Is this
the house of Barbonak?"

The servant shifted the reed cage into her other hand. "You'll
find Barbonak in the yard, out around the corner and first door."

"I'm a friend of Corn-Tassel Woman."

The girl looked up and down the alley, then back through the
kitchen yard to the ramada under its covering of sticks. She lowered her voice. "She all right?"

"I don't know," said Shaldis. "I'm trying to find her."

The lines around the girl's eyes twisted with genuine anger
and concern. "Damn it," she whispered. She was a plump girl,
probably a few years older than Shaldis, dark hair damp with
sweat from the kitchen's heat. "Master Enak, he goes on how it
was that concubine of the king's, that claims to be a Raven, but
she'd have sent word. I know she'd have sent."

"Threeflower!" The cook emerged from the kitchen door
into the striped shadows of the loggia. "Three, you gonna marry
Chicken Woman or what?" She stepped out, a small thin
woman like a hen sparrow, and Threeflower waved her over.

"Lady here says she's a friend of our lady."

Cook looked up at Shaldis with both interest and suspicion.
"You heard from her? Can you take her a message?"

Shaldis unwound her veil from over her face and shook her

head again. "What happened? How did she disappear? All I heard from Enak and his father was cursing."

"That's all you're bound to hear." Cook gave a quick sidelong glance toward the glass yard. "Cursing from him, and whining from Master B. They were on at her—again—to put a word on Ebrem's furnace, to crack it so it wouldn't heat evenly. Seemed to think the Good God gave her power just so *they* could run every other glassblower in the city out of business and then go on to run out the ones in the City of White Walls as well. That's what they were planning—I heard 'em."

She took the wicker cage from Threeflower, frowned at the chicken within it and appeared to be mentally calculating how best to prepare it. Then she looked back at Shaldis. "My lady said she wouldn't, which was what she started saying after she started talking to whoever it is at the Marvelous Tower. She used to do little cantrips like making other people's glass crack or furnace cool, just to keep Enak from taking the strap to her. When she made that strap disappear—and he must have looked for it for three hours before he gave up, cursing the lot of us for hiding it—you should have seen his face."

She shook her head, with her tight little gap-toothed smile. "He said if that was what the king's whore was teaching her—it is one of His Majesty's concubines, isn't it?—then he'd see her in hell before he'd let her go there again, and locked her in her room. Tied her to the bed since she'd got out of that room before, and set one of the boys to sit on the ladder outside."

"Should have sent her up to the sun singers, that's what he should have done," added Threeflower, nodding her head wisely.

"Think any of *them* would take help from a woman?" Cook spit into the dust. "Two weeks they been up there tootin' their horns—*two weeks!*" She jerked her head in the direction of the bluff, whence the groan of the horns drifted faintly into the untouched sky. "And have we had one single one of 'em come knockin' on the door askin', *Does a Raven lady live here who could maybe help us?* Huh! You right!" She shrugged her skinny shoulders. "Like everybody in the district doesn't know what she can do. But do they listen?

"Any rate, Enak comes up next morning to give poor Corn-Tassel Woman another yelling-at, like *that's* just what she needs, and finds his boy asleep at the foot of the ladder and Corn-Tassel Woman gone. He runs through the house yelling—he's a great yeller, Enak—then turns out the room swearing he'll burn everything of hers he finds in the big kiln. But of course since he done that already the first time she crossed him, he didn't find a thing. Place has been a holiday with mice ever since. You aren't the king's concubine, are you?" She peered at Shaldis with bright black eyes, taking in the cheap finery and sorrily hanging veils.

"I'm a friend of hers," said Shaldis. "Did you see the room before Enak sacked it? Were the ropes he'd tied her to the bed with cut or untied?"

Threeflower looked puzzled, but Cook said, "Cut. You can come up and see the room if you want. Neither Enak nor his dad'll be back till near sunset. If you can find her, at least let us know if she's well, if she's alive." She squinted at the sun, halfway toward noon, and handed the chicken back to the maid. "Get Leather Legs here killed and plucked, and start the rice. Remember to split it into two pots before you slice the sausage in. Master Barbonak doesn't hold with overfeeding his men," she added to Shaldis as she led the way to the ladder that mounted the kitchen's outer wall. "Two dequins' worth of rat meat in their rice would make too rich a diet for their tummies. He's willing to run the risk of it himself, though."

"Noble of him."

"She was a good lady, the Corn-Tassel, and good to us all, 'cept when she got into one of her bossy moods. But there, who doesn't get bossy when you've the likes of Threeflower to look after? It's not knowing, and wondering what's become of her. . . . There's another way into the room from where I sleep with the maids." The old woman climbed nimbly up the heavy rungs and opened the door at the top. "I heard naught and neither did any of the girls, and I think I would have, had anyone come through the room itself. It's got a real lock on it, not a latch, and Enak locked that up and kept the key to it."

Shaldis looked down at the ladder behind her. At a guess, the "boy" who'd mounted guard here had done so at the bottom where he could doze. Even a mediocre mage could have planted the idea in his mind and made it seem reasonable, to keep him from falling and rousing the household.

The room reminded her almost unbearably of her mother's. It was the sort of cramped cubicle that the principal son of any moderate household and his wife made do with until Grandfather was in his grave. Even in his absence Enak was very much in evidence: shirts and trousers and coats folded on the shelves behind a plain blue curtain, spare boots and dinner slippers on the floor beneath the single window. Most women, Shaldis had observed, decorated their rooms, even the poorest: a clay statue of Rohar, a bright-colored hanging, a gourd of flowers, something.

This was a man's room. She couldn't imagine how poor Corn-Tassel Woman had endured it, feeling the magic stir and grow within her and not having a place to be alone in.

Except, as Shaldis had learned to do, within her mind.

And that, she guessed, was what Enak most resented: a door he could not break down.

"I'll fetch the ropes," said Cook. "I kept them to unravel for kindling."

When the other woman went downstairs Shaldis looked around her again. The shutter latched from the inside, but the window looked straight down onto the alley, twenty feet below. Someone had come up the ladder, easily reached from the gate.

The sleep spell that had put the "boy" out could easily have encompassed the women in the dormitory next door as well, but a kidnapper wouldn't have wanted to risk carrying a Raven wife through inhabited rooms. A sleep spell might not have worked on her—many times they didn't on mages.

She opened that door and put her head through nevertheless. It was only the usual harem dormitory where female servants and sometimes the older daughters of the family slept. Divans of the cheapest sort—little more than peg-footed benches lined with corn-shuck cushions that obviously doubled as beds—stretched along three walls, while cupboards held blankets and sheets. There was a brazier in the middle of the room but the scuttle beside it held barely enough charcoal to keep the room warm an hour. She wondered how much fuel Barbonak rationed to his son.

"It was real, wasn't it?" Cook came back in, carrying half a dozen short lengths of rope in her hands. "Men around the neighborhood made jokes for most of a year about some wizard being hid in the next room—that's when they finally admitted that she could make fire, or draw spells that'd keep the rats out of the kitchen—though with all this talk about magic not being what it was, why would any man hide behind a woman? But there must have been seven or eight people saw her make Little Dog Woman's ulcer quit bleeding. Barbonak was fit to spit blood. He knew she had power and he'd got her to use it for him, but once she cured Little Dog Woman, he knew it wouldn't take Ebrem and the other master blowers long to figure out why their glass clouded. He'd been swearing for months she was faking. He's a sly one, Barbonak."

She handed Shaldis the ropes. "Here you go—I picked apart the knots." Shyly she added, "We were all proud of her, the Corn-Tassel. Sometimes she made a mistake—like with that poor dog of Normac the wood seller—but at least she tried to help folks, which is more than can be said of some. If there's anything you can tell us, anything you can find . . ."

"Thank you. Was there a knife in the room?"

Cook shook her head and tucked callused hands into the waist of her apron. "All Enak wanted was things to be the way they were again. When his father goes, the place'll be bought out from under him inside a year, and he'll be lucky if he gets a job shoveling frit. Just you wait and see."

Shaldis sat on the bed, the ropes lying loose in her hands. Yesterday's fruitless efforts in Turquoise Woman's room had yielded her something after all, she found. She didn't need to consult her bag of tablets. Each sigil, along with the words and images attendant upon its making, was clear enough now in her mind that she could simply call them into being, tracing them on the ropes, on the blue-and-yellow blanket, on the wall at the head of the bed.

The Retrieval of Dreams.

The Summons of Lost Voices.

The Double Sigil, summons and night.

Corn-Tassel Woman had lain here, she thought. On this bed—and who knew if the magics she had learned included one for unfastening ropes?—watching the light dim behind the cracks of the window shutter. Listening to the household prepare for bed. The whispered gossip of Threeflower and Cook downstairs. The clank of pots, the smell of ashes. The bray of an ass in the street and the slow boom of the horns from the Citadel.

Shaldis sank into the images, seeing her mother in her heart, seeing her sister. Knowing the world this woman had lived in. Feeling her thoughts, her patience, her need to help others, to entangle herself in their lives. Her fear that night, her recollection of ominous dreams.

Darkness coming. Silence deepening, though it was still early in the night. There had been a bitter chill, for Enak had not lit the brazier and the shutters fit ill.

Then the scent, the awareness, of the sleeping spell that had curled like poisoned smoke through the house. The woman on the bed—face hurting where her husband had struck her, hands numb from the cut of the ropes—turned her head toward the outer door. She felt the darkness growing in the yard below, flowing up the ladder, a rolling storm of alien chill and rage. *She's felt it before*, Shaldis thought. *This isn't the first time it's come to her door, sought to get in.* She recalled her own desperate struggles to keep the spells of ward on her window shutters while the latch jerked and rattled in its casing.

She knew—almost—what was trying to get in. Felt the jangling, edgy power, the growing storm of freezing malice and rage. Smelled the blue-flickering lightning of alien magic.

The woman on the bed struggled, tried to summon some magic, some power, to loosen or break her bonds. But she knew no words for that, could frame no spells. Tried to summon the breath to scream, but that, too, bled away from her with the trickling approach of that icy hatred.

She heard the latch click on the door.

And screamed in the moment before darkness swallowed her up.

Oryn's first intimation of trouble ahead had been the return of the young guard Jethan in the chill of the previous night. "It was the Believers," he said, dusty and bruised as he walked back into the aqueduct camp. "They've got guards on the road; they took my horse."

So Oryn hadn't been terribly surprised when the stream of cartage from town had thinned to a trickle midmorning, and ceased altogether shortly after the king's party started out themselves on the road back to the city.

"There's a hundred of 'em or more," reported the foreman of the last train of water-laden asses, which met them halfway along the empty road. "And more coming out from town all day. No fighting yet . . ." He wiped his balding forehead with the back of a sunburned arm. "Just yelling, like they haven't honest work to do themselves." He spit in the dirt, shielded his eyes against the hard, bright sun to squint back through the dust cloud that hid the road. "Whoresons."

"But they let you through." Bax settled back in his black mare's saddle, his soft voice almost conversational.

The foreman shrugged. "We appealed to their better natures." He held up his whip, and the dirty men leading the other asses laughed.

Oryn nudged his own mount over to Bax's side, leaned from the saddle. "Did they try to stop you?"

It was curious, he reflected: If one looked sufficiently ridiculous it seemed to have the same disarming effect as looking inconspicuous. The man would never have glanced up at his father that way. But the sheer incongruity of the iris-embroidered gold-and-violet coat—one of Oryn's best designs, if he did say so himself—in the midst of the dusty guards evidently had its effect. Though the foreman clearly knew who he was, he only gave him one startled, bemused stare—*I've seen the king and by gosh the stories don't lie!*—then shrugged.

"Don't know as how much they tried, m'lord. There was yellin' and cussin', but we was more of 'em than the Believers. More was comin' out as we got under way again, though." He scratched at the hair on his chest. "The wells over in the market are dry, see. What with the cattle all along the lakeshore, there's folks been walkin' around the city all day yesterday tryin' to get water that's halfway clean. There's a lot of crocs down at water's edge, too, but you just got to pick your place."

Oryn glanced at his commander. Word had come the previous evening that the wells in the city were dangerously low; city guards and palace guards both were working at the lines of bucket hoists that stretched out across the dry mudflats to the receding waters of the lake. Oryn had sent word that more lines of hoists were to be built and unemployed men drafted to construct and man them if necessary. A messenger from Barún had arrived this morning as they were breaking camp, with word that though the nomad An-Ariban's tribe had been turned back from the Lake of the Moon, two other bands of nomads had invaded the Sarn lands on the far side of the Lake of the Sun.

"Bunch of Believers gathered in the square outside the Citadel gates about three hours after noon, cussin' and shoutin'. Didn't come to much."

Oryn rose in his stirrups and peered through the glittering curtains of dust. Geb had brought three parasol bearers among his retinue, with orders to shade him during the ride (*"I won't have you coming back sunburned as you did from the desert, my lord, I simply cannot endure it!"*), but Oryn had dismissed them to the servants' train after the first mile. It is difficult enough to shade a man on a horse at a walk. Among mounted cavalry the whole idea became merely a massively useless annoyance. As a result Geb wasn't speaking to him—the gods only knew what vengeance the valet would take when Oryn returned to the Marvelous Tower.

At present he could see the city walls after a fashion, a low line of matte dun through the fog of gold. The road was empty for the hundred yards or so that he could discern, but there was a great deal of dust in the direction of the city, as if from a host of trampling feet. Around him the drovers leaned on their beasts' rumps and looked back too, trading remarks in low voices: By the Summer Concubine's curtained litter, and the carts of the baggage train, servants and guards muttered among themselves. All had been given weapons when the king's camp had packed itself up that morning. Most weren't happy about it.

Dim with five miles' distance, the Citadel horns still sounded, steady as a sick man's groaning breath.

"It's mostly loafers and beggars," said the foreman reassuringly. "Stirred up by the levies for building water lines, belike. Nobody armed, not with real weapons. Sticks and bricks, some of 'em. But there's a lot of 'em, so you want to be careful."

"We shall do that." Oryn urged his horse forward and bent from the saddle to give the man a silver piece. "Many thanks."

"And you might want to change that outfit." The foreman pocketed the coin and looked up at him again with a grin. "They throw shit, and you're a big target."

"Dear me. And here I've always taken pride in my figure. . . . Well, alas, it would take me at least three hours to get myself properly rigged out in something less conspicuous—if I could convince my valet to unpack anything—and I'm afraid we simply haven't the time. Thank you all the same."

The foreman laughed and saluted; the water caravan moved on eastward toward the aqueduct camp.

The king's cavalcade resumed its westward course, and slowly the mob emerged before them from the dust. It stretched across the road just where the rangeland gave way to the market gardens that ringed the city's walls—thousands, not hundreds. As Oryn and Bax left the guards and the baggage train and rode together toward that wall of restless men, Oryn could hear the unmistakable shouting of the Mouth of Nebekht: ". . . ancient days the kings had the welfare of the people at heart, yes, our welfare and our welfare only! It was the king's responsibility to sacrifice himself, even his very life, if necessary, to appease the angry gods! How different now, when the king spits, yes, *spits* upon the very commands of he who wrought the universe. . . ."

Bax's glance slipped sideways to him. Oryn raised his brows.

"I don't like the sound of that."

"It's treason, my lord. And incitement to riot."

"And absolutely dreadful grammar: 'the commands of *he* . . .'? I shall have to speak to Hathmar about the quality of speech lessons at the college."

"In those days the rains fell!" Lohar shrieked, waving his arms wildly. "Not by the manipulation and coaxing and lies of mages, but as the free gift of the patient Nebekht. . . ."

"Here they come!" shouted someone.

"It's the commander! The commander of the king's guard!"

"Tell him!" yelled someone else. "Tell him to tell the king . . . !"

"Here is your king!" Bax spurred his mare forward, made her caracole; his black cloak spread like a wing from his outflung arm. "Behold him, and tell him yourself what you will!" And he drew his sword, watching the mob with those sharp, pale blue eyes.

Counting them. And, Oryn was willing to bet, calculating the ground for an attack.

Lohar strode forward, without a salaam, without a bow, without even the gesture of courtesy. "How long, O King, will you spit in the face of he who commands the universe?" And from the men behind him—a coarse, dusty brown blanket curving in crescent wings on either side of the road and stretching a hundred yards back toward the city—came a deep-throated and angry roar.

He's had all afternoon to work them, thought Oryn. *They're thirsty and hot and looking for someone to blame.* To blame not only for the drought, but for all the other disappointments of their lives.

More dust plumed in a sudden column at the back of the mob. He saw the crimson house flags of the palace guard, and the blue of Sarn's personal troops. Metal glittered in the sunlight, and as if he'd read the whole tale in a scroll Oryn thought, *We're surrounded on both sides. If they try to cut through to us the mob will close in before they can reach us.*

"Sound the signal for them to hold fast," he whispered to Bax, and the commander nodded. As the two sharp horn blasts sliced through the shouting of the mob, Oryn thought, *And here's where the hero of the ballad quells the mob with a word.*

He gritted his teeth, spurred forward, and hoped he'd be able to come up with the correct word in the next five seconds.

"Lohar, my dear man, what on earth is the problem?" Oryn sprang down from Sunchaser's back, tossed the rein to Bax—who'd ridden up behind him—and walked forward, holding out his hands to the astonished Mouth of Nebekht. "You can't seriously believe that everyone in the city is going to die of thirst with seven lakes full of water there under our noses, can you?"

"And when the lakes themselves run dry?" Lohar drew himself up to his full height, which was almost a foot shorter than Oryn's, and narrowed his bulging, pale eyes. "What then?"

"Why, I have no idea," admitted Oryn, praying that nobody here was going to give him the same arguments he'd been giving the clan lords only a week ago. "But with seven of them, and each of them—oh, I think the White Lake is fully a hundred miles long, isn't it? I'm simply *terrible* with cubic feet of water, but I don't think we have anything to be concerned about for quite a while, do we?" Oryn looked around him at the mob as if for further information. Mostly men, though there were a few women, heavily veiled—the wives of the True Believers, despite Lohar's stated doctrine that Nebekht preferred women to remain in the harem and silent. "There's plenty of time for the aqueduct to reach the Springs of Koshlar, you know."

"The aqueduct is an abomination in the eyes of Nebekht!" boomed Lohar in the trained, carrying voice of a Sun Mage.

He'd clearly sacrificed that morning: Dust gummed thick to

the blood on his arms and calves and he stood in a buzzing column of flies. His mouth worked and his eyes had a frantic glitter—once a man started taking *ijnis*, Oryn found himself
remembering, it was a hard habit to break, even after no trace of
magic remained.

"Those apostates. . . ." Lohar jabbed a finger in the direction
of the city and the golden wall of the Citadel butte. "Those
apostates are an abomination in the eyes of the Lord of the Iron
Girdle! Thus he has withheld the rain from the lands!"

"I understand that's how you feel." Oryn, too, had been
trained by the Sun Mages, and his voice, a beautiful natural
baritone, carried as clearly as, and farther than, that of the
Mouth of the god. "And I respect your opinions. But you know
you're quite welcome to come to the Marvelous Tower and tell
them to me. Any man is. You didn't need to bring all these good
people out here in the hot sun. Have you all been waiting here
long?" He looked around him again. "It can't have been good for
the ladies among you. And truly, it isn't good for anyone."

"I have no fear of your threats!"

"I'm delighted to hear that, I'm sure, and I'll remember it if I
ever think of making any against you. But I worry more that
your own men might hurt one another, as I understand they did
in the Slaughterhouse the other day."

Someone in the crowd let out a crack of laughter. Lohar's
harsh little walnut of a face turned red with fury.

"You jest with the Mouth of Nebekht!" he bellowed, raising
his hands and turning to the crowd. "You *dare* to jest?" White
gleamed all around the pupils of his staring eyes. "Thus do the
madmen mock at the voice of Nebekht! Hear me, O King!" He
whirled again, jabbed a stubby red finger at Oryn. "In three days,
Nebekht will demand a reckoning of you! For three days more
will he tolerate the yappings of your godless wizards! For three
days more will your wells be barren, will the cisterns on your

roofs swirl with dust—will the realm go thirsty, yes *thirsty!* because of *this man* and his stubborn adherence to that which Nebekht abominates!"

Oryn drew back, unprepared for the violence of this outburst. From the tail of his eye he saw Bax, still mounted, motionless, but he knew the commander was calculating from second to second the movements of the thickening mobs along both sides of the road. It would take very little to trigger a fight, Oryn thought, and even should he make it back to his horse and his guards—always supposing he wasn't too stiff to mount—the ensuing riot would not only, in all probability, result in the death of everyone in the train, but trigger civil war.

"The patience of Nebekht is exhausted, King!" screamed Lohar, spittle flying in Oryn's face. "In three days, if the rains do not come—and they will not!—admit that it is Nebekht who holds the mastery of the rain! Submit yourself to the will of Nebekht—or suffer the consequences!"

Even had Oryn had a reply to that, it would have been drowned in the bellowing of the True Believers. *Thank the gods,* he thought, as Lohar turned away, *that Barún wasn't close enough to hear. He'd certainly have screamed "Traitor!" and plowed in with sword swinging.*

The crowd along the road parted, opening a way for Barún and his troops. Already men were leaving the edges of the crowd, streaming back to the city gates. Someone shouted, "The king's whore!" and men crowded toward the pink-curtained litter. Guards formed up close around the conveyance, swords drawn. Oryn was fairly certain the Summer Concubine had gotten out of it as soon as the trouble started and would meet him back at the palace, which in fact proved to be the case. Falling back from the litter, men rushed upon the baggage wagons instead, tearing at the food stores and the tents.

"Thieves!" bellowed Barún, and led a sortie against them.

They scattered at once before him, while Geb screamed, "Vermin! Dung beetles! Bring those back!" and chased after a trio of looters with their arms full of ointment bottles and silver plates. A great quantity of dishes, water vessels, hangings and clothing were left scattered in the dirt.

"Don't worry about it," said Oryn quietly as Bax came up cursing to his side. "There aren't enough of us. Reaching the gates will be cheap at the price."

"Rabble . . ." muttered the commander, but signed for the train to form up again.

"Quite well-armed rabble, as a matter of fact—did you have a good look at them?—and with a lot of friends in the Slaughterhouse for us to ride through before we can make the gate." Most of the crowd had dispersed, but knots and stringers of men followed on the cavalcade's flanks like stray dogs as it passed through the reeking city middens, and the narrow streets of the dirty suburb closed them in. From street to street, from square to square, in crumbling courts and teetering tenement doors, Oryn heard the chant taken up:

"Three days! Three days! Three days!"

Like a cliff the East Gate loomed. Men jostled Sunchaser, and Oryn was aware that his knees were shaking, aware of just how close he had come to having the situation explode into violence that could end anywhere.

And however it ended, he thought, even a small rebellion would destroy all chance of the aqueduct being completed in time to do any good, much less others being built. In the event of violence, probably the first thing to be destroyed would be the aqueduct—followed very closely by Oryn himself, the Summer Concubine, their daughter, and large sections of the city.

Within the gate, the Avenue of the Sun was quiet as the bedraggled train passed along it. Barún and his troops brought up the rear. No one lingered to cheer them. Those who weren't fetching water from the lakes were presumably standing in line for the muddied dregs of the city wells. The slanting evening sunlight caught the dust in the streets and seemed to fill the city with burning fog. Behind them voices echoed from the district outside, and now and then within the walls as well: "Three days!"

"Don't worry, lord." Bax glanced sharply left and right down the wider streets, at the pale green walls of the Grand Bazaar and into the courtyards and alleys past which they rode. "It won't take but a day or two for Garon and Brodag to get their levies down here to support you in case of trouble—they're loyal—and word can be got out to the farther Jothek lords as well. Lohar's boys are only city rabble when all's said. They won't last long."

"No," agreed Oryn quietly. If the Jothek House clans arrived, and weren't out chasing nomads—or worshiping Nebekht themselves.

Take the water out of anything, he thought, and even stone will crumble into dust.

He wondered exactly where Mohrvine had been during the afternoon.

TWENTY-THREE

I've been in this place before, thought Shaldis, clouded, shaken, struggling in the darkness of dream. *Or is this only the déjà vu of dreams?*

"Help me, Rohar God of Women, help me," a voice sobbed

in the echoing blackness, and Shaldis followed the voice. Rough stone scraped under her fingers. (*Why can't I see?*) The walls around her narrowed; she felt them brush her shoulders. Corn-Tassel Woman: She knew the voice belonged to the woman who'd slept in the bed, who'd been bound with those ropes. Whose screams had echoed in her mind as she'd plunged into unconsciousness. The woman who'd felt the confusion and resentment and love imbued in those walls she had touched in waking. The woman who'd tried to meddle with such helpful intent in other people's lives with her magic, not aware that in doing so she made herself a target.

She wanted to call out to her. Reassure her.

But if she called she'd be heard, and not by the woman she sought.

The thing in the darkness would hear her. The roiling, cold storm of hate.

I have to get to her. She's tied up, I have to untie her, free her, get her out of this place. . . .

Wherever this place was.

She screamed. . . .

She felt as if she'd been lost here, wandering, for hours.

Don't give up. Don't give up—I'm coming.

But the cold around her seemed to deepen. The darkness writhed, alive, as if the air were snakes or fire. As if the air listened for the straining gasp of her breath.

It was behind her. As she had in the Ring at the Citadel's crown, Shaldis ducked behind the corner of a wall—for a moment it seemed that it was the same wall—and buried her face in her arms. *Soof, soof, I am the darkness. Soof, soof, hide.*

Before her in the darkness the woman screamed again, *Help me!*

And in reply, out of that churning stink of dark and terror, she heard a voice that wasn't a voice scrape on the words, *Bitch. Thief. Thieving hag.*

It passed her by. Blue fingerlets of lightning; corpse-glow edging a robe. The glint of edged metal, the queer, lightless glitter like falling fire.

The woman screamed, *No!*

Shaldis knew she should turn and run, run as fast as she could, but she didn't know the way out of the place. *If I scream it will find me. If it finds me I'll die.*

This is only a dream but if it finds me—if it becomes aware of me—it can follow me back to the waking world. It will know where I am.

But it already knows. And I can't leave her.

She reached out, feeling and probing with her mind as if she thrust her fingers through the barred windows of a prison. Trying to find Corn-Tassel Woman, trying to lend her some of her power, some of her strength.

The Sigil of Sisterhood, she thought, trying to find the other woman's thoughts, to lend her strength. *We are sisters of the Raven.*

But the sigil had not been with Corn-Tassel Woman then. Raeshaldis understood that she saw what had already happened—there was nothing she could do. Fragments of spells rattled in the dark like blind insects. Spells of escape. Spells of invisibility. Spells of protection. Spells to make whatever it was go away, have a bellyache, forget all about it, trip and fall down . . . anything.

Dear gods, anything!

She felt its anger as it brushed them aside.

You dare do this, dare do this, bitch, dare throw magic at me. . . .

Knife-glint. A woman bound on what looked like a carved stone table, squat obsidian images staring down at her with mirrored eyes from shadowy niches in the wall. Blood on her wrists and ankles where the ropes cut with her struggles. Something gold glinted in the darkness, a jeweled thing crawling out of the center of that wickering storm of shadow and blue lightning. It crept up the length of the woman's body, over the torn blue rags of her dress, claws pricking sharp on her plump flesh, digging, drawing tiny spots of blood.

The woman's mouth stretched in a soundless scream of horror.

"No!" Shaldis threw herself forward, reaching to snatch it away, to throw it against the wall. But in her dreaming her fingers passed through the thing like shadow. She was struck aside, swept from her feet, smashed into stone, into darkness. Corn-Tassel Woman shrieked, animal noises spiraling into realms of pain only guessed at. Shaldis ran, and the purple, vibrating darkness followed her, reached for her, sought her. She blundered into walls, cold stone, smelling dust and corpses. Tried to see, and only glimpsed a confusion of images: blood on carved stone, a thing of gems with horns and hooks and pincers outstretched, creeping out of torn flesh covered in blood. She ran, and the darkness ran after her.

I have to get out. I have to wake up. To get away. If it catches me it will have me, it will give me to that thing. . . .

Light ahead, a single candle.

Screams battered her. Her own? Those of the dying woman on the stone table? Horror and pain and despair dragged like clutching hands.

This way, whispered a voice, very close in her ear. *Follow the light. Wake up. You can't help her.*

The screams were mortal, dying. Darkness like a lightning-seamed storm. It saw her now. No spell, no rhyme, no illusion would blind its vision, and it came fast, like the dust storms that overtake desert travelers, filling eyes and lungs.

Bitch. Thief. Thieving hag . . .

The light was a cheap tallow dip stuck in a puddle of its own wax on top of a packing box. Shaldis could even see the maker's mark on the box, and the carter's cryptic white chalk X. Behind her, darkness loomed like a cloud, seeking her; and in that darkness, something cold and tiny and vicious, wrought of gems, blood covering its jeweled claws.

Come back here, bitch. I'll find you. I'll have you.

You won't run from me. . . .

Shaldis ran toward the light.

She fell and woke, clutching at the hands that touched her face. Someone took her wrist and she tried to yank free. The hand was iron strong: she screamed "No!" and struck at the woman who bent over her as the darkness had bent over Corn-Tassel Woman on the carved stone.

"Wake up," said the woman again as Shaldis tried to pull loose, tried to flee, striking at the leathery, wrinkled hands that seized her. "Wake up! You're safe!"

Shaldis made an inarticulate noise, a cry that echoed the screams she still heard from the dream world in which she had been trapped. The woman said, "She's dead."

She stared up at her through the tangled wrack of her hair.

The candle whose light she'd followed back to waking burned on an upended packing box beside the cot where she lay.

"She's dead," said the woman again. Her voice was gentle, a hoarse, husky alto like very gritty brown bread.

"Who are you?" Shaldis looked around her—the grubby shed behind the kitchen brought back to her the visit to Bar-bonak the glassblower's house, the stifling bedroom . . . sitting on the edge of the bed with fragments of rope in her hands.

They must have moved me. Moved me to the kitchen, away from where the men will be at this hour. Maybe Enak came home. She hoped that really was rat meat they put in his supper.

A couple of lamps augmented the firelight that trickled back to this little closet from the kitchen hearth, providing more smoke than light. They were pottery, glazed ocher banded with black—she didn't know why she shuddered at the sight. The sky visible through the shed's slit window was the color of mountain lupine.

And clear as azure glass.

The horns of the Citadel were silent.

A flea bit her. The scraps of old carpet and fleece that covered the cot were alive with them.

The woman said, "Pomegranate Woman, they call me. And you're the Old One, that used to go about the market dressed up as a boy."

Shaldis flushed. She'd been careful to keep clear of the wizards in those days. She hadn't thought anyone else knew.

Cook appeared in the door between the shed and the kitchen, gray hair bundled in a kerchief and sweat oily on her face. "You all right, sweeting?"

Shaldis nodded.

Cook handed her a posset, goat's milk and a little honey with an egg beaten in. "We thought we'd lose you when you fainted like that. Our good lady disappearing the way she did, I didn't feel right about sending Three up to the Citadel, and neither of us knew which of His Majesty's ladies it is that our lady was friends with. But Threeflower went looking for Pomegranate Woman out in the Slaughterhouse."

Shaldis looked back at Pomegranate Woman. "Are you sure she's dead?"

The older woman nodded. Lamp flame hovered golden and

steady in her dark eyes. "Like the other," she said. "The amber-eyed girl."

Shaldis regarded her for a time in the flickering circle of light. She was little and sturdy and wiry, burned brown by sun. Her long white hair hung mostly in a couple of mismatched braids wrapped in bits of leather and cloth, but here and there long locks of it were wound up on sticks, as the nomads wore theirs, or held with jeweled clasps. Her clothing was a shabby mix of men's and women's, and none of it fit. Half a dozen necklaces glittered over three tattered shirts and a dress, cheap glass, painted paste and one of them emeralds and gold.

"Xolnax's daughter," she said.

Pomegranate Woman shook her head. "I don't know. She was the first I saw. Pontifer here saw her too—didn't you, Pontifer?" She addressed thin air near the side of the cot. "Pontifer sometimes dreams the same thing I do," the woman confided. "He's very clever, for a pig."

"I can tell," said Shaldis doubtfully. Either the woman had a far more powerful cloak on her pet pig than she'd ever encountered, or she was completely crazy.

Not that insanity had anything to do with magic, of course.

Pomegranate Woman said softly, "The amber-eyed girl was the first one it took. It wanted me, but I could hide from it. It wanted you, but you hid too. Hid behind the wall in the Ring. I saw you. It seeks those of us whom none will help; seeks us in the places where none will come when we call."

A woman tied to her bed in a dark room, waiting in dread for the night to pass.

A woman alone and shunned in a rented chamber, in a courtyard where a woman's screams, if she uttered them, were not so unusual as to rouse those sober enough to help.

A girl sleeping alone in a chamber, whose only neighbors

were boys who hated her; boys sunk in the sleep of exhaustion that followed the day of fasting and song.

"What does it want?"

Very softly, as though fearing that the thing that hunted in darkness would hear, Pomegranate Woman said, "It wants our blood and our hearts, child, devoured within our living bodies. It wants our power, to feed its own. It wants our lives."

It was full dark by the time Shaldis reached the Citadel. From the Glassblowers Quarter to the Square of the Mages, she kept to the side streets and alleys, her nape prickling at the shouting of men, the flare of torchlight, the atmosphere of anger that washed through the city like turbulent winds. The mutterings that she'd encountered all through the streets that afternoon looked to be building to some thunderclap of violence, infecting the whole city with fear. Shops and houses were shuttered, an hour before the usual closing-up time, but bands of men roved the streets. Every café was jammed, voices spilling out like the red guts of slaughtered sheep. As she passed, veiled and wrapped for good measure in a gray cloak, the spelling of which gave her a pounding headache, Shaldis heard Nebekht's name over and over, mingled with fragments of diatribe against wizardry, against taxes, against the nomads, against the aqueduct, against the king. Sometimes she heard Lord Sarn's name, other times Mohrvine's. Sometimes Lord Akarian's, and mostly only the confused outpourings of rage and fear.

Two weeks' frustration, fed rather than slaked by that single, disappointing shower of rain, was ready to explode.

"Three days," people said. "Three days . . ."

Lunatic, she thought, ridiculous. The garbled account that

Pomegranate Woman had given her of Lohar's attempt to block supplies to the aqueduct couldn't be true. Could it?

Lohar and his followers, threaten the king?

Give him an ultimatum?

He could have Lohar seized, killed.

Dear gods, had the Summer Concubine gotten safely away?

Shouting down an alleyway: a struggling mass of figures. One of them wore the blue leather helmet of the city guards; she saw him tear himself from the mob, flee bleeding into the darkness. Heard triumphant shouting: "Three days!"

Did she really think the king's men could get through the narrow mazes of the Slaughterhouse as far as Nebekht's Temple without being annihilated from every rooftop, every window, every alley mouth?

"For once the land has surrendered to the rulership of Nebekht," a crop-haired man was shouting to a crowd that filled the street. "Once all have demonstrated their repentance and acceptance of his will . . ."

Demonstrated how? As she passed the Grand Bazaar she wondered if her mother lay awake behind the shutters of the harem, listening to those yammering voices and watching torchlight jerk outside. Wondered what her grandfather was doing on this troubled and terrifying night.

"By the gods, girl, where have you been?" demanded Hathmar when she'd finally convinced Shrem the gatemaster to open for her and she'd climbed the long, lamplit stairs.

Standing in the old man's workroom doorway, where his words had stopped her, Raeshaldis opened her mouth to shout, *Outside the sacred Citadel of male magic, where you asked me to betake myself lest my dirty presence foul your precious ceremonies.* Then she closed it again.

This is Hathmar, she told herself. *Not some dirty-mouthed fellow novice like Soral Brûl.*

Sitting behind the table in his workroom, the Archmage looked as though he'd aged ten years in the last three days. Behind his spectacles, his eyes were hollowed by fatigue in a face gaunt with fasting. His unwashed hair had lost what crispness or strength it once had and lay on his skull like watered milk. His hands had a steady, ceaseless tremor of exhaustion whenever he moved them from the tabletop on which they were folded.

"Someone tried to poison me, sir, when I went down to the city to speak with the Summer Concubine," she said. "I was ill. After that I was afraid to come back here."

"Afraid to come . . . ?" For a moment all that was in his sunken, peering eyes was affront, that she could have for a moment imagined that danger would touch her here. And then, brows drawing together: "Poison *you?* Poison a *mage? Now?*"

"Maybe they thought they could get away with it," said Shaldis quietly. "Maybe they thought the masters here wouldn't much care."

She met his eyes as she spoke. It was the Archmage who looked away.

"Child . . ."

"I understand you thought you needed the other novices—the boys—as much as you needed me," said Shaldis quietly. "I understand how fond you are of Soral Brûl, how he treats you like a grandfather and brings you tea and cakes and is always asking your help with this and that. How you'd rather not hear anything against him, or know the kind of things he says about me, not only to the other novices, but to masters and adepts. I understand how you'd be afraid to change what has worked for so long and exchange it for something you didn't know." In the speckled lamplight Hathmar seemed to shrink behind the scroll-strewn table. "I can even understand how you might have felt envy yourself, as well as fear. But you could have done more than you did, sir. And, not having done it, you cannot blame me for seeking to protect myself as well as I could."

"No," he whispered. "No. And I have been—paid—for my hesitation. And for my fear."

He rose from the divan, took Shaldis's arm and drew her to the window of his workroom, flame-headed arches that overlooked the lowest of the Citadel's courts and the gate that led to the street. From up here, Shaldis could see the black-tiled lodge just within the gates in which she'd sat, a year and a half ago, waiting for Hathmar and the others to come and tell her whether they'd let her in.

Please tell me you're joking.

Gods help us, I think Hathmar's serious.

And Xolnax's amber-eyed daughter, haughty and perfect in her veils, had regarded Shaldis in her boy's things and dusty sandals with a remote wariness, as if wondering what such a creature was doing in the same room with her lovely self.

When Shaldis had come to the gate, the street outside had been empty. Now the reflections of torchlight flared over the painted walls of the houses opposite, and Lohar's voice sawed the warm spring night.

". . . degenerate monarch and his filthy sycophants . . . keeping good men down, keeping true men from doing what they know in their hearts to be right . . ."

"The city guards have come three times to try to take him." The lamplight blinked across Hathmar's spectacles as he pushed them up on his forehead to rub the red marks they'd left on his nose. "Each time he's returned as soon as they leave to quell fighting elsewhere in the streets. He's stirring up the whole city, like grassfires on the hills at summer's end. Four of the adepts and all but three of the novices have fled."

His voice choked on the words and he turned away. A lamp stood on the table amid a vast confusion of tablets and papers, diagrams and scrolls, signacons and little pots of inks. Oil had dribbled where the lamp had been filled. Of course there were no niches for lamps in any wall in the Citadel. The Archmage's hand fumbled as he picked up the lamp scissors, trimmed the burned wick, as clumsy as a child. Shaldis, shocked at the merest idea of the defection—even Soral Brûl couldn't be that contemptible, surely!—barely stopped herself from taking the implement from him, completing the task herself. The last time he'd had to trim a lamp wick this aged man who could have been her grandfather's father had *been* a child.

". . . demonstrate their repentance and acceptance of his will—yes, the true will of Nebekht! Demonstrate that they'll follow Lohar, or whoever he chooses to appoint! Cast out every wizard that can go against him . . ."

"The king can crush them, surely!" She seized on the first thing she could think of to draw his thoughts from that devastating betrayal. Boys he'd taught for years, men he'd known, some of them for decades.

"If he can bring in the troops to do so, perhaps. But word has come that the Greman levies aren't coming. There are nomad bands all over the Jothek ranges on the White Lake and moving toward the City of Reeds. And he can't defeat the whole city, child. The clan lords have been muttering since the aqueduct began building—wanting to believe there's an easier way. And each clan lord only watches for the opportunity to put himself and his house on the throne."

He sighed again and rubbed his eyes, staring unseeingly at the litter on the low worktable. Shaldis came to kneel beside the divan where he sat and said, "I'm sorry I didn't send you word, sir. I didn't realize what was happening, but you must have thought I'd just fled like the others. How were you to know that I wouldn't do that? Not even," she added, "if my magic had deserted me, as theirs did. You're my teacher."

He looked up, and she saw the tears in his blue eyes. "For all the good I've been at it," he said, and touched her face with one fragile hand. "Child, we both owe each other apologies, so let us let them swallow each other up and think no more on them. It may be that the adepts, and the boys, left for another reason. I have sent word to the Summer Concubine asking her to bring her ladies here, her Raven sisters. Asking her help, in bringing the rains."

Shaldis stared at him, her mouth open in shock.

He smiled, and put a finger under her chin. "Only now do I realize how stiff-necked I was—the whole of the order was—seeing your astonishment, which is no compliment to me."

Shaldis hastily closed her mouth and he laughed.

"And I have deserved no compliment. But I see now—or I think I see—what must be done. Whatever has caused our powers to wane, it has gone beyond the point of our being able to Summon the rains at all. We cannot allow our pride—*I* cannot allow *my* pride—to destroy the realm, maybe to destroy all hope of survival for the people who dwell in the Valley of the Lakes. I know you have become the friend of the Summer Concubine. Do you think she will come?"

"Of . . . of course. Yes. She would never hesitate."

"She is more forbearing than some men I have known." And he sighed again. His thin fingers brushed the sheets of papyrus and vellum that lay scattered over the worktable, the styli and pots of ocher and iron and ink. "I have invited the mages to take part, all those who still seem to have some power left. Aktis, and Ahure, and Isfan of the City of White Walls, and Nars the Pyromancer from the Lake of Reeds."

"I don't know about Isfan and Nars, sir," said Shaldis, "but neither Aktis nor Ahure has any power left. Judging by the machinery in Ahure's house, he's been faking his effects for years. Aktis certainly doesn't have the power to undo door bolts or keep Mohrvine's pages away from his rooms, and he's been drinking so much *ijnis* I'd worry about the effects of whatever power he may have left on the rite as a whole."

The Archmage's mouth tightened, and his thin shoulders slumped a little, like a clan lord receiving word, on the eve of battle, of the defection of key landchiefs to his enemy. But he only said, "For the sake of their pride I think I must ask their presence anyway: their pride, and the help their masters can still give to the king. My poor Oryn," he whispered. "My poor boy, to have to deal with all this. Mohrvine will do what Mohrvine will do, of course." He shook his head. "Yet if I excluded Ahure, do I not know that Lord Jamornid would take such a pet that he might well forsake the king's cause? And Lord Sarn—if . . ."

He hesitated, and his glance touched Shaldis, then fled away, not willing to betray what she'd already guessed: that Benno Sarn, too, was as Empty as the rest.

From the street below voices rose, a broken shouting, fragments of words: ". . . bitches . . . demons . . . the will of Nebekht. Three days must the false king hold dominion still over the land. Three days . . ."

Raeshaldis drew forth the silk pouch from around her neck and took out the disk. "What is this, sir?"

Hathmar took it in his shaky fingers, turned it over, squinted at it in the wavery light. "It's very old," he said, passing light fingertips over the incised runes. "I feel . . . There was a time when the spells and power within a thing would have sung to me like the djinni sing in the sandstorms, but these days my ears are all but deaf. Still, the runes are those of absorption, of drawing lightning and fire to them. Perhaps it was a hex eye. How did you come by this, child?"

"I can't tell you the circumstances, sir, though I will another time." Shaldis fought the urge to snatch it out of his fingers, the fear that he would not give it back. "It—it is a secret that isn't mine to reveal. Those look like Earth Wizard runes."

He shook his head and handed the disk back to her. "It's a very old system, an order that died out at the end of the Hosh Dynasty. After all is over—one way or another—I shall take you to the library and we'll search the scrolls for record of it together, but until that time, child, I beg you not to carry it, for who knows under what circumstances it will suddenly become active again? Promise me you will take care."

Shaldis smiled, and slipped the disk back into its bag. "I'll take care." She glanced toward the window. Firelight flared brighter on the other side of the courtyard wall. She heard the sudden rattle of hooves on the pavement of the Court of the Mages, men's shouting and the percussion of hurled stones.

She shivered, remembering the ugly currents of hatred that swirled like riptides through the streets.

The jangling shiver of malice and hate rattling her window in the darkness. *Bitch*, the voice had whispered. *Thief . . .*

"Nebekht and his followers won't like it that women are being asked to bring the rain. You'll have trouble from Lohar."

"That's why we're keeping this as quiet as possible, child. Benno Sarn and I have worked all day, while the others sang, to make a new Rite, a new Song. A Song that will incorporate the Earth Wizards, and the Blood Mages, and the Pyromancers. We have tried, too, to incorporate the powers of the Raven sisters, though we know so little of them—I have hope that the Summer Concubine will come here tomorrow to help us continue the work. Though she has had little formal training, still she knows the most about the powers of women. My child, we cannot fail."

He turned toward the window again, where the torchlight

was fading and silence whispered in the wake of the ebbing voices.

"We dare not fail."

TWENTY-FOUR

The Summer Concubine sat still for a long time after she finished weeping, looking sightlessly out at the brittle early sunlight on the garden pavement, her hands pressed to her mouth. She had not uttered a sound. Shaldis wondered if this was something Pearl Women were trained to do. To weep in silence lest they disturb their men.

Feeling awkward as she always did, Shaldis took refuge in the commonplace, fetched a linen towel from the washstand behind its inlaid door in the corner, wrung it out in the scented water of the basin there. When she came back to the bed, her friend was sitting with hands folded, long tracks of black and green marking where her tears had flowed.

"Thank you." The concubine's voice was barely a whisper as she took the towel. "He will pay for that."

"If we catch him," said Shaldis. "And we will."

"I don't mean the killer." Her hands trembled as she wiped away the remains of her paint. "I mean Enak."

She sat still again, the cloth forgotten in her hands. Shaldis took it from her, looked around and saw the breakfast tray on its spindly-legged stand. Beside it, a brazier warmed the blue-and-golden inner chamber from the morning chill. She folded the damp cloth onto the tray, felt the side of the coffeepot. It was tepid, but she poured a cup anyway, and rang the silver bell on the tray. The stout maid Lotus appeared at once:

"More coffee, if you would, please." Shaldis went to hand the woman the tray, and Lotus hastened to intercept it, visibly scandalized that a visitor should even consider doing a servant's work. She glanced at the motionless figure on the edge of the bed.

"Is there anything else I can do? Any way I can help?"

Shaldis shook her head. "Bad news about a friend." She replied in the same whisper Lotus had used, though she knew quite well that the Summer Concubine could hear the flutter of a hummingbird's wings in the terrace garden outside.

"One of her ladies, that disappeared?"

Shaldis hesitated, knowing the speed with which any tale, any scrap of information, spread through the servants' quarters, then only raised her brows. Lotus nodded, both at the mild rebuke—*Of course you know I can't speak of it*—and at the reply that lay behind it: *Yes*.

"I'll pray for her," Lotus whispered. "The god of women—he must be getting stronger these days. And they're saying that maybe he hasn't been a god all along, but a . . . a lady god in disguise."

When Lotus had gone, Shaldis turned back to the bed. "He was within his rights, you know. Enak. If he had killed her himself, he would still have been within his rights." She was thinking about her grandfather as she spoke.

Almost inaudibly, the Summer Concubine said, "Even so."

Shaldis wondered how long that state of things would last. The world was changing indeed. No wonder men clung in fury to those like Lohar who promised to keep things as they were.

The set of the favorite's mouth, the look of infinite weary anger in her eyes, did not bode well for Enak and Barbonak.

Then the Summer Concubine sighed and got to her feet,

pulling more closely about herself the robe of embroidered white wool that covered her pale green underdress and chemise. "And this woman who called you back out of the darkness, Pomegranate Woman—I hope she slept somewhere safe last night?"

"I tried to get her to come to the Citadel with me." Shaldis followed the Summer Concubine to her dressing table, neat with its porcelain pots of ointments and paints. "She refused. She said she's been a shadow for the past ten years and wants to remain that way. *He can't catch a shadow*, she said. He or it, as the case might be."

"You're thinking of the . . . the wight, the thing, whatever it was . . . that Urnate Urla tried to trap among the tombs? But surely it was a living man who attacked you?"

"It was a human being, anyway," said Shaldis. "I'm pretty sure it was bigger and heavier than the Red Silk Lady, at least as tall as I am—and I'm ready to take oath it was a man. But I was taken by surprise, and of course I couldn't see anything. Now that I think about it, I can't even swear that he was alone. There could easily have been two of them. . . ." She paused, her mind snagging on a thought that would not quite form. "You don't happen to know where Lohar was on the first night of the full moon, do you?"

"But Lohar has no power. I know he's supposed to spend every night in the temple, in communion with Nebekht."

"Which tells us exactly nothing." Shaldis sighed. "Having followers everywhere, he'd have known about Corn-Tassel Woman, and Turquoise Woman . . . and me, of course." She watched for a moment while the Summer Concubine smoothed ointment on her face and rubbed a trace of cochineal powder on her cheekbones and lips. Her eyes she painted again with kohl and malachite, fine lines with a squirrel-hair brush: Shaldis wondered, even with her thoughts of power and murder and blood black in the moonlight, how it was that this looked so beautiful on the Summer Concubine and made her, Raeshaldis, look like a girl acrobat in the circus whenever she tried it.

"Pomegranate Woman said that the attacker was looking for her, that she'd dreamed about it," she said after a time. "Did you? Or did you ever feel that you were being watched?"

Only a Pearl Woman's training, thought Raeshaldis, kept the Summer Concubine's hand from jerking at the question; she saw how she froze, and how the delicate muscles of her back and shoulders tightened at memories of things half forgotten. "Yes," she said slowly. "Sometimes. There have been times—in dreams, or in the shadows of night—that I felt that I wasn't alone."

"But whoever it is," said Shaldis, "knows better than to come after you, because if anything happened to you, the king wouldn't rest in hunting him down. What about the other Ravens, Cattail Woman and Pebble Girl? Did they ever speak of . . . of this sense of being watched in their dreams?"

"No." The Summer Concubine turned from her mirror, set the fragile brush back in its holder, a frown pulling at her brows. "Cattail Woman I don't know: She'll never admit that there's anything she can't cope with. But I asked Pebble Girl and she said she's never had this . . . this experience of someone trying to take her. Unlike the others, she's kept her powers a secret, even from her family." She smiled with gentle indulgence at the young woman's simplicity of heart.

"She used her powers mostly to make flowers grow in the harem courtyard of her father's house, and to make pictures appear in the flames when she told her younger brothers and sisters tales around the nursery fire at night. Her father's a contractor, as I think I've said, a kindly, simple man who depends on her. Sometimes she'll heal his mules when they get ill, but she doesn't tell him because she's afraid he'll be shocked. She's a solitary girl, and shy—a little slow, I think, judged by the ways of the world. But such a treasure inside."

She folded her hands, gazing out through the doorway to the terrace, where the big cat Gray King stalked a lizard along the tiled edge of the pool. Uneasy stillness lay on the city, like the pall of smoke from the scattered fires that had been started and quenched in last night's sporadic rioting. Shaldis's nape prickled, and she went to the dress stand to fetch the gown the Summer Concubine would wear to consult with Hathmar that day, gray-blues and greens, changeable silk like lake water.

The Summer Concubine went on, "Last night when I reached here after the attack by Lohar's mob on the road, a girl was waiting for me, the Moth Concubine—she belongs to one of the silk merchants allied with House Jamornid. She's had dreams of power for nearly a year, she told me, and never dared to put it to the test. But when I asked her to, she could make fire by looking at a candle and find things that I hid. I don't know the extent of her power, nor what she's capable of. Like Pebble Girl, she's never felt any sense of threat."

"So it's only women who were known to have power," concluded Shaldis. She helped her friend into gown and jacket, sashes and veils and scarves, all the intricate embroidered costume of perfection. "Maybe we've been looking too much at what the attacker is, and why he still has power, and haven't asked the simpler questions: Who knew about the victims and where to find them? You can't scry someone who has power, not against their will. And the answer to that"—Shaldis gathered up her own veils and wrapped them over her tawdry dress—"lies back in Greasy Yard."

"Spare nothing in finding that answer." The Summer Concubine finished tying her three sashes in pleasing knots and came over to lay her hands on Shaldis's shoulders, looked up into her eyes. "For you can be sure that whoever he is, he is watching. And once we go up to the Citadel tonight—once we start with the new Song at tomorrow's dawn—even those who are hidden, like Pebble Girl and the Moth Concubine, will be known to him too."

Shaldis made her way toward the Golden Court and the outer gates of the palace compound, but a thought crossed her mind and she turned her steps aside to the smaller Court of the Guards. It lay like an enclave off the larger, semipublic space, bare walled and unbroken by the usual arcade, forbidding and stark. If nothing else, Jethan deserved thanks for his willingness to act as a messenger. The Summer Concubine had told her that he had gone straight to Greasy Yard upon his arrival in the city with the king's party, only returning to the palace that morning. He would be annoyed, Shaldis feared—of course by the time she'd thought to send a message from the Citadel telling him not to wait, the city gates had been closed. He was entirely too arrogant and he'd go on and on about how she shouldn't be gallivanting around the city by herself.

But she didn't want him to be angry with her. And he had had a difficult couple of days on her account.

So she went to the Court of the Guards, and one of the men there said Jethan was in the baths, they'd send for him.

"No, please don't trouble him." That was all Jethan needed, thought Shaldis, to clinch his contempt for her, that she call him out of the baths.

"Sweetheart"—the guard grinned—"if you knew how many of the boys here have been waiting to see our Jethan take up with some pretty little fox from the city . . . Don't deprive us of the sight, I beg of you."

So Shaldis, blushing under her pink veils, which the Summer Concubine had redraped for her, settled on a marble bench to wait. She felt more flustered than she had thought she would, to be described as a pretty little fox. It was certainly something no one had ever said of her before. She was still waiting a few minutes later when Lord Mohrvine and his guards rode into the court.

The court was long and narrow, running back from its gate to a fountain at the far end. The clash of the hooves echoed against the bare cobbles and walls. The guards dismounted, bringing their horses to drink at the troughs around the fountain; Mohrvine on his black mare was still speaking to Aktis, who rode beside him, and such was the tone of his voice, and the swift, angry gestures of his hand, that none dared come near.

"Soth used to be a wizard and is now nothing but a chamberlain," the king's uncle was saying, his beautiful voice hard. "And by the gods that's what you'll be if there are more humiliations like that one! Love potion forsooth! After all your vows that there was power in it."

"There *was* power in it," returned Aktis doggedly. "I swear to you."

"If that's the best power you can come up with these days, you'd best learn to keep household accounts, then, because that's what you'll be doing for your bread. Do you have *any* concept of what's at stake? The king has two days, and then we must prove our strength."

"I won't fail you." The Earth Wizard looked half dead, cheeks hollowed and eyes sunken with fatigue. Sweat stood glittering on his balding forehead and his hands shook as they gripped the pommel of his saddle. Did he see, Shaldis wondered, the fate of Urnate Urla waiting for him? To be cast out by his patron, to finish as a clerk to some water boss hiding in his dung-spattered house for fear of the True Believers?

"Best you don't." Mohrvine swung from his saddle and strode through the doorway that led to the Green Court and the inner realms of the palace beyond, trailed by a small army of his black-clothed guards. Aktis stayed mounted for some moments, clinging to the pommel and swaying slightly, his face waxen with weariness and despair.

Shaldis went over to him, took the reins in one hand and held out the other to him. Aktis's hand groped for it gratefully, and he dismounted with the slow care of one who has not the strength to get down alone.

"Thank you, child," he whispered. "I shall be better presently. It passes." His hand was as cold as dead mutton in hers.

She left the horse ground-reined and led Aktis to the bench. When he sank down on it, she went back, wrapped the horse's rein around one of the wall rings by the fountain and held one of the public cups beneath the trickle of cold, rust-tasting water. Looking back, she saw the Earth Wizard slumped on the bench, hands folded on his knees to stop their trembling, narrow shoulders bowed. With the amount of *ijnis* she knew he was taking, it was no wonder some important spell went awry—it was only a matter of time before one did, she thought. Like Ahure, he had probably been fighting for years to maintain the illusion of the power that was his only way of making a living. Five years ago, he would have gone with Lord Mohrvine to see the king, and not be left here in the harsh open sun of the guards' court with the horses.

Five years ago there would have been half a dozen of the palace guards who'd have come out and offered him the hospitality of the barracks watch room, a drink of wine, jockeying to sit by him and talk.

What would he be, she thought, when it was shown that that power was no more?

And it would be shown. Sooner or later, he would be able to hide his weakness no longer. He would stand stripped before their eyes, revealed not only as a failure, but as a fraud for many years. And then what?

She had the feeling Mohrvine wouldn't even keep him to do the accounts, as he'd threatened, but would turn him out, as her grandfather had turned out his hunting dog when it grew too old to run.

He looked up at her as she handed him the water, squinting a little at her eyes between the diaphanous pink folds of the veils. "Do I know you, child?"

She raised and lightened her voice, and thickened her Market District accent, lest he realize that she was someone who had known him in better times—that she was someone who now had what he did not. "I don't think so, sir, though I seen you in the markets. Are you all right, sir? Can I get you aught?"

Aktis sighed and forced a smile of politeness, though it was clear he only wanted to lie down somewhere and rest. "Thank you, no." By his tone it was clear he thought her only one of the barracks whores, veiled or not. "What I most need these days no one can bring. But I truly appreciate your kind thought."

Jethan appeared in the main doorway of the barracks looking impatiently around the yard; Shaldis was aware of half a dozen other palace guards suddenly loitering around the several lesser barracks doors in the sun. Afraid that Jethan would call out to her, she dipped a quick salaam to the wizard, hurried to the door: "Where are you bound for?" he demanded, running a disapproving eye over her gaudy—and now much tattered—dress. "You can't be going down to the Slaughterhouse again, surely? Don't you know the whole city's on the edge of riot? They were burning cafés and astrologers' houses last night—and any place else where they thought there was money to be looted—and it looks like there'll be worse trouble tonight."

"Then I'll watch out for myself tonight," retorted Shaldis, keeping her voice low and glancing back at the little brown-clothed form of the wizard slumped on the bench in the sun. "Anyway, tonight I should be back where it's safe. Keep your voice down."

"Why? So those louts I share quarters with will conclude that I'm whispering words of love to you?"

"If you don't," said Shaldis, "I'll throw my arms around you and kiss you."

"What's so important that you need to go back to Greasy Yard?" whispered Jethan. His dark hair, slicked back into a warrior's knot, was still wet from the baths; standing close to him, she smelled the soap scent that lingered on his flesh and the faint muskiness of ointment. Somewhere in his journeys to and from the aqueduct camp he'd taken a small cut above one eye. "I understood from her ladyship's message that you'd learned what you needed to learn, elsewhere than—"

She put a hand over his lips. "I need to speak to Melon Girl," she said. "That's all. We can't talk now. I only wanted to thank you for doing what you did."

"I did no more than her ladyship commanded." Jethan's voice was stiff, but she saw worry and puzzlement, as well as disapproval, in his blue eyes.

"That doesn't make it less appreciated—or less difficult for you." She reached toward the cut on his forehead but did not after all touch his skin. For a moment they stood awkwardly facing one another, unsaid things flickering in the air between. She noticed how his nose had once been broken, long ago, and that he had a small curved scar near the corner of one eye. That his eyes were bluer than the lobelia that blossomed across the highlands on the other side of the Lake of the Moon. "Thank you."

And turning, she hurried away across the long courtyard, to disappear into the wide arcades of the Golden Court beyond its gate.

Without the voices of the mages, without the groaning of the horns, the silence in the Yellow City was shocking. Such merchants and market women as remained on BoSaa's Square were barely pretending to do business, and crowds lingered on every street corner talking angrily among themselves. Now and then Shaldis would see men lugging buckets of lake water on yokes, but there were still long lines around the city wells, where the water was cleaner and there wasn't the risk of crocodiles or competition with the herds. The murk that slopped out of the lake-water buckets didn't look remotely drinkable. Near the East Gate men were selling charcoal to boil it into some semblance of potability. When she passed through the square a brawl erupted around one man who everyone shouted was charging too much. His cart was overturned—boys and young men snatched up the fuel in their clothing and ran away into the Slaughterhouse's impenetrable maze.

In the Slaughterhouse itself, streets were barricaded, carts and furniture piled into walls where the water bosses' bully-boys lounged with arrows and bows. The crop-haired Believers were much in evidence, on the barricades as well as in the streets. The cafés were empty, but men clustered uneasily in the squares and intersections; half the streets were choked with herds of skinny cattle and sheep being driven down to the lakeshore and back, trampling the dry dung underfoot into a haze of stinking dust.

Rosemallow Woman sat as usual in her doorway, spinning goat-hair yarn, which she sold to one of the big jobbers; she was teaching her little Five-Fish to handle a spindle and distaff as well. "You'll always be able to make your own living, girl," she was saying as Shaldis came into Greasy Yard. "You won't have to depend on a man for your bread."

Arrayed in last night's tawdry finery, Melon Girl straddled an old saddle buck beside the door, her usual stool, and pestled up coffee beans. They both greeted Shaldis with pleasure and Rosemallow Woman sent Five-Fish into the house for some of yesterday's grounds to eke out the fragrant grit in the mortar. Both complimented Shaldis on the drape of her veils ("A friend did it for me," Shaldis said, knowing she'd never get them right again, and slung them back over her shoulder).

Both women seemed perfectly willing to provide any information Shaldis wanted about Amber Girl, Xolnax, Urnate Urla or anyone else.

"He always did keep her close," said Rosemallow Woman. "Sounds funny, that a bullyboy's daughter should be raised right here in the Slaughterhouse—in that big old palace he's taken over for his own on Sheepbladder Court—but it's true."

"I think he was always afraid she'd fall in love with one of his thugs, or with somebody else's," added Melon Girl, dumping the ground coffee into the top portion of the brass pot. "So he raised her to be stuck-up and la-di-da—when she'd go out in her litter you'd just catch a glimpse of her eyes, cold as topaz above her veils. Even as a little thing she thought she was someone special and didn't have a good word to say to servants or Xolnax's boys or anyone. She had servants following her with parasols by the time she was six. And after all that, to run off with some thug after all! Serves old Xolnax right."

Shaldis, who knew what had become of the girl, only shivered. No one deserved what Pomegranate Woman said had befallen her. "You said before that he had her educated to be an astrologer. Do you remember who her teachers were?"

The women looked at each other. "Urnate Urla would know about her, if anyone would," said Rosemallow Woman.

"If you can sit through how Urnate Urla used to be the best mage in the city, and could heal the sick by looking at them and raise rainstorms all by himself." Melon Girl's painted mouth twisted with the memory of the former wizard's private pleasures. "Nasty old bugger."

"Now, whatever he did with his powers, it's got to be a comedown for him to be just a clerk," said the softer-hearted Rosemallow Woman. "Damn those rats!" she added as a huge one streaked out through the doorway behind her, hotly pursued by Murder Girl. "I swear I should have got Turquoise Woman to do a rat guard while she was here. Did you ever find her, honey? Or hear what happened to her?"

"Urnate Urla says she was a fake." Melon Girl got to her feet, stretched her spine, and went into her friend's room to fetch the coffeepot and the water bubbling on the little stove.

"Urla hated her because she could do spells and he couldn't anymore." Rosemallow Woman wrapped her skirt around her hand to take the water pot. "He never had much good to say about Amber Girl, that's for sure. He taught her High Script, and the gods know what-all else, but he felt it was a comedown, as I said. I gather she wasn't a very nice pupil."

"Well, would you expect her to be?" Melon Girl resumed her seat on the saddle buck. "He'd come out of lessons and go straight to the Eyes of Love tavern—that was before Lohar and his men took over the temple and were still meeting at his house and weren't enough to cause him trouble. And the mess they left of that house, with blood all over the walls!"

"He said Amber Girl was an eager pupil," said Rosemallow

Woman, "but he'd go on to anybody who'd listen about how she was a stuck-up liar and a whore."

"Well, he called most women whores." Melon Girl dribbled the boiling water, a few spoonfuls at a time, through the coffee grounds. "He said that about Turquoise Woman—you ever notice how that's the first thing men say about Raven girls, that they're whores?—and about Cattail Woman down in the Fishmarket, which she isn't, though she's just about the bossiest woman I've ever met. And anyway I think Urnate Urla is sick. For two days now when I've seen him in the streets, he looks like a dead man, creeping around like he just learned his parents had died and left him a chamberpot. He didn't even spit at Lohar last time he passed the temple."

"Who were the others?" asked Shaldis. "The other tutors?"

The two women looked vaguely at one another. "Xolnax got just about whoever he could get, like I said." Rosemallow Woman set down her distaff and took the small coffee cup from her friend's hand. "Starbright Woman. Mooncircle Woman—whose horoscopes are all over Starbright's, if you ask me. He got old Lord Mohrvine to send his court mage Aktis over, the gods only know how."

"Lord Mohrvine has a deal with Xolnax, of course." Melon Girl cocked a wise eye at her friend. "I mean, look at it! Xolnax has always gotten favors—look how his bullies never get cleared away from the wells, the way Rumrum's do. If your pal Jethan's boss, whoever he is, wants to do business in the Slaughterhouse, girl, he'd best be careful how he deals with Xolnax. Most of the other clan lords don't think there's power here in the slums, but—"

Her head jerked up, and at the same moment Shaldis heard, like the throbbing rush of wind in the date groves, the rising storm of voices.

"Shit."

"It's another riot." Rosemallow Woman scooped up distaff and wool, ducked through the door of her room to set them on the table with the half-brewed coffee. Through the door Shaldis could see a mouse flee for its hole at the sight of her. "A big one."

It sounded like battle as the three women hurried through the streets. People were emerging from doors, running in the direction of the shouting—some of them, Shaldis saw, carried weapons, clubs or knives. Others simply carried sacks.

They turned three corners and she realized the trouble was in BoSaa's Square, just in front of the city gates.

As she came out of Chicken Lane, Shaldis's first impression was of dozens of individual struggles, of knots of men beating and kicking downed soldiers, or soldiers doing the same to laborers, beggars, workmen who'd fallen to the ground. Men ran between the groups, or fell on combatants from behind with walking sticks, ax handles, pieces of lumber or firewood; men in the red-lacquered armor of the king's men struggled to hold their ranks, to thrust their way out of the gate and through the square to the East Road. Dust churned into the air, burned Shaldis's eyes, and through the haze she could see flame—bonfires of café tables or overturned barrows. Rocks flew, and she ducked back as one splintered on the corner of the house that had sheltered her and her two companions. Horses whinnied crazily, donkeys brayed. Men yelled rumors about an attack on the Slaughterhouse—a square, red-mailed form on a black horse shouted to the troops for order.

But there was more here than just fighting. The air seemed weighted with hatred, like the lightning in the air of a summer thunderstorm, as if the very air would explode. Around her, behind her, Shaldis was conscious of men and women running to the square, and of others running along the streets, yanking on the doors of houses, looking to seize what they could. Fights were starting there, too, as servants or householders defended their property—more than one small moblet of thieves formed up, hammering at locked doors with benches or beams.

"What started it?" yelled Rosemallow Woman, catching the arm of a boy pelting by.

He skidded to a stop and said, "Nebekht's lot. They was throwing rocks at the soldiers and yellin'. I gotta go get a stick." And he plunged away down the street.

More shouting, and from beneath the shadows of the gate a second column of riders appeared. The men were armored as if for battle, helmed and bearing shields against which the rocks and bottles clattered with a terrible sound. Shaldis recognized the blue armor of Lord Sarn's men, and flinched as the riders plunged into the melee swinging battle maces and flails.

Men were down, crawling in the dust of the square. Horses rode over them and fleeing rioters trampled them. Somewhere a child was screaming in pain.

"You all right?" A hand touched her arm from behind, and, swinging around, Shaldis saw it was Pomegranate Woman. She felt around her the shimmer and flicker of some kind of cloak—not a spell she knew, but one she guessed was like her own childhood zin-zin rhymes, one the old woman had made up and used because it was all she knew. Rosemallow Woman was still watching the clamor and shoving in the square as if it were a play put on for her edification: Melon Girl had disappeared into a nearby house whose inhabitants had gone running to see the fighting. Shaldis nodded back along Chicken Lane and she and Pomegranate Woman ducked around a corner into a quiet alley where they wouldn't be seen.

"I'm fine," said Shaldis. "Thank the gods I've found you! We need you—the Sun Mages need you—need us. They've made a new Song, a new Summoning, a Song that's centered around the Ravens' power. All of us, all the Ravens in the city, must be up there tomorrow before daybreak."

"Us?" whispered the ragged woman, her bright eyes growing wide. "Us, in the Ring? At last? Singing?"

"They have to," said Shaldis. "You heard about Lohar's challenge to the king: If the rain doesn't come by midnight tomorrow all of his followers will rise."

"Huh!" Pomegranate Woman sniffed. "Midnight tomorrow I don't think!" She twisted a hank of her ash-gray hair and the trailing end of one of her scarves into a knot, stabbed it into place with a jeweled fork. "They'll be at it long before that, it looks like. I've seen 'em," she added when Shaldis stared. "I've seen 'em all morning, coming in and out of the temple by that side gate, the one they bring in the animals through. And I've heard their voices over the wall. They're bringing in weapons, and when they come out, it's to go straight to the men on the barricades. I didn't know what it was about, but it's plain as a pikestaff somebody's got word about this new Rite, this new Song. And they mean to stop it."

Damn it! Shaldis shivered, heat rising through her, anger mingled with disgust that she'd simply assumed Lohar would keep to the three days he himself had declared. Probably he'd say Nebekht had changed his mind.

"Can we get into the temple? Or at least have a look?"

The two women passed along Chicken Lane as they spoke, down Pig Alley and Shambles Court, leaving the riot behind. Rioters fleeing from the battle behind them hurried past. As they went deeper into the warren of alleys away from BoSaa's Square, the noise behind them grew less, the streets nearly deserted save for housewives in veils taking advantage of the shorter lines at the wells to go for water.

"Pontifer"—Pomegranate Woman looked down at her imaginary friend—"what do you say?"

When they reached the narrow court before Nebekht's Temple, the iron-strapped doors were shut. The porch before them stood empty, as if it were the fourth hour of the night instead of the fourth hour of the morning.

Yet the place had not the feel of a deserted building. A little distance down the lane, Shaldis closed her eyes, reached her mind out toward the building. She heard immediately the mutter of voices within. She thought she identified Lohar's hoarse mumbling—instructions, it sounded like. Certainly not his usual harangue. She caught the words "Rite" and "Citadel" and "morning."

Among the strands of bead and chain wrapped around Pomegranate Woman's neck Shaldis saw a mirror hung on a long red ribbon. "Let's see that," she asked. In the shelter of a doorway she angled the glass to the daylight, concentrating on the gloomy maze of old cells and courtyards she had from time to time glimpsed through the narrow gate where the meat was doled out; on the flat, dark stone of the facade with its empty niches, its defaced statues of other gods.

She saw nothing but her own face in the glass, and the walled gloom of the street behind her. Whether this was because she had the position and timing of the sun slightly wrong or because there were scry wards on the temple, she didn't know.

Like so much else about the magic of women, she thought. She simply didn't know. No one knew.

Hot wind sniffed down the alley like a jackal questing for food. She smelled incense from over the temple wall and the metallic, sour reek of rotting blood: the stink of the Slaughterhouse District rising with the day's heat. Now and then distant voices from BoSaa's Square gashed the day's stillness, but here things were ominously quiet.

Still listening for the slightest preliminary scrape of the temple's great doors, Shaldis stepped out of the sheltering niche and tiptoed across the garbage of the lane to the dark porch. She drew—swiftly—the double sigil on the black panels.

And she felt it. Evil, alien, burning, jangling . . . felt only a glimpse, a glancing breath, then obscured again in the shadow.

She fell back trembling, hearing Lohar shout, "Who's that? Who's there?" and retreated, fast, across the lane, to grab Pomegranate Woman's arm and drag her away. Men shouted behind them, pouring into Chicken Lane, but they'd turned the corner already. Shaldis felt Pomegranate Woman's spells cover her, hiding her from sight as men, heavily armed with pikes and swords, ran past them without a glance.

She was so shaken, so shocked, for a few moments she could conjure no spell of her own.

"There's something in the temple." Shaldis had to lean against the adobe wall for support. The silver disk on its ribbon around her neck felt warm, as if it had passed through flame. "Something . . ."

What? Magic?

Oh, yes.

Evil?

Yes.

Sane?

No.

Human?

She didn't know. She didn't think so. But whatever was in the temple, whatever power imbued those black granite walls, it felt very similar to the rotting hum she'd felt in the air when Urnate Urla struggled with the thing among the tombs. And even more similar to the power that had muttered and snarled as it hunted her in the darkness.

Slowly she stammered, "It feels like the thing that killed the

other women. Xolnax's daughter, and Turquoise Woman. . . .
Like the thing that came after me."

And like the thing among the tombs, the corpse-wight Urnate Urla had summoned and tried to capture.

She drew a shaky breath. Pomegranate Woman stood close
to her in the doorway of Greasy Yard, and her blue eyes were
dark with horror and shock.

"So what can we do?" she asked. "Do we send word to your
lady? Get her to help us?"

Shaldis was going to say, *Of course*, and then thought, *The
Rite. The Song.*

*I can't take them away from the Song. Not from the first time
they'll have to be recognized for what they—we—are. Not with
Lohar waiting for them to fail.*

Her heart sank and her hands and feet felt like ice.

*Shit. Damn. God of Women—Lady God of Women . . . I'm
really going to need your help.*

As are they. Every bit of it.

She said, "No. What they're doing is more important. It
can't wait. The gods only know what Lohar has in mind, or if
they'll get another chance. I've got to take care of this—or at
least see what it is—alone."

TWENTY-FIVE

I t was true.
      Foxfire Girl sank trembling back onto the divan and let
the image in her silver-framed mirror fade.

The note in Gecko Woman's almost unintelligible scribble lay like a dirty leaf on the turquoise silk cushions:

Opal-G ws hurrt bad burnt in fire in Hunysukl-L's room & burnt all over she axses for you—yr hmbl servt Geko-W

Foxfire Girl closed her eyes, trying not to see what the mirror had showed. She was shaking all over, hands and feet cold as ice.

God of Women, no! God of Women, no, please, I didn't mean bad luck for her! She's my friend.

Would you have wanted it to be Honeysuckle Lady lying there in agony instead?

No, Foxfire Girl whispered to that cold, honest voice inside her. *No. I didn't know bad luck would mean that.*

Opal Girl alone in her attic room. The image she'd called in her mirror wouldn't leave her sight. Where the bandages didn't cover, the sight of the flesh was horrible, red, black, yellow with blisters. She was conscious, her hands tied to the bed to keep her from picking at her burns in her half-delirious state. Her eyes were bandaged. *Don't let her be blind . . . !*

Don't let her be really hurt.

She clutched her arms around herself, trying to stop trembling. Her throat hurt, her eyes hurt, she hadn't cried since she was a tiny child; her father had never liked women who cried. Pearl Women didn't cry.

Darkness lay on the garden outside her room. On the top of the wall, when she'd looked out, she'd seen three of her father's guards; far-off firelight tipped the points of their halberds. The familiar noises of the city at night, a delight to her since infancy, were changed now: no carts, no late-walking vendors singing songs about flowers or hairpins or gingerbread, no cats yowling cat poems of eternal love to their sweethearts.

Even here in her father's house, behind the safety of the extra guards on the walls, she heard the occasional shouting of

men in alleyways. Smoke hung heavy in the air, not the comforting woodsmoke of kitchens and supper, but the charred
stink of things burning that had no business in flames.

Burning . . .

She pressed her hands to her mouth.

*There has to be a way to heal her. Wizards healed people. I can
do magic—maybe I can heal her, too. Maybe I can't do much right
now, but I can do a little, and I can learn. I'll make Aktis teach me
all about healing.*

. . . burnt all over she axses for you.

Oh, Opal Girl, I'm so sorry!

Foxfire Girl stumbled to her feet, snatched a dress from its
stand, for the first time in her life not worrying about which it
was or what color. *Aktis*, she thought. She knew her father had
gone out—to speak to the king? To check on the guards in the
vicinity of the house? To make some deal with the True Believers? To tell Lord Akarian that she loved him? She didn't
know. But Aktis might well have come back already. She'd
take Aktis with her to the House of Six Willows.

Shouting—dim and distant—from Great Giraffe Street; the
crash of something breaking, audible even over the walls. The
clatter of running feet.

*Aktis will never take you. Not with rioters all over the city. The
True Believers hate wizards, and hate women who do magic even
more.* She'd heard Lohar spout on for hours about that.

Foxfire Girl had no idea what the rioting was about and
didn't care, but her heart hammered at her next thought:

I'll go by myself.

Wizards were supposed to be able to make people not see
them. How did they do that? Pretend they were shadows?
Imagine they were really cats, make other people think that
what they saw was just a shadow, or a cat, or a mouse running
along the wall? She'd had dreams about doing that. About

thinking veils of cobweb on their eyes and minds. The thought terrified her, because never in her life had she been out in the streets without the protection of a maidservant, but she thought, *I can't leave Opal Girl lying in that awful attic alone.*

With the riots going on, goodness knew whether old Chrysanthemum Lady would be able to hire enough guards to keep looters away from the House of Six Willows. She had a lot of clan lord friends, but would that make any difference now? Foxfire Girl didn't know. And anyway, lying bandaged in that attic, Opal Girl must be scared to death, if she wasn't in too much pain to care about anything.

. . . she axses for you. . . .

I'm coming, sweetheart, she thought frantically, and gathered up a handful of veils. *Please, please forgive me for what I did. I'll be there.*

And I'll get past the guards how?

She stepped out into the garden, scanned the top of the wall. The garden that opened from her rooms was tiny, like all town gardens, but exquisite with tilework and water, thick at night with the scents of roses and jasmine. Usually at this hour—not more than an hour after full dark—lamps burned in the niches of the high walls, but no one had come to light them. If she concentrated, she could see nevertheless. There was far-off shouting still, audible over the walls, and the crack of wooden weapons, clubs and chairs. The guards were gone.

Gone to see what it is, she thought.

And the servants in this part of the palace, which was wedged between the harem and the dormitories of the servants, seemed to be gone too. The place was unnaturally silent.

This may be my chance.

Foxfire Girl . . .

The whisper was so soft she thought for a moment it might

only be in her mind. But she turned and saw a shape in the darkness, hidden among the sable clouds of the jasmine vines. "Foxfire Girl." Something—the smell of the chamomile wash he used in his hair, maybe—told her it was Iorradus. At the suppers she had noticed it. Had loved it then, had woven it into her spells and her dreams. Her preoccupation with him seemed impossibly trivial now, childish and appalling beside what she had done.

Done for nothing, done out of pure spite, without thinking . . .

"My darling, I've come for you. . . ."

Thank the gods!

"You have to help me," she whispered urgently. "A friend of mine is hurt. I need someone to take me to the House of Six Willows."

She ran toward him as she spoke, reaching out her hands. But she stopped a step or two from touching him, fighting to pierce the darkness with her eyes, which sometimes saw his shape and sometimes saw . . .

Something else.

Was that really him? She couldn't tell.

"Iorradus?"

"I'm here for you, my beloved. I've come to take you away."

"Don't be stupid," she whispered impatiently. "I need help. A friend of mine is hurt. It's my fault, I have to go to her."

"I'll take you wherever you wish, my darling," murmured that wind-soft voice from the darkness, and somehow she couldn't make the shape be that of Iorradus; couldn't fit that voice into his voice. She backed away.

"Who are you?"

And when there was no answer, but only deepening silence, she turned suddenly, plunged back toward the lamplight of her chamber, wondering suddenly where the maids were, and the guards, and why this quarter of the house was so silent.

As she reached the threshold darkness enfolded her, terrible strength, smothering cold.

Why hasn't she come back?

The Summer Concubine walked to the window, listened through the shutters for some sound on the gallery outside.

Midnight was past. Throughout the hours of the night she had listened: She'd told Hathmar to send Shaldis up to her, at whatever hour the girl came back, and had cast her mind, again and again, to the court below where the great gates of the Citadel of the Sun were shut against the city. She had heard the shifts of guards go past in the gallery above the First Court, where visitors were housed; had listened to Cattail Woman's too-audible complaints about the bedding in the next chamber, and to the nearly silent tread of the college cats. Two or three hours after full dark, the streets outside the Court of Mages had been quiet. Later—her ears tracked the sounds, and she'd asked the guards for news—there had been rioting, in the Bazaar, and the Dyers Yard, and northward where the metalsmiths plied their trade in long alleys shaded with striped awnings. She smelled the smoke on the wind.

"Every time the rioting is quelled it flares anew someplace else," a guard had told her, a sturdy young man in the red of the Marvelous Tower. "Someone keeps starting it up again, Bax thinks; keeps stirring people up. You'd think at this hour they'd all be in their beds."

The Summer Concubine knew he was wrong. She knew the Yellow City's rhythms, knew there were portions of the population—the thieves, the whores, the vendors in the Night

Market, the entertainers, the ne'er-do-wells with no work and
no stake in the quiet lives of others—that never slept.

Go to bed, she told herself. *You'll be of no use whatsoever in
the Singing if you don't have some sleep.*

Maybe that was the point?

She returned to the narrow bed, drew the blanket up around
her shoulders. The small guest chamber of the college was
nearly bare, its few furnishings sparse and clean, as all things
were in the Citadel of the Sun Mages. A low bed that was
barely more than a widening in the divan in one corner, a
plain cupboard on one wall. A lamp, though she hadn't lit it,
a washstand, a jug with a little water. All old and worn and
comfortable. With the red-clothed guards walking the gallery
outside it should have felt safe, but it didn't.

Did you ever feel that you were being watched?

Turquoise Woman dead. That sweet oval face, those lovely
blue-green eyes framed in the dark hair.

The way the cats in the Marvelous Tower had flocked to the
Summer Concubine's garden when Turquoise Woman came
there, even the skittish Black Princess, the aloof Gray King.
Curling around her ankles, sitting on her knees. Playing with
the ends of her cheap blue-green veils as if they were permeated with catnip.

Corn-Tassel Woman, big and bustling and so astonishingly
vulnerable and frightened beneath that air of busy meddling.

The Summer Concubine pressed her hands to her face
again, trying not to remember what Raeshaldis had told her of
her vision in the house of Barbonak the glassblower.

Raeshaldis . . .

As the afternoon had lengthened and news had come in of
an armed attack by nomads on the farmers south of the Lake
of the Sun, the Summer Concubine had tried to call Shaldis
to mirror or crystal or water bowl—anything to hear that she

was safe. The effort had resulted in nothing but a headache, and at last she'd desisted, fearing to further drain her powers, which would be desperately needed in the morning.

Not her too, she prayed to the god of women, that beautiful flowered deity with her braided hair and secret smile. *Not her too*.

Bax and Lord Sarn had ridden out with a great company of their men to meet the nomads, who were driving their herds across the tilled fields to the lake waters. They had been attacked on their way through the Slaughterhouse; the rioting that had been triggered had spread, dying down and flaring anew through the night. Had Shaldis been caught in that? The girl could cloak herself against ordinary notice, but if her concentration were broken, if she were struck by a random brick or an arrow? Would she be able to hold the spells?

What would they do without her? She was the only one among the Ravens to have received the formal training and discipline of the college, the only woman to have both power and thorough teaching. They had twenty-four hours, a full cycle of the sun, to bring the rain. After that Lohar and his followers would rise up.

And what?

The Summer Concubine shivered and drew the blanket closer about her, cold as she was always cold.

Oryn is right, she thought. *If we do not hold together now, we will all perish.*

And yet if they succeeded, what then? Would the next request be *Help us keep the teyn enslaved*? Yet how would they finish the aqueduct in time without the teyn?

Tiredly her mind slipped back to the aqueduct camp, to the hexed coins and the bloodstained ruin of the scaffolding. *The lands are perishing for want of rain and someone with power is using it for* that? The sense of power glimpsed—scented like a smoke-whiff—in the Dead Hills near the sealed Hosh tomb came back to her. . . . What of that?

It wants us, Raeshaldis had reported that the old Raven Pomegranate Woman had said. *It wants our power.*

For what? For that?

But what, or who, would have enough power to seize women who had at least enough magic to defend themselves? *If it has such power, what does it want with ours?*

And if it has no power, how could it do what it does?

On the stairs of the court below she heard the rustle of the day porter's robe as he descended, lamp in hand, to the gate-house. Was day already so near?

The creak of the courtyard gates below: hooves clattering and gaudy ribbons of torchlight in the cracks of the shutters. Aktis's voice, and Mohrvine's: "You'd best go up. I'll wait for the king."

The voices of guards. Many guards.

She supposed, if the Citadel itself were attacked, she and the women could call up enough of a cloak of spells to smuggle the Sun Mages out. But where would they flee? And after that, what?

What would happen if the rains never came?

The light is fading, Hathmar had said at supper, with twilight waning beyond the refectory's open doors. Around the tables, those who had remained at the Citadel sat with grave faces, watching their guests, these new holders of magic who had come to start the new Song. The masters and adepts looked exhausted; the three young novices who remained, frankly scared. *But if we can accomplish this one task yet,* the Archmage had said, *we may win for ourselves the chance to light candles to take us through the night. If we fail, we face darkness indeed.*

And of course Cattail Woman had delivered herself of a harangue on the unjust incorrectness of the old man's metaphor, nearly triggering a quarrel with the two northern wizards Isfan and Nars. Soth had listened in silence, looking as tired as if he'd been pulled through a mangle. Pebble Girl and the Moth Concubine had looked as if they would have disappeared had they known a spell to do so.

The Summer Concubine smiled as she thought of them. Last night after supper, when the women were alone and the last pink glow of evening was fading from the sky, Cattail Woman had overpowered the conversation, demanding of the others details of spells and magics, only to find fault. Despite the fears for Shaldis already growing in her heart, the Summer Concubine had drawn the gruff, dark-faced woman aside and into tête-à-tête conversation—Cattail Woman could be hilariously funny in her acerbic way—to let Pebble Girl and the Moth Concubine get acquainted. Now and then, behind the brassy wall of Cattail Woman's monologue, she had heard the younger women laugh, the sunny humor of the contractor's daughter dissolving the shy, young concubine's fright.

We are the first, the Summer Concubine had told them after Hathmar had given all the newcomers their instructions for the Song. It was nearly midnight then, and Oryn—who'd come in quietly on the heels of latecomers Aktis and Ahure—was silently making coffee. *It has never happened before, that even other mages have been called in to help the Song of Summoning Rain. Now we have been asked to take our place, serving as the mages have all these years so selflessly served.*

Cattail Woman had preened, Pebble Girl had looked grave but calm and, judging from her expression, the Moth Concubine only refrained with difficulty from asking whether her master would still love her if she did such an unwomanly thing.

But they were the first, the Summer Concubine thought. *We are the first.*

As Corn-Tassel Woman, and Turquoise Woman, and even the luckless Amber Girl should have been.

And afterward Oryn had flirted with all the Raven ladies and even got a smile out of Cattail Woman, though she'd told him that, king or no king, he ought to follow a diet of green-stuff and water.

Raeshaldis should have been there. Raeshaldis and Pomegranate Woman.

The predawn chill bit the Summer Concubine's feet as she washed her face. Another knock on the gate—a boy's voice asked for Mohrvine.

Where is Raeshaldis? Somewhere near, a man was pacing his room, like an old steer trying to outwalk screwflies in a bad summer; this sound she had heard all night. Elsewhere a boy's voice asked anxiously, "What if we can't do it? What if the rains don't come? They can't really close down the Citadel, can they? They can't send us away?" and a young man's voice replied angrily, "Shut up."

"But I showed him," Cattail Woman declared in her grating voice to Pebble Girl. "Every time he spoke to that hussy, a spell of sickness would come on him that would have him puking the rest of the day. He'll get the message. . . ."

Mohrvine's voice, sudden and harsh in the courtyard below, demanded, "Where is she?"

The young messenger's voice panted, "My lord, we could find no trace of her. Her jewels are gone; her mare is gone from the stables. The stablemen say they heard nothing, but they're saying in the king's barracks—"

"What has the king to do with this?"

Long hesitation, and the Summer Concubine went to the window, pushed back the shutters. Mohrvine had brought a substantial troop to add to the Citadel's guard—city men, with short hair and close-fitting trousers instead of the deep-desert riders he had of late surrounded himself with. Had she been less frantic with worry about Raeshaldis, the Summer Concubine would have smiled, for the moment the nomads had started causing trouble Mohrvine had quit dressing in their billowing robes and gone to the style of a soldier, close-cropping his hair overnight.

"Nothing, my lord. Only they're saying in the guards' barracks that Iorradus Akarian is gone too."

The Summer Concubine turned her attention away, returned to dressing in a loose-fitting gown of white linen—the most comfortable thing she owned, if she were going to be standing all the day in it—and veils and a mantle of pale blue. "You know that linen's going to be wrinkled like your granny's backside before the second hour of the morning," pointed out Cattail Woman, opening her door without knocking. "Have they brought you breakfast yet? I've heard they make bargains here with Lord Sarn to get coffee cheap. Is that true?"

She had the other two with her, and as the college servants arrived just then with barley, curds and honey, all three came in to share the meal, dashing any chance of further listening in the Summer Concubine's duties as hostess and mother, as it were, of their small new family.

The Red Silk Lady is a mage, she thought, as she poured tea, spoke gentle encouragement to the Moth Concubine. *Mohrvine's mother . . . in secret, like a snake in a wall. What is she doing in this time? Hiding, watching, waiting?*

"The woman is positively blackmailing the poor fellow into staying with her, Willow Woman says." Cattail Woman, though her power was real, never shut up. She had received ill the Summer Concubine's suggestion that she be less ready to "help" everyone around her—all of her friends and relatives, in any case—without more training in how to limit the effects of her spells, not to mention in what was and wasn't her business. "He really loves her, if only he'd admit it to himself. But he's positively cowed by Honeybee Woman. So Willow Woman asked me if I'd put a little word on Rynak, to make him realize how much he cares for her, and in the meantime bring that awful Honeybee Woman down sick."

Surely, the Summer Concubine thought, *the sigil would have let me know last night at least if she is alive.*

But it hadn't. No more than it had let her know that Turquoise Woman and Corn-Tassel Woman were dead.

She had no more been able to detect Raeshaldis's presence anywhere in the city, in the Valley of the Lake, in the range-land beyond, than she could scry the girl in a half-hour's ineffective staring into water.

Raeshaldis, she thought, despairing, *speak to me. Reach out to me.*

All the day the Summoning will absorb me, my mind and my magic and my heart. I won't be able to search for you, even in thought.

"Don't go up there just yet," snapped Mohrvine's voice from the gallery stair. "I need you. I'm sure you'll excuse us, Lord Soth."

"We were just on our way to see Hathmar," said Aktis's voice, presumably the moment Soth was out of hearing. "Lord Soth has come from the Marvelous Tower, with things for the comfort of those mages and women-who-do-magic who are not trained to the exertions of the rites."

"Bugger Soth." Mohrvine's voice was hard as iron. "Foxfire Girl has run off with that blockhead Iorradus."

Just what Oryn needs, thought the Summer Concubine despairingly. *A scandal to drive Lord Akarian farther away from the House of Jothek and into the arms of Nebekht.* Not that she blamed the girl for being unwilling to wed Lord Akarian, as her informants had told her was being planned, but the repercussions would be fearful. Odd, that even with handfuls of jewels at her disposal the girl had been able to get past her father's walls.

"Find her."

"My lord, there isn't time. We must go to the Ring."

"If you're no better calling rain than you were making a love potion to get her to accept Akarian, they're better off without you. You find her—you scry for her—and when you've located her, send me word and send word at once to Mohrhaddin—he came in last night with more of my troops—and have them bring her back. And not a word to anyone, understand? Mohrhaddin's her brother; he'll keep his mouth shut. If we catch them now, Akarian need never know."

That proves it, she thought. If Mohrvine knew the Red Silk Lady had powers, he'd have asked her, not Aktis.

And what did it mean, if anything, that the clan lord had called his son down from their lands near the Lake of Gazelles?

"My ladies?" A discreet fingernail scratched the door.

They would be in the Ring all day and all night. She thought about the exhaustion of scrying, the ravenous hunger that followed any magical effort, as if the power were drained out of her flesh. As a Pearl Woman she'd been disciplined to concentrate, to put aside hunger and thirst and the need for sleep, and even so she shuddered. What it would be for women who had never had the training she couldn't imagine.

She slung her mantle around herself, checked the mirror one more time. Cattail Woman draped her own veils and was redoing those of the Moth Concubine: "Only old ladies drape them that way these days, let me do that—I'll get yours in a minute, Pebble Girl. I don't care what those busybodies tell me—I need food if I'm going to use my power. . . ."

"My lady," said the servant's voice. "It's time to go."

TWENTY-SIX

"A re you sure you want to do this?" Raeshaldis ducked her face into the bucket of water Pomegranate Woman had brought from some secret cache among the warren of ruined villas where they'd spent the night; icy cold, it took her breath away, but it did wake her up. "You've spent this long keeping in the shadows. If there's something in that temple, it'll see you if you go in with me."

"It knows I exist," the old woman pointed out. "I've heard it whispering through the walls. If it isn't stopped—if it isn't found out—it'll run through all the other ladies that're up in the Citadel now, and it'll get to me sooner or later. The two of us might be able to stop it. The one of you sure won't."

"What?" Shaldis grinned at her shakily. "I didn't impress you with my power?"

And Pomegranate Woman grinned back.

Shaldis had spent the night in the crumbling kitchen quarters of one of the old villas of the deserted Salt-Pan Quarter, tracing the precise patterns from the surface of the protective silver disk onto the only silver disk she could find—a big double-royal coin, the last of the money the Summer Concubine had given Jethan for rent on Turquoise Woman's room—and weaving about it every spell she knew, to call lightning, fire and malice from whatever wight it was she had seen in the Redbone tombs. *And if you've been debasing your currency, Your Majesty,* she thought grimly, *and this turns out not to be real silver, shame on you.*

The rest of that money Pomegranate Woman had taken to

the markets, traders and receivers of stolen goods throughout the Slaughterhouse, and in spite of the rioting and chaos that had punctuated the day had come up with most of the implements and substances Shaldis had seen Urnate Urla use in his summoning of the wight. Shaldis now tied little sacks of silver, ocher and iron filings to the belt she'd wound on over the pantaloons, shirt and tunic Pomegranate Woman had unearthed for her—a little ragged and odoriferous, but preferable to going into what might turn into combat with that gaudy green dress tangling her feet. She'd also acquired two six-foot cottonwood saplings stripped of bark and branches, and to each of these she tied a siver disk: one of them Urnate Urla's, the other her own makeshift copy, which she hoped would do what it was supposed to do and draw away whatever fire and lightning might be flung at her.

They'd be on the move, if they got into the temple at all. There was no question of drawing a protective circle and staying put within it. The temple was scry warded from here to next week; if they wanted to see what was inside, they'd have to go look.

The gods only knew what they'd meet.

Shaldis held out both staffs. "You pick which you want."

Pomegranate Woman shut her eyes, turned around three times, then stopped with her back to Shaldis and groped out with one unseeing hand.

She touched the copy, closed her hand around the pole.

"You can still go up to the Citadel," said Shaldis quietly as they stepped out into the chilly starlight of predawn. Her mind hummed with sleeplessness and with the effort of working ward spells around herself and Pomegranate Woman protecting against every evil she could think of. She had wrought, too, the Sigil of Sisterhood between them; its warmth was comforting, like a heated brick wrapped in cloth on a chilly night. "The Summer Concubine needs every helper, every Raven." It gashed her heart not to be there for that triumph of the women-who-do-magic, the Raven sisters—the vindication of that cloth dyer all those years ago who'd been lighting bits of kindling in the street.

But if Lohar and his henchmen were going to try something today to disrupt the Rite, today was the only time she could be sure of finding the temple empty.

Empty, of course, except for whatever it was whose magic she'd felt through the door.

And if the new Song did not bring rain, and Lohar's followers did rise up in open rebellion tomorrow, it would almost certainly be impossible to get into the temple—maybe not even possible to get near it.

Would her absence from the Ring—and that of Pomegranate Woman—make the difference in the rain coming or not coming?

She didn't know.

Pomegranate Woman's breath made a thin mist in the starlight. "You can't go alone into there, honey." She sounded like a mother trying to talk a bullheaded twelve-year-old out of going into the local tavern to look for Papa. "I've dreamed of the Ring all my life—dreamed of the Song of the Sun Mages. Pontifer has too. If we get rid of this thing in the temple—or find out what it is, so that something can be done about it—maybe I'll have my chance to sing for the rains some other year."

Some other year, thought Shaldis, as they slipped from shadow to shadow under the flickering protection of the strongest cloak they could summon. For many days now—since the night she had been attacked, the night of the full moon—she had looked only from one day to the next, trying to outrace or outdodge or outfox her attacker. To Summon this spring's rains. To survive till tomorrow.

That there would be another year—whatever happened today—came as a surprise, and somehow the thought of it lessened the blind, frantic hammering of her heart.

As they halted at the corner of Little Pig Alley with the heavy black reek of old blood from the temple rising to their nostrils, she murmured, "If I don't get to say so . . . thank you for coming with me."

And Pomegranate Woman soundlessly patted her shoulder.

Pomegranate Woman had been correct in her observation of the temple yesterday; Shaldis had been correct in concluding that Lohar would try something today. Chicken Lane was full of men: laborers, beggars, small-time artisans, out-of-work stockmen and butchers from the yards. All of them sported the cropped hair of the Believers. All of them were silent, disciplined and alert. And all of them were armed.

From their position in the gateway of Greasy Yard, Shaldis glanced sidelong at her companion, raised her brows. They'd talked last night, in between Shaldis's completion of the copied protective disk and her painstaking review of Urnate Urla's diagrams and spells, about sending word of their suspicions to the king, warning him that the True Believers were more than likely going to try to disrupt the Rite. The king's a smart man, Shaldis had said. He's going to be ready for something like this, I think, whether we send him a message or not. And if we send him a message that's intercepted, that may be enough for Lohar to leave someone guarding the temple.

Watching Lohar move from group to group—watching the glint of swords, of halberds, of serious weapons of warfare in the thin glow of shuttered lanterns—Shaldis prayed she'd made the right decision. More men were moving into the street and under the darkness of the temple porch, and these, she could see, wore not the cropped hair of the True Believers but the topknots of professional swordsmen.

"They have to be guards from one of the great houses," she breathed to Pomegranate Woman.

"Tcha!" the old woman whispered. "That's not right! Pontifer, do you see that?" And she glanced down at her heel where presumably her imaginary pig had followed them from the Salt-Pan ruins.

Which? Shaldis wondered. Akarian? Mohrvine? The Summer Concubine had mentioned both as unreliable in the ever-shifting quicksands of alliance that shored up House Jothek's rule.

We'll have to walk past those men, she thought. *Maybe past the man who seized me in the darkness.* She felt cold, her hands sweating; she wished she had made herself sleep last night. They would certainly have to pass by Seb Dolek, anyway. The young former Sun Mage was right there at Lohar's elbow, handing out weapons, speaking to this man or that. He seemed, in very short order, to have made himself indispensable to the half-crazed prophet—from somewhere she recalled that Lohar had been a Sun Mage himself. Clever and educated, the young man was almost certainly better at dealing with the real world than was the Mouth of Nebekht.

Lohar had better watch out in a couple of years, Shaldis thought, watching them together. *If he can't be a Sun Mage, I'm sure Seb Dolek will settle for taking over leadership of a powerful cult.*

The temple door opened, a cubit-wide postern in the huge iron-bound portal. A big man with a scarred chin and a fanatic's cropped hair started handing out halberds and spears to those who didn't have them already.

Now or never. Whatever else could be said about that cold terrible magic, Shaldis knew that it was stronger than any cantrip of hers would be if she tried to move the iron bolts once the door was shut.

Zin, zin, we are the wind. . . .

The two women drifted among the crowd like shreds of mist, Shaldis nearly sick with dread as they passed within a few feet of Seb Dolek. Not a shadow flickered in their wake along the wall to the door. Not a dust mote stirred with the light passage of their clothing. They stood for a time at the far end of the porch in the shadows of the pillars, watching the man with the scarred chin and waiting for him to move out of the way. He moved off a few paces to hand someone a bow; Shaldis lengthened her stride, let go of her companion's hand, darted through just before him as he turned back, her heart in her throat. Pressed to the wall inside, she turned her head just in time to see him shut the postern door and throw the bolt.

Her heart turned to cold iron with dread. *No* . . .

She was trapped in the temple alone.

"Damn," muttered the doorkeeper. He bent to pick up a halberd that had fallen to the floor, shot back the bolt again and opened the door.

Pomegranate Woman was through like a cat, pressed to the wall, panting, at Shaldis's side. "Here, Pontifer!" she whispered—loud enough, Shaldis would have sworn, for the doorkeeper and Lohar and every man in Chicken Lane to hear. She nearly screamed, *Damn you and your stupid imaginary pig!*

The doorkeeper lumbered away to one side of the vestibule, where an open door showed a table, a lamp, a bed. Shaldis looked around her quickly, orienting herself: The high-ceilinged, windowless vestibule in which they stood stretched across the front of the temple, which she knew from her previous stay in the Slaughterhouse was a long rectangle whose short side faced south onto Chicken Lane, and whose length stretched back north some three hundred feet into the warren of mud shacks that had grown up around it. The courtyard where they brought in animals for sacrifice lay along the east side, though not for the whole length of the building.

The great doors before them now, as they stood in the vestibule, would lead into the sanctuary if the place was anything like the temples of Koan and Ean and Neriki the god of merchants that she was familiar with. Mold-stained frescoes loomed around them, flaking from the walls, overscrawled with crude drawings of the sword and the iron girdle that were Nebekht's symbols. Shaldis wondered if she should put a sleep spell on the scar-chinned porter immediately to keep him out of the way, and remembered the way Lohar had cried out the moment she'd placed the Sigils of Listening on the door.

The darkness lived. It watched them.

It also stank. Shaldis's neck prickled with the stench, which was worse inside than it had been out in the Slaughterhouse all around.

Somewhere she could hear pigs squealing, shrieks of pain picked up by stone vaulting, echoing fit to split her head.

Pomegranate Woman's hand closed hard around hers. "It's all right, Pontifer," she whispered reassuringly, bending down so the nonexistent animal could hear. And to Shaldis, "It scares him, even though he isn't a real pig and they can't hurt him. It's just the idea, you know."

"Absolutely," said Shaldis.

If Lohar's out there, who's killing the pigs?

When the doorkeeper disappeared into his room she led the way across the chipped and filthy marble floor to the sanctuary doors. The statue Lohar had reputedly taken from the tomb should be in there, and she was curious to see it. But when she pushed the doors open, she saw instead a transverse hallway broken by curtained openings at several points on the opposite wall. The wall itself was plastered, and the plaster looked new, cleaner by a dozen decades than that of the wall that separated vestibule from what had been the original sanctuary. Looking down, she saw that the pattern incised in the floor was cut clean across by that new wall.

"What is it?" breathed Pomegranate Woman. Hesitantly, Shaldis touched the pale roughcast only a foot or so before her.

"It's a defense, I think. Maybe a maze. Anyone who enters the sanctuary of Nebekht has to make at least one jog down a short passageway. Maybe more."

She pushed on the wall. There was no give to it—Lohar must have drilled the marble to plant studs to hold it in place—but looking at the floor she could tell that this had originally been part of the sanctuary. "Whoever comes into the sanctuary has to pass between certain points." She looked up. The ceiling was low, planks laid between the walls and painted black. Somewhere she smelled damp leather.

"That's crazy."

"In the temple of a god, yes." Shaldis backed out into the vestibule again, closed the doors very quietly. "Gods don't actually dwell in their temples, of course; they exist where they please. But in a house where some kind of jiggery-pokery is going on, it makes a lot of sense." She remembered the house of Ahure, the narrow doorways and the careful arrangement of the furniture, to make sure that the petitioner stood in exactly the right place for the cold stream of the hidden ventilators to chill him or her to the marrow.

Only this, she thought, was deadlier.

And very odd, for someone who clearly did have genuine magic.

"There'll be another way into the sanctuary through the court of the animals," she whispered, her eyes searching the darkness of the vestibule's eastern end. There was a door there corresponding to that of the doorkeeper's little room on the west side; that meant there'd be a little room there, with luck opening in its turn into the court of the animals. The door was locked, with a sliding bolt and internal tumblers. Counter-spells scratched and grated on Shaldis's thoughts the moment she put forth her mind to feel for them clumsily.

"They'll know if a spell is worked here." Shaldis's voice was barely louder than a moth wing brushing stone. "Sometimes it's simple, like a spell that triggers a bell to ring, or a candle to light. I don't think that's what this is, though."

"Makes sense." The old woman fished in one of her many pockets and produced a half-dozen bent wires. "I never could make these things work but once in ten tries when my brother taught me. But now I can listen through the wood for the scratch on the tumblers. . . . He'd have turned up his nose, my brother." She probed into the keyhole, ear pressed to the wood, turning and manipulating delicately. Shaldis realized that the old woman's hands were as supple as her own, and saw again Hathmar's arthritic joints and stiff gait, his pale eyes blinking damply behind crystal lenses.

"Pontifer," admonished Pomegranate Woman severely, glancing down beside her. "You be a good pig! Sometimes they just forget their manners," she apologized.

Shaldis didn't even want to ask.

There was, as she'd suspected, a chamber corresponding to that of the doorkeeper from which wide doors opened into the court of the animals. Even through the shut doors and barred shutters the stink of the court penetrated, and when Shaldis and Pomegranate Woman slipped through into the court it was staggering. Morning light was just beginning to stain the sky, but already the roar of the flies above the dung-splotched dirt was like the muttering of an angry mob.

"I guess Nebekht doesn't approve of fly wards," muttered Shaldis. The court, stretching along the temple's east side, was separated from Little Pig Alley by a twenty-foot wall. Between that wall and the dark basalt side of the temple, the dung lay nearly ankle deep, as if no one had bothered to shovel it in years. The only place it had been scraped away was around the two wells, eight or ten feet from the temple wall and covered with round slabs of stone, chained and barred with iron. Shaldis supposed that if she were dying of thirst she'd bring herself to drink the water seeping from this soil.

At the far end of the court, in the temple wall, there was a wide door, closed but not visibly barred. A mushy path beaten in the dung amply indicated that this was the route taken by the animals to sacrifice. Dimly she could still hear the pigs screaming.

As they stole down the length of the court, Shaldis paused to touch the well covers in passing, felt the water deep below.

Water and magic. An echo of that jangling, uneasy, alien power, like the sound of chains shaken far away.

Crazier, she thought. Edgier. She tightened her grip on the cottonwood pole and hoped that if someone or something started flinging fire and lightning at them the silver disk would draw it aside the way it had for Urnate Urla.

She struck at a fly that swooped at her unveiled eyes, tangled in the strands of hair that had worked loose from the knot at the base of her neck. "That door should lead into some room behind, or next to, the sanctuary," she said softly. "Someplace where they hold the beasts for sacrifice." She thrashed her hand at another fly. "You have to use your own judgment here. If something happens to one of us—*damn* these flies!—the other one has to retreat *immediately* and get word to the Summer Concubine about what we've seen here so far. If we're attacked by anything, we stick together as long as we can and protect each other, but if I yell for you to run, *run*. All—"

"Listen." The older woman turned her head, her blue eyes

narrowing as she struck at the swarming insects. "Wasn't it lighter a minute ago?"

Shaldis looked around her. Dawn had been in the sky—and with it the sounds of the Citadel horns, an accusation that cut at her heart.

The horns were gone, as if the two women had slipped over into some place other than the temple court. There was darkness and cold, like the winter fog that rose from Sulfur Lake, and, somewhere distantly, the agonized screaming of the pigs.

But wherever they were, the flies remained. They swirled around the two women, clung and bit. Shaldis struck at them with her hands, called on the fly wards that were one of the first formal magics she'd learned, but they struck and tangled harder. She pinched her eyes shut, twisted her head as they tried to crawl up her nose and into her ears—Pomegranate Woman pressed one of her many scarves into her hands and she wrapped it around her face, trapping a number of flies against her skin but protecting herself from the growing attack. Somewhere she could hear the pigs still screaming. *Why don't they finish those poor things off?* she wondered. *How many of them are there? And who's killing them?* She pushed forward, groping through the darkness for the wall.

But there was no wall. Blindly, she stumbled in black fog. The ground was soft under her feet, sucking at them like mud. *I'll sink*, she thought. *I'll sink and be trapped.* Panic clutched her and she felt as if she'd somehow wandered into a dream, a dream that clung and stank. Air that first whispered, then roared with the screaming red wildness of alien power. Pain ripped at her calves. *There are snakes in the mud, poisonous snakes.*

Her breath came short, and for an instant she saw herself toppling over out of the real world, into nightmare. . . .

"Follow Pontifer!" she heard Pomegranate Woman shout,

muffled in veils and flies. "He knows the way through to the door!"

She pressed forward, holding hard to Shaldis's hand. Shaldis stumbled, eyes shut, feeling as if she were suffocating, as if the biting, crawling things would devour her. Feeling as if in another moment she would wrench her hand away from the old woman's and run screaming to her death in the darkness.

What am I doing? she demanded of herself furiously. *She's following a damn imaginary pig.*

But under her feet she felt hard-packed dust and filth, no longer the fearful black mollience of that other world into which she'd been drawn. Eyes shut tight, one hand holding the folds of the scarf over her nostrils, she conjured in the air, in her mind, all the runes of clear seeing, weaving them into sigils of what was real. The bites on her legs, like jabbing needles, were those of big slaughterhouse horseflies, not snakes at least. The memory that could reconstruct spells after one viewing reconstructed the tilt of the courtyard ground, the differences between the temple's stone wall and the plastered brick of the wall that surrounded the court. *If I touch stone, I move right; if I touch brick, left.*

She touched stone. Pomegranate Woman's big hand clung to her wrist, leading her. *I'll have to ask her what nightmare world she's seeing. . . .*

"Good boy, Pontifer," she heard her say through the roaring of the flies. "Good pig!"

Good pig indeed.

She felt the doorjamb, the hinges, the latch of the door into the temple. Whatever place it was they had stumbled into, drawn by those alien spells, they had for the moment fought their way clear. A few of the counterspells clinging to the iron of the latch were old, spells placed by what felt like Earth Wizards long ago, not that hot red lightning of the temple's newer power. The heavy panel moved back. Blind as she was, she felt the cold within. Malice waiting. Watching.

She slipped in behind Pomegranate Woman. Together they pulled shut and latched the door.

Flies buzzed away as she unwound and shook out the scarf. A last one bit her on the hand. Pomegranate Woman was slapping them off her arms, out of her hair, her clothing. "Thank you," Shaldis gasped. And then, looking down in the general direction of the floor, she said, "And thank you, Pontifer. You saved both our lives."

Pomegranate Woman smiled.

They were in a short corridor that led into the bowels of the temple; trails of trampled dung disappeared into darkness that Shaldis's eyes could not pierce. Fear gripped her again, nauseating in its intensity. The blackness seemed about to explode, with violence, with hatred, with power, with blood. She felt her hands grow almost numb.

When a spark leaped close beside her she almost jumped out of her skin. It was Pomegranate Woman with a striking kit, lighting a scrap of tow. "First thing I did when I knew I could was put a word on it so it won't go out," the old woman confided. "More than just looking at wood and making it light, it always drove me crazy when I thought I'd have a spark going and then it'd up and die. You got a candle?"

Shaldis shook her head. It hadn't occurred to her to carry one for years.

Pomegranate Woman fished a stub from one of her purses, cupped her hand around the flame. The light made Shaldis feel better and showed her for a moment the dim shapes of double doors at the corridor's far end. Word or no word, she suspected the moment they moved toward these, the tiny light would puff out. She spoke Words of Light, but the darkness swallowed them; darkness that crept, as if invisible fire were falling through the air.

She held up the silver disk of protection on its staff, extending it out to the side and as far from her body as she could, and moved forward into the dark.

She hadn't thought of the flies, but she had thought of rats. When she heard their rustling, smelled the sweetish pissy stink of them growing stronger and stronger until it drowned even the stench of the pig dung in the wide, short hall, she called to life one of the ward spells she'd worked on last night. It flared like a ring of blue-burning flame moving just above the floor around them, and though the fingerlets of fire threw little light, she saw the rats. They moved like a black blanket, coarse velvet rippled and seethed by the wind. Jeweled velvet, spangled with a thousand thousand wicked ruby eyes.

She had meditated long, trained long, not to lose her concentration in the face of fear, but it was a near thing. Pomegranate Woman pressed strong wrinkled hands to Shaldis's shoulders, and she heard the old woman's whistling singsong, a little homemade spell like the zin-zin song. She had to force her mind shut against it. A rat nearly the size of a cat threw itself at the barrier, squealed and backed away. A line of its flesh smoked as if struck with a red-hot rod.

The others closed in. The noise of them was horrifying, the stink of burned fur, charred flesh, enough to distract anyone.

Shaldis shaped the spell, sang it as it had been taught to her in her mind; held it intact. As a child the only space she'd had for her own, the only place where she could be by herself, had been one of the attics at the top of the house: suffocatingly hot, but away from her grandfather, who would look all over the house for her. There had been rats there, skittering along the rafters now and then, or scratching in the walls.

She stared them down, her hatred pure. Like Buttereyes the

kitchen cat, whom she'd found once trapped in a dry well the first time she'd claimed her power, she saw them only as flesh to be destroyed, as blood to be drunk.

Piercing, probing, shocking, she felt a mind touch hers. *Who?* Like an echo of rage from far away. *Who?* Lohar's voice yesterday afternoon. *Who?* Human or alien, she couldn't tell—it didn't feel like anything she'd ever known before.

Not Lohar, she thought. *Someone else . . .*

There could have been two, she had said to the Summer Concubine. *There could have been two.*

She didn't touch the doors at the corridor's end, but thrust on them with the tip of her staff. It was fortunate that she did so. Flame blasted out of them, a blinding glare of blue and orange swatting like an angry animal. Shaldis felt the oily heat on her face, then burning her hands as it swirled into the silver disk. Shaldis held out the staff as far as she could, at the full extent of her arm, shielding her face with her other hand. The air seemed to be full of falling fire.

And cold, burningly cold.

Pigs filled the lightless room beyond the doors like battle-field dead. Some still lived, savaged hideously—throats torn, bellies torn, hamstrung, crying and kicking weakly as the life bled out of them. Shaldis thought of the three dead children the Summer Concubine had told her of, circled by vultures in the red-and-yellow rock of the Singing World. The room, Shaldis guessed at once, must lie immediately behind the main sanctuary: the ceiling was as high as that of the vestibule, and in one wall, set back in what appeared to be a tall, narrow niche, stood the idol that she knew immediately had to be the one Lohar had found in the desert tomb.

A hawk-headed man, nearly life-size and armed with sword and shield: a core of crystal, sheathed from throat to feet in gold.

At the college they had taught her the characteristics of ancient art: Durshen Dynasty, she identified the style with barely a conscious thought, they'd been very fond of the technique. The hands were left bare of the gold, wrapped around a sword of iron, and the dark-gleaming surface of the yellow metal was crossed by bands of iron: girdle, necklace, anklets.

All this she saw while the rest of her mind was still crying out in horror and disgust at the shambles of the room. The floor was awash in blood, and blood spattered the walls above head height, blood years old and black, staining the stone, overlain with blood so fresh it dripped ruby red.

Something moved, swirled among the carcasses—white lines of light that flowed among the blood like phantom snakes. Lines that poured, shining in the puddles, across the floor and up the flanks of the idol, disappearing into the crystal eyes.

Driven to her knees, focusing her mind on the rat ward, the runes of protection—trying to keep the cold, howling voice of the thing itself at bay and out of her thoughts—Shaldis watched the ribbons of shining plasma until only the light of them remained. Crystalline, hard and steady, those eyes seemed to watch her. The rats fled away among the dead pigs, but a muttering persisted at the edges of her mind, blurring her ability to think.

Bands of iron, Shaldis thought. *Three bands of iron on gold. Where have I seen that?* Blue-burning lightning played around the idol's head, chill and infinitely distant. *A crystal heart . . .*

The lamp. Urnate Urla's lamp.

And, she thought, something else, something she'd seen . . . where?

Recollection hovered on the edge of her mind.

She held the silver disk warily out to one side and called

out, *"Drinata! Drinata! Meliangobet!"* And hoped she got the pronunciation right.

For one instant, for one second of suspended time, she saw in her heart the image of Meliangobet.

A thing of fire and dizzying power. A thing of love such as she had not imagined could exist—nothing like human love. Of strange games and delights. A reaching-out and a folding-in. A juggling with water, sand and cloud.

Songs.

A smile she would have followed to her death in the wastelands.

And a taste—just a taste—of the power she had felt among the tombs, when first the dead thing staggered to Urnate Urla's bloody lure.

Then silence. She stood alone in darkness before the gold and crystal shape of Nebekht.

Pigs' blood and rats, and the thin crackle of the rat ward all around her. But she could no longer see it, or anything but those steady, shining crystal eyes.

"What is it?" whispered Pomegranate Woman from the darkness behind her. "Pontifer says—"

"I don't know what it is." Shaldis knelt—not daring to look away from those crystal eyes, not daring to spare one thought from her mind, from her spells of protection—and began to mark the floor. "But I'm going to find out." There was no need, here, of the long, looping net of sourcing lines she'd seen Urnate Urla draw: She stood in the heart of the place of power. She drew the core of his diagram: a pentagram, and a triangle within it. A square and a hexagon. Other figures within them, smaller and smaller, except that they weren't. They only looked that way because they were farther and farther off, the way Pontifer only looked invisible and imaginary.

"Tell the Summer Concubine . . ." She didn't know how to

finish, didn't know what to say. "Tell the Summer Concubine what's here. Tell her I'll contact her through the Sigil of Sisterhood, if I can."

She heard Pomegranate Woman call out something to her—she didn't know what. Blue lightning flickered down the golden shoulders, the gleaming thighs, and formed up in the air before her a continuation of the figures that she drew, stretching away into distance that wasn't distance.

And at the end of that line of symbols—which only looked like a series of concentric figures—Nebekht waited, watching her with his crystal eyes.

She walked toward him along the road she had drawn, knowing that he had the answer, or part of the answer.

Blue fire swallowed her up.

TWENTY-SEVEN

As the shouting of the rioters drew nearer, racketing off the walls of the Avenue of the Sun, Oryn reflected that he really should have ordered that suit of armor before he left for the aqueduct camp. If he was going to go in for the heroism of leading troops into battle, the least he could do was to be properly dressed for it in something kingly that fit instead of some portly cavalryman's borrowed cuirass with six inches of very undignified peacock silk bulging through the lacing at each side.

He shifted his sword in his sweating hand and thought, *I have never struck a man with a weapon. Not really. Not to kill.*

Dear gods. The thought turned him sick.

"Traitorous dogs!" Barún strode to Oryn's side on the walkway above the Citadel gate in an enormous swirl of crimson cloak. "Lohar swore his word!"

He sounded genuinely indignant—and genuinely surprised. Oryn sometimes wondered if his younger brother lived in the same world as everyone else did.

The True Believers came into sight at the end of the street, some of them armed with sticks and baskets of rotting meat, sacrificial scraps too putrid for even the very poor in the Slaughterhouse to take. Others bore the weapons of the district: meat axes, ox goads, clubs. Others still carried the businesslike gear of professionals.

They'd be within bowshot soon. Half a dozen of the palace guards grouped at the top of each pylon that guarded the Citadel gates, and fifty more, mounted, waited behind the shut gates themselves. Lohar dashed at the rioters' head, waving them on, practically daring Oryn to trigger the fighting by having him shot. He was unarmed, of course, ostentatiously so.

Would Bax order a volley of arrows? Would Taras Greatsword?

Taras would have had the man put down a year ago, like a rabid dog, reflected Oryn. *Maybe I should have too*. There'd been riots yesterday not only in the Slaughterhouse and the Grand Bazaar District, but spreading into the Circus, the Flowermarket District, the Spicemarket District. Dozens of teyn had escaped, and when cornered had fought like beasts.

No word from Bax or the nomad sorties.

Sweet and strong, the voices of the singers lifted into the morning air.

"Nebekht rules!" screamed the voices in the street, and rocks, bricks, hunks of adobe clattered against the shut Citadel gates. "The Will of Nebekht is the only law!" accompanied by the juicy, stinking splat of rotted goat entrails and handfuls of goose guano. "All praise to the goodness and mercy of the Iron-Girdled One!"

A fight had developed where the Street of Yellow Lanterns debouched into the Avenue of the Sun. A squad of city guards from the Flowermarket had heard the ruckus and come to reinforce the men there—commendable, thought Oryn worriedly, but potentially deadly. Somewhere above the patchwork of tiled roofs and dry garden vines, smoke was pouring up.

"Any word from Bax?" he asked quietly as young Jethan came out onto the walkway above the gate. "Or Lord Sarn?"

"No, Majesty. But the guards over on the walls near the bluff say they can see men coming up the gorges. Armed, they think."

"I'll get over there," said Barún. "Half a dozen should be enough to turn them back." And he strode away, calling to the guards, who followed him with the same delight they'd always shown in following Taras Greatsword wherever he led.

Oryn shook his head. *If he wasn't such a blockhead I'd have abdicated in his favor years ago.*

"And my uncle?" He turned back to Jethan. The Square of the Mages beneath them was now dark with men, ragged men for the most part, though many of them looked cleaner and better fed than any beggar Oryn had ever seen. "He was supposed to be here."

"He left before it grew light. A messenger came. Something about his daughter."

Foxfire Girl, remembered Oryn. A pretty minx. Who, according to his sources, was going to marry Lord Akarian, the gods help them all. "Get a man to find him. And see if you can find someone to ride out and get me word of Bax. . . . Not you, dear boy," he added as the young man showed all signs of dashing down to the courtyard and springing onto the first horse he

saw. "Find one of the Citadel servants, if you can. I'm afraid,"
he said, "that in a very short time we're going to need every
trained man we've got."

Raeshaldis saw that she was in the Jasmine Garden, where she
had first met the Summer Concubine, seven days ago. Her
grandfather was there, shouting at her, striking her with a
whip. She was naked, and when she fell to her hands and
knees, she saw that the grass was beaded with blood.

This is a dream, she told herself, though she knew she was
wide awake. *It is only a dream.*

She got to her feet, staggering—the blows of the four-
thonged whip smarted on her flanks with the stinging burn of
reality—and made herself face him.

He was made out of blood. He was made out of fear, the
shrinking, suffocating fear of a six-year-old child who knows
she cannot escape, who knows that without this man's love
and approval she will be turned out into the streets to die. She
thought, *I did love him, back then.* She remembered loving him
without any recollection of what it had felt like.

She'd forgotten at what point in time her love had turned
to hate. She wondered if he were still alive.

He was shouting at her, but the words were only a shrill
squeal, like a pig in agony. She crossed her arms over her
breasts, willing herself not to feel the cut of the whip, facing
him, putting aside her fear. Putting aside her memories, her
pain, her self. Searching for what lay beyond and outside.

It was more difficult than she had supposed, to see things
not in terms of herself.

Who are you? she asked. *Who are you?*

Her grandfather screamed at her. Hathmar screamed at her. Jethan screamed at her.

Who are you?

I'm in pain, I'm in pain.

I'm afraid, I'm afraid.

Echoing confusion, like a hysterical drunk, words and thoughts looping back on themselves. The whip thongs wrapped around the cottonwood pole that she held out to block them.

Who would you be if you weren't afraid and in pain?

The place around them transformed itself into a palace of crystal, wrought of air and light. But the scintillant pillars were all held together with rotting blood, like a kind of black glue. The blood still lived, and the creatures it had been taken out of—pigs, geese, chickens, rats, a lot of rats—were still in it in some fashion. The heat of them made it liquid, and thus able to hold the bits of crystal and light and air together. From the corners of her eyes she could glimpse the animals themselves, or gray, cloudy shapes of what they had been, in their own thoughts and in those of humankind. Tiny flecks of lightning—the sparks of thousands of animal lives—ran up and down the pillars, up and down her grandfather's body, holding him together too. Giving shape to the thing inside.

Who are you?

Nebekht.

The voice was still a pig's hoarse grunt, but the face became the crystal face of the statue. The gold and crystal gleamed, but they were soft as flesh. The staring crystal eyes were streaky with blood, and blood held every atom of the statue together: the heat of blood, the life that had been in the blood.

Waves of madness came off him like the stench of the blood, like the dark reek of *ijnis*. Animals, torn apart and dying in agony, wondering at their suffering and only wishing it would stop. The pain and the heat of their lives hammered at Shaldis, skinning her brain, her nerves. She saw that in this place—in the god's mind—she, like the god, could make whatever place she chose, and people it with whom she would.

A corridor opened through the palace, behind Nebekht's shoulder, clear as in a shadowy dream. Down it she saw the Citadel library, every book open to her, every fragment of knowledge hers for the savoring. In that Citadel—in this place—all her spells would work. She never need leave.

In the shadows of that library her mother smiled and beckoned. *Dearest, I have grapes for you, fresh from the market. . . .* Her father waved, big and rosy and happy, joyful to see her. *Sit down, Old One, drink coffee with me and let's talk. I've missed you. . . .* Exactly as she remembered them.

Because, she thought, with a curious sad clarity, *what I see is only my memories of them.*

The whip had ceased to strike her. She was dressed again in the white robe of a novice. The pain was gone. The crystal pillars, the near incomprehensible chambers of light and floating air, retreated to the periphery of her vision. The library came closer. She could run into it, and from it into the rooms that she knew lay beyond: her own attic at home, her hidden sanctuary, but without the rats. Her mother's kitchen, always with honeyed apples waiting for her. The market as she remembered it. Or as she had always wished it would be, though it never was, quite. The market without the camel drivers and the dogs dying in the ditches, where all the beggars were clean and friendly and not really hungry.

If I turn away from them, will these memories disappear forever out of my mind? Will I ever be able to remember them again, this clearly, this lovingly?

Smells of apples, smells of ink, smells of water and books and her father's favorite soap.

She crushed them out, looked back into the god's blood-filled crystal eyes.

Who do you want to be?

Prince of the Sunflash. Naruansich. Lord of the Thousand Lights.

She saw him, like a revelation. As the book of the djinni described him, as old Gyrax the windmaster described him, whose friend he had been almost eighty years ago. Saw him in the swirling column of dancing light, that bright, elongate form: "His face is like flame and alabaster," Gyrax had said to the small group of novices when speaking of his own experiences with the djinni. "Sometimes like a young man's, sometimes serpentine, as if it is made of jewels. His hands are white, and clear as diamonds. Heat spreads from him, even in the coldest nights, and the sands beneath his feet glitter like living diamonds."

She said, "You're a djinn." And she remembered where she had heard the word *meliangobet.*

It was one of the list of djinni's names that she'd had to memorize. One of those endless lists that the loremaster gave her: types of rabbits, shapes of cactus flowers, textures and colors of sand. Names to be memorized so that they would hear her when she summoned. So that they would obey.

Awareness crashed down on her as if she stood in a building whose roof had collapsed without warning: awareness of what had happened to the djinni. Awareness, and horror, and grief without end.

She saw in her mind Urnate Urla in the graveyard, conjuring the walking dead with a trap of crystal and iron-girdled gold. Saw the ropes of white light stream from the dead mouth, the flame snake along the ground and out of the brick of the tomb. Saw the flame and the light and the smoky plasma dissipate, dissolving into the night, disappearing forever.

They are dying.

Tears flowed from her eyes, like weeping in a dream.

Men lost their magic and remained living men. But magic was not only the art of the djinni. It was the stuff of their bodies, of their world, of their selves. Whatever magic was now, it was not what it had been.

Around her, the crystal pillars, the halls and chambers and gardens wrought of air and sunlight, floating like bubbles high over the endless sands of the deep desert, all these darkened again as the dirtied life forces of sacrificed beasts reclaimed the Sunflash Prince's mind. He stood before her, wrought of decaying blood as her grandfather had been, held together by blood, renewed each day by the life energies of the sacrifices, more and more each day.

They have no flesh, and so must build themselves bodies of magic. That failing, they must take refuge where they can. In corpses, it seems. And in houses of crystal, gold and iron . . . It must be some specific spell, or combination of elements, that can hold them.

And earning his keep, thought Shaldis, looking into those alien crystal eyes, *by bringing water to the temple well, so that Lohar—or more likely the cleverer Seb Dolek—could bind the thirsty and frightened to him.*

Shouting echoed around them, voices growing louder, coming closer. With an abruptness that shocked her, Shaldis was standing in the sanctuary of the temple—naked again, so she knew (or earnestly hoped) that this was a vision within the Sunflash Prince's dream. He was beside her, a blob of shadow that stank and dripped, a crouching shape like a huge boar pig, stupid malice in his crystal eyes. None of the men pouring into the room paid either of them the least attention, and Shaldis reached into the shape of her own mind to clothe herself in her white novice's robes. Like her grandfather's whip, hate and terror and malignant resentment seemed to fly around the torchlit cavern of the sanctuary like broken glass in a sand-storm, tearing at her flesh. Stinging her like the flies.

Pomegranate Woman, she thought, but could see no sign of her in this dream-union of the actual temple and what existed in Nebekht's mind and Nebekht's perceptions. Oddly enough, she could see Pontifer Pig appearing and disappearing among the pillars along one side of the room. Men jostled, shoved, as they poured through the single small door that opened from the de-fensive maze. Lohar, an outsize sword in one hand and a club in the other, blood on his grimy tunic and clotted in his dirty hair. Seb Dolek, a satisfied smirk on his dustless face, as if all things were working out well for the benefit of Seb Dolek.

Three men dragged Jethan between them, and Shaldis al-most cried out his name. The young guard was struggling, though the men struck him again and again to quiet him; his face was covered with blood and his arms with cuts and mud and dust. He was shouting, "Traitors! Traitors! Let him go or by the gods you will pay!"

People were starting to shout, "Sacrifice! Sacrifice to Nebekht!" and Lohar's eyes, wilder and madder, showed that he was being drawn into the whirlwind he had himself whis-tled into being. Someone came running from the back room with an ax, its handle clotted with years' worth of animal blood. "Let he who commands the universe have blood!"

Shaldis guessed what had happened even as she recog-nized—barely—the other man the mob thrust forward, sprawl-ing in a great crash of armor and blue-green silk at Lohar's feet, like a peacock snared and half plucked and beaten by mali-cious boys. Oryn son of Taras rolled to his feet, curiously grace-ful for a heavy man—Shaldis had noticed that physical grace the day she'd seen him at the Citadel—and struck aside the bullyboys who would have thrown him down again.

"Jethan, keep still! That's an order! It's no good!" He strode to the shoving knot of captive and captors and seized the man with the ax and flung him back, his strength literally lifting him off his feet. Someone struck the king over the back with a bloodied club and someone else yelled a tired jest about the king and pretty boys, but the king paid no heed to it, only commanded, "Don't!" when another of the three captors pulled out a knife. He turned back to Lohar. "This man has nothing to do with your quarrel with me. Let him go."

Shaldis turned to the Sunflash Prince, shocked and frightened. She saw, in the crystalline eyes, some change, some expression—an understanding of what he beheld. The air around him jangled like flaming bells—the quality of djinn magic, thought Shaldis. Like that of Meliangobet among the tombs. She had never heard it described so, but then all descriptions had been written by men. They would perceive it differently because their magic was different.

In the dark around them she could see that the temple was like the magic palace of the djinn's memory, a construct held together with the blood and life glimmer of animals dying in pain. But it was a construct aligned with the reality that lay beyond Nebekht's trapped mind, true events passing in the landscape of his dream. The men who moved through it were real. They shoved each other and muttered; she recognized the scar-chinned caretaker who'd handed weapons out through the door, and old Zarb the drunk from Greasy Yard. Jethan spit at Lohar and was struck down. Shaldis cried, "You idiot!" knowing it was really happening, feeling the thudding echo of his pain in her own skull.

"You idiot!" The king thrust away the blow of a meat ax, taking a cut on his own hand.

It was the closest Shaldis had ever seen Oryn son of Taras. That first day in the Citadel, at a distance, she'd found him both impressive and comical in his robes of purple and green with his feather fans and extravagant, velvety voice; she couldn't imagine what the beautiful Summer Concubine could find in him to bring such delight to her eyes. He wrenched the ax from its wielder and immediately flung it from him; he must have known that holding a weapon of any sort would make him a target and there was no chance of his cutting himself free in this mob. In the blood-stringy frame of his hair she saw even now, in panic and exhaustion, the bright intelligence of his eyes, and his hands, clasped one around the other with blood welling through the fingers, were a musician's hands.

Casting away the weapon made the men step back a little from him. He stood alone among them, over Jethan's body, and silence settled on the sanctuary though the crowd now packed it from wall to wall.

"Oryn son of Taras." Lohar flung up his arms impressively. "Nebekht calls you to justice for the crime you have committed against your people and against the chief of all the gods! What have you to say?"

"I say that you are mistaken." The king, too, had been taught how to make his voice carry, and it was, as Shaldis remembered, deep and musical. He was certainly in pain, from the cut on his hand and the terrible bruising that showed through his torn and bloodied clothes, but the ringing majesty of his tones dominated the sanctuary. "I say that you are the false prophet of a true god, a god whose words you claim to interpret but who is in fact only a mask for your own greed for power. I say that this disgraces Nebekht as surely as it disgraces every man here who seeks to *truly* serve Nebekht's will."

Beside her, Shaldis was aware of the Sunflash Prince, like a tongue of flame almost unseen over the slumped darkness of the animal that he had now mostly become. She felt the dancing glimmer of his applause, and saw—as if looking down a long dark corridor, much like the one that had led to the library of her mind—a fat, curly-haired child standing in a protective circle in the desert, wide-eyed with wonder at his first sight of the djinni. A child stepping over the boundary, no fear in his hazel-green eyes.

His mouth working inarticulately, Lohar lunged at the king. Oryn caught his wrists, holding off the clutching hands from his throat but offering no attack. "How dare you!" screamed the Mouth of Nebekht, spittle flying from his lips. "You blaspheme Nebekht! All who believe, hear the words of the Mouth of the god!"

"All praise to Nebekht!" The response swept the temple like wind going through the date groves at night.

During the commotion, somebody—probably the scar-chinned caretaker—had opened the veil before the statue. Shaldis guessed the statue had been turned on its plinth. The niche in which it stood was really a tall opening between the sacrificial chamber and the sanctuary. With the curtain parted the stink of the chamber of sacrifices was enough to knock down a man in the sanctuary. On either side of the image, slow fires began to glow—hidden air tubes, thought Shaldis, like the one Ahure had. Looking up, she saw again the sculpted gold over the crystal, the iron girdle around the waist, and the bands of black metal around the ankles and on the feathered throat. Like the bands of iron on Urnate Urla's golden lamp. An ancient device of the Durshen Dynasty to trap djinni, she thought, and wondered how well it would work if not reinforced with powerful spells.

In his hands Nebekht bore his iron sword. In the dream that mingled with her consciousness the very walls of the temple, with their leprous frescoes and patched plaster, were held together with gore.

"When he stepped forth from among the other gods among whom he had concealed himself," said Lohar, tearing himself from the king and stepping back, "Nebekht made his will clear to us. He is the giver of all good, in his time and in his way. By his will alone do men live. Those men who play with magic have *always* sinned, tampering with the will of Nebekht. Always Nebekht the Merciful has hoped that men would see their error and put their sin aside."

Beside her, Shaldis could sense the dark, jangling presence of the djinn; could smell the blood and feel the heat, not the pure fire of which he had once been composed, but the twitchy, flashing bursts of life energy he had taken. She felt, too, the drag of his consciousness on her—she could think of no other way of describing it. Felt his awareness of her, and the slow growth of his shadow engulfing her.

She looked down now and saw her own hands, her own white novice's robe, spotted and streaked with oozing blood.

And, raising her head, she saw his eyes. Animal, and greedy, wanting only to devour her as he devoured the sacrifices.

Revolted and terrified, she stepped back from him; raised the staff with its protective silver disk.

"Do you repent?" Lohar demanded.

The king replied, "I repent only that I didn't shut you in prison when first I heard the lies you told about Nebekht." Angry shouting drowned his words. The stone walls, the flat high ceiling, the plastered pillars picked up the noise, but to Shaldis everything was darkening, as if the growing cloud of the djinn's greedy power clotted the air like a dirty cloud.

"When Nebekht brings the rain," Lohar was saying, "it will be a sign to us that your reign is over, Oryn son of Taras." Seb Dolek handed him the sacrificial ax; he held it up over his head. "It will be a sign to us that the protector of what is abominable to Nebekht is no friend of his. There are others of Greatsword's blood worthier to rule."

Shaldis, backing away from the growing clot of darkness

that once had been the Sunflash Prince, turned in shock, watching the men crowd past her to lay hands on the king. Jethan struggled to stand next to his king and was beaten to the floor, and Shaldis felt rage wash over her, at those who would hurt him. *Don't get yourself killed, you imbecile!*

"I accept, Lohar son of Krek." The king flung up his arms in the filthy tatters of his peacock robe; his voice echoed impressively in the sticky darkness that had now overcome all Shaldis's vision of the temple. Even through her fear she thought, *Well, if he's their prisoner he couldn't very well do anything else.*

But his response clearly took the True Believers by surprise.

"But what about yourself?" he asked, with perfect timing, into that startled silence. "Surely you can't make one rule for others and keep another for yourself? If the rain does not come when *you* Summon it, will it be a sign to *you* that *your* term is over as the Mouth of Nebekht? Will it be a sign to *you* that *you* have deceived yourself and others?"

And just as Seb Dolek was drawing breath—probably to scream *Blasphemer!*—Oryn, again with the perfect timing of a thousand after-dinner tales, added, "Or don't you trust Nebekht's belief in *you?*"

Seb Dolek then managed to yell "Blasphemer!" but his timing was off, and there was no responding roar.

Instead, the scar-chinned temple porter said thoughtfully, "That's fair."

And other men looked at each other and nodded.

"If, as you say, the Iron-Girdled One is not the god of war, but the lord of all created men," Oryn went on, "surely he cannot want his lands destroyed by fighting. You've given us three days, for which I do thank you." He placed a hand on his breast and inclined his head without a trace of sarcasm or irony, a genuine gesture of gratitude. "If, after three days, Nebekht has not sent you the rain either, will you agree that

he has some other message for humankind? Then you and I together can seek what his true will is."

The vision—the dream of the temple—was falling apart,
coming to pieces like rotting meat, and all that remained was
vile darkness roaring with flies. Shaldis heard, as from a great
distance, Lohar cry something unintelligible as the darkness
thickened around her. She saw the thing in the darkness, the
thing Naruansich had become: greedy and hungry—hungry for
the life-heat in which it renewed itself from day to day.

Only in that life could it continue to live, she thought, raising the silver disk on its staff. The floor seemed soft beneath
her feet, as it had in the magic enclave of his defenses. Flies
clung and crawled and stung in her hair again, and the world
smelled of rot. The darkness trembled with pain, and with fear.

The thing in the darkness clung to her, groped for her mind;
the cold pressure of alien magic, the flicker of those firefly
burns of stolen life. *Animals*, she thought, *thousands of animals*.
She felt here and there among them the brighter flame of teyn,
and felt a stab of anger that someone had sacrificed teyn pips
to the greedy god. It sought her now, too, and she forced it
back, concentrated all her mind, all her strength, all the magic
she had for eighteen months now been trained to wield.

I will not become part of you, she thought grimly. *I will not*.

Down a corridor in darkness she could see the library again,
and her mother and father, smiling and alive. Loving her.

Down another corridor, a room in the Citadel she recognized
as Hathmar's . . . the quarters of the Archmage. Abstruse volumes lay on the desk; petitions from all the lords of the great
houses waiting ready to be perused. A statue of Nebekht in a
niche, a statue that lived, that smiled with its crystal hawk face,
that gave good advice and brought good fortune.

Lohar's dream, Shaldis realized. The dream the Sunflash
Prince gave him, in trade for all those dying animals.

The world in which he lived now, for longer and longer at a time.

Her head pounded, as if all the veins in her skull would burst. She couldn't breathe, as if she were choking in sand.

Other dreams.

Long-ago memories, incomprehensible visions: the hot, sweeping winds of the desert, the glittering presence of those magical beings whose loves and feuds and diversions had spanned decades, lifetimes, cycles of stars. A thousand avenues of magic, of knowledge, of ancient secrets forgotten by time, drawing her, tugging her, like the hands of children playing blindman's bluff—distracting her, she was aware. (*I see you must have been a champion,* whispered a voice in her thoughts.) Trying to break her concentration, to get her lost, so that he could swallow her, absorb her. Children—she saw the fleeting visions of children who'd wandered from their homes, from their villages, children who'd seen the djinni riding, children who'd never returned.

They devoured them, she thought, suddenly understanding who and what the escaping teyn of Dry Hill had been trying to conjure in the red-and-yellow wastes of the Singing World. *They swallowed up their energy, their lives.* Of course the teyn, the dwellers in the wastelands, would try to summon the djinni to their aid using the only bait they knew.

Her own body, her own self, she conjured against that rending darkness, as if she built her own flesh again out of magic, as the djinni had. Not the luring illusion of her memories, but the simplicity of who and what she was: Raeshaldis. Big Sister. The Old One. Raven's Daughter. Pain tore at her, trying to drive her forth, and she heard her grandfather screaming at her out of the dark, felt his whip cut her naked flesh.

The screaming was the shrieking of dying pigs. The pain was their pain, not hers.

Into the darkness she said, *I can free you. I can get you out of this place.*

For she knew she could. Around her feet she made a solid floor. She thought she'd have to conjure chalk and silver into her hand, but instead she drew the diagrams in her mind. Triangle and pentangle, square and hexagram, linked and leading away.

There were three hallways. Three corridors stretching into darkness.

Down each, she could see where gate circles had been drawn, the marks to lure and capture the djinni.

Only the power symbols, the sourcing, differed.

One gate circle was in the temple's sacrificial chamber, where amid the dark lumps and rotting offal the signs she had drawn still glimmered. Of Pomegranate Woman she saw nothing, but she glimpsed something that might have been an imaginary pig just trotting out the door.

One circle glimmered in faint starlight, and she thought she saw the white shape of tombs, the ghostly gray shades of jackals among the gullies. A broken funeral cake lay by the scuffed diagram of runes, marked on the top with a G.

From there in the Redbone Hills, she thought, she could simply walk to the palace.

In the third place . . .

She saw a golden bottle with a crystal stopper, and near it the obsidian image of a god of the Hosh Dynasty, buried in the Hosh tomb.

The third diagram—the third gate circle—was inside the Hosh tomb in the Dead Hills. The place whose entrance the Summer Concubine had sought.

There could have been two, she had said to the Summer Concubine not long ago.

She knelt, and with her finger drew the sigils that matched those of the place where she wanted to go. Then she rose, and spoke to the panting thing trapped in the darkness of the temple, the darkness of the crystal image, the darkness of its past and its unfit survival. She said, "I can help you leave."

The Sunflash Prince stood before her again, in the shape of a young boy with diamond hands. The light of him sparkled on the dust around his feet, illuminated all around him the ghastly lattices where stolen life and stolen blood kept him in semblance of what he had once had.

There is nothing for me out there, Old One. There is nowhere for me to go. I cannot even be, for there is nothing to make up my self. Only in this place—in a trap of crystal sheathed in gold and ringed in iron—can I exist. And then, only if I am fed.

He was magical before her, a wonder that she would have followed, willingly, across the desert to her death, only because of his glory. She wanted to say *I am sorry*, but couldn't. She ached, her mind half blinded, bleeding, as if she had fought him back like a rapist.

And still she pitied him. There was nothing else for him to be but what he was.

Or nothing.

She stepped into the diagram and went away.

TWENTY-EIGHT

W hat's happening?" The Summer Concubine sank onto the low bed that had been set up on the terrace below the Ring, beneath an awning of canvas white as ancient bone. "I heard shouting just after sunrise."

"The True Believers attacked the Citadel." Soth handed her a towel that had been wrung out in hot herbed water. Mohrvine could say what he liked about Soth being no more than a chamberlain, but she understood what it had cost the librarian to take on the charge of the well-being of those mages not inured to daylong fasts. To no longer pretend to be what he was not, or lose himself in the longing for it, but instead to help where he could. Oryn, ever solicitous of his own comfort, had provided amply for the comfort of others, sending up pavilions, beds, curtains to separate the shelters into cubicles and servants to be on hand with lavender water and citronade.

"They managed to get into the lower court," went on the librarian after a moment's hesitation. "There were . . . some bad moments. They were driven out, but there were injuries. They're being taken care of."

He handed her a cup of chilled lemon water. There'd been a long debate among the mages whether the fasting actually concentrated power, and whether the fasting had to be absolute or not, a debate that would have made the Summer Concubine smile in amused exasperation had the stakes not been so high.

"Can I do anything?" She started to rise, though her head was throbbing from concentration and she felt giddy—Soth put a gentle hand on her shoulder, pressed her back down to the bed.

"Yes," he said. "You can lie down for two hours and then go back to the Summoning." He stood and drew the curtain around the bed. "Everything will be fine."

She heard the lie in his voice as she lay back, closed her eyes. By the smell of the air, there wasn't a trace of cloud in the sky. It was the eighth hour of the day. The warm, still air was soundless, save for the gentle *hoon* of the desert wind. The clamor that morning had sounded serious, first the shouting of rioters, coming closer and closer, then the clash of weapons. Cries and curses, unmistakably battle, had sounded as if they were right beneath them in the Citadel. She had smelled smoke. When the wind set right, she had smelled blood.

None of the Sun Mages had so much as paused. Last night when Oryn had come up to speak to the Summer Concubine's ladies, he had told them he was expecting Lohar to make trouble: "Well, he's the sort of man who'd knock over his cup on purpose just as you're making your cast at darts, isn't he?" Which had brought a laugh from the shy Moth Concubine. "Of course he'll make trouble. Someone will come and tell you, if and when something needs to be done on your part. Otherwise, don't worry about it. Only do that which the gods in their wisdom and generosity have given you the power to do."

And not one of them—not even the Moth Concubine, who was so uncertain of herself and was halfway persuaded that Lohar was right about women and magic—had broken the rhythm of their responses during the battle. Whether their concentration had stayed focused, either during the trouble or afterward, the Summer Concubine did not know.

But it was a good guess, she thought, closing her eyes, that Soth hadn't told the whole truth. Nor would he, until the Song was done.

She breathed deep, trying to retain the focus of her mind. Seeking sleep and dreams. But despite herself her mind quested down through the sun-drenched yellow stone of the Citadel, listening to the wind among the courtyards and passageways and endless, narrow, winding stairs.

She smelled blood soaking into dirt. Bax had not yet returned, and Oryn had had only a small company of the palace guards to divide between the palace and the Citadel. She listened more deeply, seeking the sounds of the infirmary: a confused murmur of men's voices somewhere—no more. Through the centuries the Citadel must have been dotted like a wedding pastry with spell wards and scry guards.

Raeshaldis hadn't come back. What had she learned yesterday about who had known of Amber Girl's power? Unlike Corn-Tassel Woman and Turquoise Woman, Shaldis and the Summer Concubine herself, Xolnax's daughter had never used her powers outside her home. And now the others—Pebble Girl and the Moth Concubine—were revealed to whoever had sources of information in the college. Ahure and Aktis certainly, and thus their respective patrons. Benno Sarn. Whatever spies the Red Silk Lady maintained there.

She prayed that Oryn's extra guards, added protection, would be enough.

Had Shaldis learned something that drew her further on her hunt? Had she found the mysterious beggar Pomegranate Woman? The Summer Concubine guessed it might be so, for last night, half in dreams, she had felt a change in the energies of the Sigil of Sisterhood, as if some other energy had been added to it.

But she couldn't be sure. She reached her mind for it again, but her weariness pulled her over the edge into dreams.

Sweet dreams, of sitting on the edge of the fish pool in the Jasmine Garden watching Rainsong Girl feed bread crumbs to the fish. Her daughter—Oryn's daughter—was small, like herself, but she had Oryn's long oval face, and Oryn's hands, large and deft. Even at eight years she could play quite complicated tunes on the harp. Illyth, alive again and older than he'd been at the time of his death, practiced cuts at the shadows of the vines with a wooden sword: The Summer Concubine's heart ached at the sight of him. *Are you happy, my son?*

She could hear Oryn playing the harp in her dream, though she couldn't see him: that light, tripping tune he'd woven out of a singing game three of the kitchenmaids played. The notes flitted butterflylike through the garden, and when her dream shifted, returned to the Ring, she saw the notes still, blue and orange butterflies dancing disrespectfully around the heads of the Sun Mages as they called on the distant rains.

She saw old Hathmar, calling the Summons as he'd called it every year for fifty years—as the Sun Mages had been calling the rain in the third full moon of the year for five hundred years, ever since the yearly rains had ceased to come down from the north of themselves. For five hundred years the Realm of the Seven Lakes had bowed to the Sun Mages in thanks for this, and their Archmage had been hailed as the greatest in the land. Was that over now?

He looked old, exhausted, worse in her dream than in waking sight. With his spectacles laid aside, his thin face had a sunken appearance, like a corpse already. On his right, Benno Sarn looked as if his mind were on something else—what?

The fact that he'd lost his birthright, and now was losing the birthright of magic that had taken earthly power away?

Or just anger that things were changing and he had not given his consent for that change?

The other masters of the Citadel gathered around close, Rachnis and Brakt, and Yanrid with his face still haunted by grief for his vanished friends. Men she had counseled with over the years, men who had been puzzled by her, offended that a mere concubine—be she never so much a Pearl Woman—had manifested powers that had previously been theirs alone. Men who, like the angry novices, had been looked up to, praised by their families and friends and by everyone who met them. Men who from the age of four or five had known that the sun shone specially upon them. Men who had pursued their duties and their studies conscientiously for the most part, but in the knowledge that they were special.

Men who were no longer special.

Who understood, to one degree or another, that they were now no more than curiosities.

And that women were taking their places.

An ugly whisper passed like the wind through her dream. The cold scent of lightning, the harsh jangling of the air, like metal clashing far away. A shadow stood at the edge of the Ring in her dream, a shadow that the sun could not dispel.

She saw Ahure, impassive and impervious. He'd arrived at Hathmar's instruction last night late, his head bleeding from a dozen gashes, his mutilated hands clotted with blood, and blood leaking from the punctures of his lips and tongue. He had let it be known—rather thickly, since the latest mutilations of his mouth impeded his speech—that he'd been fasting for two days, and looked down his nose at the plump Pebble Girl without a word to say.

The Summer Concubine thought, *For a man who works steam vents with his feet under his robes to impress his patron, you have a lot of room to sniff.*

In her dream she saw Aktis, briefly glimpsed in one of the Citadel guest rooms, stretched on the low bed in exhausted sleep, with the black stains of *ijnis* around his mouth and an empty bottle at his side.

Then she was in the Ring again, looking out over the Citadel's walls. She saw the Lake of the Sun, and in her dream the lake was empty. Flat stretches of baked mud reflected the glare of the sky. The long lines of Oryn's water lifts stretched across that terrible waste, thin as threads: bucket hoists and troughs all still. Below the voices lifted in the Summons she could hear the empty creak of the ropes in the wind.

We are ghosts, she thought with shock. *We are ghosts haunting this place, after everything has died. . . .*

"Did you look for her?"

Mohrvine's voice. Close.

The Summer Concubine's eyes snapped open to twilight, luminous within the white canvas of the tent. The dusty scent of desert evening. The dry smell of a cloudless sky.

"I did, lord." Aktis. Hoarse, the gasp of a dying man. They must be standing close to the pavilions of rest, near where Soth had placed the big jars of citronade and ginger water. "I can't . . . I saw nothing."

"That I can believe." The king's uncle spoke barely above a whisper, but the scorn was as if he shouted. "If this is all you're going to be able to do . . ."

"Lord, I'll be well tomorrow. Truly I will. I will be able to accomplish what you've asked, I swear it—"

"You had better." Mohrvine's voice sank, but the Summer Concubine reached down after it with all her wearied concentration, seeking its whispers beneath the singing of the mages in the Ring, the groaning of the horns. "Because that whining fanatic may go back on us—him and his sniveling Believers—unless you can do as you say you can. And if you can't, believe me . . ."

"I will, my lord. I swear it."

"Like this? Like you were going to turn her love upon old Akarian with that worthless philter? You stink of *ijnis*, man! If this is the best you've been able to do in a day's scrying . . ."

"I'm—this passes, as you know. Give me a few hours more to rest and I'll try again to find your daughter."

"Save your strength," said Mohrvine bitterly. "I've got Xolnax and his informers out asking questions. You'll need your strength for bigger things."

Again no mention of the Red Silk Lady. Her own informers had hinted of Mohrvine's alliance with Xolnax. The concubine wondered if Mohrvine's mother had heard of her granddaughter's elopement yet. It was none of her business, of course, but beside her own agony of concern about Raeshaldis, she was conscious of a desire to be a fly on the wall of my lady's courtyard, to hear how the old woman would break the news of her granddaughter's whereabouts—if she did scry her—without letting her son know how she'd acquired it.

Achingly she rose, washed her face and straightened her simple dress. She was starvingly hungry, but one of the tenets of the Song was fasting, which the Sun Mages practiced for concentration. Was that something that worked for men and not for women, or was she only unused to it and weak?

Climbing the steps to the high place where the day's last light clung, the Summer Concubine looked up and saw the sky exquisite lupine blue, and cloudless to its farthest borders.

She thought of the True Believers rejoicing in their temple in the Slaughterhouse. Rejoicing and preparing—for what? What had Mohrvine meant by *May go back on us*? He'd clearly made a bargain with them. For what? And at what price? *Save your strength . . . for bigger things.*

"Honestly, it's ridiculous that they don't allow us to eat!" she heard Cattail Woman complain as the older woman passed her and went down to the little pavilions on the terrace. "*I've* never found my magic improved by starvation."

You've probably never made the experiment, my dear.

The Summer Concubine took her place again, gathered her thoughts. Watched the rhythm of the chant as she'd have watched a partner in a complex dance, waiting for her moment to step into the movement again.

Then poured out her heart and her mind and the secret energy of herself that was magic. Nothing further existed for her except drawing up the power through the long curves of conjoined sigils on the paving stones and weaving that power into a great shining net that covered the sky.

Above and around her the last bronze light faded, stars of the night came forth.

And so the Song rolled forth like a wheel into the night. Twice more the Summer Concubine went down to the terrace to rest, as she felt her strength and her concentration fail. Lamplight swayed with the desert wind, moving shadows against the white of the tent walls. If she'd suspected Soth had a honeyed fig on his person she would have killed him for it. On neither occasion did she even ask him what was taking place in the city, or what had befallen in the fighting that morning, though she guessed, from the noises she heard in the early night, that there was rioting again. Smoke stained the wind from several quarters. She had the sense, now, of husbanding her energy, like a housewife making a jar of water last through a dry spring, and did not remain awake for more than a second after lying down. Yet there was a kind of strength, a growing exhilaration, that came in the last hours before dawn. The power increasing, it almost seemed, when it should have been ebbing, until the whole earth and sky seemed to glow with it, pulsing with the pulse of the chants.

The sun dreamed, and the sun slept deep, and in the last two hours before morning the Rite called upon the magic of the Sun at Its Prayers, in many spell systems the strongest and most magical time. As brightness slowly filtered back into the dark, outshining the pallor of the waning, late-risen moon, the Summer Concubine watched the mages who had slept, or rested, return to the great round Ring. The three boys—Minktat, Ynor, and dark-browed Kylin—novices unused to the physical demands of the long ceremony, harsh-faced Cattail Woman and serene Pebble Girl, Ahure and even Soth. White robes seemed to shine in the moonstone light; blue robes claimed back their color with the first colors of the singing day.

On Hathmar's sleeves, and around the mouths of the horns, a flash of gold.

The long Rite circled to its close; in the silence afterward, the whole world lifted up, shining in the sky.

And the sky was clear, and without cloud.

The Summer Concubine went down to the room she had slept in the night before last and went to sleep at once, too exhausted even to recall that anything had taken place while all their energies were concentrated on the rain and the sun and the sky. Thus it was only an hour or so before noon when Soth woke her with the news.

During the fighting the previous day the king had gone missing. With outbreaks of rioting everywhere in the town, no one had been sure until now where he was. Barún had left immediately after the first fighting at the Citadel, to head off an attack on the Marvelous Tower itself. He'd been here and there about the city all day.

"But there's a woman here now who claims that she's hidden all night—and most of yesterday—in the Temple of Nebekht." Soth kept his voice low, kneeling beside the bed. His clothing smelled of the dates and meats, the eggs and cheeses and sweet breads, that he'd brought up to the Citadel: The scent pierced the Summer Concubine with the realization that she'd been too beaten with weariness that morning even to eat.

She sat up, pushed back her fair tousled hair from her face. "The temple?"

"She says she entered with Raeshaldis at about the hour the Rite began."

"Pomegranate Woman . . ."

"Yes, that's her name. She says Raeshaldis vanished within the temple. She waited for her for many hours before she became convinced she wouldn't come back. By that time Lohar and his men had returned, and transformed the temple into a fortress. All the streets in the district are barricaded, the place is an armed camp. Bax has closed the Eastern Gate and set it under guard."

"He's back?"

"Yes, though he says the nomads haven't withdrawn far—they just fade back into the desert, waiting. They won't have long to wait, either, if genuine war breaks out. Even within the city walls rioters have barricaded whole districts. . . ."

"What happened to Raeshaldis?"

Soth shook his head. "All Pomegranate Woman said was 'vanished.' But she says she saw Mohrvine at the temple later on, conferring with Lohar. This was about noon, she says. She's seen him enough about the marketplaces to recognize him, she said." He wiped his balding forehead, his long, slender hands shaky with fatigue.

He went on, "And she says they have the king."

TWENTY-NINE

There'd been rioting in the Circus District through most of the night, and the strewn rubble of what had been a café still smoldered in the square at the end of Great Giraffe Street. Concealed in the tiled doorway of a small temple of Bennicy, god of acrobats, the Summer Concubine could hear shouting a few streets away. It didn't sound bad: a street fight between two factions, not a riot.

"Is Mohrvine in there?" whispered Pomegranate Woman. The Summer Concubine shook her head, withdrawing her mind from an intense aural scrutiny of the House Jothek and retreating a little deeper into the doorway.

"It's hard to mistake his voice," she said. In the strange, chilly glare of the afternoon sun the place was still, save for the guards in their black-lacquered mail who stood before the gate. More guards watched both ends of the street.

"I'd guess he'll be in Nebekht's Temple," whispered Soth. He had insisted on accompanying the women on their quest, though the Summer Concubine had not told him whom she sought in the House Jothek, or why. "If they have the king there it would make sense."

The Summer Concubine had thought to go alone to speak to the Red Silk Lady, but Soth would not hear of her leaving the Citadel, cloak or no cloak, without protection, or at least someone to take note of it if she entered a place and did not come out. And Pomegranate Woman—a curious figure with her rags and her jewels and her imaginary pig—would not hear of anyone going to seek Raeshaldis without her.

"There was a hell of a quarrel between Mohrvine and Lohar," provided Pomegranate Woman now. "I didn't understand all of it, but it sounded like Lohar had made some kind of deal with His Majesty—in front of most of Lohar's faithful, which near as damn it gave Mohrvine a palsy-stroke from rage—and Lohar said he wanted proof that Nebekht was with Mohrvine. . . . I've never seen a man's face turn that color. Mohrvine said, *Kill him,* and Lohar just kept saying, *I must know that Nebekht is with you,* whatever that means."

That whining fanatic may go back on us. . . .

Save your strength . . . for bigger things. . . .

"At a guess," breathed the Summer Concubine, "Aktis has to come across with something—probably getting the wells to fill. No wonder he's been at the *ijnis.*"

"Not that it'll do him any good," said Soth. "It was just after sunset when he left—looking like death in a teacup—so that must have been immediately after you heard them speak. Bad enough that Mohrvine treats him like a slave . . ."

The shouting came nearer. The guards grew tense, hands on their swords, and looked in the direction of the Street of the Goldsmiths: "Should we go see?" asked one. Before leaving the Citadel, the Summer Concubine had attempted to scry both the Temple of Nebekht and the House Jothek, with equal lack of success. This hadn't surprised her. If Raeshaldis was correct about the Red Silk Woman, the house would be covered with scry wards.

And whatever it was that dwelled in the Temple of Nebekht, it clearly had a power of its own.

"Just how good are you ladies at the casting of illusions?" asked Soth a few moments later. "That shouting we heard—can you repeat it, call it back, but stronger, more frightening, into the minds of the men at the gate? Danger down at the end of the street, around that corner—bad danger, fear, coming closer." He sketched a Rune of Focus on the wall that the Summer Concubine recognized as one of the illusions of duty.

"What about the porter inside?" she asked. "We won't have but a moment, even if I can make the illusion work."

"Oh, that's easy," said Pomegranate Woman. "I'll send him away to take a piss about half a minute before the trouble starts."

The Summer Concubine traced the Rune of Duty two or three times with her finger, forming it up in her mind. Formed, too, the constellation of dream-thoughts that surrounded it: heroism, reward, scorn for lesser men. Loyalty to simple ideas: the House Jothek, the way of the warrior, the good old days when teyn and women knew their place. Fear and bravado. Love and respect.

Looking across the street, she saw and named the guards in

her mind for purposes of the spell: Mended Boots. Scratches His Bottom. Unshaved.

Pomegranate Woman closed her eyes briefly. *We'll feel terribly silly,* thought the Summer Concubine, *if we go charging through that gate and run smack into the porter on the other side.*

But in any case, once we're through, the Red Silk Lady will know we're here. She'll have a ward on the main gate.

I would, in her position.

She took a deep breath and slipped her mind into the dream world of magic and thought.

The porter was gone when the two women slipped the bar on the main gate and darted through. "Show me how to do that, when we have time," whispered the Summer Concubine. They fleeted across the courtyard, through the gate to the inner courts in a flutter of gray illusion. Soth would give them an hour before opening the sealed paper the Summer Concubine had given him. It contained the information that the Red Silk Lady was a Sister of the Raven, the only bargaining tool, at this point, that the Summer Concubine had.

There were fewer guards about than she had feared—where were those two sons Mohrvine had brought from the Lake of Gazelles?—and most seemed to be stationed on the outer perimeter of his house. The rest were away beefing up Lohar's troops, guessed the Summer Concubine angrily. She hoped nomads burned Mohrvine's rangeland to the roots of the grass and sowed salt in his fields.

Twice, on their way from the Citadel to the Circus District, they'd seen Bax's men dispersing rioters, putting out fires; Sarn and Jamornid had called in men from those patrolling their lands. In a few days, all other things being equal, the city would be returned to quiet. . . .

But a few days would be too late for Oryn.

She knew Mohrvine too well to think he'd let this chance slip through his fingers. Whatever bargain Lohar thought he'd made with the king, Mohrvine would disregard it. An unguarded minute—something simple, like access to the water the king would be offered to drink . . .

And the True Believers would absorb whatever blame there was for Oryn's death.

Would Mohrvine claim the throne himself? she wondered. As Greatsword's brother? Or would he run himself in behind Barún, who could probably be easily convinced that in fact Mohrvine had had nothing to do with the rioting, nothing to do with Oryn's death? Particularly if the body were discovered in a burned building somewhere, far from the temple, or anywhere else incriminating.

Prove that Nebekht is with you. . . .

Oryn has to have thought of that one, she thought. *He can sound so* reasonable.

In the second passage crossing that led to the harem quarters of the house, the two women fell into step behind a pair of serving maids, who bore heavenly morsels, baba cakes, and a tall tea vessel of silver and glass. Pomegranate Woman frowned, puzzled, but the Summer Concubine gestured that she knew what she was doing, and indeed she did. The courtyard was as Raeshaldis had described it: run-down and filled with potted trees and plants. Caged finches twittered and hopped from perch to perch. The wards on the gate, as Shaldis had said, were Pyromancer wards and badly drawn: The Summer Concubine brushed her fingers over them in passing, seeking some sense of the magic behind them.

It felt strong and clear even to her inexperienced touch.

She and Pomegranate Woman waited in the tiny courtyard, in the shadows of the bare jasmine vines, until the servant women left empty-handed. "Wait for me here," she breathed, and Pomegranate Woman nodded, puzzled but willing.

"You behave yourself now, Pontifer," she admonished the ground at her feet.

The Summer Concubine went to the door of the garden chamber and said, "May I come in?"

The Red Silk Lady was just pouring out the mint tea. On the divan beside her, half hidden by the cushions of black and gray silk, was a crossbow, drawn and cocked. The Summer Concubine remembered the stories about the Red Silk Lady being the daughter of a deep-desert hunter—she'd never known whether that was true or something Mohrvine had made up to claim kinship alliance with the nomads.

It looked like it was true.

"Would I be able to stop you?" the Red Silk Lady inquired with a lifted brow. Evidently she hadn't thought so: There were three glasses on the tray, and three little painted plates of heavenly morsels.

"I'm afraid not, lady," said the Summer Concubine apologetically. "My friend is in the courtyard, so if you would prefer to write what we have to say . . ."

"It's kind of you to give me that consideration." The Red Silk Lady tonged baba cake onto a plate, set it on the low table beside which the Summer Concubine knelt on a leather pillow. "I heard you were too skinny and they didn't lie. Call her in—if she's one of your Ravens she's likely to hear whatever we say anyway, isn't she?"

The Summer Concubine nodded. "I ask the indulgence of your secrecy for her," she said quietly, her eyes meeting those of the Red Silk Lady as Pomegranate Woman came in and knelt in curiously catlike quiet. "She has lived for some time in hiding."

And Mohrvine's mother nodded slightly, understanding that she was not only being asked for her silence, but being promised that of the Summer Concubine in return.

"She fears the man—or thing—that the girl Raeshaldis is hunting. The thing that has been killing the Raven sisters."

"Lie down, Pontifer, and mind your manners," instructed Pomegranate Woman in a whisper, and what could have been the faintest trace of amusement flickered in the Red Silk Lady's jade eyes.

An instant later the cold, green glance returned to the Summer Concubine: "What has she learned?"

"That a part of the answer lies in the Temple of Nebekht." The Summer Concubine passed a quick questing finger across the top of her tea glass, just to make sure there wasn't anything in the mint tea except mint tea. Shaldis had been poisoned, and nothing had ever shown that it wasn't the Red Silk Lady who had done it.

But the tea was perfectly safe and, when she sipped it, excellent.

Her hostess's eyes narrowed. "It does, does it? That doesn't surprise me. Filthy, prating hypocrites. I remember that Lohar when he'd stand on a box in the marketplaces screaming to everyone who passed about what his god had said to him, as if even a minor god like Nebekht would pass the time of day with a potter's son like him."

"Your son has an alliance with him," said the Summer Concubine quietly. "They've taken the king prisoner. They're holding him in the temple in the Slaughterhouse. I want you to come with us there, and to tell your son to have him freed. If you do not do this I will go myself, and speak to Lohar about matters that concern us both." She met the Red Silk Lady's gaze as she spoke. "These are excellent moonjellies."

"Thank you," said the Red Silk Lady. "Jamornid is forever trying to steal our dessert chef. Why do you think Lohar would believe a demon? Which is what you are, in his eyes. You and all women like you."

"I don't think he'd believe me right off," said the Summer Concubine and, after a cautious inspection of the confection with every spell of poison detection Soth had taught her, took a small bite. "But I leave it to you to imagine what sort of test Lohar would think appropriate to force a woman to choose between it and exposure."

"And you think my son would have nothing to say of this?"

"Oh, I'm sure he would." The Summer Concubine sipped her tea. "The question is, What? There has to be some reason you never told him of . . . the matter at hand . . . in the first place."

The Red Silk Lady watched the Summer Concubine silently for a time from pale green eyes. She was dressed simply but richly, in dark silk with her white hair coiled and lacquered and sparkling with jewels; her hands on the teacup were big and capable, marked with old scars beneath her ruby rings. The Summer Concubine did not speak, only waited for the older woman's thoughts to bear fruit. Pomegranate Woman, too, sipped her tea without asking questions, though she glanced narrowly at the Red Silk Lady from time to time. Perhaps she guessed, thought the Summer Concubine—she sensed in the strange old derelict enormous power and enormous wisdom. But for the moment she only broke a vanilla wafer in half to set on the floor for her imaginary pet.

At length the Red Silk Lady asked, "Do you trust my son?"

"Your son is a man of greatest honor and probity. All speak of his wisdom and generosity with praise."

"Neither do I." She considered the matter a few minutes more. "I understand you trust the king."

"With my life."

"So you let him make you his tool. Like a good little Pearl." Her glance flicked to Pomegranate Woman, then back. "And with you all those women whom you've been gathering around you and flattering into doing your bidding—which is actually his. What's in that temple?" She transferred her sharp glance to Pomegranate Woman. "What did you see there? Does Lohar have magic?"

"There's magic there," said Pomegranate Woman slowly after a questioning glance at the Summer Concubine, who nodded. "It's strong magic, cold magic. Ugly magic. I can feel these things, feel the stories the walls tell. I felt in the walls what Lohar says to that idol in the night, and when its spirit comes forth in the early morning to tear apart the animals they bring to that room. The magic dwells in the idol. It's inhuman magic. That's why Lady Shaldis thought it might have been the person or thing that's been killing these women."

"And is it?"

"I don't know. She disappeared trying to learn what these things are that have this magic, and why one of them would be attacking our kind."

"Disappeared?"

"Yes, lady. She made a power circle in the chamber of the beasts, where the dead pigs were, and the blood—I have a little pet pig myself and it fair made me sick. She stepped into the circle and—and walked away. Walked away without leaving the circle."

"Then this thing didn't take her?"

"That we don't know," said the Summer Concubine. "It's what we're trying to learn. Three women so far have been killed, by something whose power felt nearly the same. Two of those women lived near the temple, a young woman named Turquoise Woman, and Warfin Xolnax's daughter."

"So that's what happened to her." The old lady's painted lips drew tight. "I thought that business of Amber Girl running off with a suitor was all my cat's behind. The girl had no more suitors than I have. She was all business, that one, and cool as steel."

The Red Silk Lady poured out another cup of tea, her movements curiously controlled and feral, like a gladiator pitting a cherry.

"Ordinarily what my son chooses to do and who my son chooses to ally with doesn't concern me. Thinks he's too clever by half, and he isn't nearly as clever as he believes. But I watched this girl. Part of the reason my son allied himself with Xolnax was because of her, because he wanted to have her educated so that he could use her himself, the way he's having his daughter educated as a Pearl Woman. As I told your girl Shaldis, he uses everyone—as your precious king uses you. But he'd have found his mistake. It's one thing to deal with a weakling like Aktis, and another to have to do with a bully-boy's daughter who doesn't know the meaning of the word *no*.

"He came here on the night after the full moon, begging Aktis to find her." The Red Silk Lady waved at a finch, which had flown in from the garden and perched on the edge of the divan. The bird fluttered to Pomegranate Woman's side and pecked at the wafer she'd left on the floor for Pontifer. "Not that Aktis could have done so, for I'm told it isn't possible for a mage to scry a Raven sister. You say she was killed?"

"I saw it in a dream," Pomegranate Woman said. "At the full of the moon. About four hours after the same . . . the same person, or thing, whoever it is who holds this power . . . tried to seize Lady Shaldis. He killed her, tore her to pieces."

"Well, it wasn't Lohar, at any rate," remarked the Red Silk

Lady thoughtfully. "If the moon was full, Lohar was at House Akarian, preaching to that gullible booby that's supposed to marry my granddaughter. Which brings us," she said, her ice-colored glance sliding back to the Summer Concubine, "to the original figure of the dance. That I will speak to my son, if you will keep your silence—I don't suppose you've spoken to that overdressed capon of yours about it?—and scry for my grand-daughter. I understand you do it quite well, something not every Raven's sister is adept at," she added significantly. "Or so I have been told."

"Thank you," returned the Summer Concubine politely. "I'd be most curious to know from whom you received so glowing a report of my abilities. Do you have an alabaster vessel? I usually use a shallow bowl."

The mother of Mohrvine rose from her cushions, disappeared through the latticed screens that surrounded the doorway of the inner room and reappeared a few moments later with a footed cup of the kind lovers share wine from. The Summer Concubine took it out into the courtyard again and felt, to her shock, chill wind blowing down from the north.

She looked up quickly and saw clouds in the sky.

Thin clouds, puffs and streaks of white.

The high walls of the house prevented her from seeing to the horizon, but she felt her heart turn in her chest.

I should be rejoicing, she thought, panic fluttering her breath. Her hands trembled as she dipped water from the tiny fountain in the court. *Am I so selfish that I grudge salvation and life for everyone, if it comes from the hand of someone I don't like?*

The wind swirled and lifted her gauze overdress; there was a smell of water and dust in the air, and above it all a whiff of magic.

Aktis, she thought. *Dear gods, has Aktis actually found a Summons that will bring the rain?*

That must be what Mohrvine meant. How dare *he use such power—such a blessing—only as a tool for the domination of other men?*

The spell that would bring the rain would bring Lohar to power. It would be Nebekht's mark of approval, for Lohar and Mohrvine. *How can he do this?* her mind was shrieking. It would place Mohrvine on the throne, and cost Oryn his life. *I must know that Nebekht is with you. . . .*

Dear gods!

She felt sickened, shocked, shaken to her bones. *I will be able to accomplish what you've asked.*

If the rain came before they spoke to Mohrvine—before they got Oryn out of the temple . . .

Briefly she closed her eyes, praying to Rohar for strength.

Then she set the bowl on a bench beside a potted jasmine where the afternoon's graying light could fall on the water. Drew three deep breaths. Let her mind slide into the shadowy place of magic, her body relax into its working.

Called to mind the child she had briefly glimpsed on two or three occasions, that laughing, black-haired girl who'd cajoled for dolls and ribbons.

Mohrvine's treasure. The child of the Waterlily Concubine, the one girl out of so many whom he'd truly cared for, dead now twelve years. The one weakness, in that cold, serpentine strength.

The surface of the water glimmered in the dappled light. The finches twittered in their cages. The daylight itself seemed to soften and refract in the cup, colors moving in the shallow depths; ghostly at first, then brighter. Her bones ached, from the endless Rite of the day before. Her head throbbed. *Please don't let me be too exhausted.*

The colors seemed to clear away suddenly, leaving her looking at the polished grain of the stone.

Snakes and turtles, she cursed, a ladylike little oath and all that Pearl Women were permitted even to think. She closed her eyes again, drew several more breaths and looked into the water once more.

After the third attempt, she turned her mind not to the daughter of Mohrvine, but to Moonjelly the maid. Almost at once she saw the girl standing in the kitchen court of the House of the Marvelous Tower, towel in hand, looking up at the lowering sky. The palace pastry chef came out and gave her an order: Moonjelly trotted inside obediently, and the Summer Concubine let the image fade.

So there was nothing wrong with the way she was attempting to scry. She was not too exhausted—except that she *was* too exhausted, and in spite of the excellent heavenly morsels she was beginning to feel cold and giddy.

Wind clashed the tops of the tubbed orange trees and blew down a scatter of sand from the roof.

Temptation pulled at her to summon Oryn's image, and she thrust it away. *He's in the temple*, she thought. *Hidden by the magic of whatever is there—whatever is Summoning this rain. I'll never see him, and I will only waste my strength.*

So why couldn't she see the daughter of Mohrvine?

She's with a mage, she thought. Or with a Raven, some Raven we know nothing of. It's the only explanation.

And then, raising her head to look at the shadows of the pavilion again, hearing the Red Silk Lady's bark of laughter at one of Pomegranate Woman's tales of her husband's encounters with Nahul-Sarn: *Not the only one. She is a Raven herself.*

It's in her blood, after all.

She looked back at the bowl, drew a deep breath and called to mind the image of young Iorradus Akarian. Formed his face in her mind, golden and handsome, as he'd stood so many times at the head of Oryn's horse, or on guard outside the baths. A dull young man, but without malice.

The colors in the bowl deepened to darkness. Then like a pearlescent mist they rolled away, showing her more darkness still.

She recognized the place at once. The sandhills southeast of the city, not far from the old Salt-Pan Quarter, on the other side of the Slaughterhouse. She saw the arches of the aqueduct in the distance. The district was long deserted now, and the dunes were creeping in. The sky was the same as that above her own head: deepening blue streaked with gray and white. Wind flung sand along the ground, tossed and twisted the sagebrush and the thorns. Her first thought was *Clever of them to escape in that direction.* They'd be sought along the lake's southern shore, toward the Akarian lands.

Then she saw, more clearly, what it was that scuffled and circled in the sagebrush.

Jackals.

Jackals scraping at a shallow hole in the sand where a dead body lay.

THIRTY

B uildings burned everywhere in the city now. Warm, moisture-scented winds flickered among the alleys, whirling dust devils of dry leaves and rumors: *The king's been killed. Prince Barún was behind it all along. The nomads are coming. Bax has gone over to Lord Sarn. Bax has gone over to Jamornid. The king's fled to the City of Reeds. . . .*

As the Red Silk Lady's curtained litter passed the barricades of the Circus District the Summer Concubine reached out with her mind to the men clustered in the cafés: *Who's in charge now? Did Sarn break with the king? I heard Akarian's men came in on the side of the Believers.*

The Believers are behind the drought. Have been all the time. They've put the whole land under curse.

No, it's the Sun Mages themselves who aren't doing their job, like grain speculators holding out for a higher price.

In the Potters Quarter the clash of weapons, the shouting of voices, blocked their way. The bearers turned silently aside, through the sewery alleys behind the Charcoal Yard. Intent on keeping the cloak around the whole party—and around Soth too, who followed at a distance, still ready to go for help in case of betrayal or disaster—the Summer Concubine had no energy, no mind to spare for Oryn beside the small, desperate prayer, *Keep him safe till we come.*

She did not know to whom she prayed.

Through the curtains of her own litter—such as a serving maid would ride in, behind her mistress's greater palanquin—she could feel the daylight dimming above the saffron walls. Could feel the tension of the slow-gathering clouds.

Aktis, she thought. *It has to be. He's the only one who would have known of Foxfire Girl's powers. And if Mohrvine knew of Amber Girl's, Aktis would have known too.*

The bloody crosses and circles of the teyns' sacrifice came back to her mind, all noted in Oryn's neat hand. *It's a sacrifice of some kind,* she thought. *It's the way he's raising power—raising power with their deaths.*

Dear gods, don't let it be Raeshaldis who was sacrificed to the bringing of the rain!

Twice and thrice they detoured around fighting where Bax's troops, or Sarn's, or Barún's, engaged the rioters in small, ugly struggles under the barricades. Usually the cloak worked, though on a barricade near the East Gate—the narrow streets around the Grand Bazaar filling steadily with blue shadow—a man with the cropped hair of a True Believer strode up to them with sword in hand, calling out to them to stop.

The curtains of the leading litter slashed open; the Red Silk Lady's unmistakable voice snapped, "Garmoth, get back to the house! And your squad!"

Garmoth stopped in his tracks, eyes widening. "Ma—madam . . ."

"And don't say madam for everyone in the street to hear. Let us through."

He must have been related to Jethan, because he bowed deeply—an announcement to anyone who saw them about who was in the litter—as they passed; the Summer Concubine half expected the Red Silk Lady to hit him with her cane as they went by. It didn't surprise her that Mohrvine's men were stiffening the ranks of the rioters. *Please let us be in time.*

Oryn talked his way into a delay. *That whining fanatic may be going back on us. . . .*

I will be able to accomplish what you've asked. . . .

And why not? she asked herself in bitter fury. *They're only women.*

She forced her mind to return to the thin mists of the cloak spells, to such effect that when Bax's men at the East Gate gave the Red Silk Lady an argument about passing through into the Slaughterhouse—"It's not secured, lady, and you don't have any guards"—she wasn't even certain that they knew there were two other litters in the party. Pomegranate Woman had had to have help getting into her litter. Doing so without oversetting the chair was a trick one learned as a child if one was wealthy—or if, as a teenager, one was in training to be a Pearl Woman.

Let him still be alive.

Let this not be Raeshaldis's blood that has called this rain.

She wasn't sure whether Soth managed to slip through the gate on their heels or not.

The streets of the Slaughterhouse teemed with beasts taken from the shambles by the True Believers, driving them toward the temple in tangled mobs. Goats, sheep, pigs kept escaping, running madly through the darkening alleyways. Shrieks of animal pain came to her as they neared Chicken Lane, animals slaughtered by the dozens in the temple as Lohar performed whatever filthy rites his madness suggested to Summon the rain.

And the rain was coming.

She fingered apart the litter's curtains, saw the temple, square and black against the fading sky. The smell was horrific, and the screaming of the animals seemed to be coming from somewhere deep in the ground.

The litters halted. "Fetch my son. Don't tell me you have no idea where he is because I know he's here. And I won't appreciate it if you mention to anyone but my son who is here to see him."

"Madam . . ."

She must have recognized that guard, too.

"And don't bow! I've just told you I'm here in secret—who else would you bow to? If I were your mother my husband would divorce me for bearing fools."

"Yes, madam." Footsteps fled. A gate opened somewhere, closed. The bearers set down the litters. The Summer Concubine parted the curtains again. They were in Little Pig Alley, around the side of the temple by the gate to the court of the animals, hidden in the lane's darkness. Torches burned in

Chicken Lane, and she heard the mutter of men's voices, and the occasional clunk of a spear butt dropped on stone. The place stank like a shambles.

Small magic, dirty and ugly, filled the air. Pointless spells, like the magic wrought of *ijnis*. Magic that would go nowhere, that would expend itself attaching to other spells and twisting them askew, or peter out in eddies of ill luck, anger, madness.

Nowhere near strong enough to call the rain.

"Get away from here," snapped Mohrvine's voice. "All of you. And not a word of who you saw, do you understand?"

His gesture must have included the litter bearers, because when she pushed the curtains back the Summer Concubine saw Little Pig Alley empty, save for the three litters and Mohrvine himself. He was plainly dressed in dark blue, as he had been yesterday, though she glimpsed a steel cuirass under his cloak. His cropped hair glittered in the far-off reflection of the torchlight, and his face, stripped of that silvery dark frame, was haggard as he leaned over his mother's litter.

"Do you have word of her?"

"I do, my son."

"Aktis scried for her this morning. Said he could see nothing. She must have coaxed a scry ward out of someone. Not that that love philter he made to bind her to Akarian had the slightest good to it."

"That philter didn't work because your daughter is a Raven child."

Night-sighted as a cat, the Summer Concubine watched Mohrvine's face as his mother spoke the words. She saw his jaw drop, his green eyes flare wide, not so much shocked, in that first moment, as uncomprehending. Like a man who's taken a step down in the dark where there is no stair.

The Red Silk Lady added then, "As I am. And this the

Summer Concubine will tell Lohar—and all the True Believers—unless you release the king and release him now."

He made as if to speak then, but no sound came out of his throat.

"Your daughter is in deadly peril, my lord." The Summer Concubine stepped from her litter, and his head snapped around. She saw by his eyes that he could barely distinguish even her shape, but she knew that he knew her voice, and her perfume in the darkness. "As is my king. Where do you think Aktis was getting the power he used to put a curse on the aqueduct and to call the rains? Even to make the love philter you demanded. He has found a way to raise power from the deaths of women who have it. And he will use your daughter."

"You're lying." Then, reaching her with the savage speed of a tiger, he grabbed her arms, dragged her from the litter, face twisted with rage and horror. "You're lying!"

She twisted from his grip like an eel, breaking his hold. At the same moment the Red Silk Lady snapped, "Let her be! I think she's telling the truth about Foxfire Girl, and I know she's telling the truth about what she'll do if one dyed curl of her precious Oryn's head comes to harm."

Mohrvine stepped back, shaking his head like a man who's taken a hard blow, trying to recover his balance. From beyond the temple wall a holocaust of squeals knifed out: agony, terror, pain.

The Summer Concubine said, "I've scried Iorradus's body. It's in a sandpit south of here."

Mohrvine's voice was a snake's hiss in the dark. "I can't tell Lohar to release the king! The man's insane, and those followers of his are worse! Do you know what he's doing in there? Bathing in blood, talking to that statue in one breath and to the slaughtered pigs and teyn and goats in the next! That thing—the thing that comes out of the idol . . ."

"I didn't ask you to tell Lohar anything," the Summer Concubine said quietly. "I asked you to get Oryn out of there. Quickly—we have no time to lose. Your daughter has no time to lose. We can probably track Aktis from Iorradus's body, but I swear to you I will not stir a step in your aid or your daughter's until Oryn is with me. Look around you, man—do you really want to rule in partnership with Lohar?"

"Don't be stupid," snapped Mohrvine, probably meaning that he intended to put Lohar out of the way as soon as he conveniently could.

His mother retorted, "Don't *you* be stupid. What she's saying makes sense and whatever power it is that Aktis has found, he's the only one who *could* know Foxfire Girl was Raven born. The gods know I'm lucky he didn't come after *me*. Now get the king. Foxfire Girl is my only granddaughter, and I won't have her sacrificed to your ambition or your refusal to believe that you've been defeated. Get him."

He hesitated. *He still wants to believe he can use Lohar,* thought the Summer Concubine. The old lady added softly, "Get him—or I swear to you, I will not forgive." And she held out her hand, and for an instant threads of blue fire flickered from the ends of her fingers, gleaming in her cold, green eyes.

"I can't." Desperation edged into Mohrvine's voice. "He's guarded. They'd never let me take him. I couldn't even trust my own men not to give me away."

"Here." The Summer Concubine took a stub of red chalk from her reticule, and a scrap of paper. This she tore in half, and on each half inscribed the glyphs of the spell she had laid on the men at the gate of the House Jothek: *duty, unthinking, obedience. Dreams. Forgetting.* She remembered to lay a limitation, as Soth had instructed, and to circle each sigil with wards. "Give these to two of your men; tell them to swallow them. What are the names of the men you'll give them to?"

"Ram and Boaz." He took the papers unwillingly and looked at his mother, who met his gaze with stony, unflinching eyes.

"Keep the cloak around the litters," said the Summer Concubine softly to Pomegranate Woman, who came over as Mohrvine went down to where his guards waited in Pig Alley. "Can you turn people away from coming down this lane? Good."

"You need this?" Pomegranate Woman held out to her an enormous skinning knife she'd taken from her boot.

"Thank you." The Summer Concubine hefted it. It was a fact little known outside the Blossom Houses that Pearl Women were trained also in a startling variety of weapons. To be a true Pearl Woman was to be able to defend your man in nearly any circumstances, although most men didn't know this until and unless the situation arose. Most found it tremendously disconcerting. She'd certainly never mentioned the matter to Oryn.

"D'you want Pontifer to go with you? He's good in a fight." Pomegranate Woman looked down to the ground at her side. "Aren't you, sweetheart?"

Mohrvine opened his mouth to speak, then closed it.

"Thank you," the Summer Concubine said again. "But let's leave him on guard here with you."

Turning, she reached out with her mind to the three men coming back from the darkness, glints of armor under concealing cloaks, the soft creak of sword belts and boots. They felt their way along the temple wall; the last blue light had faded from the sky, and against the dim starlight visible over the walls, gathering clouds could be seen. *Ram*, she whispered the name. *Boaz* . . .

And cradled the minds, the names, into a gentle dream.

Drawing her veils about her, and with them the black cloak,

the thickest spells of concealment she knew, she followed Mohrvine through the beast gate and into the temple court.

The stink of magic here was strong, sawing and plucking at her thoughts with tweezers of fire. Insane magic, bloodied fragments of formless spells. Goats ran crazily around the narrow yard, leaping on and off the well covers, their thin bleating like the wails of frightened children. A flock of geese charged from wall to wall, wings spread—pale, terrified ghosts. Underfoot the pavement was ankle deep in dung and even in the evening dark, flies swarmed. Far off the Summer Concubine could feel other magic, the crazy, jangling magic Pomegranate Woman had described. As Mohrvine led the way through the beasts' door the air thickened with it, all pervasive.

There was something here. Something that tasted, felt, a little like the spells she'd felt in the hills while searching for a way into the Hosh tomb, alien and cold.

But it was far off, brooding. Drawn in on itself. Its madness permeated the walls, the air.

Rats fled and squealed in the shadows. Somewhere, the Summer Concubine could hear Lohar singing, and the half-ecstatic crooning lifted the hairs on her scalp. Anger and joy mixed. Delight in his martyrdom. Soul-deep satisfaction mingling with bitter rage. The smell of blood and dung was like a battlefield, and the tiny lamps in their niches, far too widely spaced along the corridor wall, burned brownish and sickly in the choking atmosphere. Now and then the flies that swarmed around the lights would ball themselves into tight knots and fall squirming to the muck underfoot, rolling along the ground; once one of these burst into spontaneous flame. A chicken ran squawking along the corridor, then seemed to entangle itself in one of those eddies of stray magic and began to circle helplessly and to fling itself against the walls. Mohrvine flinched at the sight, but Ram and Boaz moved along ahead of him in their private dream, and the Summer Concubine, guiding them with her spells, dared not think too much about the crazed magics that dripped from walls and ceiling like slime.

It was enough that she kept them in their dream of obedience, and herself in readiness in case of need.

They met no one. She heard a deep chorus of male voices lifted in singsong response in the sanctuary—their leader had to be Sun-Mage trained, a young voice, beautiful—but none walked here. Mohrvine passed through an archway barely taller than his head and down a flight of steps, extending his arms to the walls on either side and groping with his foot in the darkness. A lamp burned somewhere at the bottom, but the light outlined no more than a riser or two.

There were two guards outside a room that had probably once housed the temple's treasure. The brick of the corridor floor was broken with age; the shadows beyond the lamp in its niche smelled as if the guards used the far end of the passageway as a privy. Mohrvine and the Summer Concubine stayed in the blackness of the stairway, shoulder to shoulder in the dark. Ram and Boaz went to the guarded door.

"They need you up at the sanctuary." Boaz nodded back toward the stair. "We'll take over." If she had to say it herself, the Summer Concubine was pleased at the naturalness of his voice.

One of the guards grinned. "Get him to tell you the story about Wenthig Sarning and the masseuse."

The Summer Concubine laid a corner of the black cloak over Mohrvine as the guards passed them and went on up the stair.

Ram was already unbolting the door as Mohrvine and the Summer Concubine approached.

Oryn got to his feet, blinking against even the dim gold of the corridor lamps as Mohrvine opened the door. He was in shirtsleeves, the garment torn and bloody, and he shivered; he had wrapped the unconscious Jethan in his peacock robe against the night's cold. He recognized Mohrvine, and his eyes went past him to the men with drawn swords. But all he said was, "Would you do one thing for me? Send the boy back to the palace. He's—"

"Not a word," said Mohrvine. "Come with us."

Oryn stepped forward; it was only then that he saw the Summer Concubine standing in the shadows at Mohrvine's back. He stopped, eyes widening with shock and hope, and looked at his uncle. "Hurry," the Summer Concubine said. "Before the guards come back."

Oryn turned back and scooped Jethan up and onto his own wide shoulders—not easy to do given the unconscious guards-man's size. But Oryn was a good deal stronger than he looked. He halted beside the Summer Concubine, and wordlessly bent, his free hand cupping her face, kissing the flesh of her eyelids and brow, the only unveiled part of her, and whispered like a secret breath in her ear, "Oh, very good, my Summer Child . . ."

"Leave him," muttered Mohrvine, as they bolted the cell door behind them, climbed the winding stair. Oryn had to turn sideways and sidle, with Jethan's bulk on his shoulder. "We can't take him to where the body is—"

"What body?"

"That blockhead Iorradus. And believe me, nephew, you're coming with me, and if this—this *woman* of yours has lied to me about my daughter, or Aktis—"

"Iorradus? Oh, dear gods, the poor boy! Jethan tells me he has a room near here—something I'd scarcely have expected of him. He can be left there. . . . Your daughter? Foxfire Girl? You've found her? Is she all right?"

"Aktis has taken her," said the Summer Concubine, her

voice barely a breath in the dark of the stinking corridor. "To—to make magic with her blood, with her heart."

"Can he do that? Is it possible? I've never heard—"

"Neither have I," whispered the concubine, "but I believe it is he who's been killing the Raven sisters. I don't understand it all, but . . ."

"Explain on the way. If the girl is in danger . . ."

"That," said Mohrvine grimly, "is exactly our problem. To find where he's taken her. Aktis has always kept rooms in other parts of the city, in the poor districts where he had friends. Or is it part of madam's training as a Pearl Woman to be a desert tracker as well?" His voice twisted with sarcasm, now his only shield against horror.

Oryn blinked at him, surprised. "I should think he'd take her to the tomb where he laid out the hex marks to damage the aqueduct, wouldn't he?" They had reached the alley—horses stood there, nomad-bred desert steeds that the Summer Concubine knew Mohrvine prided himself on. "The poor districts are too dangerous with the rioters coming and going—not to mention, I sincerely hope, Bax and his bravos."

"The tomb was sealed," said the Summer Concubine. "Soth and I searched for an entrance but never found one; I think now there must have been spells preventing us from doing so."

"If it was that enormous Hosh tomb that looks south out of the Dead Hills I know there are at least two robbers' tunnels leading into it," said Oryn. "My jewel dealer Noyad's been selling Hosh rubies to me for years, not that he'd ever have any dealings with anything so dishonest as a grave robber, you understand. He sold some to you, too, didn't he, Uncle? Or at least someone did—that cloak clasp you bought last year. The pink tinge in the heart of the jewels and the beveled carving are unmistakable." He eased Jethan down from his shoulders and looked inquiringly at Mohrvine.

Mohrvine's eyebrows snapped together. "Xolnax sold me those," he said. "He claimed they came from Yarbekt the Strong's tomb."

"That's only in the next wadi." Oryn's studies of Durshen music had given him an almost familial acquaintance with that corrupt dynasty's rulers and the location of their tombs. The king's fund of obscure knowledge never failed to amaze the Summer Concubine.

"He sold my mother a ring that he claimed he 'found' near Trosh II's tomb at the same time; it looks like the same workmanship to me."

"Trosh's tomb is just on the other side of the hill," mused Oryn. "Astonishing, how Durshen jewels would be so fashionable and Hosh gems considered passé simply because the Hosh were so dull. I really will have to write a treatise on public taste in illegally obtained antiquities. "

"Iorradus's body is in a gulch south of the road, not far from the aqueduct," said the Summer Concubine. "If Aktis took her out there while he was supposed to be scrying for her at the Citadel, it would be a logical place to conceal the body."

Mohrvine signed impatiently, and Boaz and Ram stepped forward to receive the Summer Concubine's instructions to take Jethan to Greasy Yard and leave him in the care of Rosemallow Woman and Melon Girl.

"You'll have to pay them for their trouble, I expect," warned the Summer Concubine, and Mohrvine dug in his purse.

"Just a moment," said Oryn as the two guards were moving off again. "May I?"

And he took Boaz's sword and thrust it through his own gold-stamped belt. "And if you might lend me a cloak as well? It will be cold out in the Dead Hills."

THIRTY-ONE

Lying in the darkness—aching as if she'd fallen down a flight of stairs—Raeshaldis smelled the coming storm and thought, *He tricked me.* There was no reason, she thought, why the Sunflash Prince couldn't have sent her back to one of those unknown places she'd heard of in the scrying glasses. Or, since she smelled the familiar wildness of the desert, he might have sent her to some other year in the history of men, when the rains came every winter without being called.

She rolled over. Her bones felt stiff and her flesh was bruised all over, and she felt sick with the recollection of the tales of mages who had gone with the djinni to their floating palaces of invisible crystal. They had read unknown books, feasted, rode, made love for a night or two, only to return to find their families dead of old age, their houses decayed and abandoned, and the kings they'd served only memories centuries old.

Time was not the same to the djinni. It did not work the same in their halls of crystal and air.

A power circle was drawn on the floor beside her, exactly as the Summer Concubine had guessed it would be. From niches in the walls, barely visible through darkness that seemed thick as velvet over her sight, squat obsidian images glared with huge, round, mirrored eyes. The gods of the Hosh Dynasty, such as she had seen in Aktis's room in the cupboard beside the golden bottle with the crystal stopper, wrapped in three strands of iron.

He has a djinn.

Come back tomorrow, Aktis had said. *Don't forget, now.*

She would have, too, she thought. Was that how he'd lured Turquoise Woman to him? Xolnax's amber-eyed daughter? That pleasant, gentle friendliness, the memory of his reputation for kindness—before his magic started to fail. If she hadn't feared the Red Silk Lady she would have gone to him, hoping to learn what the Sun Mages had not been able to teach.

And now she was trapped in the tomb.

Jangly alien magic filled the cramped space of the tomb's outer chamber as if she'd been trapped in some monstrous lute's sounding box. She got to her feet, steadying herself on the stone table of a false sarcophagus. The loremaster's voice droned for an instant in her mind: *Hosh tombs are characterized by their unpainted walls and the obsidian images of their gods— you'll find the list of their names in the library and I want you to have them memorized by next week—and by the arrangement of an outer or false burial chamber near the main entrance, with an inner chamber cut deeper in the earth.*

They say every tomb in these hills was robbed, she thought. *Even if the main entrance was sealed there has to be a passageway out through one of the neighboring crypts.* At worst she was in for a four- or five-hour walk to the aqueduct camp. Always supposing the Sunflash Prince had not sent her to some other year, some other era . . .

She stilled herself, trying to quiet the frightened pounding of her heart, listening. Seeking the soft draw of air against her skin that would speak of a tunnel to the outside.

Then a moaning from the darkness, from the passageway that led into the cut rock. A girl's voice sobbed, "Don't! My father will kill you. . . ."

And the terrified bleat of an injured teyn.

Shaldis pressed back against the wall. Above the dry scents of dust and stone she could smell parched greenery from somewhere. A quick search revealed the tunnel, behind one of the tall, darkly gleaming images—too tall to steal, though the gold that had at one time covered its carved kilt and boots had been stripped off. A hole barely wider than her shoulders led away into darkness, but, putting her face close to it, she smelled the desert again, and felt the wind.

Smelled rain, too. Coming close, clouds filling the sky.

He's using the magic to call the rain.

From the inner tunnel on the other side of the chamber, steeply slanted and choked with debris, she smelled other things. The reek of mingled sulfur and incense, the stink of hot metal. Farther off, the smell of old blood.

The air was full of magic, the smell of lightning, of jangling malice and hate.

She glanced again at the power circle, Earth-Wizard signs mingled with runes similar to those on the silver protective disk. The cottonwood staff, with the disk still attached, lay at her side. She felt safer once she had it in her hand again.

He must have killed them all here. It was a four-hour ride on a good horse—after failing to take her, he could have retreated here, to raise power for that first rain by killing Amber Girl at dawn, the time of Pomegranate Woman's dream. *Rain fell the following morning, the night he kidnapped Corn-Tassel Woman. It must have been her death he used to build up power to hex the aqueduct.* She edged closer to the mouth of that downward-leading tunnel, blinking in the darkness. She remembered reading how the old tombs had pit traps in them, sometimes a hundred feet deep, for robbers to stumble into in the dark. *He must have a bridge or a plank somewhere, or footholds cut into the wall.*

I should run, she thought. *I should get out through that tunnel into the next tomb and flee to the aqueduct camp.*

By which time that girl in the deeper crypt will be dead, whoever she is.

She couldn't recognize the voice, but she sounded young. Maybe someone who didn't even know her own power, someone Aktis had watched through his connections in the Slaughterhouse, as he'd watched her in the Citadel.

How can he be here? He's supposed to be in the Citadel today, taking part in the Rite with everyone else.

If today is the same day I went into the temple.

Which it obviously isn't.

How many days have I lost?

She crouched at the passageway's entrance, listening ahead of her into the dark of the deeper crypt. Probing with her mind through the vile cold of the alien magic—djinn magic, she recognized it must be now, mixed with and glued together by the stolen life energies of the dead Ravens, as the Sunflash Prince's existed in the pallid matrix of dead animal lives. She smelled the pong of teyn, and a scent of jasmine perfume.

"Thieving bitches." Aktis's voice was thick with *ijnis*, drunkenness teetering back and forth across the line of madness. "I'll teach you. I'll find out how you're doing it. How you're taking it away from us. I'll make you give it back."

"Daddy . . ." The girl's voice was thinned with terror. "Daddy, come get me. Daddy, please . . ."

Djinn-fire and darkness blurred Shaldis's sight as she crept down the passageway, the plaster of the wall behind her smooth and cold. It was harder and harder to see chunks of rock and rubble that half filled the tunnel guarding the ancient king whose body lay in the crypt somewhere before her, and she didn't dare make the small glowing finger marks that wizards made to guide them in unfamiliar labyrinths.

He trapped a djinn, she thought again. *He's using it exactly the way Lohar uses Naruansich. Its name will be in the lists.*

There were three hundred and seventy-five in the lists, including possible duplications and obscure single appearances.

And who knew how many more who'd never deigned to establish human friendships at all.

Don't think about that, she told herself. *If it didn't have human friends it wouldn't have been trapped by Aktis. If its name wasn't in the lists, Aktis couldn't have lured it the way Urnate Urla tried to lure Meliangobet.*

At least I can eliminate Naruansich and Meliangobet himself. Two out of three hundred and seventy-five—I'm almost there!

A man and a djinn together. One without magic, the other without the physical body to sustain his life. . . .

It's powerful now. It's got the magic in it of Corn-Tassel Woman and Turquoise Woman and Amber Girl and who knows how many others the Summer Concubine never even knew about. He'll have a room here, like the one behind the sanctuary at the temple, a place where he lets it out of that golden bottle I saw in the cupboard.

At least Lohar only fed his djinn on the lives of beasts. At least it was only life alone that the Sunflash Prince sought.

No, she thought. He had tried to swallow her in the idol. Had tried to absorb her power. It had taken all her strength, even bestialized and weakened as he was, to hold him off.

"I'll make you give it back." The deep, drunken muttering made her nape prickle with horror. "Make you give all men their power back." And there was a faint metallic clink, like the lid of a golden vessel being removed. The darkness was absolute, riven through with sparks of bluish lightning that illuminated nothing. The air was icy and filled with the abrasion of hatred, like heated chains.

Frantic with horror and agony, the teyn's voice rose to a death shriek.

Magic filled the canyons of the Dead Hills like a noisome reservoir. The horses snorted, fought their bits: "Can we go up on foot?" asked Oryn, bending from the saddle to catch the rein of Pomegranate Woman's mount before it bolted. "Is it far?"

"That's the mouth of the Hosh tomb there." The Summer Concubine pointed to a dark square in the cliff face at the top of a ghostly pale talus slope. In the desert starlight the tall cliffs were barely an outline, and with the clouds moving in, even that would soon be gone. "Yarbekt the Strong's is that way— that's the big one with the colossi outside its entrance. And there's another one around the side of that promontory back there that must be Trosh's—it's the only one back there. We must have explored every one of these looking for the power circle. We didn't know then, of course, that he had enough power to place wyrds on the spot to make us miss our way."

"I never trusted the man." The Red Silk Lady dismounted stiffly—Oryn sprang down to help her, although he staggered himself—and tied back her veils like a robber's mask behind her head, the way the nomad women did, leaving her face modestly covered but her arms and shoulders free. She'd brought along her crossbow, with a quiver of arrows; her stick she'd left in the litter. Mohrvine was likewise armed. "All that rot about *ijnis* helping him until wizards' powers started to return . . . which is what they all say."

For all her appearance of decrepitude in the city, the Red Silk Lady had scornfully refused offers from both Oryn and her son to permit her to ride pillion behind them: "In my day a woman kept up or was left." The Summer Concubine, who'd been about to pick out the gentlest of the cavalry mounts for her, had stepped back at that point and let her select her own.

"I don't suppose you've another of those coins that your girl made that are supposed to draw djinn magic?" the old lady asked now. "Ah, well: I had no little magic coins when I was a girl, and I'd go with my father to hunt lions. We'll just have to watch for our chance. It's as that girl of yours said: *We don't know what we can do until we have to.* You, me, anyone. And after ten years of doing nothing but watching and experimenting and weaving webs to protect myself, I'm curious as to what I can actually do. Good luck to you, girl." And she made a sign of blessing, like a nomad sorcerer.

At her mention of how long she'd known she had power Mohrvine glanced sidelong at her, but said nothing. Only cracked flint and striker, and touched the resultant bit of burning tow to the wicks of the lanterns that had been borne on the saddle bows. The Summer Concubine wondered what his reflections were that his mother hadn't trusted him enough to tell him, and what would be said between them when all this was over, if any of them survived.

And what the results might be, for the House Jothek and for the realm.

The Red Silk Lady followed Mohrvine up the narrow way toward the promontory of rock, keeping up with him, as far as the Summer Concubine could tell, as nimbly as a goat. The yellow light of the lantern was visible for a long time, like a single firefly in the dark.

"Now, you all stay close," she heard Pomegranate Woman whispering to the horses, stroking their noses and scratching their ears. "You run away if jackals come—here's a little luck mark for you . . . and one for you . . . but you come back when I call. Pontifer, are you ready?" The Summer Concubine wondered whether the imaginary pig had run beside the horses or been carried on Pomegranate Woman's saddle bow.

"Are you all right?" Oryn limped up beside the Summer Concubine, laid a big gentle hand on her shoulder. Under his borrowed military cloak his shirt and pantaloons were ragged, and she could see bruises on his face and arms, and a crude bandage wrapped his left hand. He shivered with a chill born of exhaustion. *He must be starving*, she thought—she couldn't remember when she herself had last eaten, and she had a raging headache—but gourmand though he was, it apparently didn't cross his mind to mention it. He held Boaz's sword with a kind of awkward firmness, and she wondered if he'd used his own in the courtyard fighting before he was taken.

She hefted the cottonwood staff Pomegranate Woman had given her with its makeshift disk that might or might not draw off spells of lightning. Her mind probed at the darkness, listening for the Sigil of Sisterhood. Praying Raeshaldis was somewhere, alive. She willed her power into it, releasing magic to that invisible sourcing sign: *Take of it what you need. Add it to your strength.*

She felt drained by the rite, as if she had no strength to give. "Yourself?"

He smiled. "Beloved, to stand here with you in starlight—albeit I'd rather I were a bit more stylishly dressed—is the greatest felicity of my life. And shall be, should it end tonight."

He gently kissed her hand.

Then she felt it, like the sharp impact of a ward spell on her mind, like the note of a bell, or a cry.

Raeshaldis.

Calling for help.

In the hills around them, all the jackals began to howl at once.

"Great heavens." Oryn hefted the sword. "Here they come—can we make it around the hillside to Yarbekt's tomb?" Though it was harder to see now than it had been—the darkness seemed somehow thicker—the Summer Concubine could make out the shapes of the dogs racing down the hills, out of the gullies. Feeling cold and very unlike herself, the Summer Concubine called on the name of fire, which Soth had given her, and around them fire blazed up like a wall. Scrubby thorn and sagebrush ignited, and she caught the storm winds, twisted them to fling the flames at the yelping beasts.

Some of the jackals turned tail. Others, jaws yellow with foam and eyes crazed, plunged through the blaze at them. Oryn, who ordinarily loved the palace dogs to the point of absurdity, hacked at one that sprang at Pomegranate Woman's throat, slashed open the side of another right behind. The Summer Concubine called on the name of fire again and the jackals' coats caught. They ran squealing, to roll in dust or vanish into darkness—"Now!" called Oryn, beckoning to the thin track that led around the shoulder of the hill.

As they broke into a run the wind shifted, turned, blowing the fire back at them. The Summer Concubine put forth her mind, her magic, and the fire flattened, scattered as if it were a live thing driven two ways. They came around the rocks and saw the colossi that dominated the wadi. *Thank the gods it isn't one of those inconspicuous little holes in the rock that the later monarchs favored.*

Her breath stabbed agonizingly in her lungs. A stitch bit her side, turned from a cramp to a stab as if a sword had been run into her, then a ripping avalanche of pain. At the same moment the wind increased, blowing up out of the south against the course of the storm. Curtains of dust whirled before them; hard little specks of bone and rock and broken pottery tore at her veils, her body, her hands.

"This happened in the temple!" she heard Pomegranate Woman shout—or maybe she only heard it in her mind, as if from a great distance off. "Darkness—we were lost . . . led out of the world, into someplace else." The dust was so thick in the air she could see nothing. The pain made it almost impossible

to concentrate, but she fought to whisper the word of a chan-
neling spell and felt the pain pour along her arm, into the staff,
into the disk, leaving her free.

Free and blind, stumbling . . .

"Follow Pontifer!" shouted Pomegranate Woman, and
through the dust—as if it were only a fragment of light pro-
jected onto the dust—the Summer Concubine thought she
did, in fact, glimpse the ghost of a little white pig trotting over
the broken ground that she could no longer see, out of the
fringes of the dream world toward the tomb invisible behind
the screaming maelstrom of dust and darkness and stones.

Blue fire flashed, outlining the broken slot that tomb robbers had made in the sealing stones. On either side the tall images of the ancient king stared bleakly, scoured by sand and
wind. Darkness and magic seemed to flow from the opening,
and the Summer Concubine heard a girl scream in pain.

Oryn caught her arm, dragged her forward. The pig, if it had
ever existed, had vanished. The Summer Concubine felt the
draw of Raeshaldis's mind on hers, calling on her magic, calling on any power she could summon. Heard her crying out,
spells of escape, of the breaking of magical bonds—

Crying out names.

The names of the djinni.

One by one—the Summer Concubine could almost see the
list Soth had written up for her in the palace library, the same
list.

Crying them out hoarsely, desperately, her breath broken
with exhaustion. And around her, in the dark of the crypt, the
howling of wind and worse than wind.

Within the tomb the darkness was still more dense, and the
wind—impossibly—worse as well. The carven walls chan-
neled it, strengthened it; it seemed to blow from all directions
on her, confusing her as she clung to the stone for guidance,

support. Fragments of things she couldn't see cut her, and she felt blood on her face and sticking to the rags of her veils and her dress. Behind her she heard Pomegranate Woman cry out in pain, felt Oryn's hand on her wrist sticky now with blood. The light of his lantern flashed briefly on a pit, bridged by a grave robber's narrow plank—it was covered with spells of ruin and collapse, and the Summer Concubine crawled across first, her mind touching, counterspelling each of those ragged, grasping, invisible hands before the others could cross.

In the painted passageways of the maze she felt other spells, ripping and shrieking, but she never really felt in any doubt about where the Sigil of Sisterhood was leading her.

As they came into the inner crypt she saw Raeshaldis cornered against the wall with an old ceremonial halberd in her hands. She slashed at a thing that lunged at her, tried to seize her with crystal talons—a huge thing that was hard to see exactly, hard to distinguish from the darkness and the wind and the whirling, blinding black glitter of the air.

But it was solid enough to tear the girl's face and hands, to rip at the younger girl who stood next to her, likewise wielding an ancient weapon, her long raven hair pointy with blood from the cuts on her face. The thing, whatever it was—it looked sometimes like a vulture, sometimes like a spider, sometimes like an enormous scorpion of crystal and gold—had ripped the dark-haired girl's leg, dragged her away from the wall, and Shaldis strode out, stood over her, cutting at it and crying out spells and names as she cut.

Lightning flared forth from it, striking at the two girls. The Summer Concubine felt Shaldis draw on all the power of the Sigil of Sisterhood, on the power of all those who had participated in it—Turquoise Woman and Corn-Tassel Woman and Pomegranate Woman and herself—desperate to gather enough strength for a counterspell. The lightning struck at a silver disk tied to a stick and lying a little distance from Shaldis's feet; the creature tried to lunge in past it, and Shaldis struck at the grabbing claws with the halberd that required both her hands to wield. The Summer Concubine cried out, put forth her own power and at the same time held up her own sigil, drawing some of the lightning away. The thing—djinn, or whatever it was or had been—cried out in a man's voice, thick like a drunkard's, "Bitch! Slut!" and sprang at the Summer Concubine, and Shaldis, gasping, fell to her knees.

"*Nachosian, kamaa!*" Shaldis cried out the words of the spell of freedom, the spell of escape, for the dozenth time, or the hundredth. "*Alvorgin ea amar!*"

And the djinn—surely this thing could not be a djinn?—evidently wasn't the djinn Nachosian, because it struck, slashing, at Oryn, at the Summer Concubine, at Pomegranate Woman as she ran forward under its hammering wings and grabbed the black-haired girl, dragged her and Shaldis toward the passageway to the outer air.

Thief, the thing cried, in that thick, hot voice that seemed to come from somewhere else. *Thief, robbing us of what is ours. . . . I'll make you give it back. Make you give it back.*

Wind tore at them in the darkness. They were in the labyrinth of painted tomb passageways again—the Summer Concubine tried to remember the way out, but the whirling dust, the fire that seemed to spring from the walls, to pour from the mouth of the thing that struck at her and at Oryn again and again, blinded them. Oryn fell to his knees, slashing at the creature with his borrowed sword. The branch on which the protective sigil was tied caught fire twice, and twice the Summer Concubine felt another power—Shaldis or Pomegranate Woman—reach to put it out while she drew all her own strength in just holding the thing at bay. When they reached the pit the plank was burning, flames that were swept aside as

Pomegranate Woman ran across, dragging the black-haired Foxfire Girl. The others followed, staggering. A claw tore the Summer Concubine's arm and she felt again the deep stab of pain spells, racking her body, bleeding her from within.

A dark mind reaching for her. Devouring her.

"*Mathrashiar, kamaa!*" Shaldis cried from somewhere. "*Alvorgin ea amar!* Redfire the Wondrous, *kamaa . . .*"

"You shall not keep it from me!"

Ahead of her in the dark outer chamber of the connecting tomb, the Summer Concubine saw Oryn fall, struck by something that seemed to whirl down out of the crazed winds. She barely recognized the white face, the black sunken eyes, the whirling rags of hair as Aktis. Oryn caught the wrist that slammed down at him, staying the knife in midstroke—

"*Tharuas, kamaa . . . !*"

"I won't let you!" gasped Aktis, strings of spittle trailing from his lips. "It's mine!" With the horrible strength of the mad he thrust the knife down at Oryn's throat; Oryn grappled, blind in the darkness. The Summer Concubine seized Aktis's arm and the mad wizard flung her aside as if she'd been a child. In the same moment, foul and glittering, the thing—djinn, monster—emerged from the tunnel behind them, lunged at Pomegranate Woman and Foxfire Girl, trapped in a corner. Oryn rolled, fingers scrabbling at his dropped sword in the blue, unearthly aureole of the djinn's fire. The creature struck at him with its four-pronged tail stinger, catching his arm—

"Ba, take him!" screamed Aktis. "Kill him!"

And from the dark of the passageway that led back to the crypt, Shaldis's voice sliced out: "*Ba, kamaa!*"

The creature stopped, the gold claws pinning Oryn to the stone.

The winds swirled, died; flurried in a hundred little dust devils in the corners, then lay still.

Aktis shouted, *"Ba!"* which the Summer Concubine realized had to be the djinn's name—she even recalled it from the
list Soth had given her—and she added her voice, her magic,
her will, to Shaldis's as Shaldis cried:

"Kamaa! Alvorgin ea amar!"

Come forth and be free.

Come forth and be free.

Aktis screamed, *"No!"* and rushed forward, knife upraised,
striking not at Oryn but at the black-haired Foxfire Girl, who
was still kneeling, gasping, in the shelter of Pomegranate
Woman's arm.

And from the depths of the inner crypt passageway came
the hard, vicious thwack of a crossbow firing. Aktis stopped
midstride, coughed. Put up a hand to grip the bolt that had appeared so suddenly through his throat.

Above his head, the glittering shadow of gold and lightning
began to melt away.

A second bolt slammed out of the tomb's painted darkness
and pierced the wizard's skull. The impact flung him sideways
against the wall. At the same moment Shaldis plunged from
the shadows, ripped something from the folds of Aktis's robe.
Gold flickered in the wan glare of Pomegranate Woman's
lantern. Shaldis threw the golden bottle to the floor and
snatched up a piece of rubble, smashed it again and again. The
Summer Concubine heard a crunch, like fragile glass or crystal breaking within its soft sheathing of gold.

The shadow of the djinn evaporated with a final flicker of
lightning, with a last frail sigh of wind.

The air, filled with dust, seemed terribly, restfully still.

Mohrvine and the Red Silk Lady emerged, bows in hands,
from the inner passageway into the glow of the lantern. Oryn
scrambled to his feet, held out his arms even as the Summer
Concubine ran to him. "Summer Child," he whispered, and

caught her in a crushing grip. Mohrvine lifted the weeping, bleeding Foxfire Girl, who clung desperately to his neck. Pomegranate Woman helped Shaldis stand up, looked around—obviously for Pontifer—and with a whistle to her unseen pet, picked up the protective staff and led the little group to the outer passageway and into the night. By the time they'd brought everyone safe from the tomb and dragged forth Aktis's body, the clouds overhead had broken, letting through a vast drench of desert moonlight.

By morning they had scattered, rainless, away.

THIRTY-TWO

I think I knew it had to be Aktis," said Raeshaldis, gingerly reaching out with her good hand to take the teacup the Summer Concubine offered her, "when I saw the djinn in the temple go back into the statue of Nebekht. I didn't know what it was then, but I understood that whatever it was, it was a thing such as Urnate Urla had been trying to imprison—and that Aktis had to have one too. The magic didn't feel the same, but it felt similar enough. And it struck me that the statue of Nebekht was a giant version of Urnate Urla's golden lamp, and of the bottle I'd seen in Aktis's rooms. Gold and crystal, with three bands of iron. Then I called out the name of Meliangobet, and Naruansich showed me who that was . . . and I knew."

Twilight lay again on dust-dry gardens of the city; twilight and silence. Pomegranate Woman, sitting on a cushion near the door that led to the Summer Pavilion's hanging gardens, was brushing the dust from her ash-white hair after a day's work on the relays of water hoists that bore lake water, bucketful by patient bucketful, up to the thirsty fields. Even the lords of the great houses, Mohrvine and Akarian and Sarn, had gone down to work on them, though privately Shaldis didn't think this would last long. But it was important that they be seen to work on them, especially as Oryn himself did such work daily. It was nobody's business how much he groaned about it in the baths afterward.

Shaldis hoped Mohrvine's blisters would suppurate and he would die of them.

Small chance, with his mother and his daughter studying magic. But she could hope.

"That's a very old technique," pointed out Soth, who had walked over from the library with more notes about water wheels gleaned from the transcripts of scrying-stone conversations generations ago. "There were half a dozen Durshen Dynasty combinations of crystal, metals and spells that were supposed to contain or imprison djinni, but I don't think I've ever read of a case where such traps worked for very long."

The court mage had met the king's party halfway back from the Dead Hills, three nights ago now, with spare horses, two litters and a squad of House Jothek cavalry, newly arrived from the wide royal holdings along the north shores of the Lake of the Sun. The nomads had been turned back there after a sharp battle, and Lords Jamornid and Sarn, seeing the strength of loyal troops, had suddenly realized that they *could* spare men from their own lands to help the king after all.

"The djinni have a way of . . . of absorbing any construct," Soth went on, "be it material or imaginative, to draw magic out of it. Generally dreadful things happened to the wizards who wrought the traps. They could literally make the magic of escape from the material of their prison."

"If they wanted to," said Shaldis. "And if they had the power that they used to have."

"The poor things," said Oryn softly.

The Red Silk Lady sniffed. "One of those 'poor things' nearly tore the heart out of your breast, boy, and went far toward destroying the realm."

Once the darkness was too far advanced for work on the water hoists to proceed, the Summer Concubine invited the members of the newly established Sisterhood of Ravens to dine with her in the pavilion. Cattail Woman and Pebble Girl were both on the night work shift—checking ropes, repairing sluice gates, resetting the water wheels that Soth claimed would make the work easier—and the Moth Concubine had chosen to spend the evening with her master, a middle-aged merchant who traveled in silk. But Soth had come, looking better than anyone had seen him in years, and full of engineering schemes. And, rather to Shaldis's surprise, Foxfire Girl and her grandmother put in an appearance as well.

Very little wind stirred the white gauze curtains of the pavilion's upper room. Instead of rain, it appeared that the summer heat would come early this year. The work on the aqueduct was already being carried on only in evening and morning. Shaldis couldn't imagine how it would be finished in time to do anyone any good.

Oryn continued quietly, "We are creatures of the flesh as well as of magic." He poured out coffee for the Summer Concubine's guests. The supper had been a simple one—an uneasy reminder, perhaps, of hard days to come. "If our salvation is not to be from magic, at least we can seek it through the flesh of the physical world."

His grandfather's concubine prodded him irritably with her walking stick, and said, "Some with more flesh than others."

He smiled graciously as he held out to her a gold-rimmed glass cup. "Some of us are gifted with flesh, and others, like yourself, with magic, madam. And beauty as well, which I consider a bit unfair . . ." She jabbed him again with her stick, but looked pleased. "We must each honor our own gifts. We—men—humankind, I mean—we at least have the option—if certain imbeciles in charge of the major houses of the land would only see it, present company of course excepted—to bring in our means for survival from elsewhere. Or, if worse comes to very worst, to move on somewhere else, or to alter the way we live . . . to do *something*. Being creatures utterly of power, and apparently only of a certain kind of power, the djinni have fewer roads to try."

In billowing garments of rose-colored silk, earrings twinkling in the speckled light of a dozen lamp niches ranged in the wall behind him, the king looked every inch the dandy again, a perfumed and fan-waving disgrace to his father's name. But Jethan was alive, Shaldis knew, only because of Oryn's stubborn refusal to abandon him. Why this should concern her she couldn't imagine. The young man was straitlaced, provincial, had no imagination, was wholly given to the pursuit of arms and disapproved of half the things she'd said on the two occasions she had gone to the infirmary to have coffee with him—though of course she would be sorry had the king lost so loyal a retainer. She'd gone with Bax the day before yesterday to Greasy Yard to fetch him back as soon as the king had returned from the desert, and had heard then that it was Oryn who'd carried him out of the temple.

"He is—a true king," the young man had said, when Shaldis had visited him yesterday. He was obviously uncomfortable about the idea of a true king who spent more time having his hair curled than he did leading his troops, but at least, Shaldis had replied, having your hair curled didn't result in dead men's bodies scattered to the horizon. This had led to a lively argument. She hoped he'd be more tractable when she called on him tomorrow.

"Did you learn anything at the temple today?" asked the king, dividing his glance between Soth and Shaldis. It was Shaldis who shook her head.

"The place was empty," she said. "Locked up. It took us a while to get in, but there were no traps, no magical summonings of rats or flies."

"Though the gods know," added Soth, "there were plenty of both on hand. And stink enough to knock you down."

"I asked—and Soth asked—about what was happening, to magic, to the rains, to the world. About why all of this was going on. And Naruansich said nothing."

The Summer Concubine asked softly, "Was he there?"

"Oh, yes." Shaldis wasn't sure how she knew this. A whisper of magic, the faintest rustle of air. "He was there."

She sipped her tea, steadying the cup with her bandaged hand. "I suspect somebody in the past must have tried exactly the same thing Lohar actually did—tried to trap a djinn in the cult statue of a god, for the purpose of extorting 'miracles' to impress the 'faithful.' It wouldn't have worked—and certainly didn't work—when the djinn had any power, or could have existed outside the statue. The maker of the statue must have had it buried with him."

"Damn those tomb robbers," sighed Oryn, settling back into the cushions of the divan. "Something really will have to be done about them. Particularly now that the spells of protection put all throughout the necropoli are fading away."

"I think it likelier," said Shaldis, "that it was the Sunflash Prince who found the statue and took refuge in it, and called

Lohar to him to be his servant. The same thing may have happened with Ba and Aktis. I have no idea how old that golden bottle was that I saw in his rooms with the things he used to make *ijnis*. Did you find a silver protective sigil, madam"—she turned to the Red Silk Lady—"in Aktis's rooms?"

Foxfire Girl started to reply, but her grandmother cut her off with "Certainly not."

Yeah, thought Shaldis, *you right*.

"But I did find these." The Red Silk Lady held them out: hairpins with heads of elaborately worked glass such as the wife of a glassblower would wear. A few strands of blond hair still tangled in them. And a cheap blue-green veil such as vendors sold in the Slaughterhouse of a color that would look good on a woman with turquoise eyes.

The Summer Concubine whispered, "Thank you," and gathered them into her hands.

"And nothing," said Oryn, "to show why he was sacrificing a jenny teyn, before—er—dealing with my cousin?" He glanced in the direction of Foxfire Girl, who sat quietly on the divan near the garden doors. She had come in from her curtained chair leaning on a crutch, and when she'd removed her veils had revealed the bandages that covered the wounds she'd taken from Aktis's djinn on her cheekbones and neck. Shaldis guessed her grandmother would use her magic to make the scars disappear—she'd already asked the Moth Concubine about healing—but for a girl that beautiful, she had an abashed air, a silence as if laboring under some shame or pain.

"Nothing," said Shaldis. "I thought it odd, myself. But lucky, since I never would have gotten you out of there otherwise."

For a long time no one spoke. Then Soth asked, "If you saw the bottle in Aktis's room—when? Only the day after you learned that other women had disappeared—"

"I glimpsed it before I knew it had anything to do with who we were looking for," she replied. "I was thinking then in terms of who had power—and Aktis clearly didn't."

"Does anyone anymore?" asked Foxfire Girl softly.

And just as softly, with a proud secret smile through the steam of her coffee, her grandmother replied, "We do."

Foxfire Girl sighed. When Shaldis had gone the previous day to the House Jothek to see her, she'd found the girl in the servants' quarters with another girl—a young maidservant, it looked like—who appeared to have been quite badly burned, just sitting and holding her hand. She had asked then about learning the spells of healing: *There has to be something I can do,* she had said.

"And that was enough to lead you to Aktis?" the Summer Concubine asked, settling her gossamer shawl around her shoulders.

"I didn't think I'd find Aktis in person," said Shaldis. "I only wanted to see what was in the crypt of the Hosh tomb, to see whether my suspicion of him was correct. I lost about a day in the idol—when the djinn tried to . . . to take over my mind. I stepped through that gate a full day later than I thought I would. I thought Aktis would still be at the Citadel and that it would be pretty safe to look around."

"What will become of Nebekht now?" asked Foxfire Girl. "You say he—it—is still trapped?"

With the dispersal of the rain clouds, Lohar had hanged himself in the sanctuary of the Temple of Nebekht. Since Seb Dolek had managed to offend so many of the god's other followers by his swift rise to power, a schism among Lohar's successors had resulted within a day. There had been no resistance when Bax had taken palace troops into the Slaughterhouse.

In fact, of all the ragged, furious men who'd manned the barricades, none were found who would even claim to have been there. They had all been home, minding their own business, and knew nothing of the affair. No one knew who had burned down all those buildings, looted those shops, stolen the expensive green-embroidered shirt Rosemallow Woman had been wearing when Shaldis had gone to get Jethan or the quite excellent ham she'd been feeding the young guardsman on.

And Shaldis only said, "I don't know."

"But at least," said Oryn, "we know he's there. Perhaps only the mad or the mage-born can hear him."

"I suppose the question should be," said Soth, stroking Gray King's wide, rounded head, "are there any more of them trapped or hiding somewhere that we ought to know about?"

Oryn sighed. "I'm sure we're eventually going to find that out."

"Oh, good," said the Summer Concubine. "Something to look forward to."

And the look that passed between the blue eyes and the hazel was like a kiss.

How much of the djinn Ba—whose name and attributes Shaldis had looked up last night in the college library—had been left, she wondered, in the thing she'd struggled against in the painted labyrinth of the old kings' tombs? It had fed on the stained and alien magics of the women, trading what magic it had still been able to work for the life Aktis was willing to let it continue in the crystal bottle. How conscious had Ba still been, there at the end? She had been able to speak to the Sunflash Prince in his poisoned dreamworld within the idol. Had Aktis ever actually spoken to Ba?

When she'd reached with her mind into the numinous blue lightnings that hung, in that last instant, around Aktis's head, she'd sensed only Aktis's malice, Aktis's rage. Aktis's grief.

Had there been any crystal world of borrowed dreams in that bottle, for Aktis to live in for a time?

As people got good and tired of working sweeps and buckets, there was less and less talk in the marketplaces against the construction of the aqueduct. Even Mohrvine had quit writing scurrilous little ballads about it to circulate through the poorer quarters, though the Summer Concubine had probably had something to do with that.

As human beings, we do have options, thought Shaldis. *At least some of them still appear viable.* She hoped so, anyway.

Or are we, like the djinni, doomed as well?

She gazed out into the darkness of the garden, the trellis still almost bare against the star-powdered, velvet sky. From here she could see the lights of the Citadel, citrine flecks as tiny as those of the intricately pierced lamps behind the king.

An admission of defeat.

An acceptance of how the world now was.

With most of the novices gone—and Benno Sarn as well—Shaldis had found the quiet of the Citadel both restful and sad. The three novices who had elected to remain had been asked to sit with her at the masters' table, and there was no more whispering or jokes.

Something moved in the darkness. Shaldis thought it was a late-fluttering bird, but for a moment it seemed to her she glimpsed a small white pig lying on the edge of the empty pool, looking across the tiled basin at her with crystalline eyes that glowed with light unlike the gold of the pavilion lamps.

Then it was gone.

No one else in the pavilion appeared to have seen it. But Gray King, sitting on the low table dipping a paw into the king's coffee, turned his head and met her eyes with a reflection of that pale, steady, alien fire.

Meliangobet, she thought, had taken refuge in a corpse. Ba, and the Sunflash Prince, had sought crystals and gold to house the structure of their personalities, their minds, when the ambient magic of the air had changed so much that it would no longer suffice. But she wondered, suddenly, if that was the only sort of house that the refugee spirits could seek.

We could exist in their dreams. Can they perhaps exist in ours? Or in the minds of our cats?

"We don't know anything about anything, when it comes to it." Shaldis turned on the divan, looked back into the lamplit blue and golden room. Seeing their faces in the warm faceted glow, like the family she had never had: the king holding his Summer Lady's hand; the white-haired dowager disparaging the fig balls to Soth; the cheerful old crone offering to teach some spell—Rohar only knew what—to the dark-haired girl.

It's up to us, she thought, and knew that wasn't entirely true.

The gods who ruled the universe had put them together for a reason. She simply couldn't imagine what.

"We only know that the world is changing, and that we were given this gift, for this time, for reasons that we don't understand. All we can do is make the best use of it we can, in the time we have."

"And that," said the Summer Concubine, "can be said of anything, and of everyone."

Three days later, while all the remaining Sun Mages—and nearly everyone else in the Yellow City—were working on the water relays, clouds gathered in the north and poured down rain on the lands.

A WORD ABOUT
WOMEN'S NAMES

While the names of men are largely based on archaic clan surnames, those of women are traditionally given to them by their husbands when they marry (usually between the ages of fifteen and eighteen), or by the masters to whom their fathers sell them outright if they don't. In the wealthier households female children are given individual names, but the general custom is simply to number the girls, giving them a standard name (usually Flower or Fish or Rabbit, or sometimes simply Daughter). Theoretically a husband can change the name of even a nobly born wife, like Foxfire Girl, but this would be regarded as a tremendous insult to the girl's father.

Though the translations used in this book sound clumsy, what I have translated as Woman, Girl, Concubine, Lady, etc., are actually very brief suffixes indicative of the woman's status. To have only one name—Flower or Fish—is an indication of no status at all.

ABOUT THE AUTHOR

Barbara Hambly was born in San Diego on August 28, 1951, and grew up in Southern California amid daydreams, Beatlemania, and Flower Power. She attended the University of California, Riverside, where she obtained a master's degree in medieval history and a black belt in Shotokan karate. She later taught a year of high school, waited tables, taught karate, shelved books in the local library and was "downsized" out of the aerospace industry two days after signing her first book contract in 1981. For many years she was best known for writing sword-and-sorcery fantasy, with occasional excursions into vampire tales, *Star Trek* and *Star Wars* novels, but has recently branched out into a series of well-reviewed historical whodunits as well. A world traveler, she has served as president of the Science Fiction Writers of America, and at one point in her life wrote scripts for cartoon shows. She currently lives in Los Angeles.